WILD IS THE WOMAN
●●●●●●●●●●●●●●●●
LOVERS DON'T SLEEP
●●●●●●●●●●●●●●●●●●●●●●●●
BY LORENZ HELLER

INTRODUCTION BY GREGORY SHEPARD

Stark House Press • Eureka California

WILD IS THE WOMAN / LOVERS DON'T SLEEP

Published by Stark House Press
1315 H Street
Eureka, CA 95501, USA
griffinskye3@sbcglobal.net
www.starkhousepress.com

WILD IS THE WOMAN
Originally published by Rainbow Books, New York, and copyright © 1951 by Magazine Productions, Inc., as by Laura Hale.

LOVERS DON'T SLEEP
Originally published and copyright © 1951 by Falcon Books, Inc., New York, as by Laura Hale.

Copyright © 2023 Stark House Press. All rights reserved under International and Pan-American Copyright Conventions.

"Lorenz Heller" © copyright 2020, 2023 by Gregory Shepard.

ISBN: 979-8-88601-039-8

Cover design by Jeff Vorzimmer, ¡caliente!design, Austin, Texas
Cover art by Walter Popp
Book design by Mark Shepard, shepgraphics.com
Proofreading by Bill Kelly

PUBLISHER'S NOTE
This is a work of fiction. Names, characters, places and incidents are either the products of the author's imagination or used fictionally, and any resemblance to actual persons, living or dead, events or locales, is entirely coincidental.

Without limiting the rights under copyright reserved above, no part of this publication may be reproduced, stored, or introduced into a retrieval system or transmitted in any form or by any means (electronic, mechanical, photocopying, recording or otherwise) without the prior written permission of both the copyright owner and the above publisher of the book.

First Stark House Press Edition: December 2023

WILD IS THE WOMAN

Eve Barry is a woman on a mission—to free her brother from prison for a crime he didn't commit. The man who put him there is Vance Owen, now a city councilman and soon to be major. But Vance is a liar and a rat, and Eve intends to get him to change his charge against her brother, whatever it takes. But first, she has to get his attention. Knowing that he has a weakness for strippers, Eve joins a burlesque show. There she meets Sugar, cynical captain of the chorus girls; Cheeta, a Latin spitfire with a larcenous soul; Wiley, self-effacing orchestra leader; and Jeff O'Hare, the hard-bitten, tough-talking manager. All Eve has to do now is learn how to take her clothes off on stage.

LOVERS DON'T SLEEP

Suzy is crazy in love with Harry Sloan, but to Harry, she is just a means to an end. An attractive means, sure, but Suzy is more valuable to him working his divorce racket than anything else. And what a great racket it is. A couple want a quick divorce, and lawyer Harry arranges to have the husband found by the wife and a photographer in a hotel room with a scantily clad Suzy. It's a great scam. Except that the photographer, Joe, is worried that Suzy is letting herself be used by Harry. And now that Harry's got a new deal cooking with Camilla, Suzy means even less to him. If only Joe can wise up Suzy before it's too late.

7
Lorenz Heller
By Gregory Shepard

11
Wild is the Woman
By Lorenz Heller

131
Lovers Don't Sleep
By Lorenz Heller

250
Lorenz Heller
Bibliography

LORENZ HELLER

By Gregory Shepard

"Lorenz Heller delivers a twisty and riveting crime-noir tale saturated with defining characters and a memorable storyline. Why Heller wasn't ranked higher in the crime-fiction literary echelon is a real mystery. Ultimately, Stark House Press is doing God's work by keeping his memory and work alive." —Paperback Warrior

Author Bill Crider called him "another one of those forgotten paperbackers who deserves to be remembered." Quite an epitaph. Lorenz Heller certainly does deserve to be remembered. He never quite achieved the heights of a John D. MacDonald, but as a fellow Florida crime writer, he kept close company. And he entirely supported himself with his writing, not something that a lot of 1950s authors could say.

Lorenz was born in West Hoboken, New Jersey, from fourth generation German-Americans, which might account for his first name. Lorenz is German for Lawrence. Everyone, of course, knew him as Larry. In fact, as Larry Heller, he wrote *I Get What I Want* and *Body of the Crime,* plus one short story, "Blood is Thicker." Lorenz wrote under many names, but published most of his novels under his "Frederick Lorenz" pseudonym.

As Frederick Lorenz he wrote six crime thrillers for Lion Books, beginning with *A Rage at Sea* in 1953 (a treacherous tale of revenge reprinted by Stark House Press, 2020), and quickly followed with *Night Never Ends* (a slice-of-life story involving an arrogant photographer and the couple he manipulates), *The Savage Chase* (a quirky kidnapping tale, reprinted by Stark House Press, 2019), *A Party Every Night* (about a bartender who is inadvertently framed for murder, also Stark House Press, 2020); the two novels in this collection, *Ruby* (a man is unjustly accused of murdering the town tramp), and *Hot* (in which the brother of a bank robber must deal with his conniving wife); plus a juvenile delinquent novel for Chariot Books called *Dungaree Sin,* a seedy romp through the author's Jersey days.

And then there are all the books written as Laura Hale (crime fiction with strong female protagonists), one novel written as Dan Gregory in

1956 (*Three Must Die!*), not to mention the Larry Holden stories from the late 1940s and early 50s—over 100 of them—written for such magazines as *Detective Tales, Doc Savage, Dime Detective Magazine, Shadow Mystery* and *Thrilling Detective* (the best of them to be found in the recent Heller collection, *Pulp Champagne,* published by Stark House in June 2023). Seven of these pulp stories feature detective Dinny Keogh, who seems to solve most of his crimes through brute luck more than careful deduction. But when you're writing for *Mammoth Mystery*, you don't want a main character who is too cerebral. Fast action and heavy gunplay is the name of the game.

Heller wrote three novels as Larry Holden as well: *Hide-Out* (originally published in 1953 by Eton Books), plus *Dead Wrong* (published by Pyramid Books in 1957) and *Crime Cop* (a police procedural originally published by Pyramid Books in 1959). All of these have been reprinted in new Stark House editions.

But for all that—all the many pseudonyms, and all the various publishers he worked with, all the hardboiled titles—Heller was a character-writer more than an action writer. In a 1956 interview that appeared in the *Sarasota Herald-Tribune*, he confessed to being "interested in characters, not plots." This was his defining quality as a writer. In another interview, this one from the *St. Petersburg Times* later that same year, Heller said simply, "the plot is less important than putting characters in conflict." Characters, he said, "must be alive and have dimension. The reader should be able to see every character in the book." And because he placed more emphasis on characterization than plot, Heller was able to allow the action to take a lot of unpredictable turns.

Heller always puts his characters through the wringer. He himself led quite an adventurous life. After running away to sea on a freighter at a young age, he then jumped ship with the entire crew and found work in Puyallup Valley, Washington, picking raspberries, baling hay and building barns. Heller then returned home and got serious about his life. He wrote his first book, *Murder in Make-Up*, in 1937 when he was 27, and got it published by Julian Messner, Inc., under his given name, Lorenz Heller. According to the St. Petersburg interview, it was his return home to West Hoboken that made him finally decide it was time to either get a job, or commit to his writing. Of course, like many young men, Heller took some time out of his life to serve in World War II, working at the Aircraft Radio Corporation war plant. But it wasn't too long after the war that his first stories began to appear. Then he moved to Florida.

Heller may have grown up in New Jersey, but he didn't grow old there.

"I came down to Florida because I could not stand the snow," he said. First he moved to Nokomis, on the Gulf Coast, then built his own home in nearby Venice, sailing and fishing the Keys and islands when he wasn't working at his writing. The goal was to write 2,500 words a day, and sometimes Heller would be at it for 12 hours a day. That's how you support yourself with your writing. And Heller was dedicated to it.

He wrote 19 novels in all, not counting the four Laura Hale books he adapted for Beacon Books from earlier works. Heller also wrote six TV scripts during the 1950s as Burt Sims. His last book appeared in 1962, the previously mentioned Larry Heller title called *Body of the Crime*, a cop drama reminiscent of the Ed McBain 87th Precinct mysteries and a sequel of sorts to *Crime Cop*. His only other Larry Heller novel, *I Get What I Want,* was published by Popular Library in 1956.

Both of the novels in this volume were originally published as staplebound digest books by Rainbow Books and Falcon Books in 1951 under Heller's Laura Hale pseudonym. They were presented as sexy, risqué novels for men and were mainly sold at train and bus stations. But unlike so many of the crime fiction books of this period, they were filled with interesting, quirky characters that become more of the raison d'être of the book than the actual plots.

As Alan Cranis wrote about Heller on *Bookgasm.com*, "Lorenz's characters are what keep the pages turning, as we wonder what new complications the players will encounter." Neither *Wild is the Woman* or *Lovers Don't Sleep* disappoints in this regard. Heller gives us two great stories, filled with interesting characters, and doesn't waste a word doing it.

—August 2023
Eureka, CA

Notes:
Rita Billingham's "Profiles from Venice" from the *Sarasota Herald-Tribune*, Sunday, October 14, 1956
Woody Thayer, *St. Petersburg Times Suncoast Skyway E*dition, July 22, 1956

WILD IS THE WOMAN
BY LORENZ HELLER

writing as Laura Hale

BURLESQUE BABY!
CHAPTER ONE

Eve Barry looked tensely across the desk into the face of the theatrical agent and clenched her hands in her lap until the knuckles showed white and pointed. It was a dirty little office and he was a dirty, skinny man, with an Adam's apple as sharp and pointed as an arrowhead. His eyes were faded and discouraged.

"Girlie," he was saying, "there ain't a thing in the world I can do for you. You can't sing, you can't dance, you ain't got a specialty. Sure you got a beautiful chassis, but what can you do with it? Look, even the dumbest chorus girl in the business can wag her body in time with the music. That's what they call talent. You gotta have it."

Eve said desperately, "I ... I could learn."

He flapped his hand at her and jeered, "Sure, and so can a million other good-looking dames that want to bust into show business."

"Please, isn't there anything, anything at all?"

"Nothing for amachoors, girlie."

She laid her hand on the edge of his desk and leaned toward him. "I really need a job," she said pleadingly. "Really I do."

For a moment he eyed her greedily, his glance dropping from her wide-mouthed face to her full, challenging breasts. He had caught that pleading note in her voice, and in the past it had meant only one thing. She wanted a job, she needed it, she would do anything to get one. Ten years ago he would have lifted his cynical eyebrows and told her exactly what she would have to do. He had jobs on his list. There was always an opening somewhere—a night club up on Mt. Prospect Avenue, something in TV. Ten years ago he would have made the effort, but now, though he knew she would be worth it, he was too ruined by his enervating cynicism to arouse himself.

Instead, he asked flatly, "Why?"

The question caught her by surprise, and she quickly turned her head away so that he would not see the hot, embering fury in her eyes. Why did she want so desperately to get into show business? That was the one thing she was not going to tell him or anybody else. That was the thing she was going to keep hidden until the moment was ripe and bursting. Already she had shown him too much urgency. She would not make that mistake again.

She affected a self-conscious little laugh and said, "I ... guess I'm stage-struck."

This was definitely not the reason, but he accepted it because it fit into the estimate he had made of her, and curiously he felt an unaccustomed urge to be generous. There was, however, a liberal sprinkling of malice even in his generosity.

"You'd take anything, girlie?" he suggested slyly.

"Oh, yes! Do you have something you … think I could do?"

"Yeah," he drawled, "yeah. I just remembered. Jeff O'Hare, over at the Rivoli needs a show girl." He waited until her face lighted up, then gave it to her. "The Rivoli's a burlesque house on Market Street down near Penn Station."

He expected her to flinch and turn it down flatly, but he was disappointed. Her full mouth thinned a little, but her chin came up and she nodded shortly.

"Good," she said. "It'll give me experience. What will I have to do?"

His momentary generosity evaporated. "Nothing much," he said nastily. "Just stand around on the stage. With your clothes off." Her calm acceptance had spoiled his fun. Even professionals turned down burlesque jobs, and amateurs regarded them with horror.

Eve knew what he was thinking. He resented her youth, her beauty and her vitality, because he had squandered his swinishly, and he wanted to humiliate her. She smiled.

"I think you're wonderful to do this for me," she said sweetly.

Grudgingly, he scribbled a note of introduction to Jeff O'Hare, manager of the Rivoli, and as she was leaving, he snapped spitefully, "Don't forget, this ain't for nothing, girlie. My fee's your first week's pay."

Eve walked down the dark, narrow stairway to the street, filled with an acrid bitterness. She had not missed the grubby flare of desire in his eyes, and she felt as if she had been touched in the dark by something loathsome. But that feeling passed quickly. She had gotten what she had come to get. Her spirits rose with grim elation. She turned off Broad Street into Market and walked briskly eastward, her head high.

Thus far, burlesque was only a word in her mind, a word shabbily linked with sex, but only a word. She had never seen a burlesque show, but she knew vaguely that it was a pretty low form of entertainment, not ordinarily attended by nice girls. She had heard the usual pious lies about it, but had not really been interested enough, one way or the other, to be curious. Burlesque. She did not shudder. It wasn't what she wanted—she had tried to get a job in the City Hall. That would have been best, but she had been naïve. Those plump political faces didn't give you City Hall jobs unless you had something to offer in return—such as votes, for instance. But burlesque would serve just as well; perhaps even better. A man like Vance Owen might be a little more impressed with a show girl than he would be by a stenographer or a file clerk.

So occupied was she with these bleak thoughts of Vance Owen that she did not realize how Market Street degenerated as she neared McCarter Highway. There were pawn shops every few feet, their windows filled with heartbreak; second-hand clothing stores; and saloons that boasted, WHISKEY—15¢.

But when she reached the Rivoli Burlesk Theatre she stopped and looked with growing dismay at the grimy façade and the marquee that advertised in tired, weather-grayed letters, 20—GIRLS GIRLS GIRLS—20. Beneath this, in smaller letters, was, Laughs Laughs Laughs. She was a startlingly vivid figure in that dreary neighborhood, and even the Skid Row characters that shuffled down the street, bent on God knows what obscure, alcohol-fogged errand, turned their heads with a brief reawakening of interest.

She had a full-mouthed, violet-eyed face, high in the cheekbones, crowned by smoldering red hair, on which was set an insouciantly smart hat of deep forest green. It was a lovely face, a face that seemed to have been fashioned solely to arouse both the most tender and the most tumultuous emotions, and the grim resolve that lay behind it had not yet hardened or sharpened it. Her suit of dark green silk shantung had been tailored shrewdly, lovingly, to accept the challenging body it clothed. It was a body that could be used supremely for love—or as a weapon.

She stood before the theatre, hesitating, feeling nervously in her handbag for the note of introduction the theatrical agent had given her.

From where she stood, she could look into the dim, shallow lobby, which was faced with mottled marble. There were three wide double doors, painted a particularly repulsive shade of mustard to simulate golden oak. These were closed now, for the matinee was on. Every available inch of wall space was covered with life-sized, colored blow-ups of girls in that interesting stage of undress that just misses nudity by the thickness of a feather, by the width of a tiny, held bouquet, by the seemingly casual position of a hand. A policeman stood leaning on the ticket box on the right side of the lobby, smoking a cigar. His uniform coat was unbuttoned and his cap was pushed back, revealing his baldness. His eyes widened as Eve walked into the lobby. She was clutching her handbag at her waist. Her color was high, as if she had steeled herself to come this far into the theatre.

But her voice was steady as she said to the policeman, "I'd like to see Mr. O'Hare, please. Is he in?"

The policeman goggled at her for a moment, then hurriedly straightened his cap. "I'll see, lady," he mumbled. "I'll take a look. Be right back."

He kept staring back at her over his shoulder as he sidled through the door to the right of the box office.

A few moments later, a tall, lean Irishman with harsh carrotty hair, slouched out. He had a hard, reckless face, and a lopsided smile dug wickedly into his right cheek. In another era, he might have been a gunman in the deadly days of the Western frontier, a buccaneer, or a soldier of fortune. Now he was a tough manager of a tough theatre in a tough neighborhood.

Eve felt her heart begin to beat thunderously. O'Hare was not at all what she had expected, he was not the kind of a man whose masculine ego she could flatter with a smile or a glance. A hard intelligence gleamed in his blue eyes, and she knew she could not fool him as she had fooled the agent. And he was sure to ask the same pregnant question—why did she want to get into burlesque?

Her hand flew nervously to her hair, patting it over her ear to make sure it was in place. "Mr. O'Hare?" she said.

"That's me," he said warily. "What can I do for you?"

His eyes were passing judgment on her—a Junior Leaguer (they told his busy brain) snooty, a social worker, a troublemaker. He gave her a polite and frosty smile. When you ran a burlesque house, you had to be careful. There was always some do-gooder ready with a knife to stab you in the back.

Eve fumbled in her purse and handed him the note the agent had given her. He took it as if it were a subpoena. He glanced quickly into her face, then opened the note. His brows came down in a hard line across his eyes, and he looked up into her face again.

"You want a job here?" he said incredulously.

She swallowed. "That's right, Mr. O'Hare."

His mouth pursed until it was a hard, bitter pink bud in his face. "Let's go in the office and talk it over for a minute," he said drily. The office was a narrow alley of a room, eight feet wide and fifteen feet long, filled at the far end with an assortment of accumulated theatrical junk such as old cut-outs of undressed girls, a battered ticket box, a pile of dusty red curtain velvet, and so forth. O'Hare's scarred flattop desk was a barrier across the middle of the room. Pasted to the walls with scotch tape were glossy 8 x 10 photographs of burlesque "greats"—Margie Hart, Gypsy Rose Lee, Joey "Tramp" Regan, Abbott and Costello.

O'Hare sat down at the desk and waved Eve into a massive gilt chair that had once served as a throne in a harem scene. He reopened the agent's note and read it a second time, as if looking for some concealed message between the lines. Then he raised his head and gave Eve a long, clinical stare. He saw a richly curved body with beautiful legs. He had learned, in show business, to strip the clothes away with his eyes. He saw a body that needed no art to emphasize its breath-taking shapeliness. The face was lovely, with promise in the wide full mouth. But it was the clothes that made him suspicious. They were too smart. Show girls often wore expensive clothes, but there was always a touch of theatre in them, a flamboyancy. Not these. They had style.

O'Hare rolled back in his swivel chair. "Okay, sister," he said. "Now what's this all about?"

Eve faltered, "I ... I want a job."

"Yeah. That's what it says here, but the guy that wrote it'd do anything for a fin, and for a sawbuck he'd chisel the gold teeth out of his own grandmother's dead mouth."

Eve felt her assurance slip away from her. "But he said you had a job open for a show girl. That's what I came for."

"Let's not kid each other, sister. You came here for something, but a job ain't it. Who put you up to this? The Purity League? Did they send you here to get evidence that the Rivoli's nothing but a cat house with music? Is that it?"

Eve shook her head dumbly, close to tears. But they were tears of anger, anger at herself. This was only the first hurdle, and here she was, falling on her face. What was going to happen later when the jumps got higher, the race longer, and the trophy was for keeps? Her chin came up and she took her driver's license from her handbag. She threw it on the desk in front of O'Hare and glared at him.

"Nobody sent me," she said. "Nobody like the Purity League. I don't know anybody in Newark. This is the first time I've been on the East Coast. I came here for a job, not to make trouble."

O'Hare glanced at the driver's license. "From Frisco," he murmured. His eyes became a little less wary. "College girl?"

"Stenographer."

O'Hare didn't believe her. He sighed and gave her a wry grin, but there was friendliness in it now. "You know," he said, "you college kids give me a bang. Every so often I get one of you nosing around. You walk in, look us over, and think to yourself how dumb these poor slobs must be to work in a joint like this. Sure you want a job. But you don't want to work at it. You just want to hold it long enough to get material for a thesis on something like Environmental Immorality As Related To Exhibitionism."

He grinned wider. "I learned all those big words the hard way," he said gently. "I was taken over the jumps by a little black-haired sophomore from Vassar that had a pair of gams that would knock your eye out. I gave her a job, then after she went back to school, she sent me a copy of this thesis. Don't ask me why. Maybe she was showing off, or maybe she thought I'd be proud of her. But it taught me a lesson, sister, and you smell like a college girl to me. Not that you can do me any harm, but I don't like to be taken for a sucker."

Conscious of her own insecurity, striving to hide it, Eve gave him a lazy smile and, leaning back, slowly crossed her legs.

"If I'm a college girl, Mr. O'Hare, I'll let you butter my diploma and feed it to me on a fork. I want this job because I want to get into show business, and if there's any way I can prove it, short of beating you over the head, please tell me."

He laughed delightedly. He liked spirit, and he found himself wishing he could use this girl. But he had to be sure. He nodded.

"Okay," he said. "Take off your clothes. And don't think of me as just one guy sitting here looking at you. Think of me as a thousand guys, all with their mouths wide open, yelling at the top of their lungs every time you take off another undie, a thousand guys that ain't gonna let you get away with showing a little leg. When they yell, 'Take it off!', they mean take it all off. Of course, you don't have to do this for me. It's only a suggestion."

This was the little test O'Hare had developed for his own protection. He didn't care particularly whether Eve took off her clothes or not. He had seen the best strip women in the business take it off, and over the years, he had come to look at the female anatomy as just another piece of stage scenery.

His words seemed to hang in the air like smoke until they were punctured by Eve's gasp. But she stood proudly, unzipped her skirt and let it fall to the floor at her feet. She knew she was blushing furiously, but she hooked her fingers into the elastic of her half-slip and stepped sinuously out of it. Something electric crackled in O'Hare's blue eyes and almost involuntarily he leaned forward. Her legs were not merely beautiful. They had something else—a breath-catching quality, an excitement. They were long and tapering and between her stocking tops and brief black panties, her thighs were softly rondured, yet firm, glowing with a golden sheen. O'Hare felt something rise in his throat at the sight of them. His hand jerked as if he were suppressing with difficulty an intense desire to reach out and touch them. He was suddenly aware that this lovely girl with the smoldering red hair and smoldering eyes was something far more than a stage decoration. And it made him combustibly aware that he, too, was something more than the hard-boiled front office of a burlesque house. He was a human being, and things like this could hit him just as hard and unexpectedly as other men. And as deeply. He held up his hand as Eve's fingers went to her throat and she started to unbutton her blouse.

"Okay, okay," he growled. "That's enough. I'm convinced." He felt an inexplicable sense of shame at having done this to her. "The job's yours, sister, and God help you."

And he was angry with himself for another reason. He had prided himself that during business hours he was impersonal about women—but this girl had aroused him so sharply that desire had raged within him.

You're getting soft, O'Hare, he told himself with fierce self-mockery, *the next thing you know, you'll start to twitch every time a dame crosses her legs!*

Something warned him that if he fell for this girl, he was in for a bad time. He was shrewd, and he could look deeper into the human soul than most, and what he saw behind Eve's violet eyes made him wary. In this business, he had met a lot of dames on the chisel, and they never gave anything away for nothing, but this was different. This Eve Barry wasn't out just for the old moola. It would have been simpler if she were, because that was something he could understand. She was after something else. He did not know what it was, but it made him uneasy. There was a fire in this girl that could consume him, a destroying flame. Yet, he could see that if Eve ever did give entirely of herself, without reservations, without holding back, it would be something so wonderful, that the thought of missing it was a poignant stab of pain. But there was hope, there was always the bait of hope that he would be the lucky guy, the one exception who could live in this fire of hers and not be devoured by it.

Eve dressed slowly. She knew he was being kind, that he had stopped her when he did because he had not wanted to humiliate her. She felt a surge of gratitude. She gave him a tremulous smile.

"Thank you," she said. "Thank you for the job and ... everything."

She was surprised at the sudden torment that twisted his face.

"Don't thank me yet, sister," he said harshly. "You don't know what you're letting yourself in for."

He thrust a cigarette into his mouth and avoided her questioning eyes. Eve became thoughtful. In the month since she had left San Francisco, she had learned to identify the dawning of passion in the faces of men. On the train, there had been an advertising executive, a witty and chatty man, whose light conversation she had found delightful until the night in the observation car when he had seized her in urgent arms, pursuing her twisting face with hungry, demanding kisses. His groping hand had found her breast, and she had slapped him. At the moment, she had been bewildered at the anger that blazed out of him, not understanding it. Then, again, when she had gone to the Newark City Hall for a job, there had been a plump, pink, manicured Councilman, who had been willing to give her anything, excepting a job, and had made himself perfectly clear by running the tip of his finger over the curve of her hip. She hadn't slapped him—she was learning—but she had walked out. There had been greedy desire in the eyes of the theatrical agent, and now, there was O'Hare—but, somehow, she felt that O'Hare was different from the others. He could be violent, but he wouldn't try to take her by surprise or subterfuge. When his passion could no longer be controlled, he'd be honest with her. He might be brutal, but he'd be honest. She'd always know where she stood with O'Hare. Whether or not she'd be able to handle him was another question, and she did not try to answer it at the moment, because there was a kind of savagery in his eyes that left her breathless and opened a tiny wound of fear inside her.

"Exactly what will my job be, Mr. O'Hare?" She tried to sound business-like.

"Parader," he mumbled.

"Parader? What's that? I was told you needed a show girl ..."

"Same thing, only in burlesque we call it a parader." He took hurried refuge in the familiar slang of his profession. "We call it a parader because that's what you do—you just parade around the stage in just enough of a costume to bring the men in and keep the cops out. Or you stand around on a platform and try to look interesting while the chorus goes into a routine. There's nothing to it. A moron could do it if she had good-looking gams, and you won't have any trouble in that direction. You'll get fifty bucks a week. But maybe, after a while," he eyed her speculatively, "we can give you a featured spot, if you can learn to move around the stage without looking as scared as a cat in a dog pound. There's a trick to it. You've got to make every man in the audience feel that you're doing this just for him. You've got to make him think that if it wasn't for that s.o.b. of a manager, meaning me, you'd come right down off the stage, sit in his lap and put your arms around his neck." Suddenly his face flushed and he said heavily, "But that shouldn't be tough for you to learn. You can do it just by standing there and looking at a guy." He glowered at her, then laughed thinly. "How does it sound, sister?"

Eve had the panicky feeling that his suppressed violence was about to burst its bonds, but when he laughed, she knew that he had himself in hand, that this was not the way it would happen.

"I'll do my best, Mr. O'Hare," she said guardedly.

He waved his hand carelessly. "Call me Jeff. That's what they all call me, and I don't want you to be different than anybody else. Now there's one more thing," his voice hardened. "What you do with your life outside the theatre is your own business, but while you're in the theatre, you'll take orders and keep your nose clean. And I might as well tell you this, if you start playing around on the outside, sooner or later it's going to show, and the minute you start looking like a tramp, you can consider yourself canned. My girls are clean, hard-working kids, and I don't want any bums around. Is that quite clear?"

Eve said faintly, "Yes. Quite clear."

"Okay." He glanced at his watch and his eyebrows shot up with surprise. "The show's been over for fifteen minutes. Let's go backstage, and I'll introduce you to your boss." This was safe, familiar ground to him and he was friendlier now, more relaxed. "You'll have three bosses, Evie. Me, Sugar Russell the chorus captain and Wiley the orchestra leader. We'll go back and meet them."

The house porter was wearily sloshing a wet mop over the tiled lobby floor when they left the office. The auditorium was empty, but the sound of a piano came from the orchestra pit. Someone was playing softly, playing the same phrase over and over again with slight changes, as if he were trying to build the music for a special effect.

O'Hare took Eve down the center aisle and leaned on the brass pit rail. A thin, sandy-haired man, who looked a little like Hoagy Carmichael, was hunched over the keyboard of the piano. A sheet of manuscript paper was propped on the music rack before him, and he leaned forward and quickly dotted in four bars of notes. He sat back and regarded them with sardonic eyes, then let his fingers ripple over the keys. The music, this time, came out with a kind of heartbreaking yearning, blues with a sob. Blues that cried out for love.

"What is that, Wiley?" asked O'Hare curiously. "I like it."

"It's the music for Sugar's routine next week." Wiley did not look up; his voice was a little bitter. "It's called *Frustration*."

"I like it," O'Hara repeated, and Eve was surprised at how gently he could speak. "By the way, this is Eve Barry, our new parader. Think Sugar can get her in shape for tonight's show?"

Wiley shrugged his thin shoulders, gave Eve a disinterested glance and extended a limp hand.

"Meecha," he mumbled. "I could use her in the Sunflower number I guess. All she'll have to do is stand on a trigger step and look like a sunflower without clothes, and she looks intelligent enough for that." He shook his head uncertainly, "But you'd better talk to Sugar first. She's the chorus captain, not me."

O'Hare nodded and, taking Eve's elbow in his hand, led her toward the stage door at the right of the stage.

"The poor mug," he said softly. "He's so nuts about Sugar that he don't know which end is up. She'd give him a tumble, I guess, but he won't let her. Don't ask me why. Some guys are like that."

Eve felt a mounting excitement as she climbed the steps to the stage. This was the theatre and she was going to be a part of it. There was magic even in this dingy house. They went by the electrician's board, with its battery of switches, past an area of stored stage props—chairs, tables, beds, clothes trees, hats of all descriptions. The chorus dressing room was in the basement. O'Hare knocked on the door and called:

"Hey, Sugar. You home?"

A throaty voice answered, "Come in, Jeff. I'm decent."

Eve was wide-eyed when she walked into the dressing room. It was thirty feet long and about twelve wide. There was a table on each of the long walls, and eight mirrors, bordered by naked electric light bulbs, hung over each table. Into the sides of the frames of most of the mirrors were stuck snapshots of men, and the tables were covered with jars and bottles of creams and cosmetics. There were cigarette stubs, crumbled facial tissue and empty lipstick containers scattered over the floor from one end of the room to the other; the chairs were festooned with stockings, skirts, and underwear—but the costumes for the show were neatly and carefully hung in an open closet. This was what a theatre was like back-stage. Though she had come, really, by accident, though this was merely a means to a different kind of end, Eve could not help feeling the pulse-lifting excitement that was always so close to the surface of show business.

Sugar Russell was sitting in a chair at the end of the table nearest the door. She was still in costume—a brief emerald skirt and a wisp of brassiere to match. She was sewing a dress, and the fabric spilled over the end of the table like molten gold. It was beautiful with her vibrant tawny hair. She was a tall girl, boldly curved, with strong, well-shaped legs. Her gray eyes were widely spaced in a generous face.

She said, "Hi, Jeff," and held up the golden dress. "Like it? It's for my *Frustration* number next week. It comes off in two pieces. Zip, and off comes the top, and zip, off comes the skirt."

Then she caught sight of Eve, and her face went carefully noncommittal, except for a brief, questioning glance that she shot at O'Hare from the ends of her eyes.

O'Hare caught that glance, and he said shortly, and, Eve thought, a little defensively, "This is the new parader I got for you, Sugar. The name's Eve Barry. Wiley wants to use her in the Sunflower number tonight, so tell her what to do."

Sugar said very politely, "How do you do, Miss Barry," but did not offer her hand.

O'Hare's eyes narrowed. "Don't give her the freeze, kid," he said gruffly. "Evie's okay. I vouch for her personally."

Sugar's glance sharpened on his face for a moment, then slid to Eve, and she smiled with warm good-humor.

"Once bitten, twice shy," she said in that husky voice of hers. "Sorry I slipped you the ice cube, Evie, but I was just being careful. Welcome to O'Hare's harem."

Eve took the now extended hand, and felt an answering warmth come out of herself. She liked Sugar.

Sugar went on, still half apologetic, "I was afraid for a minute Jeff was slipping me another mickey. A couple months ago he brought in a college girl that snooted us every minute she was here, then went back to kindergarten and wrote a la-dee-da-dee-da about what badgirls-they-raise-in-burlesque-all-they-think-about-is—s-e-x—naughty-word. The little tramp! She tried to make every pair of pants that walked into the theatre, and I was just about ready to can her when she quit. I wish she had stayed one more day. It would have given me a lot of satisfaction to have kicked her out on her snooty little fanny."

O'Hare said sourly, "Why don't you pull in your barber pole?" He turned and left the room abruptly, slamming the door.

Sugar's head jerked around and she stared after him with astonishment. Then a remembering gleam came into her eyes, and she pursed up her lips in a soundless whistle. She looked up at Eve.

"Well, well, well," she murmured. "Think of that, now."

She chuckled as a slow flush climbed Eve's face.

"I lived a long time to see this," she observed. "Jeff wasn't just vouching for you, honey, was he? He was keeping his fingers crossed that you wouldn't walk out when you saw this dump." She waved her hand at the littered dressing room. "How long have you known him, Evie?"

Eve said helplessly, "I met him for the first time a half hour ago. The agent sent me over for the job." Suddenly and desperately, she wanted Sugar's wholehearted friendship. She had an idea she was going to need it.

"You're kidding!"

"No. Honestly."

"You mean, you walked in and Jeff fell for you just like that?" she snapped her fingers. "What'd you do?"

"Nothing, Sugar, honestly. Just asked him for the job."

Sugar shook her head. "Honey," she said commiseratingly, "have you got troubles! Jeff don't fall easy, but when he does, I got an idea it's the works, and he's a very, very tough man. Tougher than you've ever met. And right at this point, a word to the wise might be very efficient," her face became intent and serious, "don't ever cross him up, Evie. Don't ever even think of crossing him up. He'll wring your neck with his own two hands!"

MEET THE WOLF!
CHAPTER TWO

After this somber warning, Sugar said half-humorously, "But if I know Jeff, he'll never let you know he's carrying the torch, except maybe he'll treat you a little worse than everybody else, just to show you how tough he can be, even about love. In Jeff's language, only sissies fall in love, and only morons get married. However, there'll probably be a lot of gin under the bridgework between now and then, so you might just as well learn your routine to pass the time."

She laid her unfinished dress aside with a tinge of regret and took Eve out to the empty stage. Wiley had gone and the piano was silent, though the manuscript with *Frustration* elaborately and lovingly lettered across the top, was still on the music rack.

Eve remembered what Jeff O'Hare had said about Wiley's being nuts over Sugar, and looked at the tawny-haired girl to see if she had glanced toward the unfinished manuscript on the piano. Sugar was standing over the footlights, staring down in the orchestra pit. There was an expression of haunted sadness in her eyes.

"*Frustration*, he calls it," she muttered. "Wouldn't you just know it!" She raised her head and saw Eve watching her. "I suppose Jeff O'Hare told you all about it," she said defiantly.

"About what, Sugar?"

"About me and Wiley. It's something that Jeff would think very, very funny, damn him."

"He didn't say anything to me, Sugar," Eve lied pityingly.

"Well—let's skip it then."

Sugar turned and faced the stage with her hands on her hips, her long, boldly curved legs spread wide.

"I'll give you the run-down on the number," she said briskly. "There are ten chorus girls who do all the work. They do the dancing. There are six paraders. Three come in from the left, and three come in from the right. You'll come in from the right. You'll be wearing some green stuff around your waist, like leaves, net panties and a bra. You'll be carrying a sun flower. All you do is walk on, step on the first platform you come to and stay there until the number is over. There's a song that goes with it, but I ain't got the time to teach it to you now. When we sing, you just move your mouth. It's a crumby song, anyway, and if you ask me, we'd be better off if none of us sang it. Got that, now?"

A tall, broad-shouldered man, with lovingly polished black hair, had come down the aisle and was now sitting in the first row, watching them. He was darkly handsome, and a smile sat on his self-satisfied lips. Sugar's back was to him, and she had not seen him enter the auditorium. His eyes were boldly on Eve, and she was uncomfortably aware of his calculating interest.

Eve hurriedly answered Sugar's question. "I come on stage from the right," she repeated, pointing toward the wings. "I'm carrying a sunflower. I stand on the first platform I come to. I move my mouth when you sing. But is that all I do, Sugar?"

"That's what you get paid fifty bucks a week for," Sugar said drily. "Paraders sure have it tough. You don't just stand there, though. You got to stand there in a certain way. You stand sideways to the audience, and put one leg out like this. See? Show it off, in other words. How are your legs, by the way?"

The man in the first row sat up a little, and Eve was aware of his heightened interest.

"They're ... all right," she said.

"Well, let's see them. Come on, lift it up. Don't go shy on me, Evie. You're in the wrong business. I don't care what kind of legs you got, but if they're Steinways or Knabe, I'll bury you in the back row where it don't matter."

Eve gave her a pleading glance. She had shown herself to O'Hare without shame, and she would show herself on the stage during the show, but now, with that darkly handsome man watching avidly from the first row, she refused to lift her skirt and show her thighs, pearlescent above her stocking tops. That would make her feel really naked.

Sugar caught the direction of Eve's pleading glance and looked back over her shoulder. Her face went cold. The man waved airily at her and grinned with anticipatory enjoyment.

"Don't stop on my account, Sugar," he said. "Keep up the good work."

Sugar said succinctly, "Beat it."

"Ah, now, Sugar, is that nice? After all, it would be only polite to introduce one co-worker to another co-worker ..."

"I said beat it! Unless you want me to tell Jeff O'Hare you busted up a rehearsal."

The man lounged indolently from his seat. He winked at Eve.

"See you tonight, honeybun," he said jauntily and sauntered up the aisle.

Now that he was gone, Eve felt amused.

"Who was that?" she asked.

"That," said Sugar in a flat voice, "was Gilbert Verne, our juvenile, and I do mean juvenile. He sings and does character parts. He's got a good baritone, but not as good as he thinks it is. In fact, nothing about Gilbert is as good as he thinks it is."

"He's very handsome."

"So's a rope, if you like ropes—until you get one around your neck. From the look in his eye, he's got you on his list. Watch yourself. He's made life pretty miserable for some of the kids in the chorus. He's the we-were-meant-for-each-other-it's-destiny-dahling type, and a kick in the pants for you when it's all over. But that's your business. Now, where were we?"

Eve smiled. "You wanted to see my legs."

"Forget it. That's one department you don't have to worry about, and Gilbert might be up there peeking through a knothole, the same one he crawled out of. Oh yes. We had you standing on the platform, showing the boys a leg. Now, don't just stand there, Evie. Turn your head to the crowd and give them a big smile, like you'd love it if they could come up there and stand with you. That's all you do, but you can put a lot of schmaltz in it. When the number's over, the chorus dances off, then you walk off, too, and I mean *walk*. Don't bust for the wings like you're glad it's over. And keep giving them that big smile." She forked her fingers through her tawny hair. "I guess that's all unless you want me to go over it again."

"I can remember it. I won't disgrace myself."

"Good. Now how's about going out for a plate of ribs and a drink, maybe?"

"I couldn't eat a thing, honestly," Eve confessed. "I'm ... kind of tied up in a knot."

"Sure," Sugar was warm and understanding. "I know how you feel. Go downstairs and relax. I'll bring you back a carton of coffee. I remember my first night," she began to grin. "Was I ever paralyzed! I got up on that platform and, so help me, I couldn't get off. I was still standing there, clutching a parasol for dear life, when they rang down the curtain. Did I get a laugh. But get yourself a rest. You'll be okay. There's nothing to it."

After Sugar dressed and left, Eve sat alone in the dressing room. It was unreal. The whole day had been unreal, and the crowning unreality was the fact that very shortly she would begin her career as a burlesque girl.

Her hands were shaking when she reached into her handbag. Out of a leather folder she took a newspaper clipping. This was her reality. This was what she had to cling to amid all other madness. This was her *purpose!*

The clipping showed a one-column cut of a virile, smiling man with crisp blond hair. It showed only head and shoulders, but they were the head and shoulders of a fullback. The caption said, "Vance Owen, Newark Councilman Extraordinary." The clipping was from the gossip column of a San Francisco newspaper, and Eve's face was somber as she re-read what she had already read a hundred times, what she could have quoted, word by word, from memory. The columnist had obviously written with his tongue in his cheek, yet his admiration came through despite his surface sophistication.

"Vance Owen," the clipping said, "Newark's playboy Councilman, has returned to the scene of his martial triumphs. During the war, as many a chagrined GI will remember, Vance was a Major of Military Police for the San Francisco Area. Now he has returned, unofficially, on a visit. Frankly, we wish he could stay forever. He is the life of the party. Vance is a playboy in the real, old fashioned stage door tradition, but there is nothing old fashioned about Vance, as many a pretty chorus girl can tell you. It is whispered that Vance enjoys nothing more than a good rowdy evening at the burlesque. (Who was that lady I saw you with last night, Vance? Or didn't I recognize her with her clothes on? Could it really have been Lolita, burley-Q strip-teuse?)

"But all joking aside, lads and lassies, Vance is a real firebrand. My East Coast spies tell me he is the fair-haired boy in the razzmatazz of Newark politics. Councilman of the snooty Forest Hill ward, no mean feat for an ex-MP roughneck, Vance has his eye on the ball. And it is no secret that the mayoralty chair is undergoing alterations so it will support his two hundred pounds of bone and muscle. I don't want to be the first to say I-told-you-so, but Vance Owen is going PLACES!"

Eve brooded over the photograph. She knew every line in that self-assured face with its professional personality smile. How long would it be, she wondered darkly, before she and Vance Owen met? Already, their paths were converging.

AFTER THE BALL
CHAPTER THREE

It was seven-thirty when Sugar came back with the container of hot coffee. Eve drank it gratefully. She felt all washed-out, as she always did after a session with that clipping from the San Francisco paper. First there was the surging emotion, then the let-down. The hot coffee flowed into her with strength.

The other girls began to drift in in twos and threes, giving Eve curious glances as they came through the door. Eve had been given the mirror next to Sugar's, and Sugar was showing her how to apply theatrical make-up, so they knew she was a member of the troupe. Their glances, while not actually hostile, definitely put her on probation. Sugar introduced them as they came in, but there were so many names, and such odd ones—Alabama Russell, So-So Chandler, La Verne Sardi—that Eve ended in confusion. But one girl she did remember. Vividly. A small dark girl, a lush Latin beauty, with high voluptuous breasts and an intense, sullen face.

Sugar introduced her acidly as Cheeta Rodriguez.

"Our little Mexican cactus flower," Sugar drawled. "Don't handle without gloves."

Cheeta laughed and shook her head so that her wild black hair tumbled about her face. "Tatatatatatata, don't listen to her. I am really very nice," Cheeta's voice was supercharged, like her dynamic little body. "Eve? Is your name really Eve? That is a very fonny name. Eve means the beginning of nighttime, when the day starts to go away. It is a name with a sense of humor, no? Like naming somebody Sunset or Six P.M. ... Fonny, eh? But soch lovely hair! Like slow fire, the color. How do you get it soch a color? Is it moth trobble to keep? Me, I have no trobble with my hair. It is always black. Black, like the thoughts of men when they look at you from under their eyelids, so. I hope you are very happy with us. Now I do my exercises."

She sat down beside Eve and rapidly took off all her clothes.

Sugar muttered, "If you're bleeding a little, Eve, the First Aid kit's on the wall outside. But keep an eye on her. This is what she does every day before every show."

Cheeta was sitting straight up before her mirror, naked except for her black net stockings and high-heeled shoes. Carefully, she poured scented oil over both hands from a rose-tinted bottle, then slowly began massaging her breasts, upward from the silky skin over her ribs, counting aloud each time her palms firmly lifted each breast.

"Wan, two, t'ree, four, five, seex ..."

She did it calmly and, methodically, as if she were alone in her boudoir instead of in that roomful of girls. She counted clear up to a hundred.

Sugar dug Eve in the side with her elbow and said, "Who taught you that one, Cheeta? That Portuguese boy friend of yours from the Ironbound?"

Cheeta said calmly, "If you did the massage also, Sugar, maybe five years from now you would not look like a pair of old stockings, maybe."

Sugar started up from her chair, her face fiery. "Why you ..." she began furiously.

Eve grabbed her arms and pushed her back in her chair. Cheeta merely shrugged smugly and murmured:

"She knows it is true, that is why."

It might have developed into a first class brawl, but at that moment the dressing room door burst open and a petite blonde, holding her left hand over her head, danced into the room, singing excitedly:

"Look at me look at me look at me!"

An engagement ring glittered on her finger.

Sugar yelled, "You made it!" She jumped up and threw her arms around the little blonde. "Rosie put it over!"

With shrill yips of excitement and congratulation, the other girls surged toward them, but Cheeta darted in before them, as quick and sinuously as a mink.

Eve suddenly saw that Cheeta's whole character was betrayed by her hands. They were long, grasping, avaricious. They seized Rosie's hand greedily and turned the ring this way and that to catch the light.

"Aaaaaaah!" she said, raising her enormous black eyes to Rosie's happy face. "I see that you are going to marry a scientist."

Rosie said blankly, "A ... who?"

"A scientist. I have found out your little secret, eh? It was easy. I say to myself, what would you need to find soch a teensy-weensyitsy-bitsy little diamond like thees one? Ah, I say, a microscope. And then say, who uses a microscope? The answer—a scientist. And a very good scientist, too, I can see. He has found for you the teensiestweensiest little diamond in the whole world. You are a very lucky girl. You are going to marry a scientist!"

The silence in the room fairly quivered, then somebody drawled:

"Now wouldn't you just know we'd have to be in the cellar instead of on the top floor. From these windows, you'd have to fall up if you were kicked."

Rosie's face was blanched white, but Sugar hugged her tightly.

"Pay no attention to her, honey," she begged. "She's jealous. All she gets from her boy friend is massage lessons. Hey, kids! How's about a party for Rosie after the show Saturday night? All in favor say aye, the rest are fired. Carried unanimously ..."

The next fifteen minutes were filled with shrill plans for the party. Rosie was hustled out of the room, and Sugar took charge. Everybody was going to kick in five bucks, whether she liked it or not.

There would be potato chips and pretzels, baked beans, noodle salad, pumpernickel, pastrami, salami, Swiss cheese, boiled ham, steak sandwiches and crêpes suzette from the Swiss Town House. And a keg of beer. Sugar figured rapidly, thirty dollars for the spread, which would leave fifty bucks for the gift from the girls.

"I'll promote another fifty from Jeff O'Hare," said Sugar. "The first banana'll kick in ten if I kick him hard enough first. Five from each of the strippers. Five from the straight man and five from the second comic. What does that make, somebody?"

"Counting our fifty," said Eve, "that makes a hundred and thirty-five."

Sugar grimaced. "I wanted a hundred and fifty."

"Please. I have a suggestion." Still sublimely nude, Cheeta was sitting on the edge of her table, a picture of eager innocence. "Do not buy a keg of beer. That fifteen dollars will make the hondred-and-fifty. I will go to my Portuguese boy friend and I will say, 'Listen to me, Stupeed, one of the girls is engaged and we geev her a beeg bost. You contribute all the liquor or you kees Cheeta adios.' He ees so ugly he will do it because he ees always afraid Checta will get herself another boy friend who is not so ugly. We will have scotch, not beer, and maybe one bottle of champagne for the leetle bride. Hokay?"

The silence was overwhelming for a moment, and then they began calling her names, but affectionately. Cheeta basked in it, preening herself. She shrugged.

"It is notheeng," she said. "He is so repulsive, he will do anytheeng I say. Even marry me!" she spat viciously at Sugar, then grinned. Sugar gave her a warm smile and touched her bare knee. "Of course he'd marry you," she purred. "And I, personally, will give you a pair of dark glasses when you announce your engagement. Now come on!" She stood up straight and slapped her, hands sharply together. "Back to work. Get your costumes on, get on your make-up. The curtain still goes up at eight-thirty sharp, party or no party. That leaves you exactly twenty minutes to be on stage, and you're docked if you're late."

The girls scurried for their mirrors.

The Sunflower number, the lone number in which Eve was to appear that night, was the finale, but she had on her scanty costume and was in full make-up before the overture. Still writhing to reach the final snaps on their costumes, the girls raced up the stairs and crowded into the wings at either side of the stage, talking in sibilant whispers.

The orchestra was brassily blaring the gay bars of the *Strip Polka*, which was both the overture and the exit music. Sugar was on the stage, squinting through a peephole in the curtain. She beckoned to Eve.

"Standees in the balcony," she grinned. "That's your public, kid."

Eve bent over and looked through the peephole. The air in the auditorium was blue with tobacco smoke, and for the first time she heard the jovial hum of an audience ready and willing to be amused. It was a hum that had the power of a contented dynamo. Frightening—yet reassuring. Instinctively, she knew this hum was not the thing you had to dread. The thing you had to dread was—*silence*.

The candy butcher was stalking down the aisle, holding a package of the cheapest chocolate over his head, berating the audience stridently.

"Hurry, hurry, hurry!" he bawled. "Each and every package of this delicious confection I hold in my hand contains a guaranteed prize for your amusement and entertainment. Each and every package! For twenty-five cents, a quarter of a dollar, two small dimes and a nickel, you get a box of delicious imported Swiss chocolate, plus a free gift to en-ter-tain your friends and influence people. In one of these packages is your own private burlesque show that you can take home and enjoy in the privacy of your own bedroom. All you do is hold the little card up to the light, twirl the disc with your finger, and what do you have? Ladies and gentlemen, I repeat, what do you have? I will tell you what you have! When you twirl that little disc with your finger, you have a lady and a gentleman in twelve—TWELVE!—different and interesting poses. They move! They *live!* Hurry, hurry, hurry ..."

Sugar saw the look on Eve's face, and she grinned, "Part of the show, kid. Milk chocolate with peanuts. The twelve interesting poses are Fred Astaire and Betty Hutton doing dance steps from *Let's Dance*. Sucker bait."

The overture swelled, became louder, and Sugar grasped Eve's wrist and hurried her back to the wings.

"Curtain cue," she hissed. "We're on in exactly thirty seconds."

She fussed a moment with the skirt of her costume, a wispy piece of orange chiffon that barely covered her net panties and gave full play to her bold thighs. She looked back over her shoulder to make sure the chorus girls were in place, and the paraders behind them. The music broke with three crashing chords, and almost immediately went into *You On My Mind* as the curtain slowly rose. Simultaneously, the girls raised smiles on their faces, tensed, then danced on, singing, "*You, you,*

you're on my mind ..."

Eve stood by the electrician's board, with its multiplicity of switches. The evening sped by with bewildering speed. The girls danced on, they danced off. The strippers went on in a blue-and-red blend of dramatic light, the comics and their skits crackled through the routines with the crispness of a short-circuit on a high tension line, perspiring men and girls raced by her, coming and going. Everything seemed to be going on at once—the girls coming off, the comics going on, a stripper, clad in glowing cloth like a queen, waiting to go on, knots of girls grouped to gossip breathlessly, the stage hands ill-naturedly grumbling, pushing people out of their way as they wheeled heavy preps for the next scene, the electrician standing at his board, sharp-eyed, watching his plot-sheet to mix the lights in colors like a bartender mixing cordials in a pousse-cafe.

Eve felt like a blind pedestrian in the middle of Times Square on a dark night, searching for a black hat she had dropped three blocks back on 39th Street.

Twice she caught sight of Jeff O'Hare's tough Irish face in the wings across the stage, his teeth showing whitely around a slim cigar. Twice his eyes sought her, then darted away when their glances locked—locked like wrestlers reaching for a commanding hold. But he didn't come across the stage, and he didn't talk to her.

Gilbert Verne, more darkly handsome in white tie and tails, went on between the Gazeeka Box routine of the comics and the current featured strip, and sang *On The Road To Mandalay* in a resounding baritone. He got such a hand that he went back and sang another chorus as an encore.

But this time, instead of exiting right, as he was supposed to, he exited left and wound up at Eve's side in front of the electrician's board. He looked down at her. He was a good six-feet-two.

"How was I?" he smiled.

"I liked it. You have a good voice."

He swelled his chest. "This is just experience for me," he said with elaborate nonchalance. "I need stage presence. I was talking to Schuster the other day, and he says I'm ready."

Schuster was the big, if not the biggest, theatrical agent of the East Coast.

"Next year," Gilbert patted his white tie affectionately, "New York, a marquee all to myself, the Stork Club. Sherman Billingsley and me are just like this." He held up crossed fingers.

Behind Eve, the electrician muttered, "Yare, and Billingsley's the thumb on the other hand."

Gilbert whirled. "What was that remark?" he demanded angrily. The electrician calmly munched his tobacco. He was an old timer, and Gilbert should have known better.

"I said," he grinned, "all that ham and no mustard. Better git goin', son. You gotta stooge for the comic in the next one, and you gotta change of costume. O'Hare'll skin you alive if you're late."

Gilbert said hurriedly to Eve, "Cocktails tonight, dahling, after the curtain?" His hand on her arm was urgent.

She shook her head. "Not tonight. I'm worn out."

"Lunch tomorrow."

"Please. Give me time to get my bearings."

"I'm a dope!" he said dramatically.

"For heaven's sake, why?"

"Where have I been all your life? That's what it comes down to. What have I been doing with myself, when I could have been out meeting you? You'll be at the party Saturday night, won't you?"

Eve smiled. "I wouldn't miss it."

"I'll bring you an orchid ..."

The electrician yawned, "Two minutes to git outta that monkey suit and inta ya costume, Romeo."

Gilbert gave Eve's arm a last significant squeeze and fled toward his dressing room.

The electrician grunted, "If I was you, girlie, I wouldn't pin any orchids on myself before they're hatched."

The night sprinted by. Intermission was Sugar grasping her around the waist in a panting hug and saying:

"For the luvva mud, put on some more rouge. O'Hare's not paying you to haunt the joint."

The Sunflower number. Nervous last-minute adjustments on the too-scanty brassiere, the electrician muttering:

"Gams like that and she worries about her costume!"

The Sunflower music. Eve stood on her little platform, holding a papier-mâché sunflower, conscious of a thousand pairs of staring eyes, conscious that she was more naked in public than she had ever been before in her life, conscious of her breasts thrusting out of her bra, conscious of her legs beneath her, so naked and exposed, the swell of her thighs, the net panties. She felt dazed under the impact of all those eyes.

Then, suddenly, it was all over. The curtain was down and the orchestra was again playing the lively strains of the *Strip Polka*, the exit music, as the audience filed noisily out of the theatre.

Sugar pounded her on the shoulder blades, shouting affectionately, "You're a trouper, kid, now you're a trouper. You're with it!"

Confusing, bewildering, fantastic.

And the rest of the week was just as bad. Three times a week, Monday, Wednesday and Friday, there were rehearsals for the next show, each rehearsal lasting two hours. Rehearsals were after the matinees. Matinees started at twelve noon and ended at five, two full shows an afternoon. Each night Eve fell into bed, her muscles quivering with fatigue, something crying out within her that it wasn't worth it, that there was surely an easier way, that this exhaustion was sheer cruelty.

There were songs she had to learn—lyrics for the current show, lyrics for the following show, and the shows were changed weekly. Routines in which the paraders had to dance with the experienced chorus girls, who made light work of what, to Eve, was an impossible feat of memory.

But she got through the week, and, surprisingly, each day seemed a little easier. The dance routines not quite so complicated, the lyrics of the songs pouring out of her as if her tongue were a sound track. And then there was Saturday night and the engagement party for Rosie.

The moment the curtain went down on the midnight show, the stage hands hustled the trestles on the stage for the tables, and someone wheeled in a small white piano and Wiley played, his lanky face sadder than ever above the keyboard as he followed Sugar with his disillusioned eyes filled with hope and hopelessness, yearning and rejection.

Cheeta's word had been good. There was a full case of scotch, a bottle of champagne, wrapped in tissue paper for the bride-to-be, *and* a half keg of beer for the stage hands who looked on scotch as kind of Woolworth perfume for sissies. Her boy friend, in a Glen plaid suit with a crimson thread running through the checks, stood puffing out his chest beside the case of scotch, so no one could be mistaken about the identity of the donor.

When Cheeta had said he was ugly, it was an understatement due, probably to vocabularic deficiency. He was the epitome of masculine repulsiveness. He was built as low to the ground as was possible without his being a dwarf, but, as if to make up for this oversight in height, he was wide. He had shoulders like a running back, accented just a little by padding in the shoulders of his gaudy jacket. He had the mouth of a frog, and his little eyes were burnt raisins. He strutted up and down in front of the case of scotch, he beamed on the half keg of beer, and from time to time he fondled the bottle of champagne with ostentatious hands. But every time he looked at Cheeta, who was throwing her dynamic curves in as many masculine directions as possible, his face softened, became human and somehow pathetic with longing.

He was really, Eve thought, a very nice little man, far too good for Cheeta.

The case of scotch was half empty before the potato chips could be taken from their glassine bags. The beer flowed from its keg in a never-ending stream, and the electrician began to sing, in a mournful tenor, *In The Shade Of The Old Apple Tree*, unmindful of the fact that Wiley was playing *St. Louis Blues* on the piano.

Eve was exhausted, but she forgot her fatigue in the excitement. Somebody gave her a drink and she drank it, hardly knowing she had drunk it as she watched Mersh, the candy butcher, go through a hilarious strip routine while Wiley cynically, or reproachfully, played *Frustration*, Sugar's strip music.

The girls were still in their almost invisible Sunflower costumes and, instead of feeling undressed, Eve felt an exhilarating sense of freedom. Glasses of scotch kept being put in her hand, and, watching the antics of the comics, she kept drinking them. Things got hazy.

Someone moaned in her ear, "Eve, dahling, you look wonderful, wonderful, wonderful, wonderful. You should never wear clothes. A body like yours expresses itself only when it is gloriously nude!"

She looked around and it was Gilbert, suave in his evening clothes. She giggled. It was the scotch. He had her hand and he was leading her into the darkness of the wings, murmuring in her ear.

Suddenly her exhaustion and the liquor caught up with her, and she drooped against him, closing her eyes wearily. All she wanted to do now was sleep. His arm around her felt so nice, so comforting, and so strong, holding her up.

"Dahling, dahling," he murmured, "dahling."

She felt herself sink back into something soft. The darkness was complete around them. His lips began to kiss her. Softly at first, brushing her hands, her cheeks, her neck. It was so nice to lie there and drift into sleep. The sound of the music and hilarity from the stage orchestrated a lullaby. Hands were softly running over her, experienced seeking fingers, and she found it soothing as her senses swam deeper into sleep.

Hungry lips ground into hers, and the hands became demanding. She turned her head away and moaned, and her hands weakly fended the searching. Then, abruptly, the chances of escape were gone and the hands were relentless. She struggled, but she could hardly move, as if under a crushing weight. She cried out feebly:

"Nononononono ..."

A voice panted in her ear, "Dahling ..." and his arms became resistless cables around her.

She tried to cry out ... then suddenly there was a wrenching pain as the arms were torn from around her. Her eyes fluttered open and vaguely she saw Jeff O'Hare, his face was white as death, standing and holding Gilbert Verne by the collar. Jeff's blue eyes looked muddied.

"You louse," he grated. "You cheap louse!"

His fist shot out and caught Gilbert on the side of the face. Blood gushed from Gilbert's nose. He bleated and frantically writhed to escape from the grip on his coat collar. O'Hare chopped him twice across the jaw, whirled him, shoved him toward a pale oblong of light that looked a million miles away. Jeff kicked and Gilbert, still bleating anxiously, sprawled forward on his hands and knees. He screeched and scurried toward the light on all fours, like a fleeing animal.

Jeff shouted after him, "Show your face around here again, punk, and by heaven, I'll beat it off you with a baseball bat!"

Eve was agonizingly aware of all of this. She knew she was lying, sprawled, on a pile of dusty velvet curtain, but she felt as weak as if she had just come out of anaesthetic after a major operation.

Jeff was on his knees beside her, demanding harshly, "Did he hurt you, baby? Did he hurt you? Tell me if he did. Tell me and I'll go out and kill him!"

Her head lolled. "Tired, Jeff," she breathed, "tired."

He gave her the bare bones of a smile, lifted her in his arms and walked toward the light with her.

"You poor kid," he murmured in her ear. "You're worn out, and some dope gave you too much to drink. I'll take you home."

"And tuck me in, Jeff," she said drowsily. She felt safe and comforted in his arms.

She slept lightly. There was motion, and she knew she was in a car in Jeff's arms. She walked. Her eyes were closed, but she walked. Up a set of stairs. She was in bed and someone was tucking the covers under her chin. Someone lightly kissed her parted lips. Her eyes opened, and this time it was the lean, ravaged face of Jeff O'Hare. Something seemed to pour out of her and she smiled tremulously at him. She put her arms around his neck and kissed him back. He started to draw back.

"Gotta go now," he muttered.

Panic exploded in her. There had been a nightmare, and Jeff had pulled her out of it and comforted her. Her arms tightened around him.

"No, Jeff," she pleaded. "No. Please no."

He sucked in his breath. "You don't know what you're saying, kid. You're not sober, Eve ..."

"I am, I am, I am, don't go, please don't go, Jeff!"

"You've been drinking ..." he was trying to convince somebody, perhaps himself, perhaps Eve, or perhaps it was the last voice of a weakening conscience.

She knew she had to make an effort. Otherwise, she knew, he would go and leave her with the memory of the nightmare—alone.

"I'm not drunk, Jeff," she said quite steadily, though it was the false steadiness of desperation. "I want you to stay. Please don't go."

He said wonderingly, "You know what you're saying ..."

Her emotion lunged toward him, enveloped him. "Yes. Yes. Don't go."

He cried, "Oh, Eve ... Evie ..."

Her lips opened to meet his kiss. She surged into his arms on the crest of something that was like a gigantic wave already toppling into the abyss of an angry sea, meeting violence with violence and, finally, peace with peace.

DEAD-END!
CHAPTER FOUR

Eve awakened the next morning filled with a lassitude she had never experienced before. It lay luxuriously in every long muscle. It pervaded her mind with a delicious haziness and made her want to stretch, sensuously, like a cat. It was as if something that had been long pent up within her had started to flow, warm and deep. The sunlight streamed through the windows and lay across her bed, like a lover. She pushed her covers from her, baring herself to the solar fire. It seemed to penetrate to the bone and to the marrow of the bone until it was an almost living thing within her. Her long thighs curved and she smiled, her head back in the pillow, her eyes closed.

It was several minutes before memory of the night before began to filter into her luxuriating consciousness. It came slowly, in drifting bits and snatches, then in a wave that engulfed her. She lay rigidly in the bed, clutching the sides of the mattress. Her body had betrayed her! Her tingling senses froze. Why had she let it happen? Not for a moment did she blame Jeff. It was not his fault. Not any part of it. He had been gentle, almost hesitant—her body remembered his hands and, for an instant, reasserted itself, yearning for him, remembering the far reaches and terrible heights of ecstasy. Kisses that had been like wings ...

Eve sat up and said stonily to her reflection in the mirror across the room, "Eve Barry, take a good look at yourself. A good look. You're acting like an adolescent school girl after her first necking party. Stop it!" Then, in the most school-teacherish voice she could muster, she repeated, "Stop it instantly, do you hear? Or you'll have to stay after school and wash the blackboards."

It took just exactly that touch of self-derision to break her mood. The remembrance of the dark joys fell away and her anger shrivelled. She giggled.

"Bad girl," she said. "Bad, ba-a-a-ad girl!"

She laughed and the laughter came a little bitterly from her. She had broken the mood, but she also had the uneasy feeling that she was destroying something.

After all, she thought defensively, nothing had happened. Nothing really. Gilbert Verne had made a pass at her, and Jeff had knocked him down. She had been grateful to Jeff, that was all. It had been a gratitude, a momentary necessity. Well, the moment was gone. It was over. To continue it, or to consider it as anything else was to walk into a blind alley, a dead-end. There was nothing in it for either of them. Nothing, absolutely nothing.

Calmly, she stepped out of bed and walked toward the shower—though not without an uneasy sidelong glance at the mirror, at the soft rise of her breasts, at the long, pearlescent spring of her thighs. Somehow, this morning, her body had a new significance, a new importance.

Her glance rested for a moment on the clock on the dressing table and she gasped. Eleven o'clock! She was due at the theatre in three quarters of an hour.

She showered, dressed hurriedly, drank a cup of hot coffee standing at the stove, and ran from the room, eating a banana. She took a bus to the corner of Broad and Market Street. Quickly she threaded her way through the hungry, milling lunch hour crowd that throngs the sidewalk. Sugar, as chorus captain, played no favorites. If you were late, you took a bawling out and were careful not to be late again. At least, not for a week or two.

A half block from the Rivoli, she saw Jeff standing outside, smoking a cigarette and ostensibly examining the ceiling of the marquee, but even at that distance she could see that his eyes were ranging the street, watching for her. She flushed, but tilted her chin and walked firmly toward him.

"Good morning, Jeff," she said in a voice that was barely audible.

And passed him without another word. She turned into the alley beside the theatre and fled toward the stage door, her heart thundering. She deafened her ears so that she would not hear if he called after her. But he did not. He stared after her, his face turning a sudden dead white. He snatched the cigarette from his lips, snapped it into the gutter and strode into the lobby, where the porter was haphazardly sloshing the tiled floor with a wet mop.

Jeff snarled at him, "Get a move on there. Shake your butt! The box office opens in a quarter of an hour." He stamped into his office.

The porter's eyes sprang wide with surprise. He looked up at the cashier behind the grill in the box office.

"That's show business for you," he said sourly. "One minute you're everybody's pal, and the next minute they're yelling for the garbage man if you show your face." He swung his mop with angry vigor.

The cashier grinned. "What do you want?" he asked. "Your name in lights?"

Eve burst through the stage door and ran down the steps to the dressing room, panting. She hesitated at the door of the dressing room. She felt suffocated. She dreaded walking in there, dreaded facing that battery of inquisitive, greedy eyes. They would be watching for her, she knew. They all knew that Jeff had taken her home. They would be speculating about it, making guesses, and when she walked in, Cheeta would make one of her shrewd, malicious remarks, and everybody would laugh.

Eve's hand trembled on the knob of the door. She wanted to run away and hide, but she turned the knob and walked in. No one looked up except Sugar.

And all Sugar did was ask mildly, "Where's the fire, Evie?" and turn back to Cheeta, who was massaging her breasts with oiled, perfumed palms, declaiming shrilly:

"Something happen last night. Cheeta knows. I meet Gilbert on the street. Such a face! I do not like Gilbert, but even so I feel sorry that even he has to walk around weeth such a face! I know sometheeng happen last night."

"He fell down," said Sugar sweetly. "He fell down and hurt himself."

"Ha-ha-ha," said Cheeta scornfully. She gestured. "He fall down? Thees I do not believe. He fall down on one side of his face. Then he get up and fall down on the other side of his face, eh? Then he fall down on his nose? No. Even Gilbert could not be so stupid. He fall down once, yes. He fall down twice—maybe he is a little dronk. But to fall down three times on his face, no. Not even on purpose. Thees I cannot believe. Sometheeng happen. To fall down three times in soch a way, one must have assistance. One must be encouraged to fall down three times. Maybe," she slyly turned her large black eyes on Eve, "there is somebody who can tell us how Gilbert was encouraged to fall down three times on his face, especially when he ees so fond of that face, eh?"

Eve sat stiffly in front of her mirror, knowing that if she opened her mouth to answer, they would all know the truth instantly. She felt Sugar squeeze her knee reassuringly.

"Well now," Sugar drawled, "if you must know the truth, he made a pass at Rosie, and her boy friend took him out in the alley for a little bout."

Cheeta's eyes glittered at Eve, then she shrugged. "Hokay," she said. Then, innocently, "But for soch a little theeng Gilbert was fired?"

"Sweetheart," said Sugar, "if I were you, I'd go straight to the horse's mouth. If Gilbert meant so much to me, I'd make a point of asking Jeff why he was fired."

"Gilbert meant notheeng to me! Notheeng!"

"You're making an awful fuss about nothing, then."

"I am not making a foss, but I theenk ..."

"Don't let it bother you, sweetheart," Sugar said with mock concern. "I'll tell you what I'll do. I'll go to Jeff myself. I'll tell him how you feel about Gilbert, and see if I can get Jeff to take him back on again. How's that?"

Cheeta glowered. Her eyes rested suspiciously on Eve, and then she shrugged again. "It is not so moch of a joke, I theenk," she muttered. "Maybe someday I find out, then we will see who is laughing, eh?" She gave Eve another significant glance and went primly back to massaging her breasts, counting aloud at each upward stroke of her palms.

Eve leaned toward Sugar and whispered, "Thanks."

Sugar raised her eyebrows. "For what?"

Eve flushed. Sugar knew the story, all right. Or part of it. The part in which Gilbert Verne had taken her back into the wings, and Sugar must have known that Jeff had knocked him down. And if Sugar knew that Jeff had taken her home ... She felt a beginning surge of emotion at the remembrance and grimly locked her mind against it.

"Thanks for not letting me get in a spat with Cheeta," she said to Sugar. "I was beginning to get the idea she had me in mind. I wasn't going to let her get away with it."

The words were so obviously false, so obviously not what she had started out to say, that Eve turned her head away from Sugar's searching glance and busied herself with her make-up. Sugar reached out and patted her hand.

"Don't let it throw you, Evie," she said a little sadly. "Keep it under control."

Eve did not have time to answer for there were three heavy knocks on the door and the stage manager's weary voice called out:

"Ten minutes, ten minutes. Can the chatter and get on the ball. Ten minutes to curtain. Get on the ball in there! Ten minutes, ten minutes."

The girls broke into a frenzy of last minute repairs on their make-up and costumes, and Cheeta hurriedly concluded her mammary massage; "... ninetyeightninetyninehondredfeeneesh!"

The orchestra was playing the overture when they ran up the stairs to the wings. Eve's eyes flew across the stage. Jeff usually stood over there, concealed from the audience by the tab, smoking a cigarette or one of his thin, dappled cigars. He usually looked up and smiled when she appeared amid the brightly chattering chorus girls. She was ready for him, ready to meet his smile with a casual smile of her own—but he was not there. In his place stood one of the stage hands, grumpily chewing his cud of tobacco.

Eve felt something hard and cold knot inside her breast. If he had been there, if he had smiled, she would have known that he had accepted last night for what it was—a moment of love that they had shared, but no more than that. His absence told her that he was taking this seriously—and suddenly she began to be a little afraid, for Jeff O'Hare was not a man to be treated lightly.

She glanced nervously at the typewritten scene-plot clipped to the electrician's switch board. Sugar's strip number followed the comics' Gazeeka Box routine, and Jeff would surely be backstage to catch that. He never missed when one of the chorus kids had a specialty in the show. Eve pressed her lips together. She, too, would be backstage when Sugar did her number. If there had to be a showdown with Jeff O'Hare, the sooner it came, the better. Then both of them would know where they stood. It would be better that way, she told herself, much better for both of them. And again she had the uneasy feeling that she was destroying something.

But there was only one thing that was important, one thing that came before all else, and that was Vance Owen. Nothing, not even Jeff O'Hare, was going to interfere with that.

Eve paraded through the opening number as if it were an unpleasant chore that had to be done before she could go out and play. It was a very uninteresting routine—one-two-three-kick-one-two-three-turn- one-two-three-kick—and Wiley, as choreographer, had shown a notable lack of enthusiasm for it even in rehearsal. It was a stock routine and had nothing to recommend it but the length and shapeliness of the legs of the girls in motion. The costumes were less than inspired. Eve wore an aquamarine G-string, pimpled with red bits of cut glass, a fringed and beaded brassiere, designed originally to give tantalizing glimpses of her exciting breasts, but which in actuality hung down limply, giving no glimpses, tantalizing or otherwise, of anything. The audience talked and coughed all the way through.

Eve hurried downstairs with the other girls to change costume. No one wanted to miss Sugar's *Frustration* strip. Eve was in the wings again before the comics had finished their Gazeeka Box skit. She watched them for a few moments, then turned away. Sugar, standing placidly at her elbow in her golden dress, said casually:

"Pretty crumby. I can't stand that guy."

Eve said ruefully, "He's not very funny, is he?"

"Funny! The funniest thing that guy ever did, Evie, was fall and break his leg at his grandmother's funeral. Look at him!"

Unable to get a laugh any other way, the comic was stuffing a violin into his pants.

Bored, Sugar remarked, "He did that once and the E-string broke. He jumped ten feet. No such luck this time, I suppose."

She turned away, wrinkling her nose. Then her eyebrows arched and she cried out in a bright, artificial voice;

"Well, if it isn't our playboy councilman. What's on your mind, Councilman?"

Eve turned, and it was as if an icy hand had gripped itself around her heart. Behind her, leaning against the electrician's switchboard smoking a dark, fragrant cigar, was a big blond bull of a man. Vance Owen! She felt the blood pulse into her face. He was bigger than she had expected him to be, and the sheer animal force of him was like heat that warmed or burned what it touched. His ruddy face was broad and big-boned, a brutal, arrogant face, not handsome, but strong in a way that would draw women to him. His neck was thick and muscular, and his shoulders tremendous. He reached out and patted Sugar on the fanny.

"Hi, Sugar," his voice rumbled out of him. "Where the hell's O'Hare?"

Sugar glanced across the stage to see if Jeff were standing in his favorite spot in the wings. "Did you try his office, Councilman?"

"Yeah, but they told me he'd be back here to catch your number." His bold eye ranged her body and he winked. "Kinda thought I'd like to catch it myself, Sugar."

Sugar signalled to one of the stage hands, who turned and ran for the stage door. Eve could not take her eyes from Owen. She watched him with a kind of horrible fascination, as if she were a bird and he a powerful, heavy-bodied rattlesnake. He glanced at her, and she felt his eyes on her as if they were hands.

He stood there, his powerful head thrown back, looking at her through the silken veil of smoke that wove from his cigar.

Sugar was saying, "Was there anything special you wanted to see Jeff about, Councilman?"

He turned back to her. A surge of anger roared through Eve. In another moment he would really have looked at her, really have noticed her, for she was wearing one of the most provocative costumes Wiley had yet designed—a diminutive little frilly black corset, a wisp of a French corset that barely covered the lower halves of her breasts and sat excitingly on her rounded hips. Black net stockings went half way up her gleaming thighs and were attached to the corset by black, ribboned garters. Her black shoes had ridiculous six-inch spike heels that made her legs look longer, slimmer and more intoxicating. This was the costume for the Folies Bergère ensemble number. It was a costume that gave even the plump girls a quality of heady femininity.

But Sugar's words had distracted his attention, and now he was grinning down at her. He had forgotten Eve entirely. She stood with her hands clenched whitely at her sides, then slowly she relaxed. There would be other times, other opportunities. This was not the last time Vance Owen would come into the theatre, nor even the last time he would come backstage. She could tell from the way Sugar greeted him that he made a practice of this, taking advantage of his political position.

And Sugar was anxious about something. Eve could see it in her nervous gestures and the way she kept glancing over Owen's shoulder toward the stage door.

"I hope you're not bringing us any bad news, Councilman," she said archly, trying to make it sound like a joke.

Owen ignored the anxious question and was fiddling with her dress.

"Say, that's a cute outfit, Sugar," his chuckle rumbled. "It comes apart in all directions. I know a few dames I'd like to see in an outfit like that." He pulled a zipper and the skirt fell partially away, exposing Sugar's soft thigh. "Well, whattaya know about that!"

She slapped his hand away. She tried to make it a playful slap, but her palm struck his hand with a sharp crack. There were two angry spots of red high on her cheekbones. Owen guffawed. The electrician came stalking toward his switchboard, a satanic gleam in his eyes.

"Less noise there, less noise," he glowered. "There's folks out front want to enjoy the show." He shouldered Owen out of the way and stood grasping a switch as the comics out on the stage went into a frenzy winding up their routine. Owen gave him a mean look and pushed out his jaw.

"Don't do that again, my friend," he said nastily. "The next time you want me out of your way, *ask* me!"

Sugar said quickly, "He didn't mean anything, Councilman. He's got to ring down the curtain on cue." She glanced frantically toward the stage door for the tenth or twelfth time. "Jeff'd have his scalp if he missed his cue."

"I don't give a damn what Jeff'd do. I don't like being pushed around, sister."

"He didn't *mean* anything ..."

"Cut it out. You're breaking my heart."

Eve was glad now that she had this opportunity to study Owen before she met him. Now she could see that he was dangerous, that she would have to be careful. He was arrogant, brutal and ruthless. Never for a moment did he really relax, never for a moment did he ever forget that he was out for Number One and nobody else. And, too, Eve could see that Sugar was handling him wrong, that Sugar was fanning his arrogance, giving him the opportunity to trample her. Sugar should have made a joke of it. Owen would have gone along with a gag, not because he had an active sense of humor, but because he was the kind of man whose prime fear was to appear ridiculous. Opposition would make him stronger, but ridicule would destroy him.

Eve filed this precious scrap of knowledge away in the strong-box of her mind for future use.

Fortunately, at this moment, the stage door opened and Jeff strolled in. He had been drinking. His hard blue eyes were very bright and very cold and his mouth was a lipless slash across his lean face. He gave Vance Owen a cold glance and said:

"Hi, Owen."

Sugar said shortly, "The Councilman's got something on his mind, Jeff," and strode away. As she passed Eve, she muttered, "Remind me to get my brass knuckles sharpened!"

Owen turned to Jeff with a big jovial smile that made him look a little like Alan Hale of the movies. "Hiya, Jeff-boy," he held out a big, meaty hand. "How's every little thing, kid?"

Jeff shook hands with enthusiasm. "Fine," he said, "till you walked in."

Owen chuckled, then, leaning closer to Jeff, sniffed. "Say," he said, "that's a pretty expensive smelling breath you got there, Jeff-boy. scotch?"

"I just had a couple for lunch in the gin mill across the street. Or have you and that City Hall crowd of yours made it against the law or something?"

Owen laughed and clapped Jeff on the shoulder. "I'm just a poor, hard-working politician, kid. Don't hold it against me. But, say, I got a little business I'd like to talk over with you."

Eve could not help comparing the two men. Vance was a mastiff, heavy-muscled and big, bigger than Jeff and taller by six inches, yet somehow he did not dwarf the shorter man. Instead, his bulk made Jeff look leaner, harder, faster.

When Owen mentioned business, Jeff's eyes turned wary.

"Business?" he said.

"Yeah. I'd like to buy out the house for Thursday night. I'm throwing a shindig for the boys in the Ironbound ward, the Down Neck crowd, and I thought I'd treat them to a show. Thursday a good night with you?"

"Tuesday'd be better, but Thursday's okay. It's kind of slack." Jeff's face suddenly became alert. "The Ironbound? What's the gimmick? That's not your ward. You've been running with the Forest Hill crowd."

"It's like this," Vance grinned and winked broadly, "I'm not throwing this party at all, get me? In fact, I don't know anything about it. Know what I mean?"

"Frankly, no."

Vance dug him in the ribs with his thumb and winked again. "It's the Vance Owen Club from Down Neck that's giving the party. Now do you get me?"

"I might have known it'd turn out to be some kind of political double-talk. What's a Vance Owen Club?"

"They're springing up all over the city, Jeff-boy," said Vance with satisfaction. "A spontaneous action of the citizens who want to honor their favorite son, meaning me. I've been working on it for eight months, and now it's spreading of its own accord. Mostly. That's the reason I'm throwing this party for the Down Neck gang. That's a tough mob down there, and you know what they think of the rich Forest Hill crowd. The Ironbound was the first ward I tried to swing on this deal, but I haven't been able to make any time with them, because they think I'm a Forest Hill boy, and anybody from Forest Hill is automatically on the spit-list. Know what I mean?"

"Yeah," said Jeff drily. "Sounds to me like they got good sense down in the Ironbound."

Vance's eyes narrowed. "Y'know, Jeff," he said slowly, "I've known you for a long time, but I'm beginning to think you more than half mean it when you rib me like that."

Jeff grinned thinly. "Now for Pete's sake," he said, "don't start to go intelligent on me."

Vance hesitated, then let a chuckle rumble from his deep chest. He was not ready to make an issue of it. He was still a little afraid of Jeff's barbed wit, afraid to appear ridiculous.

"That's the reason I like you, kid," he said heartily. "You're always good for a laugh, always ready to tear the top off a Cadillac and send it in for a box of corn flakes."

Jeff turned somber for a moment and he muttered, "Could be you're right, at that." He flickered a glance at Eve. "So you're treating the suckers to a burlesque show," he said to Vance, "just to show them you're one of the boys. Is that the idea?"

"Right on the nose, kid. We got a little office down Neck, and on the door it says Vance Owen Club. Right now we don't have any members, but I'm throwing in a crew to give away tickets to the show, and I'm willing to bet you that on Friday we'll be wearing out our fountain pens signing them up."

"Sure. Give away tickets every week and I'll bet you'll keep them signed up, too."

Vance let that one pass. "Now look, Jeff," he dropped his voice confidentially. "There won't be any cops and there won't be any censors in the house Thursday night. Get me?"

"What's there to get?"

"Don't be like that, kid. You know as well as I do your comics have to clean up their routine before they come into Newark. That's something you won't have to worry about on Thursday night."

Jeff said woodenly, "The comics clean up their act because I don't go for filth. And most of them don't have anything to clean up because they can be funny without it. Funnier."

"Sure, sure, Jeff. You're absolutely right. But that's not really what I meant. But these guys from Down Neck, they're a pretty tough bunch. Nothing prissy about them. Now you got some pretty nice looking peelers in your show this week, so on Thursday night, pass them the word that they don't have to stop at the G-string. Let them have some fun. Let them take it off."

Jeff put his hands behind him. He was mad clear through, and he felt safer with his hands behind him. The worst thing he could do, he knew, would be to smack a Councilman on the jaw.

"Tell you what to do, Owen," he said in a strained voice, "*you* pass the word to the girls to take off their G-strings. They develop their own routines, and I don't interfere. *You* tell them to take it off for the boys from Down Neck."

Vance fingered his muscular chin. "I couldn't do that, Jeff, and you know it."

"Send somebody else to do it, then," said Jeff with a thin, wicked, dancing grin on his lips. "But let me know when you send him, because I want to be around to see him get his jaw slapped sideways."

"Don't give me that, kid. Look, promise them an extra sawbuck apiece …"

"*You* promise them."

"Dammit, Jeff, I told you I can't do that. I'm in politics, kid, and I can't take the chance." He glanced around and saw Eve standing behind him. He turned back to Jeff and jerked his thumb toward Eve. "She got ear trouble?" he asked.

Jeff tilted his chin at Eve. "Beat it, girlie," he said. He took Vance's elbow. "Let's go to my office and you can write me out a check ..."

Talking in lower voices, they walked toward the stage door. Eve's face flamed as if Jeff had deliberately slapped her.

Which he had.

DEDICATED TO ROMANCE
CHAPTER FIVE

There was a sobbing crash of music from the orchestra pit, and Eve whirled as Sugar came running from the stage, panting. Her number was over, and she was holding the last remnant of the golden dress to her bare breasts. Her beaded G-string jauntily swung its glittering fringe against her glistening thighs. The applause was thunderous. Sugar rolled her eyes and grimaced.

"Hold your hats, kids," she muttered.

She ran out to the edge of the stage and took a bow, flirting the edges of the dress she held to her breasts so there was a promise, never fulfilled, of something more to be revealed.

Sugar strode, scowling, into the wings, refusing to take a second bow.

"Each time I do this," she said to Eve, "I tell myself, this is the last. I don't like stripping, and I never did. Not for that slap-happy gang out there, anyway."

"They seem to like you, Sugar."

"Hell, Evie, they'd like Grandma Moses if Jeff threw a blue spot on her and Wiley played the music." She took down a dressing gown from a hook on the switchboard and swung into it, her thrusting breasts standing out hard and glistening for a bared moment. "Say, what did that big political louse want Jeff for?" She was worried again.

Eve said carefully, "One of his clubs is buying out the house Thursday night."

Sugar looked relieved. "I was afraid we were in for another police raid or something," she confessed. "I'll give Vance Owen some credit. He always comes around and tips Jeff off beforehand. They went to school together, or something. I can't stand him."

Eve smiled. "I know. Jeff doesn't like him either, does he?"

"Jeff thinks he's a jerk. Say," Sugar sounded worried again, "Jeff wasn't making cracks at him, was he? Jeff always makes cracks, maybe seeing how far he can go. I keep telling him someday he's going to go too far. Owen's no dummy, and he can be damn mean, too. If he took it into his head to close the theatre, he'd close it so tight you couldn't get it open with a fire ax. Did they get along okay, Evie?"

"As far as I could see," Eve lied. She didn't want to tell Sugar too much. She didn't want Sugar to make trouble. "Does Vance Owen come backstage much?"

"Does he ever! Some weeks we can't get rid of him. He practically lives back here. And always running his damn hand over somebody's leg or patting you on the fanny. A guy like that should be handcuffed when there are women around."

"And the chorus kids let him do that?"

"Chorus kids! He wouldn't look at one of the kids from the chorus. He's what you'd call a snob. It's the strippers he goes after, the name acts, the specialty numbers. He likes to take them out after the show, just to prove to everybody that he can do it. And dammit," Sugar added ruefully, "he usually can. But not me. If I want to wrestle, I'll go down to the Newark Arena. Say, it seems to me you're awful interested in Vance Owen. You haven't gone and fallen for the guy, have you?"

Eve's mouth twisted. "No," she said, "I haven't fallen for him. He's about the last man I ever would fall for."

Sugar blew out a breath with exaggerated relief. "Whew! You had me worried for a minute, Evie. And you keep it that way, too, Evie. You'll save yourself a load of grief. If ever I saw poison on the hoof, that guy's it. And speaking of that, what gives between you and Jeff?"

Eve said steadily, "Nothing."

Sugar looked at her searchingly, then said a little sadly, "That's too bad. You'd be good for him. You're not a tart."

Eve caught the sadness that weighted the words, and before she could think, she asked, "Are you in love with Jeff, Sugar?" She gasped.

Sugar patted her hand. "Yes, I'm in love with Jeff," she said, "but not the way you mean. I'm in love with him because he's a tough scrapper, and I'm sorry for him because he's so tough that he hasn't left himself anything to fight for anymore. If you want to fall for the guy, go right ahead. I'm only in love with him because I got the screwy idea he needs something like that, and the minute he falls for somebody, like you maybe, I won't be in love with him anymore. And if you don't know what the hell I'm talking about, that's okay, because I don't know either."

"But what about Wiley, Sugar? I thought you were in love with Wiley. He's ... in love with you."

"Wiley?" Sugar tied her dressing gown around her waist with elaborate care. "Wiley, that twirp?" she laughed a little wildly. "Sorry I can't stay to hear the rest of it, Dorothy Dix, but I got to take the body beautiful downstairs and turn the shower on it. I got to wash the eyeballs off it.

Oh Gawd, how I hate to strip for a houseful of Popeyes! There must be an easier way to raise a sweat."

She gave her dressing gown another hitch around her and walked toward the stairway to the dressing room with a deliberately exaggerated swing to her voluptuously molded hips.

Suddenly Eve saw what she had to do. There was only one thing that was important, and that was meeting Vance Owen. That was what she had come to Newark from San Francisco to do—to meet Vance Owen and get to know him as intimately as possible, to make herself important to him. As a parader in the background for the chorus, she was nothing. If Vance Owen noticed her at all, it would be only because he happened to need a quick, easy pick-up at the moment, a girl he could make without the necessity of going through all the motions. From her own brief observations and from what Sugar had said—that he picked only the featured performers—that was the way he was. A snob, a show-off.

And Vance Owen had to want her, want her so desperately that it would be a fire in his blood, that he would roar in the starless night with desire and the consuming need of her!

And there was a way. Sugar had pointed it out. There was a way, and she had to take it. Now that her resolve was made, she could hardly wait for intermission, when the musicians went down under the stage to their locker room for a quick smoke or a quick drink. When the break came, she was waiting down there at the foot of their runway. She could hear the candy butcher upstairs chanting as he walked down the aisle holding up a package of his execrable chocolate:

"Hurry, hurry, hurry! Each and every package of this delicious confection I hold in my hand contains a guaranteed prize for your amusement and entertainment ... twelve different poses ... exciting!"

The musicians came plodding down from the orchestra pit. Some of them greeted her, "Hi, Eve," or, "How's the kid, Evie," but others, the worn-out ones, the lushes, hurried by her and went straight to their lockers, reaching quickly inside for their furtive bottles. Wiley came down last, thin, tired, sandy-haired.

He gave her a small smile and murmured, "If I were a beautiful woman, I wouldn't trust myself among a lot of lecherous musicians in a costume like that."

She was still wearing the provocative little black corset and long net stockings for the Follies number.

She put her hand on his arm. "Can I talk to you for a minute, Wiley?" she asked.

He looked toward his locker, and she knew he wanted a drink. "Can't it wait, Evie?" he asked.

"Ye-es." She allowed disappointment to show in her face. "Can ... I wait outside the locker room for you?"

Everybody knew that Wiley drank like a fish—before the show, during intermissions, between shows, after the show, and sometimes even during the show he ducked down in the darkness of the orchestra pit and pretending to tie his shoelace took a couple fast nips from a half-pint bottle he thought nobody knew about. But Wiley was ashamed to show the craving. He drank in front of the musicians, but that was all right. They were not outsiders. But anyone not a musician was an outsider from whom Wiley tried to conceal his weakness.

"Fine. Wait outside, Evie," he said with relief. "I just want a minute to freshen up." He was sidling away from her toward his locker even before he had finished speaking.

Two minutes later, he rejoined her outside the locker room door, his breath fragrant with the cognac he always drank. He was smiling, and his tiredness seemed momentarily to have dropped from him.

"Now, Evie, what's so important that has to be talked about during intermission?"

She began hesitantly, "Wiley, I'd like to do a specialty." She watched him anxiously to see how he took it. She had been in the theatre long enough to know that Wiley's word, on such things, was final. Even when Jeff O'Hare made a suggestion, it was Wiley, as choreographer, who made the actual decision.

He looked surprised for a moment, then nodded, still smiling. "I'm glad to hear that, Evie," he said sincerely. "We need some new blood in this crummy business. What can you do—sing, dance?"

It was obvious that he did not think of her as a stripper, and the strippers were the queens of burlesque. Straight dancers were tolerated, and singers were only fillers, something to pad the time between the comics and the strippers. Even the chorus was more important than a dancer or a singer.

"How would it be, Wiley," she asked slyly, "if I sang *O Promise Me* or *I Love You Truly?*"

He grinned. "Make it *I Love You—Fool* and you might have something. So you're not a singer. That means you want to dance. Solo? Or do you have a partner in mind?"

"I took ballet lessons once, when I was twelve, but I didn't like it very much. It hurt my toes."

"Then I don't get it, Evie. What do you have in mind? Don't tell me you're a female acrobat. Or do you have a trained seal at home in the bathtub? What kind of specialty *do* you want to do? You know I'll go along with you, if it's within reason."

Eve took a breath. "I want to do a specialty like Sugar's."

His jaw dropped. "You want to strip!"

"What's wrong with that? Sugar strips."

"That's different."

"Different than what?"

"Different than ..." he struggled for articulation, making small, vague motions with his hands. His face got very red. "It's not for you, that's all, Evie. It's okay for Sugar. She's been trouping since she was a kid. But it's not for you."

Her chance was slipping away from her, and she reached for it desperately, trying to hold it before it slipped away entirely.

"But why isn't it for me, Wiley?" she pleaded. "Look at me. Is my figure bad? Is that it? Is it a figure the boys out front wouldn't like?"

She stood straight before him and turned slowly, lifting her proud breasts with a breath, putting rhythm into the turning of her long, inflaming legs. He looked at her and seemed to draw back into himself.

"Don't work on me that way, Lillith," he said softly. "I'm fireproof."

There was a sudden hostility in his eyes.

"But, Wiley, I was just trying to show you ..." she looked at him helplessly.

The hostility disappeared from his eyes. "I'm a fool, of course," he said. "And I'm not fireproof. Sorry I made that crack. But what I said, still goes. You're got the figure. God knows you have the figure. You could have that gang out there tearing up the seats and throwing them in the aisle—except for one thing."

"Except for ... one thing?" she asked faintly.

"That's right, Evie. Except for one thing," he smiled to soften it for her. "You're too damn ladylike. Sometimes I look up from the pit and there you are standing on your little platform, looking as if you'd gotten there by mistake, as if everybody in the house was a Peeping Tom. That's no good, Evie. You can't get away with that in show business. You can't give your audience the impression you're doing them a favor. They'll resent it. They'll give you the bird. You can't act as if you'd only taken off your clothes to take a bath and that if we were gentlemen, we'd turn our heads away. See what I mean, Evie? It's your attitude."

"You're wrong, Wiley."

"I don't think so."

"That's not my attitude at all. I may *look* that way, but I'm not *thinking* that way. Would I ask to do a strip specialty if I were?"

"Maybe not," he admitted.

"Then all I've got to do is change my expression. Like this."

She threw back her head and gave it a shake to loosen her smoldering red hair. It was a fire around her shoulders. She made her eyes heavy-lidded and parted her lips, then lazily, sensuously, she smiled. When she stopped smiling, her lips were still parted, but held up now as if for a kiss, a kiss of passion and leashed violence. She had hardly moved, but her whole body seemed to be uplifted for the kiss.

Wiley's eyes spread. The bored and weary cynicism had dropped from him and for the moment he seemed alight with excitement. He grasped her arms and his fingers bit into her flesh.

"Do that again!" he ordered. "Start from the beginning and do that again!"

She did, but changing it a little this time. Not in the actual movement itself, but in something else, something Wiley could not put his finger on, but which he knew was pure artistry. When she smiled this time, it was the languorous smile of a woman who had been kissed, who had been loved, who had risen to the terrible heights of ecstasy, who had come back wanting one more kiss, one last sweet kiss.

One of the musicians looked out from the locker room and yawned, "Time to go, Wiley. Intermission's over."

Wiley whirled. "Don't bother me!" he snarled. "Beat it. Take another five."

When he turned back to Eve, his manner was brisk, professional. "Okay," he said. "You can do that for me, here. But can you do it up there on the stage?"

"I can do it anywhere. I can do it on the corner of Broad and Market Street."

"You'd be arrested." He laughed and added, "For inciting a riot. You've got something, Evie. Believe me, you've got something! But before I can say yes or no to giving you a strip spot in the show, I'll have to talk to Jeff."

"No, Wiley!"

"What do you mean, no? Why not?"

Intuitively, she knew Jeff would turn thumbs down, but she could not tell Wiley that. Nor could she tell him why.

Lamely, she said, "I ... I want to have my routine all set before we go to Jeff. I want to be able to show him, Wiley."

He looked puzzled. "I don't get it. You don't have to get anything set. He'll take my word that you're with it."

"Please, Wiley, I don't want to go to Jeff until I've got something to show him."

"Okay with me, but I don't see how you're going to work it. Where'll you rehearse? You can't rehearse here in the theatre. Jeff knows everything that goes on here. You know that."

She hadn't thought of that. She felt a little flutter of panic. It was too soon to go to Jeff. There were other girls who wanted to do a specialty, girls who had been in the chorus longer. Cheeta, for instance. Cheeta was always after Jeff to give her a spot in the show.

Wiley glanced at his watch and swore. "I have to run, Evie," he muttered. "Look. Suppose we do this. Have dinner with me after the matinee, and we'll talk it over. Okay?"

The next moment he was gone with his quick, nervous stride. Eve turned to go back to the dressing room. She was filled with a bubbling exultation. She was a step closer. A long full step. For an instant, the remembrance of Vance Owen rose in her mind, Vance Owen, handsome as a full-blooded bull, arrogant in his thick-muscled strength, so sure of himself, so casual and brutal with women.

Never before had she hated anyone so fiercely and now, having seen him, having listened to him, her hatred burned like a clear, hot, inextinguishable blue flame. She was fervently glad that he was so easy to hate. He might have been some harmless-looking non-entity, some mild mannered sheep. She had never met him before. She had only heard about him and the things he had done in San Francisco during the war. Many men had been different during the war. Some had been better men than they had been, some had been worse. Vance Owen, with his brutal arrogance and driving ambition, had been one of the bad ones. Oh, he was so easy to hate that it seemed like a gift from Heaven. Hatred is not an easy thing. It has to be nurtured. It cannot feed forever on itself. It has to have someone like Vance Owen to keep it hard, undeviating and angry, and the anger has to be a slow anger, the kind of anger that is willing to take its time. Eve was willing to take her time—within reason—because Vance Owen was the kind of man who could feed a hatred forever.

Eve was feeling cold and dedicated when Cheeta darted out of the shadows of old stored stage furniture at the side and hissed at her like an angry cat. She leaped in front of Eve, her huge dark eyes glittering. She was wearing nothing but a gaudily embroidered kimono, and as she gesticulated, it fell open, exposing her high, pointed breasts, the muscular symmetry of her legs, the flare of her violent hips.

"Ha-ha!" she cried dramatically. "Now it ees poor Wiley you are after. Do not theenk I was not watching. I see you. Lift your face for him to kees. Do you theenk I do not see thees? Kees me, kees me! Ha. Now what are you up to, eh?"

Involuntarily, Eve fell back a step, then she stiffened and snapped, "I don't think that's any of your business."

It was the wrong line to take with Cheeta. It was defensive, and defense only inspired Cheeta to new heights of invective and fury. She clawed her hands as if to scratch Eve's face to ribbons.

"May-bee I make it my business, eh? Do not theenk I believe that nonsense that it was Rosie's boy friend that beat poor Gilbert up. I know better. So now you are working on poor Wiley. I theenk maybe I tell Sugar of thees. I theenk you are a trobble-maker. I theenk this is no place for you, Mees Nose-In-The-Air. I theenk eet is more better if you are fired, but queeck. I theenk may-bee I tell Jeff O'Hare, too, so he weel know what kind of snake-behind-the-back you are!"

Eve's palm itched with the desire to lay it with vigor across the side of Cheeta's contorted face, but that would be a mistake. They would both be fired. She fought back a growing surge of panic. Cheeta was jealous, of course. Cheeta was jealous of anyone who was the center of attention, even if it was only the center of Wiley's attention. To be always in the limelight was the very breath of Cheeta's life.

Eve pulled herself together and smiled. "Dear Cheeta," she said with saccharine sweetness. "How would you like it, dear Cheeta, if someday I were to drop a little sulphuric acid in that perfumed Mazola oil you use to rub your bony chest? Why, in no time at all, you'd hardly have any chest left, to speak of." The very thought horrified her, but she kept the smile on her face.

Cheeta shrank away from her, covering her breasts with her hands, as if Eve already held a phial of acid. Her mouth trembled, and worked spasmodically, but no sound came forth, no sound but a small moan.

Eve pressed her advantage. "Or a little powdered glass in your jar of oil," she said. "It makes you itch, and you'll scratch yourself to pieces with your own fingernails. Now you mind your own business, dear dear Cheeta, and don't forget that I haven't got red hair for nothing!"

As she walked away from the cowering little Mexican girl, saying over and over to herself, *"I couldn't have spoken those words! I couldn't have, I couldn't have. I couldn't have said those awful things!"* She wanted to go somewhere and wash out her mouth with strong soap.

Yet, she knew that nothing less than a threat of such dire violence could have shut Cheeta up so completely.

THE CELESTIAL BODY
CHAPTER SIX

After the matinee, she walked up to the Anchorage on Branford Place, a bar and seafood restaurant. Wiley had told her to meet him there. He had a little business to take care of first, he said, but when he walked in fifteen minutes later, his breath was again inflammable with cognac, and she knew that his "business" had been a quick stop somewhere for three or four straight shots. He was not drunk, however. Wiley was never drunk. At least, he never showed it. Which was more than could be said for some.

His sandy hair was crisply combed, his eyes twinkled, and his face had a healthy flush. The lights in the Anchorage were soft, and he looked as lean and fit as a fox hunter. Eve was at the bar, and he slid up on the stool beside her.

"I've been thinking about you all afternoon," he said gaily. "My Gawd, that body of yours! It sticks in a man's mind like a dagger. You don't mind if I talk about your body, do you? It's a wonderful body. Everybody should talk about it. Did you know you had such a wonderful body?"

Eve felt the pink steal into her face. "I ... hadn't thought much about it," she said.

"Good, good. It's better that way. If you'd thought about it, you might have turned out like that little witch Cheeta, who sits in front of a mirror caressing herself. Every time she crosses her legs, she's got a man in mind. No, if you'd thought about your body, you'd probably have done all the things women do to spoil it—exercises, massage, girdles. You'd have been trying to make it look like Betty Grable or Hedy Lamarr, and that's foolishness. If your body were a concerto, I'd play it with a full symphony orchestra. I'd give a concert. If I were Harry James, I'd play it on the trumpet. If I were Gregory Peck, I'd make love to it on the biggest screen in the world. If I were Congress, I'd pass a law. Hell, I'd pass a dozen laws—one for each leg, one for your breasts, one for your lips. That makes five. I'd think of seven others. But, being what I am, I'll make you the best damn strip woman in the business!"

It was the cognac, Eve decided. Normally, Wiley was as taciturn as a morgue attendant.

Without his having ordered, the bartender set a double cognac in front of him. He gulped it and twiddled his fingers, ordering a second, but never once taking his sparkling eyes off Eve, the words tumbling from him in full spate.

"As I said, I've been thinking about you all afternoon. If you don't want to put it up to Jeff O'Hare on my say-so, that's your affair. You must have your reasons," he shrugged lightly. "But you have to have a place to rehearse. You can't rehearse in a hotel room. You have to have space. You have to have a stage. Professionals can rehearse on a picket fence, but you're not a professional, Evie dear, as much as I love you. You need a stage. So, I have a stage for you!" He brought it out with an air of triumph.

She cried, "Wiley!" She flung her arms around his neck and kissed him.

"I've got two stages for you," said Wiley. "I've got three, four, five, six, seven ..."

The barkeep, who had been eavesdropping, grinned, "Sure, and it's meself that can dig up the eighth."

Eve was too happy to blush or mind what anybody said. "Where is it, Wiley?" she begged. "Where is it?"

"Know the old Opera House?"

"I don't know Newark, Wiley."

"Well, it's on North Broad Street. It's too far out, and they can't rent it. I played there once. Did you know I was a concert pianist? Once. Just once. A damn good one, too. But one day I thought, ah the hell with this, and went into show business. Never regretted it."

For a moment his eyes were faraway and wistful, and Eve could see that he regretted it very much. He reached out for the glass the barkeep had refilled and gulped it.

"Anyway," he said briskly, "I know the renting agent for the Opera House, so I gave him a ring, and he said hell go ahead and use it, Wiley. There's a good piano—a Steinway—and they have to keep it in condition just in case. So there you are. We can start first thing in the morning."

Eve grasped his arm. "Why can't we start tonight, Wiley?" she begged urgently. "I've got all sorts of ideas for the routine. I'm just bursting with ideas. I won't be able to sleep a wink tonight. I won't be any good tomorrow. Please, can't we start tonight, Wiley?"

"After the show?" he said incredulously.

"Why not?"

He looked at his empty glass and twiddled his fingers at the bartender.

"Why not," he echoed. "Sure. Let's shoot the moon. You're going to be pooped, though, Evie. You've had two matinees, and you'll have another show tonight. Sure you wouldn't rather wait till morning, after you've had a good night's rest?"

"No!" she cried "Oh, no!"

Wiley looked at the bartender. "Once in a lifetime," he said in a conversational tone, "you meet a performer like this. She's got everything except experience. And right away she wants to work you to the bone. I wish I were twenty years younger."

The barkeep gave him a clinical glance. "That," he said judiciously, "would make you about fifteen. What were you good for at fifteen?"

CHANGE OF HEART!
CHAPTER SEVEN

Eve had to be back at the theatre a half hour before Wiley, but before she left the Anchorage, she made sure that he ate dinner: He'd had six cognacs that she knew of and though he was not drunk, he was in a state of elation.

"But I never eat dinner," he protested. "Isn't that a fact, Mac?" He appealed to the barkeep.

"Yep," said the barkeep drily, "that's a fact and how are your ulcers today. If I was you I'd listen to the lady and do my ulcers a favor."

Wiley groaned. "Everybody hates me."

But when Eve left the Anchorage, he had finished a bowl of clam chowder and was glumly chewing his way through a swordfish steak with mashed potatoes and peas.

Jeff was standing outside the Rivoli, a cigar jutting from his mouth at a thoughtful angle. He was leaning against the wall at the mouth of the alley that led to the stage door.

In a low voice, Eve said, "Good evening, Jeff," and would have passed him, but he put out a long arm and stopped her.

"Don't be like that, Evie," he said softly.

Her heart began to thud. His fingers were gentle on her arm, but the remembrance of his touch sent a prickling shiver through her. Feeling the warm blood pulse in her face, she kept her head down.

"Don't hold last night against me, Evie," he pleaded. "I was out of my mind. I've been out of my mind all day, just thinking about you. Don't hold it against me."

She whispered, "I'm not holding it against you, Jeff."

His fingers tightened on her arm. "Evie!"

"No, Jeff, I ..." the words were coming with difficulty. If only he hadn't touched her! If only her senses hadn't reeled and surged toward him at that pressure of his fingers on her arm! Her emotions were clamoring, and it frightened her. "I don't want to make any demands on you, Jeff," the words came with a rush, "and I don't want you to make any demands on me. We'll have to forget last night. We'll have to forget it happened!"

His painful grin twisted into his cheek like a knife. "Ah, now," he said, "that's an impossible thing you're asking a man to do. A man who's kissed you and held you in his arms in the night when men and women turn to flame, a man can't forget just for the asking!"

She forced herself to say mockingly, "You're a poet, Jeff?" She had to break this kindling mood!

"No, not a poet. Just the man you're asking to forget he's on fire. Would you have me burn myself out and turn to ashes, Evie?"

"Please, Jeff. It was a mistake. You know it was a mistake."

"Look me in the face and say it was a mistake. Why won't you look me in the face, darling?"

She looked up into his face, intending to keep her eyes cool and self-possessed, but when she saw his mouth so close, she could feel it again on her lips, seeking the kiss that had sent them rocketing into passion.

She stammered, "Please Jeff. People are beginning to look at us."

"Let them. They're only looking because you're so heart-breakingly lovely, and they're envying me. Evie, listen," his voice dropped into pleading. "Don't let's forget last night. Let's just say that maybe we got off on the wrong foot. Let's go out tonight after the show. Let's call it our *first* date. We can take a ride up Boulevard East on the Palisades and look at the lights of New York across the Hudson, and afterward we can go down to Hoboken and have steak sandwiches in Myers Hotel ..."

His eyes were sparkling, and she knew she had to stop him before it became too real in his mind. "Not tonight, Jeff."

"Tomorrow night, then, Evie?"

"Ask me again at the end of the week."

"But why not tonight or tomorrow...." he stopped. "There I go again," he said ruefully, "trying to finish the fight in the first round. I keep forgetting this isn't just a three-round prelim. This is the big fifteen-rounder for the championship."

"But it's not a fight, Jeff," she reminded him gently.

"No?" he grinned. "Then why am I so groggy? Somebody sure pasted me one on the button, and I hear the bells ringing. Sure, it's not a fight, and I know it. But I used to be in the ring, and it's a way of talking when things are important to me. I'll ask you again at the end of the week, Evie. You meant that now, didn't you?"

"Yes, Jeff." Then swiftly, "How did you make out with that awful politician, that Councilman Owen? About the girls stripping ... all the way, I mean."

Jeff's lean face darkened, and he said shortly, "He's dead set on it."

"What are you going to do?"

"I don't know."

"Be careful, Jeff. He's dangerous."

"He's pitiful. When we were kids, I used to kick his tail all the way to school every morning, and in the afternoon I kicked it all the way home. And I can still do it. He's pitiful."

Before Eve could retort that they weren't kids anymore, Jeff made a short, dismissing gesture with his right hand and smiled at her. The smile drove all the toughness out of his face, leaving something incredibly shy and boyish.

"Ah," he said, "who wants to talk about that *schlimazl?* I want to set things right between us. You had me scared all day, Evie. Honest." He looked down at the cigar in his hand and mumbled, "I was so sure I'd made a mess of things. I ... I guess I'm still just a tough kid from Down Neck, but I'm nuts about you, honey. It's never hit me like this before. It's the old one-two. I've had dames before, but when I look at you, I can't remember them. I can't remember their names. I can't even remember their faces! They used to say I knew how to pick 'em, so they couldn't all have been Airedales—but I can't remember them."

Something rose in Eve's throat and she felt as if she were choking. There was a kind of dazed look on Jeff's face, as if he actually had been hit and partially stunned, a look of groping consternation, as if he didn't understand what had happened to him. Impulsively, she leaned forward, kissed him lightly on the lips, then walked quickly down the alley toward the stage door.

The earth had opened at her feet—not as a pitfall, but to reveal the hidden riches that lay in its bosom. She was in love with Jeff O'Hare! She was in love with him. The words began to drum on her mind—*in love with him, in love with him, in love with him!*

She pushed through the stage door. The two stage hands were playing checkers just inside, and they looked up when Eve walked in with a lilting step. One of them took his pipe from his mouth and pointed the stem at her.

"Look at the face on her," he chuckled. "What happened, Evie? You just find five dollars on the sidewalk?"

The other stage hand said scornfully, "You old fool, it takes more than five dollars to make a girl look like that nowadays. I'll bet you she just come from a beauty salon. I know that look. That's the look my daughter gets when *she* comes from a beauty salon, like she's Lana Turner, Betty Grable and Greer Garson all rolled into one. Right, Evie?"

Eve laughed, blushing. "You're both wrong," she said. "It's just that I had a good dinner, that's all." She danced down the steps to the dressing room, humming to herself.

She dropped into her chair before the mirror at Sugar's side and took off her blouse and brassiere. One of the girls down the table let out a long wolf-whistle, and Eve hastily covered her thrusting breasts with a towel. Still humming, she began to cream her face and neck before putting on make-up.

Sugar said sourly, "I'm glad somebody's in good humor."

Eve stared at her, startled. Sugar was always in such good humor herself, but Sugar's face was stony.

"What's the matter?" Eve asked.

"Haven't you heard the latest?"

"The latest what?"

"About that creep Councilman Owen. It's all over the theatre. Bobo the Dog-faced Boy overheard him talking to Jeff this afternoon."

Bobo the Dog-faced Boy was the girls' name for the grumpy electrician.

Eve felt as if a cold hand had been laid over her heart, freezing the song within her.

Sugar went on angrily, "Owen wants Jeff to make the girls strip, and he means strip. He's throwing a theatre party for his gashouse pals from Down Neck on Thursday, and he wants to show them a good time."

Eve cried, "But Jeff won't let the girls do that!"

"No? If Jeff knows what's good for him, he will. Right now, Owen's about the hottest thing in Newark politics. Don't get in his way. When he wants something, he *wants* it, or else. Don't worry, Evie, we'll get the word tonight or tomorrow. Jeff's a nice guy, but he's smart enough to know which way the wind's blowing."

"I don't believe it!"

"Don't be naïve, Evie. Jeff hasn't any choice. Owen can close this joint like that," Sugar snapped her fingers. "This is a burlesque house, sweetheart, and in this town, even the dogcatcher can get his name in the paper just by making faces at us."

"But Jeff will never, never, never ..."

"Five'll get you ten, kiddo," Sugar said drily.

Eve tossed her head. "That's a bet," she said.

Sugar reached over and patted her hand. "I used to have stars in my eyes, too." Then, gloomily, "But I'm telling you one thing. This is one little girl who isn't going to peel for that gang of jerks. Don't tell anybody, but I got inside information that on Thursday I'll be in bed with a bad case of logos-on-the-bogos. I've talked to the other two strippers. One of them's a tramp and'll do anything, but the other one's okay and she's reserved a broken leg for that night. The hell with Owen. And the hell with Jeff O'Hare, too."

Eve said faintly, "Jeff wouldn't do that."

Sugar shrugged.

As chorus captain, Sugar set the tone for the rest of the girls, and the opening number was very sloppily performed. The chorus line was very ragged. The sturdy, shapely little legs that had kicked with such precision in rehearsal, now kicked every which way, and Cheeta Rodriguez, who always had a feud with one girl or another, viciously kicked a tall brunette, named Janet, on the side of the thigh during the pinwheel routine. The moment the curtain came down, Janet whirled on Cheeta and gave her a full-armed open-handed slap across the face that sent her staggering into the wings. Cheeta crouched, spitting like a cat, then hurled herself at the brunette. Sugar caught her by the hair and pulled her back on her heels.

"You had it coming, pepper," she said casually.

"Let her go," said Janet, breathing heavily. "I'll take her apart. I'll massage her chest for her. Look at my leg. I'll be black and blue for a month."

Sugar said shortly, "Won't show if you powder it. Now cut it out, or I'll kick both of your teeth in."

The girls were silent. Ordinarily, Sugar would have fired both of them, or at the very least would have docked them a good slice of a week's pay. Something was going on.

Wiley came storming up the stairway from under the stage. He had left the orchestra in charge of the first violin.

"What's the matter with you kids?" he hissed at Sugar. "Girl scouts on crutches could have done that number better. Come on now, pull yourselves together. That was the crummiest performance I've ever seen."

Sugar flipped his tie out of his vest. "Write a letter to the newspaper, little brother," she said coolly. "Send Jeff O'Hare an inter-office memo."

Wiley's face jerked .as if she had slapped him. She walked toward the stairway to the dressing room, and he stared after her, his eyes bleak. She had never spoken so contemptuously to him before. He turned and saw Eve standing there. He fumbled his tie back into the V of his vest, making an effort to recover his dignity. He smiled at her, but it was a dead smile. She had been intending to tell him that she had changed her mind about working with him on the strip routine, but seeing him standing there so forlorn, so without hope, the words would not come to her lips. The discovery that she was in love with Jeff O'Hare had changed everything. She wanted nothing now but to please Jeff. Even Vance Owen was forgotten. Nothing mattered but Jeff. She was waiting now to see him so that she could tell him ...

Wiley mumbled, "See you after the show, Evie," and shambled away. Sugar had killed something in him. Some men could laugh off being treated like that, but Wiley was not one of them.

Wondering how she was going to tell Wiley it was all off now, Eve walked slowly down the stairs to the dressing room. Sugar was seated at her table, clutching a white envelope in her hand. She looked up at Eve, then thrust the envelope at her.

"Read that," she said harshly. "It looks like you owe me five." There was a typewritten slip in the envelope. Eve read it mechanically. It said;

"Please see me about special routine for Theatre Party Thurs. nite. J. O'Hare."

Sugar had been right. Jeff had given in. Eve knew now how Wiley had felt—stunned, betrayed. Jeff had betrayed her. He had talked big, but in the end he was giving Vance Owen what he wanted. And this was the man she had thought she loved?

She opened her purse and tossed a five dollar bill on the table in front of Sugar.

"It's worth it," she said woodenly. "It's worth every penny just to find out."

Now she was glad she had not cancelled her date with Wiley. Now she was going through with it. Nothing would ever change her mind again!

BACCHANALE!
CHAPTER EIGHT

The old opera house was on North Broad Street, about a half mile past the cemetery. It was not actually named the old opera house. The name on the marquee was the Savoy Theatre. The one-sheets in the frames outside the theatre advertised *La Bohème* with a New York Opera Company, but the sheets were several months old and streaked by the sun and rain.

Eve had taken a cab straight from the Rivoli, for Wiley had asked her to meet him at the Savoy. She waited fifteen minutes on the dark sidewalk, peering now and then into the gloomy, unlighted lobby, before Wiley boisterously drove up in another cab. He had had several drinks and carried a bottle in a brown paper bag under his arm.

He staggered a little as he paid off the cab.

"Now don't tell me I'm drunk," he said solemnly to Eve. "It's purely temporary." He fished a key from his pocket and opened the lobby door. For a moment, his head was turned toward the street light, and she saw the shine of tears in his eyes. He took her elbow and steered her into the unmoving, dusty-smelling air.

"Wait here," he said when they were inside the black vault of the auditorium. He took a pencil-thin flashlight from his pocket and walked down the aisle in a tiny cone of light. He walked very steadily. He had been right. He had been drunk, and now he did not seem drunk at all. It had been purely temporary.

She saw him trot up the stairs at the side of the stage, and then his light disappeared as he walked into the wings. The darkness closed in on her. She put her hand behind her, feeling for the solidity of the wall. The darkness was not merely quiet any longer. There was something breathless in it—not exactly menacing, but waiting.

Wiley's voice came thin but cheerfully out of the vault of blackness, "I keep getting the wrong switch. There. Did that light anything?"

"I don't see anything." Then in a sudden spurt of panic, "Maybe the electricity's not turned on, Wiley. I think we'd better go."

"Don't be silly." He laughed. "It's turned on, all right. It's just a matter of finding the right switch. Here's a big one ... ah!"

The big 500-watt work light, high in the ceiling of the auditorium, threw its sudden hard glare, showing the paint peeling from the walls like scabs, showing the tattered upholstery on the seats.

The curtain was drawn back from the stage, revealing a bedroom set. There was a queer, high, old-fashioned bed, a big box-like closet, a few chairs and a washstand with a white bowl and a white pitcher.

Wiley came out on the stage and looked around, wrinkling his nose. "That's terrible," he said critically. "There's better lighting in Penn Station. Hold everything. I'll turn on the foots."

He trotted off-stage again. A moment later the warm footlights went up and the work light went off. It was a miracle. A moment before, the theatre had seemed rather horrible and dirty, but now it was warm and friendly, and even the bedroom set on the stage looked like a pleasant glimpse into the comfortable past. Eve walked down the aisle.

Wiley strutted out on the stage. He put his hand to his chest and began to sing, throwing in a lot of ho-ho-ho's like an operatic baritone. Eve clapped.

"Very good, Nelson Eddy," she cried.

"Nelson Eddy nothing," he said indignantly. "I'm Lawrence Tibbett. Nelson Eddy doesn't have that much schmaltz."

He leaped lightly down into the orchestra pit and threaded his way through the chairs and music racks to the big black concert grand piano. He opened the lid and ran his fingers up the keys. He grinned at Eve.

"That's a piano," he said.

He sat down before it, clawed his hands and wrenched three crashing chords from it, then another three even more majestic, but when he really started to play, it wasn't Beethoven, Brahms or Mozart—it was boogie-woogie. He stopped suddenly, feeling her grave eyes on him.

"You're so beautiful," he said. He leaned forward and kissed her arm inside the bend of her elbow. "So beautiful," he murmured.

Eve put her arms behind her. "We came here to work, Wiley." "You're being mean to me."

"Are we going to work, Wiley?"

"So beautiful—but so cold, so hard. Do you know what opera that scene is from?" He pointed at the old-fashioned bedroom on the stage. "That's from *Traviata*. *Traviata's* all about a beautiful courtesan. She dies in the end. It has some very passionate music in it. I'll play some for you later. But in the meantime, you're right. We came here to work."

He took off his coat, loosened his tie and the collar and lit a cigarette.

"Now the first thing to do," he said, "is to figure out a routine for you. You can't just come out, take off your clothes, then leave. You have to take them off in a special way—and you, you have to take them off in a very special way. Now, do you have any ideas?"

He wasn't clowning now. He was very businesslike. Eve sat down on the bench beside him.

"I know what I don't want to do," she said thoughtfully. "I don't want one of those routines where I walk up and down the stage, showing a little leg, pulling first a petticoat from under my dress, then a brassiere from under my blouse, then taking off my skirt, then winding up at the end of the stage with my blouse off, giving them just a glimpse of a bare chest before the lights go out. That's what I don't want."

Wiley laughed, because Eve had succinctly described the most usual of all strip routines. "No grinds?" he asked, "No bumps?"

"They're not really necessary, are they? I mean, the girls waggle their hips like that because they can't think of anything else to do, don't they?"

"More or less," Wiley agreed. "But what *do* you want to do?"

"Well, I'd thought of something like this. I'll come out in an old-fashioned hoop-skirt ..."

"No."

"Wait till I finish, Wiley!"

"I don't have to. I don't like it. It's too awkward to take off all those draperies. There'd be yards of it!"

"But Wiley, all I need are a few zippers ..."

"And in the second place," he interrupted firmly, "it's a costume, and who cares if you take off a costume? They expect you to take off a costume, so what good is it? One of the fine points of stripping is to make the boys think they're seeing something they shouldn't—so you've got to be wearing something that doesn't look like a costume in the first place. Just a simple street dress with an ordinary brassiere and a garter belt under it is actually the most effective outfit."

"Why?" asked Eve stubbornly.

"Because it's like walking down the street and seeing a girl take off her clothes on the corner of Broad and Market. It's like looking in your neighbor's window and watching his young and beautiful wife undress. It's got an added tickle because the primary idea behind it is that it's *something they shouldn't be seeing.*"

"Ye-s, but taking off an ordinary street dress with an ordinary brassiere and an ordinary garter belt underneath, is too much like taking off my clothes on the corner of Broad and Market."

"And you don't like that?" he asked seriously.

"No!"

"Well, good for you," he laughed softly. "I said you needed a very special routine, didn't I? Well, I've got one for you. It's a honey. They'll tear up the seats and beat themselves over the head when they see it."

Eve grasped his arm. "What is it, Wiley?"

He pretended to evade the question. "Now there won't be any special zippers on this outfit, Evie. When you take it off, you'll take it off over your head the way all girls take off their dresses. You're not going to be squeamish about that, are you?"

"You're teasing me, Wiley."

"Not at all," the corners of his eyes crinkled as if he were laughing inside. "And furthermore, you're not going to be wearing any special gadgets underneath, like G-strings or beaded brassieres like the rest of the peelers. It'll be just you and your pretty underwear, and the boys out front staring with their eyes bulging like ducks' eggs."

"You're making this up!"

"No. And you'll be wearing nylon stockings, high-heeled shoes and a garter belt. Can you imagine the sensation those wonderful legs of yours'll make?"

"You're making it sound rather dreadful."

He rippled his fingers on the keys of the piano. "You're sure you want to go through with it?" he asked slyly.

"What's the routine, Wiley?"

He saw the high color in her cheeks, and he knew if he teased her further, she'd blow up. You couldn't take too many liberties with a redhead. They were too combustible.

"Okay," he said. "It's a good routine. You're a bride. You'd make a beautiful one—"

He saw the glint in her eyes, and he said quickly, "Before you sound off, just listen, will you, Evie? Remember the *Spectre of the Rose*, the ballet, where the young girl comes home from a ball and dreams of the guy she's in love with, or something like that? Well, this is the same idea, in a way. When the curtain goes up, you walk into this bedroom set, all dressed up like a bride, veil and all. You're carrying a bouquet of flowers. The orchestra'll be playing a little wedding march music, but we'll swing it, give it a nice dance tempo. You'll come in the door and you'll turn and laughing, close the door as if you're telling somebody to stay outside until you're ready. The idea is that the groom wants to come in, but you're telling him to stay out until you're ready. How's it sound so far?"

She did not have to answer. The look of horror on her face was more than a thousand vituperative words. He put his hands over hers and said gently:

"Look, darling, if you can't do this without making a mock of organized marriage, then you can't do it without cheapening yourself, which is silly. Forget all that malarkey I gave you before. Forget it. I was just making a funny. I just wanted to get you sore, and don't ask me why. Maybe because you're so goddam beautiful when you're sore. But this can be a very lovely thing. A very lovely thing—a kind of ballet, like the *Spectre of the Rose*. Here's a young girl, just married, in love with the guy she married!"

He jumped up from the piano bench, vaulted up on the stage, postured. He was the young bride; walking into the bedroom with the bouquet of flowers cradled in his arm.

"Laughing, but a little frightened, she holds back her lover-husband-to-be at the door," he was arched at the door, yet timid, closing it just a little too quickly, stepping back from it, clasping his hands together as if suddenly worried—had he (the bride) been too brusque in shutting her young husband from the bedroom? But no. She is sure of his love, and anyway, it will be for just a few moments. Wiley (illustrating) danced with the bouquet, the symbol of their eager young love.

"Here," he called down to Eve, "I'll interpolate a little of Debussy's *L'Après-midi d'un Faune* music, swinging it, of course, so the cash customers don't get the idea they're listening to *good* music and walk out on us."

He danced with the bouquet, holding it in adoration, a pagan thing.

"Love on the eve of consummation," he called down to Evie. "Get the idea? You're young, you're pure—but you're about to give your all to this young guy you just married. You're a little afraid, but you're yearning for it with every red corpuscle in your body. If you can get that across, it's art. Now come's part two, and in here I'll write in some of the *Bacchanale* music from *Samson and Delilah*, but legato and very pure. Now you are beginning to take off your wedding dress. Again, this is a symbol. You are putting behind you the uniform of virginity. You are about to enter the corridor that leads to the fulfillment of your womanhood. This part of the dance should be a little sensual, yet still virginal. For, after all, you're still supposed to be a virgin. So you take it off slowly, giving the appearance of reluctance."

He danced it, pretending to take off a wedding gown, lifting the hem of the dress, dropping it, lifting it, and then with a single sinuous movement, taking it off entirely.

"Now," he called down to Eve, "it should be obvious that you have made a definite choice. This is the point at which most young wives make it or break it. But you are going to love your young husband. You are going to give him a love that he has never known before and from which he will never want a change. You dance a moment with your wedding gown, finally discarding it as a garment you have suddenly outworn."

Wiley, a little angularly, illustrated that part of the dance, throwing the wedding gown from him.

"Now," he said, "you are standing here in your slip. You look toward the door. The groom has just called out impatiently to you. You turn shy again at the sound of his voice. You pantomime for him to be patient just a little longer. You take off the slip. You stand there in your undies—they'll be white satin trimmed with lace, and you'll have on a lacy bra. Now you have a choice of three nightgowns. You hold up one, covering yourself. You dance a little with it. You hold up another, you hold up the third, glancing toward the door behind which the groom is waiting with increasing impatience. The tempo of the music is faster and more passionate in character. You take off your shoes and stockings. You lift your arms and slip on the nightgown, down to here," his hand described a line that would cut across the meridian of her breasts. "You take off your brassiere, and the nightgown slips down to your hips, and as you take off your panties, the nightgown slips all the way down. You leap into bed. You look toward the door and raise your arm. The door starts to open, the music reaches a tremendous crescendo, there is a crashing chord. The lights go out, the curtain falls." He sat down on the edge of the bed and reached for a cigarette. "Think you can do it?" he asked in a matter of fact voice.

In a very small voice Eve said, "It'll be terrible if I don't do it just right. I mean, if I keep leering at that closed door, I'll look like a ... a ... prostitute."

"I'm not afraid of that," Wiley said. "I'm afraid you might get stage fright and look as if you're about to be raped. Let's do a quick run-through and see how it shapes up."

Eve's heart was beating very fast as she mounted the stage. The routine Wiley had sketchily outlined was a job for an experienced actress, and aside from her parading behind the chorus in the Rivoli, the only acting she had ever done was when she had made faces at Wiley that evening at the bar.

At the piano, Wiley noodled through a swing version of *O Promise Me*, then swung into the *Wedding March*. He raised his arm.

"That's your cue," he called. "Now back in through the door, laughing and keeping your young and eager groom out of the room." Stiffly, she obeyed, knowing she was doing it all wrong. Wiley brought down his fists on the piano in a disgusted discord. He jumped up, flapping his hands at her.

"No, no, no!" he cried. "Don't *smirk* at him. You've never been married before. This is your first husband, not your fifth. You've never had a man in your bedroom before. You love the guy, but you're timid. You're acting as if you're sending him down to the gin mill for a bottle of rye so you can have a real party. Now come on, get with it. You're a bride, a young bride, and you're beginning to realize that in about a half hour you're going to know what love is. We'll try it again."

They tried it again. Eve postured at the door, repulsing the eager male. Just when she was sure she had it, Wiley started playing *Minnie The Moocher*.

"We'll try it again from the beginning," he said shortly.

It wasn't until the eighth try that Eve began to *feel* like a bride. It wasn't a matter of making faces now; it was in every timid motion of her hands, in the tilt of her head.

Wiley yelled, "Wow!" and hammered out *The Stars And Stripes Forever*. "Now you're with it, kid. Next comes your dance with the bridal bouquet ..."

His fingers purled over the piano. He made the *Samson and Delilah Bacchanale* sound like a spring song, springtime in Basin Street. She snatched a bouquet of dusty paper flowers from a vase on the nightstand beside the high old-fashioned bed. She knew exactly how this should go. The train of her invisible wedding gown was draped over the crook of her left arm. She dipped her head and kissed the flowers. She began her dance. There was nothing in it of the striding, self-satisfied prowl of the professional burlesque stripper. It began very chastely. Wiley's music seemed to take her by the hand and lead her through every step of it. Not once did he break off during this phase of the routine. She went through it as if in a trance, which was just the right note to strike, for as a young bride, she was in a kind of romantic, awakening trance.

Wiley increased the tempo of the music. "Now the wedding gown is discarded," he called.

Everything went smoothly until she came to the final phase, in which she danced, holding up the three nightgowns, trying one after the other. By this time they had been rehearsing for over two hours. Eve's arms and legs felt boneless and heavy. Wiley slapped down his hand across the keys and looked up at her.

"Just what are you supposed to be doing?" he demanded. "Trying to see which nightgown is the prettiest, or are you looking for the price tag on them?"

"I'll go over it again, Wiley," said Eve meekly.

Wiley bent over the piano, and the music came out wild and throbbing, but Eve could not get the feel of it. It was just noise. They went through it four times, and each time it got just a little worse. She held up the invisible nightgown to her, but she had no sense of the gown hanging down before her. Wiley stopped playing.

"What's the matter?" he asked.

Eve shook her head. "I don't know," she said helplessly. "I feel as if I'm doing setting-up exercises."

"Listen, honey. Try to see this in your mind. You've got three pretty nightgowns ..."

"But I don't have three pretty nightgowns," she wailed. "I forgot to put them in the suitcase. I didn't bring them."

Wiley grunted. "You mean you can't feel this nightgown scene?"

"I can't feel it at all."

He forked his fingers back through his sandy hair, looking, in that soft light, just a little like a harassed Leslie Howard.

"Well," he said wearily, "maybe you've got too many clothes on. Take off your dress and slip, then you won't have to *pretend* you've taken them off. Maybe that's the trouble. You've been pretending too much, and now you've run a little dry. You've reached the limit of being able to pretend. Take off your dress and slip and let's see how it goes."

He turned back to the piano and began to play very softly the lingering sadness of Schubert's *Serenade*, barely brushing the keys with his fingers. Eve lifted her dress and drew it off over her head. She swung out of her slip. Wiley looked up. His eyes glowed. Her long, beautifully modelled legs were pink and gold in the wash of the footlights. Her breasts were lifted and pointed. There was languor in her slow body. He knew she was tired, but she was not drooping. Her face was flushed, and in her red hair that tumbled around her shoulders the fires smoldered and flamed. The passion she had shown in her bride-dance was not entirely simulated. It burned within her. She was woman. Not just one woman, standing up there on the stage in radiant semi-nudity, but the epitome of all women; a flesh and blood symbol of heartbreak and yearning, of love and ecstasy. His eyes darkened and he crouched over the keys of the piano, thundering out a self-mocking travesty of the *Liebesträume*. Love's dream indeed! What did Lizst, or anybody as far as that went, know about love? There was more than dreaming to love. There were nightmares, too.

"Ready to pick it up again?" he called harshly to Eve. "How does it feel now?"

"Better," she said with the throatiness of fatigue.

"Okay. Take it from nightgown number one. Glance toward the door. Your lover, your husband, is pacing outside, burning with desire for you, and you are making yourself beautiful for him, so put some schmaltz into it ..."

The piano tumulted into the most abandoned passages of the *Bacchanale*. It went beautifully. Her slow body wove into the rhythm, its very languor heightening the effect of surrender. She did it perfectly, but Wiley was not content. He made her go through it again, and then again,

"Again!" he cried, swaying on the piano bench. "Just once more and we've got it."

She tottered, then fell across the bed, sobbing aloud from pure fatigue.

Wiley stared at her as if he did not comprehend that she had reached the physical limit of her endurance. Then slowly he brought down the lid of the piano. He sat slumped for a moment. Weariness had seeped, unnoticed, into his very marrow.

"That's enough," he said heavily. "That should have been enough an hour ago. I didn't mean to work you so hard ..."

His eye fell on the bottle of cognac, still untouched in its brown paper bag. He hadn't even thought of taking a drink for hours and hours. He reached for the bottle, then pushed himself to his feet, shambled the length of the orchestra pit and climbed heavily up on the stage. In the wings, just beyond the electricians' switchboard, were a water fountain and a glass. He washed out the glass and started back to the stage. As he passed the switchboard, he turned his head and looked at it. There was a switch labeled orch. pit. He flipped it and a soft golden glow arose from the pit. He pulled down the footlight switch. The stage was bathed in the reflected drowsy golden light from the pit.

He plodded across the stage, carrying the bottle in one hand, the glass in the other. Eve was still lying on the bed, her eyes closed. Her hair was an embering nimbus on the pillow, framing her face. Her lips were parted and she looked as if she were smiling.

He sat down on the edge of the bed and poured the glass a third full of brandy. He slid his arm under her head, lifting her slightly. Her hair was living silk.

"Here," he said gently, "drink this. I wish it were champagne. You've earned it. You were wonderful."

Obediently, she opened her eyes and grasped the glass with both hands. She sipped it, shivering just a little as the burning liquid slid down her throat. She held out the glass to him.

"You finish it," she said.

He hesitated. "No," he said. "I don't feel like having any right now."

"You're tired, too?"

"Yes."

He put the bottle on the floor and stretched out on the bed beside her, his arm still behind her head, tilting her face toward him. Her hair brushed his cheek. He kissed it lightly, the tendrils of it washing against his eyes and lips.

"There's something I want to say to you," he murmured. His voice seemed to come from a long distance off. "Something ... but I can't seem to remember what it is ..."

She felt him slipping away from her, and she wanted him close. He had filled her with music that night—the haunting memories invoked by the *Serenade*, the savage melancholy in the way he had played *Liebesträume*, the way he had built and built and built the heady music of the *Bacchanale* to a passionate climax. All this was coursing through her blood, tingling, demanding, crying out for fulfillment. She remembered the lean sadness of his face as he had bent over the piano, and mingled in her was a great tenderness for him, a need that answered his need.

She stirred in the circle of his arm and turned her face toward him. His lips touched her face, tracing the clean and lovely line from her cheekbone to the corner of her mouth as if his lips were fingers. His hand touched her cheek, caressed the creamy perfection of her neck, slid over her bare shoulder. At first his lips and fingers were slow and drowsy, but then they quickened with life and she felt that life communicate itself to her in a rapture that was almost dizzying in its swift climb toward exultation.

He said huskily, "There's something ... there's something. I have to tell you ... something ..."

"You don't have to," she whispered, "you don't have to."

His arm tightened around her and he half rose, bending his head over hers. His lips traced the outline of her lips, then dipped. Her mouth molded against his and the richness of the kiss became a fire that melted the two mouths into one. Her body arched.

Something, some flimsy strap of lingerie, snapped, and her breasts surged with freedom from their silken prisons. His hands streamed quivering fire down her body. She gasped as the erupting emotions tore her asunder, rocking her fiercely, and she moaned as the soaring tumult carried her beyond all imagined sensation. And then the incredible peace, the buoyant ecstasy, the floating into a cloudlike sleep ...

STRATEGY AND TACTICS
CHAPTER NINE

There was the cheerful smell of coffee in the air, the sound of dishes. Eve opened her eyes and stared uncomprehendingly at the tremendously high domed ceiling. For a moment, it seemed like part of the uneasy dream she'd been having. She could not remember what the dream had been, exactly, but the brutal, arrogant face of Vance Owen had been in it, hanging in the background like a picture glowering from a dominating wall. It was the smell of coffee that dissipated the dream. Hearty odors like that were real, and the clatter of dishes were real.

She turned her head on the pillow, and there was Wiley, setting a small table on the stage not ten feet from the bed.

But what a different Wiley it was this morning! His crinkly, sandy hair was wet and ruthlessly combed flat to his head, he was shaved, and his suit was pressed. And his tie! He had always worn a green knitted thing that even a farmer wouldn't have used to tie a goat, but this morning, sprouting out of the V of his collar was a blue and white polka-dot bow tie. But contrasting oddly with his debonair appearance was the expression on his face. He looked as if he had been caught picking a bouquet of flowers from a newly laid grave. Eve said softly, "Good morning, Wiley."

He turned and regarded her with guilty, hang-dog eyes. "Good morning, Eve," he said gloomily.

She sniffed the air. "Do I smell coffee?"

He lifted a quart thermos bottle. "I went out and got some. Down at the diner on the corner. I got two grapefruit halves and some Danish pastry. If you'd rather have an order of bacon and eggs, it'll only take a minute to run down and get it for you."

"Don't be silly, Wiley. I think this is miraculous, and I think you're miraculous to have thought of it!"

She sat up in bed. The thin blanket, with which he had covered her, fell away and for a moment her bare breasts were exposed. She almost giggled at the woeful expression on his face. Unhurriedly, she lifted the blanket to her chin.

"Is there such a thing as a shower around here, Wiley?" she asked. He stood there biting his underlip and pulling at his finger joints until they cracked. Finally, painfully, he said:

"Eve ..."

She sat very still as he stiffly walked across the stage and sat down on the edge of the bed. He avoided her eyes. He tortured his fingers for another moment, then blurted:

"I'd like you to marry me, if you don't mind, Evie."

She was thunderstruck. This was the last thing in the world she ever expected from Wiley.

"Good Heavens!" she stared at him. "But why, Wiley?"

He kept his head averted and mumbled something about wanting to do the "right thing." She almost laughed aloud, but she stifled the impulse before it became anything more than a cough. It would be very bad if she laughed at Wiley.

"But, Wiley," she said gently, "whatever made you think that marriage is the right thing for us?"

"You know what I mean. Because of ... of what I did last night. It wasn't fair. It wasn't right. You were worn out. I ... I took ... advantage of ... your fatigue."

She covered his shaking hand with hers and squeezed it. "No you didn't, Wiley. Honestly you didn't. I needed you last night. I felt lost and scared." This was not true, but it was what he wanted to hear. "I needed your kindness. You don't mind if I think you're kind of wonderful, do you, Wiley?"

In a tone of wonder, he whispered, "And I thought you'd be furious with me this morning!"

Poor Wiley. She looked at him with pity. Now she knew the secret of Wiley. He was so unsure of himself. He had thrown up his career as a concert pianist because he had been afraid of failure. She knew that now. He had taken this job in the burlesque house because with his superior knowledge of music, his position was secure. And she knew, too, why he held himself aloof from Sugar, though he loved her deeply. He was afraid, he was so unsure of himself.

"Why, Wiley," she cried gaily, "in case you don't know it, half the girls in the chorus are forever scheming to get you to notice them. They'd give up the chance at a mink coat just for a date with you. I know for a fact that Cheeta Rodriguez stood up her boy friend four nights straight last week, just because she had gotten the idea you were going to ask her to go out with you after the show."

This was all pure invention, but it was what Wiley needed. He was sitting up a little straighter and though he tried to appear cynically indifferent, there was a kind of hope in his face.

"Even Sugar Russell," said Eve chidingly. "Do you know why she was so mean to you last night? She has the idea you think you're too good for her. A girl has to keep her self-respect, doesn't she?"

Wiley touched his bow tie with a self-conscious gesture and stammered, "I've tried to keep my personal life out of the theatre."

"That's all very good, Wiley, but you could treat Sugar a little more like a human being. You treat her as if you were the lord of the manor and she were just a peasant."

"I ... I didn't know. I mean ... I didn't mean ..."

"I know you didn't, Wiley. It's your nature to be shy and aloof, but you might be pleasant to her once in a while."

"I will," he said eagerly, "I will. I didn't know I ..." he blushed. "I didn't know I was hurting her feelings," he finished lamely.

Eve knew she would be forgiven these white lies she had told. There was a look of assurance in Wiley's face now. He was in love with Sugar, and Sugar was in love with him. Sometimes it was necessary to stretch the truth.

Eve swiftly changed the subject before she said too much. "About my specialty, Wiley," she said. "Do you think I can have it ready by Thursday?"

"Thursday!" he was aghast. "It'll take you at least two weeks to get your routine in shape ..."

"It must be ready to go on by Thursday. It must, Wiley!"

"Why?"

Quickly, she told him of the position Jeff was in with Vance Owen and the theatre party, which could easily turn serious now that Sugar Russell and one of the other strippers were refusing to go on that night. Wiley was shocked that Jeff O'Hare had even considered Vance Owen's proposition.

Then he said shrewdly, "Are you in love with Jeff, Evie?"

"I don't want him to get in any trouble," she answered woodenly.

"But you can't be ready by Thursday. The act'll be too rough ..."

"Any rougher than some of the strippers we've had, Wiley?"

He argued stubbornly, but in the end he gave his grudging permission, warning her, however, that she'd have to work under a dark blue spotlight to cover any mistakes she might make.

"In the meantime," he said firmly, "I'll talk to Sugar. She's a trouper, and she hasn't any right to let her personal feelings interfere with the show."

Eve did not attempt to dissuade him. With his new-found assurance, a note of real authority had crept into Wiley's voice. She contented herself with his promise that they would work together again that night after the show.

After breakfast, they left the theatre together, Eve noting with some surprise that Wiley left his bottle of cognac behind. With still more surprise, she noted that but one drink had been poured from it.

Out on the sidewalk, he said seriously, "Frankly, Evie, I think it's swell of you not to let Jeff down, and I'll tell him so."

"Do that, Wiley. Do that—and I'll cut your throat with a nail file."

He laughed and patted her shoulder. "We'll put together a show for Jeff. And I'll keep my mouth shut."

The moment she left him, she made a bee-line for the drug store on the corner and called Sugar Russell. Sugar lived in a theatrical boarding house on Washington Street, at the south end near Lincoln Park.

"Could I see you right away, Sugar?" she asked urgently.

"Sure, kid," Sugar sounded a little surprised. "Come right ahead. Something on your mind?"

"I'll tell you when I see you."

She hung up with a feeling of dismay. Should she have said as much as she did to Sugar? Yet, she had to talk to Sugar before Wiley did, and Sugar, she knew, was to be trusted.

She caught a bus at the corner and twenty minutes later she was walking across Lincoln Park toward Sugar's boarding house. To Eve, the boarding house was a wild and wonderful place. From some of the rooms came the sound of singing, all kinds of singing, male and female. The female singing was, she had to admit, worse than the male vocalizing. A strident soprano was telling the world in a reedy voice that only God could make a tree, while across the hall a more impressive baritone informed her authoritatively that the sun came up like thunder out of China 'cross the bay. Somewhere in the house, a trumpet went wah-wah-wah and laughed insanely. In the "parlor," an animal man had rolled back the rug and was teaching a seal to beat a drum.

Sugar leaned over the bannister from the second floor and yelled down the stairwell:

"Come on up, kid. It's safe." Then, somewhat cryptically, "The bear just had his breakfast."

It turned out that there was another animal man in the house, who had a bear that rode bicycles. It was a very amiable bear, however, whose delight was ice cream sodas served in a soup bowl.

As Eve, wide-eyed, climbed the stairs, a girl came from the bathroom, with a wet towel thrown over her shoulder, unconcernedly smoking a cigarette. What made her unconcern just a little remarkable was the fact that except for some very interesting tattooing, she was as naked as a peeled onion.

Sugar jerked her thumb at the girl and grinned at Eve, "Miss Metropolitan Art Museum of 1951. Her sister is a little more heavily illustrated. She got first prize. She was voted Miss Funny Sheet of North and South America. Come inside, kid, and we'll push your eyes back in their sockets."

Sugar's room was tiny. It contained a bed, a chest of drawers, a closet and a chair. There was enough room left over for a pair of shoes, which stood at the foot of the bed.

Sugar sat down on the edge of the bed, rummaged in her pocketbook and handed Eve a five dollar bill.

"It was a tie," she said.

Eve said blankly, "A tie?"

"Yeah. It was a draw. Remember I said five would get you ten that Jeff O'Hare would tell us to peel the way Councilman Owen wanted? Well, it turned out to be one of those no-decision things."

"I don't understand."

"That's your five bucks back. You gave me five bucks, remember, when we thought Jeff had turned rat. Well, I didn't win. And you didn't win, either. So now we're even. Siddown. I'll tell you about it. It's still a mess, if you ask me."

She lit a cigarette and moodily blew out a plume of smoke.

"It's like this," she said. "I went to Jeff's office and told him to lay it on the line. He gave it to me deadpan. The YMUS—Young Men's Uplift Society of the Ironbound—was offering fifty bucks extra to the strippers who'd peel down to the skin Thursday night. I asked him what he thought I should do. Just leading him on. And still deadpan, he said for me to suit myself. That if I didn't want to do it, it was okay with him. So I apologized to him. I told him I'd thought he was a rat. I took it back. He was only a mouse, I told him. He asked me if I wanted the fifty bucks, and I said hell no. In fact, I told him, I'd sprained my back in advance for Thursday night, and if he wanted to can me, now was the time to do it. So he looked out the window and told me to think it over. I told him I was saving my brains to think over more important things and he had my answer and was I canned or wasn't I? He told me to be my age, and that's the way it stands. So you get your five bucks back. It was a draw."

Eve wanted to cry. She should have known that Jeff wouldn't really pander to Vance Owen—but ruthlessly she bit off the feeling of tenderness toward him. She wasn't going to go through that again.

"But what about the other strippers?" she asked. "Did they turn it down, too?"

Sugar laughed shortly. "Grow up, kid, grow up. Show either of those two tramps a sawbuck and they'd wave their bare tails in Macy's front window. Of course they didn't turn it down."

Eve faltered over the question she had come to ask. She knew Sugar. Sugar was roiled up now, but she was a soft-hearted and generous girl. If Jeff asked her to go on, as a personal favor, or if Wiley talked to her, Eve knew Sugar would impulsively agree to anything they asked—if they made the appeal personal enough. And Eve did not want Sugar to change her mind.

"Then you're really not going on?" she asked a little breathlessly. "I mean, not under any circumstances?"

Sugar was lying on the bed, propped up by her pillow, manicuring her nails. She frowned. "Did Jeff send you here to work on me?"

"N-no ..."

"Then what's on your mind?" Sugar looked puzzled. "There's something up your sleeve."

Eve looked at Sugar and tried to say the words, but they wouldn't come. Sugar's face was friendly—but puzzled. It suddenly came to Eve how lonely she was, how starkly and terribly lonely. In this pursuit of Vance Owen she had cut herself off from every honest human emotion. The tears filled her eyes and spilled over. She tried to squeeze them back and a racking sob shook her. She covered her face with her hands and let the sobs come, one after the other.

Sugar was aghast. Her jaw dropped, then quickly she swung her long legs over the edge of the bed and took Eve in her arms, stroking the back of her neck.

"Now, now, kid," she murmured. "It's okay. You're among friends. What's the matter, Evie? It's okay. You cry it out then tell old Sugar all about it."

Eve clung to her with a strength that was almost desperation, burying her face against Sugar's soft, generous breasts. She couldn't walk alone any longer. She had to tell somebody—and little by little, in broken, sob-racked sentences, the pitiful story came out.

During the war, Vance Owen was a Major of Military Police in the San Francisco area—but his war wasn't with the Nazis or the banzai boys. Oh no! Vance Owen had a private little war. His war was with the unfortunate GIs who were stationed in his area, and a bitter, ruthless little war it was. Not that Vance Owen gave a particular damn about law and order. He didn't. Everybody else was fighting to make the world a better place to live in, but Vance Owen had a bigger idea than that. He was out to make the world a better place for Vance Owen to live in. He was out to make his reputation.

The cynical city editor of the *San Francisco Herald* once remarked, "I can't go to press anymore unless I print that fascist bum's face. I thought this was a free country."

That was an exaggeration, of course, but Vance Owen knew how to get his name in the paper and how to keep it there, too. He was the major who once put the San Francisco City Hall out of bounds for GIs because, as he said virtuously, if the City Fathers permitted houses of prostitution to operate on the Barbary Coast, they would be a contaminating influence on the American Army. That was pure hogwash, of course, but it got his name in the paper, and the next day four miserable, overworked prostitutes were sentenced to ninety days apiece in the house of correction, thus adding another laurel to the lustre of Vance Owen's name.

He made his reputation, all right, and in a spectacular fashion.

A gang of young muggers, disguised in GI uniforms had been preying on the late night club crowd. Whether it was a gang or just one hoodlum, no one really knew, but the police claimed it was a gang. Possibly because they had not been able to do anything about it. Vance Owen publicly boasted that *he* would put a stop to the activities of this nocturnal bandit. He gave his MPs an order to shoot to kill, and publicly announced that there was not an MP in his command who was not at least a marksman and that they had medals to prove it. And he had himself photographed intrepidly patrolling the city alone in a jeep at night.

Whether it was luck or not, no one ever really knew, but on the second night he blundered down a street in which the bandit had held up a car of half-drunk merry makers and was engaged in relieving them of their valuables. There was no one's word but Vance Owen's for the veracity of the events he claimed took place.

He prowled into the street, he said, and saw the holdup man at work. He left his jeep and ran down the street in the shadows, opening fire. The bandit fired once and fled. Vance Owen's story was that he gave chase. The occupants of the car corroborated this story, but later, after the trial, they furtively and shame-facedly admitted they were too terror-stricken to have noticed. And in addition to that, the moment the bandit fled, the driver threw his car into gear and bolted from the scene.

Vance Owen had been quick-witted enough to take their license number, and the next day they were summoned to police headquarters. Owen had brought in a very drunk GI who, he claimed, was the bandit. To support this claim, the GI was wounded in the shoulder, and Owen produced a Luger which, he said, the GI fired at him while resisting arrest. The identification of the unfortunate GI was a farce.

Owen *told* the occupants of the car that this was the man who had held them up, but, he said, successful prosecution depended on their identifying the man. He hinted that he would say nothing of their having run away if they made the identification. Having sobered up, they were dreadfully ashamed of having fled, and they identified the man—actually a nineteen year old boy. At that moment, they would have identified the Chief of Police as the bandit if Owen had asked them. They were grateful to him for concealing their cowardice. Also, they had no reason to doubt his word. He said this was the GI who had held them up, so why should they doubt him. After all, he had saved their pocketbooks.

Owen then turned the GI over to the city authorities—another publicity gesture. The boy was given the severe sentence of *ten years at hard labor.*

"That was my kid brother," Eve said dully. "He wrote me a letter from prison. He begged me not to believe what they had said at the trial. He wasn't guilty. He had never owned a Luger, and at the time Owen said he was holding up those people, he had been drinking with three Marines who were leaving the following day for the South Pacific. He couldn't produce the Marines at the trial because they had already left and, furthermore, he only knew them as Mac, Jimmy and Roy."

Sugar held Eve tightly. "I knew," she said harshly, "there had to be a reason I didn't like that creep. But how did he get away with it, honey? How did he get away with it?"

Eve felt sodden, drained of all emotion. "My brother couldn't prove where he had been that night," she said. "I was a WAC and I was stationed in North Africa. I tried to get back to San Francisco, but they wouldn't let me go. They thought I was hysterical. They sent me to Paris to rest, to have a good time, to forget. Then there was a man in Paris ..." She shivered at the memory.

"A *schlemihl?*" asked Sugar shrewdly.

"He was a civilian, but he said he had a lot of influence in Washington. He said he could get my brother released ..." Eve shivered again.

Sugar stroked her soothingly. "You don't have to tell me, honey," she said. "He made you a proposition. He said, sleep with me, let's go down to the seashore and have a party, let's have a party without going to the seashore, I'm crazy about you sweetheart, I'll do anything for you, I know Sam Goldwyn, I'll get you a screen test, I'm a big brewer, I'll have you made Miss Rheingold of 1952 ... it's the same old tune, honey. All wolves don't howl at the moon."

Eve began to cry again. "I didn't know there were men like that. I thought he really would get my brother out of prison. Then, after the war, I went back to San Francisco. I saw my brother, and he told me again he wasn't guilty. I talked to the people they said he held up, and I got them to admit that they were pretty drunk and couldn't have identified anybody. But they wouldn't retract their statement unless I could prove that my brother wasn't the one ... and that's what I have to do!"

Sugar said briskly, "Come on, sit up on the bed with me. Kneeling beside this chair is giving me housemaid's knee."

She jumped back on the bed. "Better take off your shoes, honey," she said. "The landlady gets sore when she sees footprints on the sheet. I don't care what you do in bed, she says, but I'll have you know it ain't Broadway and Forty-Second Street." She fluffed the pillow and put it behind Eve's back. "So, all by yourself, you're going to get Vance Owen to admit he framed your kid brother. Is that the idea?"

"You make it sound as if ..."

"I know. I make it sound like a quick way to commit suicide. You know what you are, Evie? You're a fluffy little kitten—*in a dog pound!* You think you have claws, but those Airedales'll break your back with one flip. And one Great Dane in particular—Vance Owen. Why, honey, he's a professional louse. He knows more ways to cut your throat than they can write in a book. He's a politician. Now, now, don't make like a shower bath again."

The tears had come to Eve's eyes. Sugar put her arm around her, held her close and kissed her.

"You've got friends, honey," Sugar whispered. "And you're not the only one that'd like to see Councilman Owen take a fall. I'll talk to Jeff ..."

Eve wrenched herself out of Sugar's arm and cried, "No!"

Sugar drew her back again and laughed throatily. "All right, honey, then we won't tell Jeff. You're in love with the guy?"

"Sugar, please! ..."

"All right, honey," Sugar kissed her again, soothingly. "We won't talk about that. Now, this is the idea I get. You want to do a strip on Thursday night because Councilman Owen'll be there. You want to get him all hot and bothered. Okay. Let's say you do get him all hot and bothered—then what?"

With dismay, Eve suddenly realized that her plans had not gone beyond that point. After she got Vance Owen interested, then what? What exactly *did* she plan to do? She knew what he would want—he would want her to go to bed with him. He would want her to go on a weekend with him, up at that hunting and fishing lodge he had near Rock Ridge Lake in north Jersey. She had heard about that hunting and fishing lodge. She had heard whispers of orgies, but she was smart enough to realize that "orgies" could mean anything from a harmless drinking party (stag) for fellow politicos, to bacchanalian revels, whatever they were.

But what exactly had she planned after Vance Owen had fallen for her?

Sugar said dryly, "I don't like to disillusion you, honey, but it ain't necessarily true that a beautiful dame can wrap a wolf around her little finger. Especially a senior wolf like Vance Owen. And that's the idea you had in mind, right?"

Eve nodded miserably, knowing now how adolescent her plans had been. How innocent, really, how futile. Sugar had thrown the cold light of experience on them. Sugar patted her cheek and chuckled.

"Now, now, honey," she murmured. "We'll work this out. Don't worry about Thursday night. You'll go on. That's what you wanted, isn't it? That's the first step. You're a beautiful tomato, and don't think the maidens' delight, Councilman Owen, won't notice you. Those other two peelers are just second-hand meat compared to you. He'll notice you, all right. And I'll guarantee he'll be backstage after you before you can pin up your G-string ..." her hand tightened on Eve's shoulder. "I think," she whispered, "somebody's trying to get her ear through the keyhole."

Lithely, noiselessly, she swung out of bed, grasped the doorknob and swung it open. Cheeta Rodriquez, clad only in a gaudily embroidered kimono, lurched into the room. There was a flash of golden limbs and flesh before she recovered herself and clutched the kimono to her. She flashed a white smile at Sugar.

"Ef eet eez possible," she murmured, "Cheeta would like to borrow thee iron to press her dress, no?"

Sugar gave her a smile that was just as white and just as insincere. "Eet ees possible," she said.

She went to her closet and took out her small electric iron and gave it to Cheeta, who stood in the doorway looking at Eve with calculating eyes.

"Was there anything else, sweetheart?" asked Sugar sweetly.

"Oh, no no no no. Just thee irons. Muchas gracias, muchas gracias." She darted down the hallway, and Sugar slammed the door.

Eve said faintly, "She was listening ..."

Sugar grinned. "I don't think she heard very much. I've lived in this place long enough to know when somebody's got his ear to the keyhole. But I think we might find a use for that little pepper. Don't ask me what, but I've got a feeling. There isn't a minute in the day that Cheeta isn't on the make, and I think she'll come in handy. Mighty handy ..."

THE FIRE BURNS HOT!
CHAPTER TEN

That night and every night until Thursday, Sugar went to rehearsal with Eve and Wiley. She supplied the practical details that Wiley had overlooked—the making of the wedding gown, for instance. She brought a portable sewing machine and fitted the gown, cutting and draping it during rest periods. She had it finished on Wednesday so that Wednesday night Eve could have a dress rehearsal. It was zippered all the way down the front so that Eve could swing out of it in a single graceful movement. Wiley had wanted Eve to take it off over her head, but Sugar said scornfully:

"Talk sense, Wiley! Do you realize that gown is six yards around the hem? She'd be fifteen minutes fighting her way out of it. What's she supposed to do to entertain the audience during those fifteen minutes—tell funny stories or show lantern slides?"

To take the sting out of her scorn, she kissed him lightly on the lips and patted his cheek.

Something had happened between Sugar and Wiley. There was a kind of dazed happiness in Sugar's eyes and Wiley, at long last, seemed at peace with himself and with the world. They shared long intimate glances, and when they kissed or touched each other, it was with love. Their smiles had a special meaning. It was as if they were newly married and were entranced by the wonder of it. The rehearsals went like magic.

And then on Wednesday night, during the intermission, Sugar almost gave the secret away to Jeff O'Hare. She was sitting on one of the trigger steps, smoking a cigarette and talking to Eve when he came up to her. He looked haggard, as if he had not been sleeping well. He gave Eve a pallid smile and mumbled to Sugar;

"How about it, honey, you going on tomorrow night?" You could see he felt ashamed, and he spoke as if he did not want Eve to hear what he was saying.

Eve looked quickly at Sugar and prayerfully crossed her fingers. Sugar was a forthright girl. She never lied and always said what was on her mind. She gulped, and Eve could see that she was not going to lie this time, either. She could have given Jeff a simple yes, but it was against her nature.

She looked down at her feet and muttered, "Don't worry about tomorrow night."

"You sure?"

"I said don't worry, didn't I?" she sounded angry. Then shrewdly, "Are *you* going to be here?"

Jeff said shortly, "*I'll* be across the street in the gin mill if you want me. Here's your fifty."

He shoved a bill into Sugar's hand and walked away without another glance at Eve. Sugar held the bill as if it were coated with cyanide. Cheeta hovered around them, stretching her neck, trying to see and hear everything that was going on. Sugar slipped the bill into her brassiere and whispered to Eve;

"Take a look at La Rodriguez. Her eyes are like golf balls. She'd give an arm and a leg to know what's going on."

Eve turned and smiled sweetly at the Spanish girl. Cheeta tossed her head and flounced away, but she was unable to resist a scowling glance back over her shoulder.

Thursday night came with a rush. It came with a whoop and a yell. The Ironbound gang crowded the lobby as early as seven-thirty. The burlesque habitués had never been a quiet audience, but this was something entirely different. This was a noisy, drunken crowd, a tough crowd. Within fifteen minutes, there were three fights in the lobby, the last of which might have developed into a riot had not a burly, roaring black-haired Irishman flailed his way through the howling crowd, grabbed the two combatants by the scruff of their necks and hurled them through the doors to the sidewalk, where they rolled and bit and pummelled each other while the big Irishman stood in the doorway, laughing. Finally he jerked them to their feet, rubbed their faces together and made them shake hands.

Sugar and Eve were standing on the corner, watching with wide eyes. Cheeta slipped up beside them. Her eyes were shining and excited.

"That beeg hombre," she whispered, pointing at the Irishman, "He ees Mike Lenahan, boss of the Ironbound. My boy fren tell me about heem. He ees mucho hombre. Soch a man!"

Sugar looked at Eve's white face and squeezed her arm. "Nervous, honey?" she asked.

Eve's teeth were chattering. "S-scared stiff," she managed to say, but she laughed, and then it was all right.

They slipped around the edge of the crowd and darted down the alley to the stage door. Cheeta walked boldly through the crowd, rolling her neat little hips, answering the whistles and wolf-calls with a mock-disdainful toss of her head. Many of the roughnecks were Spaniards and Portuguese, and they yelled bawdy invitations to her in Spanish. She laughed at them. She was at home, thoroughly.

Another fight developed on the sidewalk. A prowl car rolled slowly by but did not stop. They had been warned to keep their noses clean. This was Vance Owen's party, and they knew better than to interfere. When the inside doors were opened, the crowd surged into the auditorium as if it meant to take the place apart. The first five rows were reserved for the Ironbound ward heels and other notables, but the rest of the house was wide open. There were several wordy disputes over seats, but no more fights developed. The men in the balcony had paper bags which they filled with water and threw down on the heads of their luckless friends in the orchestra. The air was blue with cigar and cigarette smoke. Bottles were passed freely from hand to hand and row to row.

Eve's specialty was scheduled for the second half of the program, after the intermission. Sugar excused her from chorus duty, and Eve sat down in the dressing room, trying to keep her nerve. Down there behind the dressing room door, the noise was muted, but she could still hear the pandemonium that reigned in the auditorium upstairs. At times it sounded like a subway train roaring into the Times Square station. When the girls came down to change their costumes during intermission, they were dripping wet. Sugar shook her head as she dropped wearily into the chair beside Eve.

"It's like fighting your way through a hurricane!" she gasped. "They're good-natured enough, but my God how they can yell! Half the time we couldn't even hear the orchestra." Then she grinned, "Did you hear them scream when that stripper peeled it all off?"

Eve swallowed. Her mouth had never felt so dry. "I ... I heard something ..."

Sugar chuckled. "They gave that tramp what was coming to her. They yelled, 'Put it back on, Grandma!' They sure knew a bum when they saw one. When she finally got it all off, somebody threw her a bathrobe. God knows where he got it from." Then she saw the look on Eve's face. She laughed and hugged her. "But *you* don't have anything to worry about, honey," she whispered. "If they can tell a tramp, they'll be able to tell class when they see it, too. You'll go over like rum-and-Coca-Cola."

The crowd had seized intermission as the opportunity to lay in a fresh supply of liquor. They were singing in the balcony. They sang and threw things into the orchestra all through the first three numbers of the second half of the program.

Dressed in her bride's costume, Eve stood in the wings, waiting for the comics to finish their Pickle Persuader number. She was shaking. Sugar stood beside her, holding her hand, murmuring encouragement, but even Sugar was dismayed by the increased drunkenness of the crowd.

The curtain came down, and the comics ran off the stage, swearing. The lights dimmed and the orchestra swung into *O Promise Me*, the prelude to Eve's number. She felt as if she couldn't breathe. Then came the opening bars of the wedding march, swung to dance tempo. Sugar gave her a little push toward the door through which she would enter.

"You're on, honey!" she whispered, her voice shaking. "Do it the way you did it last night for Wiley and me and they'll be giving you curtain calls from now until Stonewall Jackson's birthday."

Sugar had warned her not to look out into the audience, but she could not help it. For the moment, the crowd sat in crouched silence, waiting, she knew, to spring at her with boos and catcalls, the way they had leaped all over the comics. All she could see at the other side of the footlights was a thick pall of tobacco smoke. Her feet felt like granite as she moved through the first steps of her little dance with the wedding bouquet. The crowd was still silent, and she gained a little confidence. She could pick out a few faces in the crowd now. Vance Owen was sitting in the middle of the third row.

She glanced shakily down into the orchestra pit. Wiley was sweating, but he smiled quickly up at her and nodded vigorously to tell her she was doing fine. Again, with his music, he seemed to have her by the hand, firmly leading her through the routine.

Then it happened, the thing she had been dreading! A swaying, drunken blond roughneck, wearing a dirty sweatshirt, lurched to his feet in the sixth row, cupped his mouth with his hands and bellowed:

"Stop jumping around up there, sister. Take it off! Show us some skin! TAKE IT OFF!!"

Eve felt as if she had suddenly been incased in ice. She stopped dead, the blood draining from her face. She froze. She couldn't move. Wiley waved frantically from the orchestra pit, whipping the orchestra into a thundering crescendo of sound, trying to give her the pick-up cue, trying to drown the drunk—but the drunk had a voice like a fog horn. He stood there chanting at the top of his lungs:

"Take it off, take it off, take it off ..."

Other voices began to pick it up.

Suddenly, out of the second row, a burly, black-headed Irishman leaped to his feet, whipped a blackjack from his pocket and threw it at the drunk with a savage overhead swing. It caught the man in the middle of the forehead with an audible *splat!*, and the drunk disappeared as if he had fallen through a trapdoor in the floor. The big Irishman—it was Mike Lenahan, himself—turned to the stage and waved his hand at Eve.

"Go ahead, girlie," he called. "You're doing swell. If another of these monkeys interrupts you, I'll bust his neck with me own hands."

He glowered around the theatre and sat down. There wasn't a voice to be heard. Miraculously, Eve came out of her frozen daze, saw Wiley motioning violently to her—miraculously, she picked up the cue. Except for the soft music, the theatre was hushed. There was a sound as if a thousand men had sucked in their breaths when she swung lithely out of the wedding gown, but Eve did not hear it. She heard nothing but the music. Her mind was numbed. The music led her gently, firmly, and when the curtain came down, there was dead silence for a moment, then the theatre exploded. Men whistled, shrieked, stamped their feet and beat their palms together. They jumped up and down and yelled themselves hoarse.

Wrapped in a white silk dressing gown that Sugar had hurriedly thrown over her shoulders, Eve took five curtain calls. She just stood there in the middle of the stage, slim and virginal, her red hair aflame, while the curtain went up and down, up and down, and the audience roared for "More, MORE!" Even they, drunk as they were, realized that this girl with the smoldering hair and proud breasts was something more beautiful than anything they had ever seen in their misspent lives, and they acted as if they were afraid they would never see anything as beautiful again. They wanted to keep her on the stage forever and feast their eyes on her loveliness.

But Sugar saw that Eve's knees were beginning to sag, and she hurried her off the stage and down into the dressing room, while the orchestra burst into *Happy Days Are Here Again!* Down in the dressing room, Eve collapsed into Sugar's arms and burst into wild, hysterical tears. Sugar held her close and kept murmuring:

"There, there, there ..."

Finally the tears stopped. Eve wiped her eyes on a piece of Kleenex and looked woefully into Sugar's face.

"Was I ... awful?" she stammered.

"Awful!" Sugar squeezed her hard and burst into a ringing laugh. "Why, honey, you were just about the most wonderful thing that ever happened to this crummy old emporium of mirth. Do you realize that you got five curtain calls? Five! And that's a tough gang to please. Why, they wouldn't give five curtains calls to Ginger Rogers, Betty Grable and Lana Turner if they strip-teased in unison. But you got it, honey. You got it. You got five!"

Eve could scarcely believe it. Her mind had practically blanked out when the drunk interrupted the number, and she didn't remember a thing that happened afterward. She only remembered the music.

"That's okay, honey," Sugar said soothingly. "You're not the only one it's ever happened to. Now go and take yourself a good cold shower. You're a success."

Eve obediently took a shower while Sugar lounged against the wall outside, smoking a cigarette and chatting with her. While Eve was getting dressed, there was a heavy knock on the door, and Sugar went to answer it.

Eve heard the heavy voice of the stage doorman, then she heard Sugar laugh a little hysterically. A moment later, Sugar staggered back into the dressing room, carrying a six-foot floral horseshoe, made of roses and green carnations. Across it was a gold ribbon that said GOOD LUCK, and pinned to the ribbon was a white envelope with a note inside.

"I'll see who it's from," said Sugar eagerly, ripping open the envelope. She read the note and whistled. "Take a look at that, honey!" she cried, tossing Eve the note.

Eve read it in bewilderment. It said:

"Dear Miss Barry,

Sorry that dope had to interrupt your act. I'd like to apologize for him personally. How's about you and me having a steak together after the show?"

It was signed, "Mike Lenahan."

Eve looked at the huge floral horseshoe, looked at Sugar. Sugar laughed.

"It's kind of a funny bouquet, eh, honey?" she said. "But I know what happened. Mike Lenahan sent one of his henchmen out to get you the biggest bouquet he could find. This was it. And I'm willing to bet if there had been a funeral wreath that was bigger, you'd have gotten that instead. What are you going to do?"

Before Eve could answer, there was another knock on the door. It was the stage doorman again, but this time all he had was a card.

Sugar handed it to Eve with a crooked smile and watched her narrowly as she read it. On one side of the card was printed, Vance Owen, and on the other side was scrawled:

"I'll meet you at the stage door in fifteen minutes."

Eve's heart began to beat wildly.

Sugar said dryly, "Don't be a dope." She snatched the card from Eve's hand and scribbled across the face of it with an eyebrow pencil—

"Sorry, too late."

She went to the door and called the doorman. "See that Councilman Owen gets this. Put it in his hand yourself," She closed the door and turned back to Eve.

Eve cried, "But why, Sugar ..."

"Because," said Sugar, "tonight you're going out with Mike Lenahan, boss of the Ironbound. That's one date Councilman Owen won't try to break up. You gotta use your head, honey. Don't go running the first time Vance Owen raises his little finger to you. Let him get a little hotter. Let him burn a little ..."

SPORTSMAN'S INN
CHAPTER ELEVEN

Lenahan was waiting at the curb in a long cream-colored Cadillac convertible, but when Eve started across the sidewalk toward the open door, Vance Owen, smiling, stepped out of the shadows beside the theatre and intercepted her.

"Good evening, Eve," he smiled. "I was just wondering if you mightn't reconsider ..."

Lenahan called roughly from the car, "Hey, what's going on there, Owen?"

Vance turned toward the car. "Why, Lenahan," he said easily, "I was just telling Miss Barry how much I enjoyed her performance."

"Tell her on your own time, pal. This is my time, and don't try to beat it, get me?"

"Of course, old man." Vance dropped his voice and said quickly to Eve, "Get rid of this hooligan. Meet me in the Tarpon Club at midnight. I'll have supper ordered—lobster, champagne." Without waiting for Eve's answer, he turned, gave Mick Lenahan in the Cadillac a mock salute, and walked down the street whistling.

Eve would have been amused at his cool assurance had she not hated him so bitterly. "*Meet me at the Tarpon Club* ..." Not, *will you meet me*, or, *please* ... No. And he had walked away without the slightest doubt in the world that Eve *would* meet him at the Tarpon Club at midnight. Mr. Owen needed to be taught a little lesson.

Eve walked across the sidewalk to the waiting car. Mike Lenahan was in the back seat.

"I'll be back in a moment, Mr. Lenahan," she smiled at him. "I forgot my compact."

He scowled. "Is this the brush-off, sister? Did the Councilman make you a better offer?"

"If you're going to talk like that, Mr. Lenahan, perhaps you'd better forget you asked me out tonight," Eve said and turned away.

He said hurriedly, "I'm sorry, Miss Barry. Honest. I apologize. But that guy gets my goat. I thought he was trying to make you."

"He was merely telling me how much he enjoyed my performance tonight." She knew instinctively that Mike Lenahan was not a man to whom you could give an inch.

"Sure, sure," he said in a placatory voice. "You just go and get your compact. I'll be waiting right here."

Eve walked slowly down the alley toward the stage door. She was not going to give Mike Lenahan the idea that she was rushing on his account. Sugar jumped up from her table when Eve walked into the dressing room. Eve had left early, and the rest of the chorus girls were just taking off their costumes.

Sugar said swiftly, "What happened, Evie?"

Eve pursed up her mouth. "Council Owen met me outside and told me to meet him at the Tarpon Club at midnight."

Sugar grabbed her arm. "Now wait a minute, Evie," she began, "you're not ..."

Eve laughed. "Of course not. But I thought, since the good Councilman is going to all the trouble of ordering a lobster supper with champagne, I ought to send a substitute in my place." She nodded toward Cheeta Rodriguez, who was watching them with dark avid eyes.

Sugar raised her eyebrows, then began to laugh softly. "It'll serve him right," she chuckled. "She's a greedy little pepper. She'll smell money on him and sink her nails into him up to the knuckle." She raised her voice, "Hey, Cheeta, come here a minute."

Cheeta jumped up and darted over to them.

Eve said gravely, "Would you do me a favor tonight, Cheeta?"

"A favor!" she gave Eve a vengeful glance. "Why should I do you a favor, eh?"

"No reason at all, Cheeta. But I thought you might enjoy it. Councilman Owen wants me to meet him at midnight in the Tarpon Club, but I have a previous engagement. I was wondering if you'd keep the date with the Councilman for me. He'd love to have you, I know. He's ordering a lobster supper with champagne. That is, of course," said Eve archly, "if you will not try to steal the Councilman away from me." She knew that would get Cheeta if anything would.

Cheeta's face turned sly. "*Si, si*, I will keep the date for you, Evee," she purred. "And why should I steal the Councilman from you? I have a boy fren, who ees reech. Don't worry about Cheeta, Evee. I will tell him all night what a beautiful girl you are. He will be busting to see you tomorrow, eh? *Si*."

She darted back to her dressing table and madly began rubbing cream into her face to remove the theatrical make-up.

Sugar worried, "I hope you're doing the right thing, Evie. If that little pepper gets her hooks into Owen, she'll never let go. Although," she added thoughtfully, "I think Owen's a little too tough, even for our Cheeta. She'll throw herself at him like a baseball, and he's not the kind of guy to value anything he gets too cheap. He'll take everything she's got and," she grinned, "it won't be the first time."

Eve smiled.

This time, when she went out to Lenahan's car, he was not waiting in the back seat for her. He was standing out on the sidewalk, holding the door open, clumsily eager to assist her into the car. He, too, had been taught a lesson.

When he settled himself in the seat beside her, he began to apologize all over again. "I guess I'm just a slob, Miss Barry," he grumbled. "But I'm telling you, that guy Vance Owen rubs me the wrong way."

"Is he really going places?" Eve asked with a show of innocence. "In politics, I mean."

Lenahan waved a hand as big as a ham, but hairier. "He wants to be the next mayor of Newark, that's all."

"The mayor! But isn't he awfully young to be a mayor?"

"What's 'young' got to do with it? It's know-how that counts, and the guys you know, see." He waved his hand again. The implication was plain. He, Mike Lenahan, was one of the guys you had to know if you wanted to be mayor of Newark.

Eve set out to pump him. "But does he stand a chance, Mike? I mean, you'd know if anyone knows."

Mike preened himself, basking in her flattery. "You're right about that, kid. I'd know if anybody does. There never was a guy that got to be mayor if he didn't carry the Ironbound on Election Day, and I got the Ironbound in me back pocket, see. In me back pocket. But is Owen gonna be mayor? That's the question, see? He's got the bug, all right, and he's sure busting a gut trying. And he's the kind of guy, he's so stuck on himself, he'll just about die if he don't make it on the first try, get me?"

"I know what you mean," said Eve slowly. And she did. It was very obvious. It would be a terrible blow to Vance Owen's arrogance if he were defeated in the election.

"But does he stand a chance at all?" she asked. "I mean, are you going to help him in the election?"

"I'll tell you, Eve," he said solemnly, hooking his thumbs in the armholes of his vest, "it's like this. Me, I don't give a hoot who's mayor of Newark—as long as he plays ball, get me? As long as he plays ball with me. For my money, Owen's a jerk, but so what? I can't let pleasure interfere with business. If I want to think he's a jerk, that's one thing; but if he shows he'll play ball with me, that's another thing, and the hell with the jerk business. Now you get the idea, Eve? It all depends on if he'll play ball."

Eve got the idea. She looked at the hand-tooled leather upholstery in that custom-made Cadillac. She looked at the driver, who was a tough, Down Neck edition of George Raft. The window had been rolled down on her side of the car, and she saw that the glass was much thicker than the window glass in ordinary cars, and she suddenly realized that it was bulletproof. Then she knew what Mike Lenahan was, and what he meant by "playing ball."

She was about to ask another leading question, when Mike said truculently, "Now how the hell did we get talking about Vance Owen anyways? Say, maybe you got a special interest in him for some reason. You got something in mind, maybe?"

Eve cried, "I? Good heavens, I thought *you* wanted to talk about him. I certainly haven't any interest in Councilman Owen. I never met the man before tonight. Let's talk about that steak we're going to have. I'm hungry." She laughed.

Mike laughed with her. "That's a dame for you," he said. "Always hungry."

The place he took her to was down in the Ironbound. It was a shabby brick building with a faded canvas canopy that ran from the front door to the curb. It was called The Sportsman's Inn.

"One of the places I got an interest in," said Mike. "It don't look like much from the outside, but inside, let me tell you, baby, it's class."

Mike's idea of class was soon apparent. Inside, Sportsman's Inn looked like a great big gaudy juke box—the same screaming color, the same pseudo modern design, the same garish blue-red-gold-green-pink lighting. The bar was a thirty-foot chromium horror and the mirror over the back-bar was blue. The tables were crowded as closely together as they could possibly be, and the dance floor was about a quarter the size of a wrestling ring. The music for the alleged dancing came from a somewhat frantic band that called itself, Swoop McJones And His Raggedy Andys.

Mike was treated with a deference that was almost awe. It was easy to see who was boss down here in the Ironbound. The head waiter practically kissed his foot, and when he snapped his fingers for a waiter, it sounded like a string of firecrackers. No less than four waiters sprang into action. They evicted a party of four from a ringside table, Eve was presented with a white orchid "with the compliments of the management," and two waiters went busily ahead of them, clearing a path to their table. Eve's eyes popped when she saw the prices on the menu—coffee, $1.00; steak, $15.00; bread and butter, $2.00; champagne,

$25.00.

"Nothing cheap about this joint, baby," said Mike smugly. "We try to keep the cheapskates out."

Eve was brought a bottle of champagne in a silver bucket, but Mike had scotch, which he drank from water tumblers.

"Order anything you want, Eve," he said. "If we ain't got it, we'll get it. And don't worry about the price. They know better than try to hand me a bill here."

Eve noticed that the tough-looking chauffeur, who had driven the Cadillac, was sitting alone at the next table, which commanded a view not only of the door but of the whole room. There was a very noticeable bulge under his left arm, and when he moved, Eve could see the dully gleaming butt of a gun in a leather holster. Mike Lenahan did not feel as secure as he tried to seem. The gunman drank only water, and his cold, thin eyes constantly ranged the room, missing nothing and no one.

Eve suppressed a wild impulse to order eagle à la King—she was sure they would try to get it for her—and demurely ordered filet mignon. Mike glared at it when it came.

"See if it's any good, Eve," he said. "If it ain't, I'll shove it down that waiter's throat with a chair leg. Go ahead, taste it."

Eve repressed a shiver, and cut off a small piece. It was delicious, but if it had been as tough as brake lining, she would still have said it was delicious. Mike Lenahan was fully capable, she knew now, of shoving it down the waiter's throat with a chair leg.

All through supper, he entertained her with stories of how he'd had this guy beaten up for trying to put something over on him, or had that guy worked over for trying to put something over on his friends. Mike's sole idea of friendship, it seemed, was to have somebody beaten up for a pal.

When they had finished eating, Mike leaned over the edge of the table and winked at her. "Howja like to buck the wheel for a little, baby. It's on the house."

"The wheel?" she said, not understanding what he meant.

"Yeah, the wheel. Or maybe you'd like to shoot a little craps. They got quite a layout in the back. Like to see it? Come on, I'll show it to you."

He was working hard to impress her.

The door to the back room was guarded by a plug-ugly with a pair of cauliflower ears the size of doorknobs, but he had the door open even before they reached it.

"Come right in, Mr. Lenahan," he fawned. "Nice to see you again, Mr. Lenahan. Did you want to see Mr. Stapp, Mr. Lenahan?"

"Naaah. Just tell him not to bother me. I'm here for pleasure tonight."

Then he confided to Eve, "Stapp runs the joint, a jerk, but he keeps his nose clean."

Eve was wide-eyed at what she saw. There were two beautifully polished mahogany roulette wheels, and several long, green, felt-covered dice tables. There were other tables at which was being played a card game similar to twenty-one. There was a different crowd entirely in this room. They were in evening dress—the women in expensive gowns, the men in white-tie-and-tails—obviously a rich crowd. Not the hoodlum rich, but the blooded rich from the socially snobbish Forest Hill section of Newark, the Oranges, Maplewood and Millburn.

This was just another facet of what Lenahan meant by "playing ball." He shoved a stack of blue chips into her hand.

"Go ahead, play anything you want, baby," he said. "This ain't gonna cost you a dime. It's on the house."

At first, Eve found it exciting—the spin and click of the little white ivory ball in the bowl of the roulette wheel, the uninflected chant of the croupier after each spin:

"Twenty-three, red, even—twenty-three, red, even ..."

And then his rapacious rake would go out and pull in the chips that had backed the wrong numbers, the wrong color. Eve lost her chips in exactly ten minutes. Mike handed her another stack of blues.

"Maybe you'll have better luck this time," he said laughing. "Tell you what, put the whole stack on red. Go ahead. The whole stack. Never get anywhere playing penny ante."

Eve could not swear later that Mike had actually given the croupier a signal, but when the wheel stopped spinning, the ivory ball nestled in the compartment of a red number. The croupier pushed an equal stack of blue chips toward her with his rake.

"Does mademoiselle wish to play the red again?" he murmured with just the hint of an accent.

"Sure. Let it ride," said Mike. Then he whispered in Eve's ear, "That guy ain't no more French than me. His name's Mush Schwartz, and he's an ex-con from Chi."

The red won again, and Eve had a tremendous pile of blue chips, now.

But the excitement had gone out of it for her. She was sure now that they were letting her win. The wheel was crooked. And, too, she'd had time to study the faces of the people around her. Some were young girls, Junior Leaguers, playing with frantic intensity, their eyes staring, their mouths hanging open as the little ball clicked and bounced around the spinning wheel. The same look was on the faces of the older men and women. They were not having fun. They were doing this because of some twisted compulsion. Eve saw one woman lose her last chip and turn away from the table with sick eyes.

Eve said to Mike, "I ... I'd like to go home now, if you don't mind. I'm a little tired."

"Sure, baby, sure. Anything you say. Hey, pal," he called over a muscular man in a bulging dinner jacket, "cash these in for the lady." A few minutes later, a thick wad of bills was handed to her. She looked at them with surprise.

"What's this for?" she asked.

"That's your winnings, Eve," he said delightedly. "You cleaned up. Fifteen hundred bucks."

"But I can't take this money." There was a ring of envious eyes around her, and she felt embarrassed.

"The hell you can't take it," said Mike. "They take your dough quick enough when *you* lose, don't they? So take it. It's yours."

She felt the hot flush wash down from her face into her neck. She wanted to run away and hide. She couldn't say, "I didn't know I was playing for keeps," but she hadn't thought about it. She had known, really, but the chips hadn't seemed like money, and she just hadn't thought about it.

She stammered, "But it was your money I bet with. This ... doesn't belong to me. It's yours."

Mike laughed at her. "Okay," he said. "Tell you what I'll do." He pulled one bill from the wad in her hand, then took the rest of it, opened her pocketbook and thrust the remaining bills inside. "There y'are, now. Buy yourself a new hat." He guffawed.

She suddenly realized he was still working to impress her, so she accepted the money with a small smile, resolving, however, that in the morning she would mail it back to him.

On the way out, he insisted on stopping at the bar for "one for the road, eh, baby." Eve barely touched her cocktail, but Mike tossed off a half tumbler of neat scotch. He was very boisterous and in strangely high spirits when he took her arm and steered her toward the front door.

She thought nothing of it when, out on the sidewalk, he said with a broad wink; "The car's in the parking lot round back, baby. Can't leave a car out in the street in this neighborhood. The boys are kinda fast-fingered. In two minutes they'd strip everything off it but the paint." He laughed noisily.

The parking lot behind the Sportsman's Inn was as black as three feet up a chimney, but Mike seemed to know exactly where he was going. He kept her elbow tight in his big fist, and he kept bumping against her as they walked past the line of dark silent cars parked there. Again Eve paid no attention to his actions. He had drunk a lot of scotch, and she thought he was a little tipsy. The Cadillac was at the extreme end of the lot, in the darkest corner. The interior of the car lit up as he held the door open for her, then he slid in beside her and closed the door.

Before Eve knew what was happening, she found herself wrestling across the seat with him. She fought him back for a moment, but only for a moment. He was all over her. He tore her blouse and her brassiere.

In the panicky suddenness of his attack, she did not realize what was happening.

His breath was coming in grunts, and he kept ripping at her lingerie. His hands were everywhere. She cried out and grasped his wrist, but it was like a bar of iron, and she could no more push him away than she could stop the piston in a powerful engine.

"Come on, Baby," he croaked. "Don't be like that. Come on, come on, come on ..."

His strength was tremendous, and she felt a spurt of terror as he crushed her to him and covered her twisting face with panting, thick-lipped kisses. She was powerless in the iron circle of his arms. She had one arm free, and she beat at his head with her fist, but the puny blows had no more effect on him than raindrops. Something hard and sharp dug into her breast, and she moaned. She pushed her hand between her breast and his chest and felt the scored butt of a gun under her fingers. She managed to pull it from the holster under his left arm. She raised her hand and brought down the flat of the gun against the side of his head with all her strength. He gasped and his arms fell away from her.

The next instant, the door was jerked open. Eve felt her arms seized from behind and she was dragged from the car.

A harsh voice rasped in her ear, "Drop that rod, sister, or I'll break your arm." Then with anxiety, the voice called out, "Are you all right, boss? Are you okay?"

It was the tough chauffeur.

Mike Lenahan lurched out of the car and staggered in a small circle. He was holding his handkerchief to the side of his face. There was blood on his chin. He stopped, stood wide-legged, swaying and looked at Eve with glassy eyes.

She had stopped struggling and sagged limply, sobbing softly. Her blouse was ripped away and her torn brassiere dangled. She made no move to cover her exposed breast.

"Whattaya want me to do with her, boss?" the chauffeur asked. He sounded scared.

Mike tried to focus his eyes.

"Let'r go," he said thickly. He waved his free hand. "Take'r home. Take'r anyplace she wants to go. Sorry, baby. 'Pologies. Guess I drank a little too much, maybe."

He turned and staggered toward a dim oblong of yellow light that was the rear door of the Sportsman's Inn.

The chauffeur was over-solicitous in helping her into the rear seat of the car. She pushed his hand away and sank wearily into the corner of the seat.

"Where to, Miss?" he laughed nervously. "He said anyplace you want to go. Here's your chance to drive to Florida."

She dully gave him the name of her hotel.

ICE-COLD REDHEAD
CHAPTER TWELVE

When Eve walked into her hotel room, holding her blouse together at her throat, Sugar was sitting on the edge of the bed, jerkily smoking a cigarette, and Wiley was standing at the window, his hands clasped behind his back, staring down into the street. At the sight of Eve's torn blouse, Sugar started up from the bed and cried:

"Holy Cow, what happened to you?"

Eve had recovered by this time, and in reaction, now thought the whole episode extremely funny. Funnier, in fact, than it really could have been.

"Well," she said, trying to make it sound humorous, "Mike Lenahan is quite the Don Juan, it seems. He gave me a ride in his nice new shiny custom-built bulletproof Cadillac. We went to the Sportsman's Inn where he fed me about seventy-five dollars worth of bread, butter, steak and champagne. After taking me into the gambling room where they let me win fifteen hundred dollars, he thought the build-up was complete, so we went in the back of his car and wrestled. I hit him on the head with his gun, and when it was all over, I was the winner and still champion."

Sugar whistled and said to Wiley, who shook his head, "It must be in the air. But dollars to doughnuts, Evie, Mr. Mike Lenahan'll be around the first thing in the morning, apologizing with orchids."

Eve pinned her blouse together with a cameo broach. "Dollars to doughnuts," she said, with a hysterical little giggle, "he'll have a headache first thing in the morning. But what are you two doing here at this hour? Did you ... get married, or something? Tell me."

"Or something," said Sugar, making a wry face. "After you left the theatre tonight, Jeff blew in, half lit, and sister was there all hell to pay! Somebody told him about your little specialty. He seemed to think somebody put something over on him."

"I don't blame him," said Eve soberly. "Somebody did."

"Yeah? Well, it was no excuse for the way he acted. He lit into Wiley first. It was, what the this and what the that and where the whosis did Wiley think he was getting off at, so Wiley threw up his job and walked out."

Eve gasped, but Sugar held up her hand.

"Hold everything," she said. "That's only the half of it. Then Jeff barged into the dressing room and started in on me where he'd left off on Wiley. So *I* threw up *my* job and *I* walked out. It was quite a night all around. We thought we'd drop in and warn you, just in case Jeff ..."

There was a brisk knock on the door, but before anyone could answer it, Jeff walked in. His harsh, carrotty hair was mussed, and his eyes were bloodshot, but his face was composed. He looked at Sugar and Wiley.

"Now listen, you two," he said. "Just because I act like a damn fool, does that mean everybody has to act like a damn fool, too?"

"Just what did you want us to do, Mr. O'Hare?" jeered Sugar. "Did you expect us to say, Yes, Mr. O'Hare, no, Mr. O'Hare, you're quite right, Mr. O'Hare, let me kiss your foot, Mr. O'Hare."

Jeff made an appeasing gesture. "I blew my stack. I'm sorry. I take it all back. We've been friends a helluva while, haven't we? So give me a break. Don't walk out on me."

Sugar looked at Wiley. "It's up to you, darling," she said with such tenderness in her voice that everyone looked at her.

Wiley smiled. "Ah," he said, "I wouldn't know what to do without the crummy old Rivoli. But, Jeff," he added, "I'm warning you right now. The next time you talk to Sugar like that, it's for keeps, boy."

Jeff said, "That's understood," and turned to Eve. "And I apologize to you, too, Evie," he said somberly.

She cried, "Oh, Jeff!" and ran into the bathroom, her hand to her cheek.

Jeff gave Wiley a wan smile. "Was she any good?" he asked.

Sugar snorted. "Any good! Tell this benighted heathen just how good she was Wiley."

"She was wonderful," said Wiley with emphasis.

Jeff nodded. "I should have known I didn't have to ask."

Sugar gave him a sharp glance, then rose from the bed, beckoning to Wiley. "It's past my bedtime, darling," she yawned. She went to Jeff and put her hand on his arm. "If you love her that much," she said in a low, fierce voice, "for the luvva mud, be a man and tell her. Make her believe it! Now get me out of here, Wiley, before I bust into tears like everybody else."

Eve's face was pale when she came from the bathroom, but otherwise it showed no emotion. Jeff was standing in the middle of the room, looking at her. He crossed the distance between them in three long strides, took her in his arms and kissed her. She put down her head and turned her face away. His lips met only the softness of her glowing red hair.

"I love you, Evie," he whispered. "I want you to believe it, but I don't know how to say it so you will. I love you. That's the reason I blew my stack tonight—the thought of you standing up there on the stage taking off your clothes for that gang of creeps from Down Neck. I love you, honey."

In a muffled voice, Eve said, "Please, Jeff ..."

His lips sought her mouth again, but she turned her face against his shoulders. She felt his arms tighten convulsively against her shoulders, and felt the surge of passion that was in him. She closed her eyes and for the moment let her senses reel. Something hot and heady seemed to gush from her heart. Her legs trembled from the momentary force of it, and she surrendered herself to his arms, feeling the long length of his hard, masculine body against her, bearing her backward. She stiffened. Now she was stone in his arms. He tried to kiss her again, and this time his lips found her cold, unresisting cheek. She did not push him away, but the soaring interplay of their emotions was gone. Desperately, Jeff tried to recapture it, tried to arouse her again, murmuring into her ear:

"Evie honey, Evie honey, I love you, darling ..."

But it was gone. The moment was over, and presently he let his arms drop from her, and he stepped back.

"Someday," he said huskily, "I'll say that to you, and you'll believe it."

Silently, her heart cried out—*I believe you now, Jeff dear, I believe you now, but can't you see I'm not yet fit to be loved?* She wanted him. She wanted his lean, hard tenderness—and she looked away, for she knew if she looked into his face, she would throw herself into his arms with all the intensity of the pent-up emotions that tumulted within her.

"Someday, Jeff," she said gently. "But not today. Not tonight."

He smiled at her, but his hands were knotting and unknotting at his sides, betraying him. "Anything you say, honey." Then with forced brightness, "Say, Wiley said you were wonderful up there tonight. Do you want to continue with your specialty?"

She wanted to cry. She nodded. "I'd like to, Jeff ... if it's all right with you."

"With me? Wiley runs the show. I just run the business end of the theatre. Tonight I kind of forgot that for a little while. So if Wiley says you're wonderful, why that's the green light, isn't it?" He started toward the door. "See you tomorrow, kid. Sorry I didn't catch your act tonight, but I kind of ran out on everybody, I guess. I threw me a wingding," a small shadow of pain crossed his face and was gone. "See you tomorrow, honey." The door closed behind him.

Eve stood there, her hands clasped whitely at her breasts, then with a low, heart-rending moan, she threw herself on the bed and buried her face in the pillow.

DEMAND FOR LOVE
CHAPTER THIRTEEN

Sugar had been wrong about one thing. It was not Mike Lenahan who called, first thing in the morning. It was Vance Owen. Eve caught her breath. In the cold light of morning, the trick she had played on him did not seem nearly so funny.

But with a great show of humor, he said, "Not that anybody can take your place, Eve Barry, but please as a special favor, the next time you send a substitute, don't send the lightweight wrestling champion of Latin America."

Eve suppressed a giggle. "I beg your pardon," she said.

"You should. Believe me, you should. That female boa constrictor just about ruined Newark's up and coming young Councilman. Before I could peel her off, she had torn my shirt, bitten a hole in my ear, pulled off my tie and got lipstick in my hair. Doesn't she have any inhibitions at all?" He sounded a little plaintive.

"Perhaps," said Eve sweetly, "she found it impossible to resist your manly charms. Cheeta is actually a shy, home-loving girl and one of my dearest friends."

Vance said, "Ha, ha, ha. Pardon my unseemly laughter at this point. I don't know where you got the idea she was your friend. Within ten minutes last night, she informed me that you were frigid, that you tried to make every man you met, that you hated men, that even the stage hands weren't safe when you were around—not exactly consistent, but you get the idea. However, I was the perfect gentleman, and I do think you owe me a little something." His voice was sly and oily.

"I do? And just why, please?"

"For not having strangled your little friend with my bare hands. So how about a little night clubbing after the show this evening?"

"Oh, I'm dreadfully, dreadfully sorry, Councilman, but I have another engagement."

"Tomorrow night, then?"

"I'm sorry ..."

"How about the night after that. Or the night after the night after that?" Very whimsical, very boyish, very eager. "Or the night after the night after the night after?"

Knowing him for what he was, this pretended boyishness set Eve's teeth on edge, and she said, "I can't say. I'm really terribly busy."

He said quickly, "Who is it—Mike Lenahan?" His good humor was beginning to slip. "You two must have had quite a night. Everybody's been asking him where he got that shiner ..."

Eve hung up. She didn't trust herself to talk with him any longer. The phone rang again almost immediately, but she did not answer it.

A half hour later a messenger came with a large flat box, and when she opened it, there was a filmy black lace nightgown. It was from Mike Lenahan.

"Dear Eve," his note said, "I'm sorry I tore your blouse, and I hope the enclosed will make it all right with you. I don't blame you if you throw it out the window. But even a dog gets another chance after he bites somebody. Can I call you up later? Mike."

She folded the note and tapped it thoughtfully against her chin. Mike Lenahan with his gambling houses, his gunmen, and God knows what other vice rackets, was somewhat less than desirable either as a citizen or a boy friend. But he had one thing—he did not like Vance Owen. And the day might come when she would need someone exactly like Mike Lenahan.

When he called her at the theatre that afternoon and asked her for a date, she accepted. He took her to the exclusive Far Hills Country Club and behaved generally as if she were made of rare Sèvres porcelain. He had taken particular pains with his wardrobe. He wore a midnight blue dinner jacket with velvet lapels, a deep wine red bow tie and a dyed carnation to match his lapel. His curly blue-black hair was a masterpiece of barbering and you could almost see the waves of scent emanating from it. He dipped his head toward her in the car.

"Smell that, kid," he said proudly. "Chanel number five, the best cologne you can buy. I used almost half a bottle. Smells nice, eh?"

"Very nice," said Eve faintly, opening a window.

When he danced with her, he was scrupulous to keep six inches of dead air between them. But several times during the evening he mumbled something about, "... there oughtta be some way for us to get together, kid ..." and, "... you and me, we could go places, baby." And he didn't mean marriage. He pawed her with his eyes, and there were times that Eve felt naked when he looked at her. But she ignored all these obvious hints and gestures, and kept him at arm's length.

She knew, however, that with Mike Lenahan she was walking very close to a narrow edge. Sooner or later, unless she were very careful, she would find herself in the hands of a raging animal. Mike Lenahan's desires were very close to the surface.

One night he frightened her by saying truculently, "You're using me for something, baby, and I'd like to know what it is."

Trying to keep the panicky tremor out of her voice, she said lightly, "Of course, Mike. I'm really a sharp little girl on the make. I'm getting you to spend all your money, and when you're penniless, I'll laugh in your face."

He stared at her, then burst into a guffaw, slapping his thigh with gargantuan delight because it was so ridiculous. Aside from taking her dancing with the incidental expenses of food and cocktails, she had firmly but smilingly returned to him the expensive gifts he at first had tried to thrust on her, just as she had firmly returned the fifteen hundred dollars she had "won" at roulette. This was something he simply could not figure out. All the other dames he had gone around with had greedily seized everything he had to offer and had given as little as possible in return. Eve wasn't "giving," but neither was she taking anything from him. He could not understand it, and he was suspicious of anything he could not understand. Eve finally saw that she was going to have to give him an explanation, or she was going to be in trouble. He was becoming increasingly suspicious and hostile.

"My father," she told him one night, "was a minister."

It solved everything.

"Ah, why'n you say that before, baby?" he demanded. "You had me gawn around in circles trying to figure you out. Your old man was a minister! That explains it. I knew there hadda be a reason."

After that, there was less tension and he even confided that he, "... went to church meself once in a while." It did not prevent him from asking her to take a little trip to Miami with him. Mike Lenahan was not a man who would be long content with an atrophied sex life.

The one problem, however, that Eve refused to face was the problem of Jeff O'Hare. She avoided him, and when she could not avoid him, she forced herself to be casual, though her emotions rioted whenever he came close to her.

Vance Owen called her up every day for a week, then fell ominously silent. Eve did not worry. Owen would not give up.

Eve's bride-dance specialty was being held over for the third week, an unheard of holdover in the Rivoli, but phone calls for reservations were still pouring in, showing no sign of letting up. People were coming from as far away as Westchester in New York, and from as far south as Atlantic City in Jersey. Daily she received offers of night club jobs in New

York, Miami Beach, Chicago, St. Louis and other incredible places, but she answered none of them and steadily refused to see agents eager to make her fortune and, incidentally, theirs.

It was a Friday afternoon, during the matinee intermission, about three weeks after her premiere appearance, that she came upon Jeff O'Hare and Sugar talking together in the wings backstage.

She heard Jeff say angrily, "I'm turning him down flat, Sugar. There's a limit and this is it. I don't give a damn who he thinks he is!"

Sugar put a restraining hand on his arm. There was worry in her face and in her voice. "Think it over, Jeff," she pleaded. "Don't be rash. When you come right down to it, the kids can take care of themselves. Don't blow your top before you think it over."

"I have thought it over."

"No you haven't. Wait till you get over being sore. Then give him an answer. Don't do anything you'll be sorry for."

"Don't give me that 'sorry' stuff! I was sorry after I gave into him the last time. I never felt more like a heel in all my life. It's not going to happen again!"

They were talking, Eve knew, about Vance Owen, and from what she could gather, Owen had made another demand on Jeff.

At that moment, Sugar caught sight of Eve and said sharply to Jeff, "Shhhhhh!"

Pretending she had not overheard anything, Eve said, "Hello," people, what's the matter? Why the long faces?"

Jeff said shortly, "Nothing's the matter." He pushed himself up from the tinselled platform on which he had been sitting and strode away, thrusting a cigar into his mouth.

Still pretending innocence, Eve said to Sugar, "What's he burned about?"

For a moment, Sugar looked as if she were about to tell Eve what it was all about, but then she, too, closed up like a clam.

"I wouldn't know," she said, holding her hand out at arm's length and looking at her fingernails. Then, tartly, "Why don't you give the poor guy a break, Evie? He's nuts about you."

Eve and Sugar were not as close as they had been. Eve no longer worked in the chorus, of course, and as a featured stripper, she had a dressing room to herself. Then, too, she did not see Sugar after the show anymore. Sugar had no time for anyone but Wiley, now.

Eve said, a little sadly, "You know why I can't give him ... a break now, Sugar. It wouldn't be fair to him. He'd only be hurt when I ... start to accept Vance Owen's invitations."

Sugar was silent for a moment, then blurted, "Then why don't you accept those invitations and get it over?"

Sugar's voice was like a lashing, slapping hand across Eve's face. Eve started angrily, "I'm not ready yet to ..." and then she understood. She said slowly, "The Councilman's making trouble again, Sugar?"

Sugar ignored the question. Under her indignation, and in her way, she loved both Eve and Jeff O'Hare, but she had a blunt tongue.

"The trouble with you, Evie," she said, "is that you want your cake and you want to slice it your own way. You won't give Jeff a yes or a no, and you're putting the poor guy through hell. So let me tell you this, you'd better make up your mind pretty quick or it's going to be too late!"

Eve was speechless, rocked back on her heels by this unexpected attack. Sugar lounged to her feet and ground out her cigarette on the stage. She pinched Eve's cheek lightly.

"Think it over," she said more kindly, "and you'd better make it fast."

She strolled away. A few moments after she was gone, Cheeta sidled up to Eve.

"I was out with your fren last night, Evita," she murmured, rolling her eyes. "He call me up."

Eve said absently, "He did?" But she had hardly heard what Cheeta had said.

"*Si* ... but I doan theenk he ees so much your fren anymore." Cheeta looked smug.

Eve came to with a start. She gave Cheeta a narrow glance. "You mean Councilman Owen?" she asked, suddenly intent on what Cheeta was saying.

"Who else?" Cheeta shrugged. "I like heem. He ees so handsome, so reech. He theenk Cheeta she ees a plenty smart girl, too. I theenk he ees mad weeth you." She smoothed her scanty skirt that came but a few inches below her hips, and gave Eve a searching sidelong glance.

"He is?" Eve pretended an interest in her fingernails. "And what makes you think that?"

"The way he talk about you. He ask what time you go on at night. He asked if you go on the same time every night. I say, so, that ees all you want to see in the show, eh? And he say, Honny, you know better than that. He say, you make exhibeetion of yousalf. No good."

"Indeed?"

"*Si*, indeed. But," she nudged Eve with her elbow and winked, "he say eef you call heem on the phone, everytheen' be hokay."

"He said for *me* to call *him!*"

"*Si*, you call heem."

Eve laughed. "And just how much did he pay you to deliver that message, Cheeta?"

"Two hundred bocks," said Cheeta smugly. "What I tell heem, hey?"

Eve laughed again at the arrogance of the message. "Tell him," she said, "that I'll think it over."

Cheeta looked pleased. "*Si*. Hokay. You theenk it over. Don't give in too fast. Thees Councilman Owen, he like to be the beeg shot. It is no good to give in too fast to a beeg shot. And maybe Cheeta can get another two hundred bocks out of heem. I tell heem you theenk it over." She grinned greedily.

Eve turned and walked away. She knew that Cheeta would do anything for a buck, but such greediness disgusted her. For a miserable two hundred dollars, Cheeta was willing to play pander for Vance Owen. Still, Cheeta had served her purpose. Eve paid no attention to the arrogant message Owen had sent. It was his last attempt to force his will on her. He was practically ready, she knew, to take her on any terms.

Her terms!

Oh, she'd be able to handle him now. He wasn't a roughneck like Mike Lenahan. She wouldn't have to wrestle with him in the back seats of automobiles. She wouldn't even have to be afraid of going alone to his apartment, unless he were drunk, of course, and she would take good care not to go anywhere with him when he was drunk. She would humble him. She had learned a lot since she had come to work in the Rivoli. She had had a liberal education in men. Now she knew exactly what gestures, what words, what glances inflamed them. She knew exactly how far she could let them go before they got out of hand. She knew when to break a kiss. She knew exactly how to deflate the masculine ego with a giggle, and she knew that nothing could stop a roving hand so quickly as saying, "I do wish you wouldn't pant with your mouth open like that. You look like a thirsty Airedale!" Cruel little tricks—but it was still a man's world, and if a girl could not defend herself, she had only one choice, to get herself quickly and safely married. She knew how men talked about the girls who let themselves be used. ("That dame? Yeah, she's a nice piece, but I look at it this way ...") Oh yes, she had heard them talking, so smug, so proud of themselves that they had put something over on a girl, so calmly superior.

Men, she thought bitterly, *men!*

She knew Cheeta would run directly to a phone and call Vance Owen, and she half expected him to call her that afternoon. But he did not.

In fact, she was more than a little puzzled when Cheeta came to her dressing room after the matinee with another message from Vance Owen.

"Councilman Owen, he say he ees having dinner at the Town House."

She eyed Eve slyly. "You go?"

Eve looked at her and said coldly, "What are you going to be when you grow up, Cheeta—a madame?"

Cheeta laughed and swaggered to the door, thrusting out her pointed breasts and walking so that her hips rolled voluptuously.

"Cheeta's all grown up," she said. "She's doing hokay. And I theenk maybe it be more better you go to dinner weeth Councilman Owen at the Town House after the matinee. Why not? He ees a handsome hombre, he ees reech, what more you want, eh?"

"Do you get a commission if you persuade me to go, Cheeta, dear?" asked Eve sweetly.

Cheeta shrugged. "Weeth Councilman Owen, I give nothing away for nothing. If he ees my boy fren, I know how to handle heem." She pressed her right thumb tightly into the palm of her left hand. "I get heem right there and I hold heem there. No monkeyshines. You wait too long, maybe I get heem yet. Cheeta, she's no dummy, eh?"

After Cheeta left, Eve sat looking thoughtfully into her mirror. Vance Owen had something up his sleeve, or he wouldn't have sent Cheeta with a second arrogant message. It worried her a little. She knew what he wanted to do. He wanted to bring her to heel. He wanted to be boss. And she knew that it would be the worst thing she could do.

She went to dinner alone, but her appetite had deserted her. The little nagging worry that Vance Owen had something up his sleeve would not leave her. Those two messages, for instance. He had sounded so sure of himself. What was he planning? She pushed her half finished plate away from her and ordered a martini.

RAID!
CHAPTER FOURTEEN

Eve did not get back to the theatre until nine-thirty. Now that she was not in the chorus any longer, she could stretch her dinner hour whenever she wanted, as long as she was ready to go on when she got her cue from the orchestra, which was at exactly ten-fifteen every night.

Impulsively, she walked first into the lobby and looked into Jeff's office. She wanted to talk to him—not about anything special. She just wanted to hear the sound of his voice. She was feeling low and she wanted reassurance. The office was empty. She peered through the grill at the box office and said to the cashier:

"Is Jeff inside, Harry?"

The cashier looked up from the tickets he was putting into "Reserved" envelopes—the calls for reservations were still pouring in—and shook his head.

"He got a phone call about five minutes ago and went out in a hurry, Evie," he said. "Want me to tell him you were looking for him when he gets back?"

Eve said, "Never mind, Harry," and turned away from the window.

She went back to her dressing room and put on her costume. She could not seem to throw off the feeling of depression that had been growing on her ever since she had talked with Cheeta after the matinee. She no longer tried to hide from herself that she was worried about Vance Owen. Had she waited too long? Had she put him off too many times? Had she over-estimated her appeal to him? Had he become, finally, bored. Was that it?

The stage manager knocked on her door and called, "Five minutes, Evie. Five minutes. Get on the ball."

She hurriedly looked into the mirror, finished her make-up and walked out into the wings, holding the train of her wedding gown over her left arm.

One of the comics cracked, "Always a bride, but never a wife."

Eve cracked back, "Always a comic, but never funny."

Two stagehands, carrying a prop chest of drawers that would give an air of realism to Eve's bedroom scene, pushed by them saying impatiently, "Gangway, there, gangway ..."

The comic murmured, "I never knew a stagehand that didn't think he was the most important guy in the house. Is it because they belong to the union?"

Eve was cold, absolutely cold, when her cue came from the orchestra—the opening bars of *O Promise Me*. Usually she got an anticipatory thrill from it, but tonight her feelings were entirely negative. She had no enthusiasm. She could not warm up even after she was on stage. She was wooden. From the tail of her eye, she could see Wiley snapping his arms, commanding her to loosen up, but she could not get going. The routine seemed interminable and she went through it as if she were wading in syrup.

She was slipping into her nightgown at the end of the act when suddenly she heard loud voices backstage, the sound of scuffling, and the curtain came down with a rush. Out front, a commanding voice shouted:

"Nobody leaves their seats. Stay where you are."

A strange man appeared in the mouth of the wings and pointed his finger at Eve.

"Get that dame!" he said sharply.

A uniformed policeman lumbered across the stage toward her. She had barely time to snatch the blanket from the bed and cover herself with it before he grabbed her arm with a hand like a vise and roughly hustled her across the stage. She tried to pull away.

"You're hurting me," she cried.

He gave her a shake. "This is a raid, sister," he growled. "Keep moving." She bent her head and sank her teeth into his fat finger. He let go with a howl, and she ran across the stage. The comic was still standing in the wings, pale but contemptuous. Eve ran to him. His was the only friendly, familiar face she could see. The wings were full of policeman. He put his arm consolingly around her. She was sobbing.

"It's just a little demonstration of law and order, miss, that's all," he murmured. "Just a little show of force by the forces of justice. Just a day in the life of a policeman, miss."

A plain clothes detective, standing at the head of the stairs that led down to the chorus girls' dressing room, was saying crisply:

"Come on, keep moving, keep moving. We ain't got all night."

Uniformed policemen were hustling the girls up the stairs and out the stage door. The raid had caught the girls in the middle of a change of costume. Some of them had on nothing but panties and were clutching whatever clothes they had been able to snatch up to their breasts. Some of them were crying, others were making jokes and laughing jeeringly at the police. A little blonde girl, new to the chorus, was fighting and screaming hysterically, as a grinning policeman half dragged and half carried her up the steps. A tall brunette, one of the paraders, walked scornfully. A grinning policeman's arm shot out and dipped behind her. She whirled, spitting like a furious cat. The policeman gave her a shove that sent her staggering toward the door.

Eve heard one cop laugh to another, "Ain't had so much fun since the cat house burnt down. Remember how the dames ..."

Eve saw Sugar, her head held high, walk out swiftly, wearing a plastic raincoat. It covered her to the calf, but its translucency showed plainly that she was wearing nothing but panties and bra. The grinning cop, who had handled the blonde, made a motion toward her, but Sugar had been waiting for him. She gave him a ringing, full-arm slap across the face and strode on, daring the other policemen, with her eyes, to touch her. They let her go unmolested, though the slapped cop was yelling:

"Stop that dame! Stop that hellcat!"

The plain clothes detective waved Sugar on and said sharply to the cop, "Keep your hands to yourself, Parker, and you won't get slapped. Come on, come on, come on, you guys, keep them moving there!"

A stocky policewoman, with the face of a wrestler and a frank moustache, strode over to Eve and wrenched her out of the comic's protecting arm.

"He means you too, whore," she said in a rasping baritone. Pretending to give Eve a shove, she tried to pull the blanket from her, but Eve clung to it desperately. The policewoman raised her voice:

"Here comes Minnie-Ha-Ha, boys. Help her along the line!"

But the comic darted to Eve's side and took her arm, walking past the line of cops with her. A cop reached out for her, but the comic jumped between her and the reaching hand and said quietly:

"I wouldn't do that, bud."

The cop looked into his face, then gave him a rough push, growling, "A wise guy, eh?" But he did not touch Eve.

There were seven police cars parked in front of the theatre, and they were loaded and driven off so quickly that only the beginning of a crowd had time to gather. The comic managed to get into the same car as Eve.

He was muttering, "Where's O'Hare? Why isn't O'Hare around?" The two frightened chorus girls in the car with them were tearfully trying to cover their nakedness with the inadequate scraps of clothing they had managed to grab before being hustled out of the theatre. And the comic said loudly, answering himself, "Hell, I know where O'Hare is. He's at Headquarters with his lawyer, ready to spring us the minute they bring us in."

But the police cars did not go to Headquarters. They turned into Market Street, after going around the block, and sped silently west. They wound up at an obscure precinct station near the city line in west Newark. The girls and actors were herded into the station through a rear door. There were no news photographers or reporters. The comic looked puzzled.

"This is a helluva raid," he said. "Whoever heard of a raid without news photographers? Somebody'll catch hell for this."

The room into which they were thrust was the locker room of the precinct force. A small table had been brought in and a plain clothes detective was sitting behind it. As the girls were brought into the room, they were lined up against the lockers by uniformed policemen and told roughly to keep their mouths shut. The line began to move slowly past the table. The detective mumbled questions and wrote the answers down on a sheet of paper. He had stiff gray hair, like a terrier. He had frosty gray eyes and his manner was hostile. Eve saw Sugar and Wiley down the line, but Jeff was not in the room. The half-naked girls looked worse than ever under the garish overhead light. Their hair was in disarray and their make-up was tear-streaked. The policemen who kept them in line were wooden-faced, but they kept nudging one another and pointing whenever one of the girls let her clutched clothing slip enough to show a glimpse of an uncovered breast. The policemen whispered comments on the shapes of the bare legs.

"Take a look at that pair of gams, Murph. How'd you like to ..."

"Too skinny, pal. Take a gander at *that* pair. There's meat on them, something a man can get his hand ..."

Once the gray-haired detective at the table raised his eyes severely, and the whispering among the cops died down for a few moments.

The comic, in the line ahead of Eve, turned his head and muttered to her, "The rats, O'Hare'll be two weeks finding us out here in this precinct. What's going on? Why didn't they take us to Headquarters like they always do?"

Eve was still too stunned to hear what he was saying.

As the girls finished answering the questions at the table, they were taken out of the room through another door behind the gray-haired detective. When it came Eve's turn, the detective gave her an icy glance and said shortly:

"Name, address, place of birth."

Eve answered mechanically, and when she finished, the detective wrote after her name, "Charge: giving an obscene performance."

She stammered, "Wha-what does that mean?"

Without looking up at her, he said indifferently, "It means at least a year in the house of correction, sister. Take her away."

A policeman took Eve's numbed arm and led her through the doorway behind the table. Behind the door were the cells, which smelled pungently from the bedding on which hundreds of unwashed bodies had lain, from the damp musty walls, from urine, from the harsh antiseptic used for scrubbing the floors.

The comic, waiting to be let into a cell, sniffed the air and said ironically, "Ah, home, sweet home." He winked at Eve. "They smell like this from Natchez to Nome. Beg to report, miss, that this is the natural odor of policemen."

The cop shoved him into the cell in which were all the other men of the burlesque troupe. The girls were in different cells. Some of the cells were small and held only two girls, but the big cell, the bullpen, held twelve. Eve was pushed into the bullpen. There were no bunks in the bullpen, but there was an open toilet and a washbasin. Eve was still benumbed. She stood there as if unable to realize what had happened to her. Sugar strolled over to her and drawled:

"Well, well, look who's here. I thought you'd called your boy friend, Mike Lenahan, and gotten yourself sprung."

Eve wailed, "Oh, Sugar!" and flung herself into the tall girl's arms.

Sugar relented. She held Eve close and stroked her glowing hair.

"I was only kidding, honey," she murmured. "But honest, you're a dope if you didn't call Lenahan. He'd have you out of this pigpen in a minute. He throws a lot of weight around Newark."

Eve dried her eyes. "Could he get all of us out?" she asked hopefully.

"I don't know about that, but he could sure get you out."

"I'll stay here with the rest of you, then."

"It might be a long stay, honey. Jeff can't get us out on bail if he can't find us. There are a lot of precincts in Newark, and this one's way out in the sticks. When a cop takes you to a precinct station instead of Headquarters, Evie, he don't want you to be found."

"But how long can they keep us this way, Sugar?"

Sugar shrugged and said wryly, "Forever, if they want to, honey. Did you notice that we weren't formally charged? I know, I know, they wrote it down on a piece of paper and 'charged' us with giving an obscene performance, but it's not a charge until they write it in the blotter. And they didn't bring us in the front door, either. In a place like this, they're supposed to take you up to the desk sergeant and make a charge ..."

Eve interrupted, "Vance Owen's behind this, isn't he?"

"If he isn't, I've never been wronger in my life!"

Eve looked around the cell. Some of the girls were sitting on the floor, some were leaning disconsolately against the walls, but all looked shamed and scared. It was damp in the cell, and the half nude girls were shivering. Eve felt a surge of anger.

"Was this the trouble Owen was threatening Jeff with?" she asked Sugar in a steely voice.

Sugar's generous mouth thinned. "He wanted," she said with loathing, "Jeff to provide six girls for a party he was giving for some political big shots from the county organization. Jeff told him off. He told Owen he wouldn't provide call girls for anybody!" Her voice rose indignantly.

Eve cut her short. "Did Owen specify which girls he wanted?" she demanded.

"Are you kidding? He wanted *you*, he wanted me, he wanted Cheeta Rodriguez, and any other three Jeff could throw in."

Eve made up her mind. "Would you go to that party if I did, Sugar?" she demanded.

Sugar hesitated and looked down the cell block toward the cell in which Wiley had been put.

"You've got something in mind?" she asked finally.

"I'm going to see to it that Councilman Owen gets more than he bargained for!"

"Then I'm with you, kid, Wiley or no Wiley!"

"Will Cheeta come?"

"Once you told her about it, you'd have to tie her hand and foot to keep her away. But wait a minute now, Evie. The three of us can take care of ourselves, but I'm not going to ask any of these other kids to let themselves get pawed over by a lot of fat politicians. You know what kind of party it's going to be, don't you? It's going to be Saturday night in Owen's hunting lodge up in the north Jersey woods, and you know what that means. It means we're there for the weekend and no holds barred. Owen wants you there, but he also wants a girl for each of his political pals, too. Where are you going to get the three extra girls?"

They looked at each other helplessly, and then Sugar snapped her fingers and laughed.

"I got it!" she said. "We'll call the agent and get three of those tramps that strip for the smokers."

Eve put her hand on Sugar's arm and said pleadingly, "But you won't tell Jeff, will you, Sugar?"

"Do you think I'm nuts?"

Eve pressed her arm gratefully. Then she said, "Now I'm getting out of here, Sugar. Do you have any money with you?"

Sugar grinned. "When you're in this business as long as me, honey, you never go anywhere without your grouch bag. How much you need?"

"Twenty dollars."

Eve took the twenty, and when the policeman brought in another girl from the locker room, she called to him. He came over and growled:

"Whatever it is, sister, the answer's no."

Eve showed him the twenty. "Could you make a phone call for me?" she whispered.

The policeman looked at the bill and said reluctantly, "Sorry, sister, but we got strict orders nobody calls their lawyer."

"I don't want you to call my lawyer ..."

Sugar interrupted in a tough voice, "This is Mike Lenahan's girl friend, dopey. She wants you to call the Mike for her."

The cop said, "Holy Cow!" and looked back over his shoulder at the door to the locker room.

Sugar said to Eve, loud enough for the policeman to hear her, "This guy's badge number is 318. When you get out, you can tell Mike he turned you down when you asked a little favor."

The cop said hurriedly, "Who said I was turning you down?"

The name of Lenahan had power even outside the Ironbound ward.

The policeman took the twenty and shoved it into his pocket. "Whattaya want me to tell him?" he mumbled.

"Just tell him Eve Barry's being held here, that's all."

"Okay, but don't tell nobody I done this for you. They'd crucify me." He looked unhappy, as if he were wishing, in spite of the twenty, that this had happened to somebody else.

He was back in a half hour.

"Let's go," he whispered to Eve.

He unlocked the door. Sugar threw her arms around Eve and gave her a last squeeze.

"Good luck, kid," she whispered.

"I'll see that you all get out as fast as I can," Eve whispered back.

The cop was standing outside the door, nervously cracking his knuckles. He led Eve down the corridor and into a small room, in which were a desk, a chair and a filing case. Mike Lenahan was sitting on the edge of the desk, smoking a cigar.

He looked at the cop and took the cigar from his mouth. "Beat it, crumb," he said. He waited until the cop had left before he turned to Eve. His eyes were bleak.

"I been thinking, Evie," he said, "it's quite a run around you been giving me these last three weeks. I don't like it no more."

Eve was standing with her back to the door. She didn't say anything, but she felt a chill go through her.

"Yep," Lenahan went on, nodding, "quite a run around. Now you're asking me to get you outta this dump. Okay. I'll get you out—but one good turn deserves another, know what I mean?"

Eve knew what he meant, but she said, "What does it mean?"

Lenahan waved his cigar. He did not smile. "It means when I get you outta here, we celebrate, see? We go up to my place. We have a few drinks, a bite to eat, and we talk things over for a little while. We put things on a different basis, get me?"

Eve said dully, "Yes, I get you." Too late she realized that this was exactly the kind of situation Mike Lenahan would take advantage of. Vance Owen was the one she should have had the policeman call, but she hadn't wanted to give Owen that much satisfaction. It was too late now. If she turned Lenahan down, she'd go back to the cell, and the policeman wouldn't make any more phone calls for her. Jeff would get them bail sooner or later, but in the meanwhile, the inadequately clad chorus girls were shivering in the damp cells.

Lenahan carefully knocked the ash from his cigarette with his forefinger. "Well, what's the answer, baby?" he asked.

She gave him a smile that she meant him to take for complete acquiescence. "Why, Mike," she said, "there's no question, is there? But first we've got to go back to the theatre for my clothes."

For the first time his heavy face cracked in a grin. "What do you want clothes for? But okay. Maybe that blanket gets kind of itchy."

His car was waiting at the back door of the station. There were no policemen in sight when they walked out. The same tough-faced chauffeur was driving the Cadillac. Mike sat in the back seat with Eve. He slid his hand under the blanket and gave her arm a squeeze.

"You and me, baby," he said, heavily playful. "You and me. From now on it's the high road for you and me. Right?"

"Right," said Eve with a shiver.

The night porters were at work cleaning up the theatre when Eve walked in through the stage door, Lenahan at her side.

"Not that I don't trust you, baby," he said, "but now that we got an agreement, I want to see as much of you as I can, know what I mean?"

There was a pay phone backstage, and Eve stopped at it and held out her hand to Mike.

"Give me a nickel," she said.

"Who you calling?" he asked suspiciously.

"I'm getting those other kids out of jail. You don't think I could enjoy myself with them in that clammy place, do you. You can stand here and listen, if you want."

"Okay, baby, okay. Here's your nickel. I was just asking, that's all." Eve riffled through the phone book, found Vance Owen's number and called him. He answered immediately.

"This is Eve Barry," she said.

He chuckled. "Well, well, what do you know," he said. "What's on your mind, Evie?"

"I want you to get some people out of jail."

"Glad to oblige, Evie. Glad to oblige," he said smoothly. "Have you heard about the little party I'm throwing this Saturday night?"

"Yes."

"You'll be there, of course."

She said, "Of course," and glanced at Mike. He was leaning against the wall some three feet from her, ostentatiously not listening. But she knew he wasn't missing a word she said.

"And the other girls," Owen purred. "The invitation was for six, you know. Will they be there, too?" He was rubbing it in, showing his power over her, gloating.

"Yes," she said shortly. "Now will you get those people out of jail?" Then for Mike's benefit, she added, "The police arrested the whole troupe and took them to that precinct station near the west Newark line. I want them out tonight."

"Arrested the whole troupe, did you say?" Owen pretended

amazement. "What are the police coming to? Just an example of misplaced zeal, that's all. I'll get them out for you, Evie, but I hardly think I'll be able to squash the charges against them until after the weekend. You know how it is." He was laughing at her.

Eve said ironically, "Do your best," and hung up.

Mike ambled along beside her as she walked across the empty stage toward her dressing room.

"Y'know," he observed, "if you ask me, that sounded just like Councilman Owen's voice back there. Funny, ain't it?"

"It was his voice. He's the one who instigated the raid."

"And now he's getting everybody outta clink, just like that?" he shook his head. His voice was still pleasant. "I'm trying to figure it out. The Councilman ain't the kind of guy to do a favor without asking for a little blood in return, know what I mean?"

"If there's any blood," said Eve grimly, "it's going to the the Councilman's."

Mike laughed softly. "You kill me, baby. But don't take me for a sucker, see. I know you hadda promise that creep something. You don't have to tell me. I don't care, see? Because after tonight nobody's gonna lay a hand on you but me. So you can forget you promised the Councilman anything. I'll take care of that end of it."

He walked into the dressing room with Eve, picking her up by the arms and lifting her out of his way as she tried to bar his entry.

"You can't stay here," she protested. "I'm going to get dressed."

He lounged against the wall. "You got something to hide?" he raised his eyebrows. "A wooden leg or something? No? So whattaya worrying about? Go ahead and get dressed. I'll watch and see that you don't catch cold."

She knew it was no use to protest further. He did not trust her, and he was not going to let her out of his sight. She turned her back to him and dressed as quickly as she could. He was grinning wider than ever when she finished.

"Baby," he said, kissing his fingers at her, "I never knew a dame before that was put together like you, believe me! Let's get outta here. We're wasting time."

He took her arm and his fingers lingered over her lightly. She clenched her teeth at his touch. They recrossed the stage together. As they reached the head of the stairway that led down to the chorus girls' dressing room, Eve twisted out of his grasp and pushed him violently. He stumbled backward, swearing. She ran down the stairs. It was pitch dark down there now, but she knew her way even in that inky blackness. At the foot of the stairs she turned sharply left and ran into the musician's locker room. From there she turned into the ramp that led up to the orchestra pit. Behind her in the darkness, she could hear Mike Lenahan stumbling heavily over the stored stage props, cursing savagely. His savage voice lashed after her, telling her with vicious detail exactly what was going to happen to her when he laid hands on her. There was a metallic crash as he fell into the bank of steel lockers.

Eve scrambled through the orchestra pit, ducked under the curtained rail and sprinted across the auditorium toward the side exit. A porter, pushing a huge vacuum cleaner down the carpeted aisle, gaped after her.

Lenahan's face, darkly suffused with blood, appeared over the rail of the orchestra pit.

"Fifty bucks if you stop that dame!" he roared at the porter.

Eve thrust the door open and ran out into the night. She flew down the alley to McCarter Highway. She ran across the street, waving frantically at a bus that was lumbering to the corner. She scrambled into it and crouched down in the rear seat. She was panting so hard that a wave of nausea turned in her stomach. Peeping through a corner of the window, she saw Lenahan's Cadillac turn the corner into McCarter Highway, and she prayed that he wouldn't think to stop the bus. She saw his violent face as he leaned out his window to search the street for her. The Cadillac prowled slowly past the bus, but neither the gunman-chauffeur nor Mike Lenahan looked up. Eve sank back into the corner, her heart pounding with sickening thuds.

She had made, she knew, an implacable enemy.

RAY OF HOPE
CHAPTER FIFTEEN

The bus stopped. Eve huddled in the back seat, watching for Mike's Cadillac. She was startled when the bus driver called out: "Penn Station. End of the line, lady."

Her heart sank. She had not ridden three blocks from the Rivoli. But she dared not stay in the bus. It would be parked here, she knew, for at least fifteen minutes, and unless she lay on the floor, she would be as conspicuous as a cat in a goldfish bowl. She hurried down the aisle and stepped out into the cool night. The yellow lights overhead shed a dreary radiance. The bus terminal at Penn Station was like all bus stations—cheerless, and as devoid of all hope as the last stokehole of Hell.

Eve stood outside the bus for a moment and shivered, then she saw a cab and ran for it. She gasped Sugar's address and collapsed into the seat. The city reeled around the cab. A scant month ago she had come to Newark, a bewildered girl, scarcely mature—how much had happened since! Her bewilderment had increased, if anything. Events had piled up until they towered like a top-heavy camel, swaying and ready to fall, engulfing her. Yet, there was within her, a small, rock-steady spot, a spot of maturity, sustaining her. There was ahead a pinpoint of light, a ray of hope. (Oh God, how she yearned for the comfort of Jeff's lean and muscular arms!) Hope. (Jeff, your lips, your eyes, your lips!)

She lay there, against the shoddy mock-leather seat, weeping, until the cabbie said gently:

"This is it, lady. Here's where you wanted to go, okay?"

She gave him a misty smile, slid out of the cab, paid him, and walked up the high porch to the front door. It was an old brownstone front, this boarding house, and the front door was always open. She went straight to Sugar's room, slipped in and switched on the light. She turned—and screamed.

There, lying together on the bed was a man and a chimpanzee. The man sat bolt upright and stared at her. The chimpanzee blinked its shoe-button bright eyes and fingered its lips, mooing.

The man said brightly, "Sorry, lady, but Ethel here has first call on my bed, and it'd make her real mad if I kicked her out. Howsomeever, if you wanted to make a reservation ..."

Eve gasped, "I ... I thought this was Sugar Russell's room."

"It was, but she changed. She's got a suite on the first floor now, but she's just as democratic as ever. It's at the back of the hall, suite 3-A. Sorry about Ethel here, lady, but she has a very jealous disposition, so you can see for yourself that there's not much chance for you and me to get better acquainted."

Eve fled, wondering why Sugar chose to live in such a madhouse. Sugar's door was open, and Eve saw that Sugar had indeed taken a suite. There was a bedroom, a kitchenette and a living room. It was certainly an improvement over that pigeonhole on the second floor, but it was not clear to Eve why Sugar wanted so *much* room now. She dropped into a chair and stretched out her long legs wearily. Sugar would be home soon ...

It was broad daylight when Sugar and Wiley walked in to find Eve curled up in the chair, asleep. Eve sat up and rubbed her eyes, smiling drowsily. Sugar sprawled out on the sofa, groaning:

"What a night! Lordy, lordy, what a stinking night!"

Eve saw that it was daylight, and she said indignantly, "Did they *just* let you out?"

"No. They let us out about an hour after you left, honey, but we spent the rest of the night trying to find Jeff O'Hare. The poor guy was going nuts trying to find what precinct they had taken *us* to. I didn't say anything to him about you and Lenahan." Sugar gave her a curious glance. "How *did* you make out with him, anyway?"

Eve told her, and Sugar shook her head and said, "Oh-oh. I'll bet he was fit to be tied."

"I'm not going near the theatre," said Eve. "He'll be watching for me, I know. Can I stay here with you, Sugar? I don't dare go back to my own hotel. That's another place he'll be watching."

Wiley looked embarrassed and shot a quick glance at Sugar, who smiled at him and said, "Build me a drink, will you, Wiley honey. The rye's in the closet over the sink in the kitchen."

When he left the room, Sugar beckoned to Eve.

"He's embarrassed," she whispered a little defiantly, "but you might just as well know we're living here together. He wanted to get married right away, but I said uh-uh, you wouldn't buy a new car without driving it first, and a wife's a bigger and longer investment than any old car. And the same, I told him, goes for husbands. I wanted to be sure what I was getting before I signed on the dotted line. That's what I told him, so we're trying it out for six months."

"Sugar, how wonderful! I know you two will make a go of it. But of course I'll go to a hotel ..."

"The hell you will!" said Sugar bluntly. "Lenahan'll have the hotels covered like mustard on a hot dog. You'll stay right here. Wiley'll just have to get over being embarrassed. You'll have to sleep on the sofa, but it's better than letting Lenahan get his hands on you. He's tough, honey, and no guy to fool around with."

Eve glanced toward the kitchen and dropped her voice. "Now about Owen's party Saturday night," she said swiftly. "Do you know a photographer who can be trusted?"

"You mean to keep his mouth shut? Sure. The guy that takes publicity stills."

"Good. I want you to get in touch with him. Now another thing. Are you friends with any of the bartenders around? I mean, friends enough to ask a favor?"

"Hell yes," Sugar grinned. "Louie Storch in the Cabana Club on Bloomfield Avenue. I've steered enough suckers into his joint for him to owe me a hatful of favors."

"Good. Now here's what I want you to do ..."

Wiley came in from the kitchen at that moment, carrying three tinkling glasses on a tray.

"I suppose she's told you," he said to Eve.

"Yes, and I think it's marvelous. Congratulations."

"Well, I don't think it's so marvelous. I wish you'd persuade her to let me make an honest woman out of her. How do I know she won't change her mind in six months?"

"Fat chance of that," scoffed Sugar. "It's you I'm worrying about, little man. It's always the man that's the first to start looking around for softer shoulders to rest his head on. And speaking of rest, this chile's going to bed. I got a full day's work ahead of me." She pushed herself up out of the sofa and walked toward the bedroom, yawning. Wiley looked at Eve and blushed.

Then, elaborately off-hand, he said, "I could use a little shut-eye myself."

Still, he hesitated, looking covertly at Eve. Then angrily he blurted, "Dammit, if we were decently married, situations like this wouldn't come up."

From the doorway to the bedroom, Sugar drawled, "Oh, stop jittering, darling. Evie won't blackmail you. Eve-honey, you'll find sheets, pillowcases and blankets in that closet over there. Now I'm going to sleep, and I do mean sleep."

Wiley mumbled something like good night to Eve and followed Sugar into the bedroom. There was a mumble of their voices from behind the closed door, and then Sugar laughed throatily. There was silence, and then another throaty laugh, a laugh of tenderness, love and emotion. Then silence again.

Eve was fast asleep when they left for the theatre. She woke up about three in the afternoon. She did not dare go out. Sugar called her after the matinee.

"Well," she said, "your boy friend, the Councilman, called me, and it's all set for tomorrow night. He'll have a car to drive us to his shack in the hills, and he reminded me again, in his sweet way, that the charges against us had not been dropped, and you'd better show up at his party or else. Nice boy. And here's something else. There's been a tough character that looks something like George Raft hanging around in front of the theatre all day. Is that one of your friend Lenahan's playmates?"

"His chauffeur," said Eve in a small voice. "He carries a gun."

"For a sweet innocent little girl," complained Sugar, "you sure got yourself mixed up with the damnedest citizens. By the way, Jeff is scouring the city for you. He looks terrible. He thinks you're hiding out someplace. He thinks the raid last night scared you into a panic. I didn't say anything to him."

"Don't," said Eve swiftly. "I'll see him myself after the party tomorrow night."

Sugar said sadly, "The things you do to that poor guy. Well, I called the photographer and he's set for tomorrow night. Right now I'm on my way to see my bartender pal in the Cabana Club. Now you stay indoors, honey, hear me? From the looks of things, half the hoodlums in town are looking for you, plus Jeff O'Hare. I gotta run now. Here comes Wiley ..."

Eve hung up. She was trembling. It was close now, so close. If anything went wrong tomorrow night, her brother would have to stay in jail to serve out his unjust sentence. But nothing must go wrong. She prayed, dear God, please don't let anything go wrong ...

SHANGRI-LA
CHAPTER SIXTEEN

Vance Owen's limousine picked up Eve at the boarding house. The other five girls were already inside. Cheeta Rodriguez sat up front, chattering excitedly at the bored chauffeur, but the three girls Sugar had gotten through the theatrical agent, were very blasé. Parties like this were nothing new to them.

One of them grumbled, "I'll bet the guy hired this car from an undertaker. Nobody but undertakers own cars like this. It gives me the creeps."

Sugar did not bother introducing them to Eve. They were greedy-faced chemical blondes, and they talked only among themselves, chiefly about the hundred dollars apiece Eve was paying them for their time.

They thought it was Owen who was paying them, and they were trying to figure ways to chisel an extra fifty apiece out of him.

Eve sat next to Sugar. They were both shaking a little. Sugar slipped Eve a small bottle without saying anything, and Eve nodded, understanding.

"The photographer?" she whispered.

Sugar pointed out the rear window. A small black Ford coupe was following the limousine about a hundred feet behind.

Except for the mumbled plotting of the three chemical blondes, and the firecracker chattering of Cheeta in the front seat, it was a silent ride up Route 6. Owen's hunting lodge was on Lake Powhatan, about an hour north of Newark. They turned off the highway into a private road that wound through dense trees. The fieldstone lodge sat on a small hill overlooking the lake. Behind the lodge were two small guest houses, made of logs. There was a cement dock at the edge of the lake, and bobbing in the water were several row boats, three canoes and a nineteen foot speedboat. The limousine stopped in front of the lodge.

"This is it, ladies," the chauffeur said contemptuously. Obviously, this was not the first time he had brought girls to a Vance Owen party, and his opinion of the girls was patent in the sneer on his face. He knew what kind of girls they were, all right.

The door opened and Vance Owen, in his shirt sleeves and holding a tall glass in his hand, appeared in the yellow oblong of light that streamed from inside the lodge. He came quickly down the steps, smiling and looking very eagerly boyish.

"Well, well, well," he cried as he saw Eve. "Welcome to Shangri-La, Miss Barry. And Miss Russell, and Miss Rodriguez. But I don't believe I have met these ladies." He smiled at the three chemical blondes. His eyebrows lifted slightly at the sight of them. He knew what they were.

One of the blondes gave him a toothy smile. "I'm Gladys," she said. "This is Eloise and that's Gwendolyn. Are you my boy friend for the evening, Handsome?"

"If I had only known you were coming," Owen sighed. "But Miss Barry here has promised to teach me how to play chess. But there are plenty of men inside, girls, and all of them free and over twenty-one. Suppose we go inside and have some drinks."

He took Eve's arm. Cheeta gave her a jealous glance, but tossed her head and walked into the lodge, haughtily waggling her tight little buttocks.

She stepped through the doorway and cried, "Now the party can start. Here ees Cheeta!"

One of them laughed. "Well say now," he rumbled. "This is what we've been waiting for all day, ain't it, boys? C'mere, Cheeta, and let me give you a little drink."

Cheeta paraded across the room and sat on his lap. "Now don't make Cheeta dronk," she cooed, "because she does such fonny theengs when she is dronk!"

Sugar whispered sourly to Eve, "That's a laugh! That little pepper can drink everybody in the room under the table and still be sober enough to walk across Niagara Falls on a tightrope."

Eve looked warily around the room. Her heart was thundering. It was a big room. At one end was an enormous fieldstone fireplace, and over the mantle hung a mounted moose head. The ceiling was high and ribbed with hand-hewn beams. At one side of the room was a small hallway, masked by a pair of fancifully curlicued wrought iron gates. Behind the gate was the stairway to the bedrooms on the second floor. There were five sofas in the big room, a television set, a radio and phonograph combination, which was now playing records.

The men had been fishing all day, and they were sunburned. They were big men with soft pampered faces and shrewd eyes. They had plump, knowing hands. They had been drinking since sundown, and it was beginning to show in the slackness of their mouths and in the noisy blare of their laughter. The man on whose lap Cheeta was sitting, patted her on the thigh and leered;

"Yes sir, this is going to be quite a party once it gets warmed up, yes sir."

Nobody was introduced to anybody. Vance Owen simply cried, "Girls, meet the men. You're on your own, so relax and have a good time."

Eve tried not to show her loathing, when Vance Owen took her elbow and steered her toward the sofa in the alcove that overlooked the lake. This sofa was set with its back to the rest of the room.

He murmured, "Can I make you a drink, Miss Barry?"

She managed a smile. "Yes, please. Something long and cool," her voice shook a little. "A Tom Collins."

She looked out the window at the calm water below. She tried to keep her teeth from chattering. Now that the moment had come, she was scared. Owen came back with her drink. It was terribly strong, and Eve was glad that she had taken Sugar's advice—she had eaten a very heavy dinner and had followed that with two tablespoons of olive oil. That wouldn't keep her from getting drunk, of course, but it would certainly slow up the process.

Owen watched her over the rim of his glass as she took her first sip. He was drinking straight bourbon in a cocktail glass. She managed not to shudder as the drink, which fairly reeked of gin, slid down her throat.

"It's very good," she said.

He gave her a wolfish grin. Nobody could drink a powerhouse like that and stay sober. He did not sit too close to her on the sofa. He was going to take it easy for a while. He waved his hand at the view through the window.

"This is a lovely place, Eve," he said. "I'd like to show you through the grounds a little later."

I'll bet you would, she thought.

Aloud, she said, "Oh, I'd love it! It's so peaceful here, isn't it?"

"That's the word for it," he said smugly. "I own a thousand acres all around here. When I throw a party, I like to be sure I won't be disturbed. There isn't a neighbor within miles of me. We've had some pretty good parties up here." He was watching her narrowly.

"It's so nice to know there won't be any eavesdroppers," she smiled at him.

He leaned back into the sofa, a grin twitching at the ends of his mouth. *A few more drinks*, he thought, *and this little number'll be doing all right, but take it easy, pal, take it easy; don't rush it or you'll scare her off.* He remembered how she had looked on the stage in that lacy lingerie, he remembered the glowing curves of her beautifully rondured legs, the sweetly swelling mounds of her breasts—and his eyes glowed with anticipatory pleasure. This was going to be a *night!*

He did not rush her. In fact, he left her alone several times to get more liquor from the kitchen for the party, to bring cigars, to change the records on the phonograph. Each time he left her, Eve quickly emptied her glass under the seat cushion of the sofa.

Sugar was dancing sedately with a florid, paunchy man. He was very drunk and his legs seemed made of rubber. He took in both sides of the room when he danced. He tried to paw her, but he had consumed so much liquor that Sugar had no difficulty in warding off his fumbling hands.

Cheeta was noisier than ever, shrieking and laughing, dancing alone with her skirts pulled up to give flashing glimpses of her exciting legs above her stocking tops. Her man was also quite drunk, his heavy head lolling as if his neck was no longer strong enough to hold it up. Cheeta bounced on his lap, chattering like a monkey, pouring drinks into his mouth.

She's smart, thought Eve, *she gives the impression of abandon, shows a little leg, but she isn't giving a thing away!*

And it was true. Her man had a silly grin on his face. He was having the time of his life. Cheeta's flashing eyes kept promising him delights he never dreamed of, but soon she would have him too drunk to move a finger, and in the meantime his roving hands encountered nothing but her arms or her hands. At the moment, she had both of his hands in hers and was pretending to read his palm. Cheeta was smart, all right.

The three chemical blondes had gone to work in a business-like manner. They, too, were plying their men with liquor, sitting on their laps, necking with a great show of passion—but all through it, their eyes remained cold and commercial. They had been hired to liven up the party. All right, they would earn their money—but when it was over, the men wouldn't have anything but a bad taste in their mouths and a shamed remembrance. One of them hauled her stumbling companion to his feet and danced madly with him for about two minutes, then fell into a handy sofa with him, screaming with brassy laughter as she tilted a bottle to his lips.

Owen held out his hand to Eve. "Shall we dance?" he asked her.

There were hot little lights flickering in his eyes.
She stood and pretended to lurch dizzily.
"Oooooooo!" she giggled. "Who tilted the room like that." She fell into his arms.
He danced with her for a few moments, holding her very close, brushing his lips against the side of her face. She kept tripping, as if her feet had suddenly and inexplicably become too loose for her.
"I think you could use a little fresh air, Evie." he whispered into her ear. "Suppose we take a little walk around outside?"
"Fresh air, thass what I need, awri'," Eve slushed solemnly. "'Sawful close in here. All at cigar smoke 'n stuff. I'll be okay with a lil fresh air."
He grinned and started her toward the door. She pulled away from him.
"My bag my bag my bag," she cried. "Girl's gotta have a lil make-up. Gets all schlmeared ..."
She reeled back to the sofa and got her handbag, wearing a loose, foolish smile. "Schlmeared, gets all schlmeared," she said to Owen as he led her out into the night.
She kept lurching against him. He didn't waste any time now. He led her straight up the path to one of the guest houses behind the lodge. The moment he had her inside, he grabbed her in his arms and began kissing her face with moist, ardent lips. Her stomach turned. She had known this was going to happen, but she couldn't help the feeling of revulsion. He switched on the light, then picked her up in his arms and carried her over to the sofa. His hands became very urgent. Panic spurted up in her and she thrust him away with a cry. He grabbed her again and pulled her close, raining brutal kisses on her face and neck, pulling her blouse from her shoulder, running his lips over the cool, satiny skin. She fought him.
"Come on, baby," he was breathing heavily. "Come on, don't be like that." She held him off stiffly, and he broke out angrily, "What's the matter with you?"
She smiled loosely. "Girl's gotta have a lil drink," she said coyly.
"You've had a little drink."
"Sure, but this iss different. This lil drink's a nightcap. Girl's gotta have a nightcap first."
"Okay, okay," he said impatiently, "I'll make you a lousy nightcap ..."
She pushed him back into the sofa and stood, weaving. "Oh no," she said, smirking. "Lil Evie's gonna make her own nightcap, see? Doan like your drinks. You're too stingy with your likker, unnerstan'?"
Owen was laughing now. "Sure," he said. "The liquor's in the kitchen over there. You can make me one, too."

"I'll make you a drink awri'," she said truculently. "But doan you come around trying to make my drink, unnerstan'? I'll go home you try to make my nightcap. You're so stingy with your likker I don't know why ..."

She staggered into the kitchen. There were several bottles on the table. Swiftly, she opened her handbag and took out the little bottle Sugar had given her in the car. She emptied it into the glass she intended for Owen, then put two fingers of bourbon on top of it. She was really shaking when she stumbled back into the other room and handed him his glass.

"Go ahead, taste that one," she said. "Thass a drink. Thass got likker in it, not like the stingy drinks you make. You can't fool me, Mr. Councilman Owen. Bottoms up, happy days ..." she giggled, "But iss nighttime, so happy nights!"

She lifted her glass and drained it at a gulp. Grinning, he did the same. Then he set his glass on the floor and reached for her. She dodged his hand.

"Lil girl's room," she said huffily. "Firss I want a lil girl's room and no backtalk ..."

His face flushed angrily and he jabbed his finger at a door the other side of the room. "It's over there," he said savagely. "Now snap it up and quit stalling."

She grimaced at him. "Snap y'self up," she said haughtily. "Girl's gotta make herself pretty, ain't she? Awri' then ..."

She lurched across the room. Inside the bathroom, she locked the door. Only a few minutes, Sugar had said. It would take only a few minutes. She clenched her hands and waited. Time sluggishly dragged itself by—then suddenly there was a crash from the other room. She opened the door and peeped out.

Vance Owen was standing wide-legged in the middle of the room.

He was swaying like a toppling tree. His mouth hung open and his eyes were wide and staring. He saw Eve and made a feeble pawing motion at her.

"Damn you ..." he said thickly. "I ... I ..."

He reeled, staggered backward and fell into the sofa. He sat limply, his eyes glassy and open. Eve ran to the door and opened it. Sugar slipped into the room. She looked at Owen and nodded with grim satisfaction.

Eve stammered, "Will he ... will he be all right. He looks so awful."

"Don't worry about him, honey. Louie said those drops would paralyze an ox, but he'll be all right in the morning."

She went to the door and whistled softly. A moment later, a young fellow, carrying a candid camera with a flashlight attachment, walked into the room with Cheeta Rodriguez.

Sugar said briskly, "Okay, let's get this over before somebody from the lodge takes it into his head to investigate. Let's go, Cheeta."

Cheeta held out her hand. "First you give Cheeta the monny, eh?"

Eve wrenched open her handbag and gave Cheeta five hundred-dollar bills. Cheeta counted it and nodded. "Hokay," she said. She began to take off her clothes.

"Leave on your panties and stockings," ordered Sugar. "Don't ask me why, but it makes a bigger impression. All set, Joe?"

The photographer laughed softly. "Maybe I can persuade the Councilman there to have these shots made up into personalized Christmas cards."

Owen's eyes were open and there seemed to be a flicker of consciousness in them. Sweat was pouring from his forehead. Agony showed in his eyes.

Eve crouched against the wall, shivering. It was Sugar who took charge. She propped Owen up, so he was really sitting in the sofa, not sprawled there. She pushed him around and prodded him into position as if he were nothing more than a department store dummy.

She looked at Cheeta. Cheeta was standing there in her stockings and panties, insouciantly fluffing her hair, but actually watching the young photographer from her lashes. She knew the impression her beautiful little body was making on him, and she showed off a little. He couldn't take his eyes from her.

"Okay, okay," said Sugar impatiently, "if you're finished getting an eyeful, Joe, suppose we take a few pictures."

Joe grinned sheepishly and fiddled with his camera while Sugar arranged Cheeta on Owen's lap. She put Owen's limp arm around Cheeta's waist, and had Cheeta pose as if kissing Owen's cheek.

"How's that look, Joe?" Sugar asked the photographer.

"He sure looks natural with his eyes open that way," he answered. "He looks a little surprised, but that's good. A guy caught like that, with a half-undressed dame on his lap would look a little surprised. Nobody'll ever believe he was paralyzed when we snapped him."

"All right, let's go, let's go," said Sugar, nervously looking through the doorway toward the lodge.

The photographer swiftly took three shots. Cheeta jumped off Owen's lap and dressed rapidly. Eve felt faint. It was over now, this part of it, the worst part. Her mouth felt dry.

"We gotta get out of here now," said Sugar. "I don't want to be around when he snaps out of it in the morning. Can you take the three of us back to town, Joe?"

"Sure, somebody'll have to sit on somebody's lap and I wish it were me," he grinned at Cheeta. "I'm parked down the road about a hundred yards."

Eve could not resist a glance into the lodge as they went swiftly and silently past the open door. Two couples were drearily dancing. The third girl was standing at the fireplace, moodily smoking a cigarette. All of the men but two had passed out. The air inside was blue with cigar smoke. One of the men dancing fell, then rolled on his side and snored.

It was dreadful. Eve felt sick.

As they drove down Route 6 toward Newark, Sugar slipped Eve a key.

"Room 412 in the Hotel Robert Clinton," she whispered. "It's registered in my name. There's a side entrance that Lenahan probably won't have staked out. Say, Joe, when'll you have those pictures ready?"

"Couple hours, no more."

"Fine. Deliver them to me at the Hotel Robert Clinton."

Eve closed her eyes. One more day, she was thinking. One more day and it would be all over. Just one more day ...

SEAL OF PASSION
CHAPTER SEVENTEEN

It was two o'clock Sunday afternoon. Eve prowled the floor of the hotel room. She knew what time it was, for she had looked at her wrist watch only two minutes before, but she glanced at it again. She had been doing that ever since she had called Vance Owen at the lodge at twelve-thirty. He was now on his way to Newark. She went to the window and looked down into the street. It was a gray, lowering day. Newark on a Sunday was bad enough, but on a gray Sunday it was just terrible. It was as bad as Philadelphia. Nervously, Eve looked down at her watch again. 2:01.

She could hear someone moving around in the adjoining room. There was a locked door between, but she found the sounds of life very comforting. She did not feel so dreadfully alone.

She walked jerkily to the bed and lifted a corner of the mattress. There lay the manila envelope that she had found slipped under her door. In it were three negatives and three photographs. Joe, the photographer, had been right. Vance Owen looked exactly like a man surprised in an amorous act. But it was Cheeta's lovely little body that made it a striking picture. No one could look at her, at the swelling curves of her stockinged legs, at the lift of her pointed breasts, at her wide and eager mouth, without knowing that this was a woman who had been made for passionate love. All the fire and emotion of her Spanish ancestry was in her dark-eyed face.

There was a knock on the door and Eve hurriedly thrust the envelope back under the mattress and smoothed the covers, before going to the door.

It was Vance Owen. His face was sallow and drawn and his bloodshot eyes small and mean. He gave her a short, curt nod and walked into the room without saying anything. Eve closed the door but she did not lock it. She was beginning to feel frightened. Owen turned and looked at her. His head was out-thrust on its thick, bull-like neck, and he looked dangerous.

"Well," he said harshly, "what is it?"

She did not trust herself to speak. She had kept one photograph out of the envelope. Silently, she drew it from inside the front of her blouse and handed it to him. He looked at it. His shoulders hunched and his mouth became a hard thin line, his eyes snapped. His hand twitched as if he had stifled an almost overpowering impulse to lash out and smash her face to bloody ruin with his fist.

Eve stepped back quickly, but Owen did not move. A muscle jumped in his cheek.

"Okay," he said in a voice that told of the terrible restraint he was putting on himself. "How much?" He snapped the photograph with his forefinger.

Eve moistened her lips. "I ... I don't want money."

His brows drew together slightly. "No? How unusual. Then what do you want?"

"I want you to write something on a piece of paper," her voice grew stronger as she spoke, as she thought of her brother. "I want you to write how you framed a poor little GI back in San Francisco while you were an officer in the MPs. My brother, Jack Barry."

"I never framed anybody," he said loudly, avoiding her gaze.

"That's a lie. I spoke to the people Jack was supposed to have held up, and they said they could not identify him, but you talked them into it. They won't change their testimony because they said you identified Jack. But they *will* change their testimony if you admit you were wrong, and that will free my brother. That's my price for the photographs and negatives!"

Owen swallowed and said hoarsely, "You're crazy. You're not giving me any choice. You can ruin my career either way. If I write anything like that, the newspapers'll get a hold of it and they'll crucify me. Nuts to you, sister. I'll take my chances with the photographs. What can you do with them, anyway? The newspapers won't print them. *Just what can you do with the photographs? Nothing.*"

She felt a growing sense of dismay. Yes, what could she do with the photographs?

"Furthermore," Owen went on, "I'm going to have the cops pick you up before you can move a step out of this hotel. Then we'll bargain for the photographs. Then we'll see if you'd rather hand them over, or serve a nice little stretch in the jailhouse for, let's say, prostitution. And don't think I can't make a charge like that stick, baby." He started toward the phone on the wall beside the door. "Let's see how loud you sing when the boys put the arm on you," he gloated.

"Just a minute!" she cried desperately. "Maybe I can't do anything with the photographs to hurt you. But Mike Lenahan can!"

Owen jerked like a boxer who has just taken a sharp body blow.

"Is Lenahan in on this?" he asked heavily.

"You don't think I did this alone, do you?" she flung back at him. Then coldly, "And your precious career needn't be ruined. This is what you can write to the San Francisco authorities. You can write that you based your prosecution of my brother on the testimony of those people he was supposed to have held up. You can tell the authorities that it has just come to your attention that those people never could identify Jack, and therefore you strongly urge that my brother be released immediately."

Owen's face had become increasingly thoughtful as she spoke. "That could work," he nodded. "That gives me an out, too. Okay, Eve, it's a deal."

She went hurriedly to the chest of drawers and took out the pen and paper she had ready for him. Her hands were trembling, but there was a great surge of relief through her. It was over. Her knees felt rubbery and weak, but it was over, now.

Owen sat down at the small table by the window and wrote rapidly. When he finished, he blew on the paper to dry the ink, then handed it to Eve.

"That sound all right to you?" he asked, almost pleasantly.

She read it quickly. He had written exactly what she had dictated. "That's ... just right."

"Fine. And now may I have the photographs, *and* the negatives?"

"Of course."

Unthinking, she went to the bed and reached for the mattress, but a warning bell rang in her mind and she straightened up with a jerk.

"No," she cried. "Not until ..."

But she was too late. He was on her like a savage bull. He jerked the confession from her hand and gave her a backhanded slap across the side of the face that sent her reeling across the room. He lifted the mattress and laughed when he picked up the manila envelope and examined the contents.

"Thanks, sister," he chuckled. "This takes a big load off my mind. But I'm going to have you put away for awhile. You're just a little too smart for your own good."

He turned toward the phone but before he had gone two steps, the door to the adjoining room flew open and Mike Lenahan's tough chauffeur scuttled into the room. There was a gun in his hand and his teeth glittered in a white grin.

Mike Lenahan's voice came lazily, "Relax, there, Councilman, relax. A big politician like you wouldn't want to get himself shot, would he? Lew, relieve the Councilman of that paper and stuff he's got in his hand. Don't make any smart moves, Councilman, because Lew, he's a guy he don't care who he shoots, even the next mayor of Newark."

Owen stood frozen while the grinning young gunman took the confession and photographs from his hand. Mike looked them over and laughed softly.

"You take a good picture, Councilman," he said. "But wouldn't it be too bad if I had fifty thousand copies of this made up and scattered from one end of Newark to the other like confetti? That'd sure make a mess out of your campaign for mayor now, wouldn't it? But I'm a good guy, see? I wouldn't think of doing anything like that to a pal. I'll just hold on to this stuff, know what I mean? Then when you get to be mayor, you and me, we'll play ball. It's going to be all right having the mayor of Newark in my back pocket, yes sir. I'm thinking of expanding. That's the kind of guy I am, Owen. A pal. I do you a little favor, and you play ball with me when you get to be mayor. Between us, we'll sew up this city like an Easter bonnet. Now beat it, crumb. I got business with the little lady here."

Owen looked thoroughly beaten. He knew what life under Mike Lenahan's thumb was going to be like. His eyes were ashes. He made a sodden motion with his hand.

"Could I ... could I have that confession?" he pleaded.

"I said scram, didn't I? I got a special use for this little piece of paper. Eve here, she's gonna do something extra special for me, know what I mean. Then after awhile, if she's a good girl, I might want to do something for her, like giving her this piece of paper and letting her get her brother out of the pokey. But like I said, scram. You're wasting my time. Beat it."

Owen shambled across the room, a defeated man. Eve saw him start when he opened the door, and there was a curious expression on his face when he turned his head and looked back over his shoulder at Lenahan, but he went out and closed the door behind him. Lenahan jerked his thumb at his young gunman.

"You, too, pal," he said. "Run along and keep an eye on the Councilman."

Grinning even more widely, Lew slipped from the room. Lenahan turned to Eve.

"You know, baby," he said, "you're not smart. You're dumb. There ain't much goes on in this town I don't know about, like, for instance, you having your girl friend reserve this room for you in her name. One of the oldest dodges in the business. The minute Lew told me she took a room here, I knew it was for you, so I got the room next door. I just wanna show you how tough it is to put anything over on Mike Lenahan."

Eve crouched against the wall and looked at him with miserable eyes. She didn't care what happened to her now. Her plans had smashed.

"And now, Eve-baby," grinned Lenahan.

Wide-eyed, Eve saw Jeff O'Hare slip into the room from the corridor. In his hand he held Lew's gun. His carrotty hair was mussed and there was a wild, reckless light dancing in his eyes.

"And now what, Lenahan?" he said.

Lenahan whirled. "Well, well," he said. "Mr. O'Hare with a great big gun in his hand. That makes him a great big guy, don't it!"

Jeff stooped and skittered the gun across the floor into the far corner. He moved toward Lenahan, balanced on the balls of his feet. Lenahan was bigger and heavier, but he backed up as Jeff advanced on him. He held up his hand.

"Now wait a minute, pal," he said quickly. "I know you're a fast man with your dukes. Okay. So far I ain't got nothing against you, and you ain't got nothing against me. Be smart and I'll cut you in on the biggest deal you ever seen ..."

Jeff said evenly, "That stuff you got in your hand. Put it down on the bed."

"Okay, pal, okay. See? There it is. On the bed. All of it. I didn't hold out a thing."

"What's the matter, Lenahan?" Jeff jeered. "You're supposed to be quite a scrapper. What's the matter?"

"Nix, pal, nix. I'm just an amachoor. I ain't scared of you. I just got good sense, that's all. I hear how you kill that guy from Detroit in the ring with just one slap in the mush. Now suppose I just get outta here and no hard feelings, okay?"

Jeff put his hands on his lean hips and looked at Eve. "It's up to you, Eve," he said.

"Eve don't have nothing against me neither," Lenahan said eagerly. "I was a perfect gentleman with her at all times except once when she smacked me with my own roscoe, which unfortunately I ain't wearing today, not that I'd of tried to pull it, because I hear you're kind of a fast guy on your feet and the chances are I'd of got smacked before I could get it out. No hard feelings, Eve?" Mike asked, edging toward the door.

Eve cried, "Oh, let him go, Jeff!"

Jeff nodded, and Lenahan lumbered out of the room, pausing only at the door to say, "No hard feelings ..."

Eve said, "Jeff ..." His face was forbidding. "How ... did you find me ..."

"Cheeta Rodriguez told me you were here. But she wasn't doing you any favor. She thought she was tattling. Come here!"

"Oh, Jeff."

She ran to him. But instead of taking her in his arms, he whirled her around, sat down on the edge of the bed, and laid her across his knees.

"You've got this coming," he said between clenched teeth.

Eve cried out with pain as his hard hand cracked down across her back. His hand came down again and she winced, but she did not cry out. She even smiled a little. She had been afraid that she had pushed Jeff too far, but now she knew that he still loved her, and he was right—she did have this coming. She stiffened, waiting for the next crack of his palm, but it did not come.

He cried, "Oh, Eve!" turned her on his lap, lifted her; meeting her eager lips with his. The wildness went out of the kiss and it became a powerful current that swept them to a peak of flaming emotion. His hand slid down her side, stroked her, leg, swept up again until it was stopped by the firm under-curve of her chin. He stood, lifting her again. He laughed, a high, reckless laugh like a wind in a mountain pass. He laid her gently on the couch and bent over her, brushing her lips with a soft kiss. His lips found her eyes, her throat. His hands proclaimed his love. Her body met his in the seal of passion ...

Afterward, in the drifting peace, Jeff laughed softly.

Eve kissed his ear. "What are you laughing at, darling?" she whispered.

"Poor old Vance Owen," he chuckled. "What's going to happen to him, shouldn't happen to a dog."

"What do you mean?"

He laughed outright. "Your little friend, Cheeta wheedled a print from that photographer, and now she's going to blackmail the Councilman."

"Blackmail!" said Eve with horror.

"Yes. She's going to make him marry her, or else."

"Poor Councilman Owen," said Eve.

THE END

LOVERS DON'T SLEEP
BY LORENZ HELLER

Writing as Laura Hale

NEVER BEEN KISSED
CHAPTER ONE

Suzy Carr hesitated just the fraction of a moment, then swiftly swung out of her dress and hung it in the closet. This was the part she hated. The undressing. She knew Frawley was standing at the foot of the bed, watching her with those avid fried-egg eyes of his.

"*Go ahead and look*," she thought resentfully. "*Get an eyeful!*"

She hadn't liked Frawley from the moment they were introduced in Harry's office. He was an aggressive, stocky man with one of those chins he kept thrusting at you like a fist, the way Mussolini used to do. She had known then that it was going to come to this, and she could have backed out, but she wouldn't do that to Harry. Harry depended on her.

He had put his arm around her shoulder and given her a squeeze, saying to Frawley, "She's the best in the business, Mr. Frawley. Satisfaction guaranteed. Right, Suzy?"

And with Harry's arm around her, Suzy had said, "Right."

So here she was again, in another hotel room with another guy she couldn't stand the sight of because he wasn't Harry. She wished Harry had enough money so he wouldn't have to be in this crummy business—but that's what this crummy business was for, to give Harry enough money to get out. Thinking of it that way made her feel better about the undressing. After all, the undressing was necessary, and it was only her dislike of Frawley that made it seem awful. The way Frawley felt made absolutely no difference. Frawley didn't matter, except that he was one of Harry's clients. Frawley really didn't matter at all, she told herself.

Now she was all right again, and she lifted off her slip with a single lithe motion and hung it in the closet beside the dress. She heard Frawley suck in his breath, but she ignored him. She adjusted the slip on the hanger so that it hung straight and smooth. This was always her worst moment, after she had taken off her slip, for she was fully conscious of the effect of her body on men.

But it was her legs that were really exciting. They were not slim and coldly patrician, nor were they heavy and sturdy. Her thighs curved strongly from her stocking tops, round and boldly feminine. The excitement in them was this utter femininity. You did not have to seek for similes when you looked at them. They were not *like* the legs of gazelles, nor were you reminded of the sleek and sinuous grace of cats. They were the legs of an exciting woman, and their appeal was so direct that there was no room for extraneous thoughts.

From the sun, her skin was the color of chocolate and cream. In the summer, she was in the sun every day, and when the months became too cold to go to the beach, she used a sun lamp. The silver and gold contrast between her blonde hair and the toasted bisque of her skin was breath-taking.

It must have been, for it had taken Frawley's breath, and he stood clenching the foot-post of the bed in his hand, leaning slightly forward as he stared at her. His Mussolini chin hung slackly.

Suzy paid no attention to him. She bent over and skinned off her stockings. She did not like to be there in her brassiere, panties and stockings, especially at a time like this. It was just a little too much like those picture post cards the slimy little men along the Prado in Havana tried to sell you when all their other fantastic entertainments failed.

It was all right in just brassiere and panties. That was more like being in a bathing suit than being undressed. She felt better now. She didn't *feel* undressed anymore.

Frawley watched her hungrily as she lifted her blonde hair and aerated it with her fingers, fluffing it. She was charged with something stronger than beauty. Her face was high across the cheekbones, her eyes were long and hazel. Her mouth was wide, promising kisses that would smolder long after the twin pairs of pressing lips had separated.

Not until she had taken a cigarette from her handbag and lighted it did she turn and look at Frawley.

"Take off your coat and tie," she said coldly. "Do you want to look as if you're lecturing me on my morals?"

He started, then cleared his throat. "Of course," he said, "of course." He hurriedly took off his coat and tie and threw them on the bed.

"Not there," Suzy corrected him. "Over there." She pointed to the chair beside the bed. "Let's do this right."

He reddened. "Of course," he said again. He didn't like being corrected, but he hung the coat and tie over the back of the chair. He heaved his expensive pigskin suitcase up on the bed and opened it. He took out a bottle of scotch and two glasses.

"Have a little snort now?" he offered hopefully.

"No thank you. And take that suitcase off the bed, too. Do I have to tell you everything? Do you want to be scrambling around at the last minute getting things off the bed? You should know that much."

His temper flared, but she held it in check with the calm flatness of her glance. His flush deepened.

"I've never done this before," he said defensively. "This is all new to me, you know. It's old stuff to you and all that, but don't expect me to know all the ins and outs."

She gave him a small, acid smile, but inside she felt the lift of relief. At least, *that* part of it was over. She had expected him to be a problem, but now that he was on the defensive, she had him under her thumb and she could hold him to the blueprint. It was always a relief when she got that far.

He held up the scotch bottle. "Sure you won't have a little snort?" he said archly.

She reached out and took the bottle away from him. She broke the seal, then turned and walked across the hotel room to the wash basin and emptied half the bottle into it.

He glowered. "What's the idea of that?" he demanded.

She looked back over her bare, golden shoulder. "You didn't expect to *drink* that much, did you?"

"I'd rather drink it than pour it down the sink."

"Talk sense."

This was not her way of talking. It was not even the way she liked to talk, but it was the only way to keep him in hand.

His eyes flickered at her long rondured legs as she walked back across the room. She took the lamp from the small wicker table beside the lounge chair and set it on the floor. She brought the table to the bedside.

She took the two glasses from him, placed them on the table, and poured a little scotch in each one. She set the bottle to one side of them. She stepped back to the door and surveyed it critically. She went back and moved the table a little closer to the foot of the bed. She glanced around the room and found an ash tray on the window sill. This, too, went on the wicker table. She took four cigarettes from the package in her purse, broke them in half and scattered them in the ash tray. All this was done in a very businesslike manner.

Frawley had moved to the side of the room out of her way, and was leaning against the wall, watching her from heavy lids. He watched her legs and how cleanly they moved. There was a growing resentment in him. She had pushed him around, and he didn't like it. He hadn't come here to be pushed around. After all, he was paying for this, wasn't he? It was his money. But he didn't say anything. He just stared at her, as if by staring he was building up a power over her. He gloated over the tawny loveliness of her legs.

She looked at him and said briskly, "Do you smoke cigars or cigarettes?"

He was disconcerted by the suddenness of her question. "Uh, cigars," he said.

"Give me one." She held out her hand.

He gave her a cigar, and she broke it in half. One half she ground into the ash tray, and the other half she handed back to him.

"Light it," she ordered. "Get an ash on it."

Her tone did not bother him this time. He allowed his eyes to linger on her legs, then indolently took the cigar, grinning a little at her as he lighted it. He'd show her she couldn't push him around.

"What time is it?" he asked.

She glanced at her wrist watch. "Nearly time."

"Mind if I have a little snort, all by myself?"

"Help yourself."

She moved quickly toward the window, but he managed to be just a little quicker and brushed the back of his hand across her as he passed her. He chuckled. He'd show her. He had one drink fast, then poured another and lingered over it, ogling her over the rim of the glass. Standing there at the window with the light behind her, her face and breasts and legs only highlighted, she was like something beautiful and Tuscan in bas-relief. But living. He savoured that.

"What do we do now?" he asked.

"We wait," she said, without looking at him.

"Just wait?"

"What did you expect to do? Set up light housekeeping?"

"It's kind of dull, just waiting."

Suzy felt her heart begin to pound a little faster. He was slipping out from under her thumb. He was beginning to wriggle. With the others, it had been clear sailing once she had them in hand, but Frawley was tough. She had seen he was tough that very first minute when she met him in Harry's office. He had looked like trouble, even then.

"Smoke your cigar," she said a little breathlessly, trying to maintain her former briskness. "Pour yourself another drink."

He laughed softly. "Anybody can pour himself a drink, baby. Anybody can smoke a cigar. Why don't you climb down off that high horse of yours? Come on, have a little snort and relax. It's all in a lifetime."

A little barb of panic caught in her throat, but it went away when he didn't move toward her. He just reached for the bottle and poured himself a third drink.

"How'd a girl like you get mixed up in this racket?" he asked.

With that question, she was back on familiar ground. It was the question they all asked, and she gave them all the same flip answer. "It's a penance," she drawled, "for killing my grandmother with her own crutch."

"If you ask me," he leered at her, "you froze her to death."

"That was first. I hit her with the crutch when she tried to come back to life."

She was warning him. He got it. He grinned.

"Relax," he said, "relax."

A few pebbles of perspiration gathered on his upper lip, and he licked them off. As harmless a gesture as it was, she shivered. If only Harry didn't have to be in this crummy business! It was worse each time she had to go through this. Something like a wail echoed through the emptiness of her. Each time she went through this, something of her was left behind in these dreary hotel rooms. Each time it was just a little harder to come back to normal again.

But she couldn't tell this to Harry. It would be too much like whining, and he did depend on her.

The phone rang, and Frawley turned mechanically toward it, dropping his cigar in the ash tray.

Suzy said sharply, "I'll take it."

"But it might be for me."

"All the more reason for me to take it. But it won't be for you unless you've been blabbing, and Harry warned you about blabbing, didn't he?"

He didn't flush, and he didn't go back on the defensive. He just grinned. It was a bad sign.

She picked up the phone and said, "Hello?"

A familiar voice asked, "All set?"

"All set," she said breathlessly.

The man at the other end caught that note in her voice and asked curiously, "Is something the matter, Suzy?"

"No, nothing's the matter, Joe. What could be the matter?"

Joe was the photographer Harry always used.

"The way you sounded," said Joe.

"Nothing's the matter."

"I hope not, Suzy. I don't want to barge in unless everything's in line."

"Everything's in line. How long will you be?"

"Ten minutes. Dammit, Suzy, you know I don't call you till I'm ready to come up. If there's something wrong, let me know, will you?"

"There's nothing wrong."

"I hope not. I sincerely hope not from the bottom of my heart. This new District Attorney is on the rampage, and he's no baby to fool around with. See you in ten minutes."

He hung up.

Suzy replaced the phone in its cradle and turned to Frawley.

"They're on their way," she said. "Now for heaven's sake, don't sit grinning when they break in. Try to look as if she were the last person in the world you expected to see."

"She's the last person in the world I *want* to see," he chuckled. "What do we do now?"

"We sit on the edge of the bed. Let me fill these glasses up first. They'll show in the photograph."

Her hands were shaking as she tilted the bottle over the glasses. She sat down on the edge of the bed.

"Sit beside me," she said. "They'll be here any minute."

Frawley unbuttoned the collar of his shirt and sat beside her. He knew what he was supposed to do next, but he pretended innocence. He wanted to make her do it.

"Put your arm around me," she said.

"You're making it tough for me," he grinned wider than ever.

"Not there. Around my shoulders!" she said sharply. "And wipe that grin off your face. It's not a joke."

"You're telling me." His hand slid over her shoulder and fingered her arm. "Smooth."

It was too late to slap him away when his fingers slid to the satiny underskin of her arm, stroking it. She turned her head against his shoulder, then lifted her blonde hair and laid it concealingly across the side of her face. Harry had warned her about getting her face in these pictures.

"It's only the body we want, honey," he had warned. "Once you get your face in, you're no good to me anymore. Those judges aren't as dumb as *The New Yorker* might lead you to believe. The second time around, they'll recognize you as sure as hell. Not that you don't have a memorable chassis. Remember what Boccaccio always said."

Boccaccio, it seems, had cynically remarked on the general anonymity of the unclad female form, with an amorous connotation. Especially with an amorous connotation. But Boccaccio was a writer, and you expect writers to say things like that. Suzy didn't like it coming from Harry. It just proved to her that this crummy business was coarsening him.

Keeping her head buried against Frawley's shoulder, she groped for one of the glasses on the table with her right hand. It would give just the right touch to the photograph. If she were snapped with the glass in her hand, it would give just the right touch to the picture. It was things like this, plus her knowledge now of how to set it up, that made her invaluable. Just the right touch, she thought bitterly. It was doing things to her as well as to Harry.

Frawley's hand wandered and she hissed at him, "Grow up, will you, grow up!"

"That's just the trouble," he said blandly. "I am grown up."

She didn't dare move. She didn't dare get out of her pose, because they would be breaking in at any moment, and Harry liked these things to be just right. Frawley was taking advantage of the situation. He had known this moment was coming, and he had planned to do just what he was doing.

Suzy clenched her teeth and lay rigidly against his side. She could hear the tiny ticking of her wrist watch, and it seemed to her that the watch seemed to draw a deep breath between each tick. Frawley's fingers trickled down her side, pausing a moment at her bra, tugging experimentally at it. His left hand lightly touched her bare knee, stroked it with his fingertips, pressed it as if curious about the structure.

Surely ten minutes had gone by since Joe had called! More than ten minutes. Much more. The watch ticked, drew a long breath, and ticked again. Ten minutes!

Frawley was not content with the knee.

"Smooth," he murmured, "smooth ..."

Something inside Suzy had begun to quiver, and the quivering was spreading, like hysteria. His thick neck was a scant inch away from her teeth.

The door burst open. Foremost in the throng of people was a tall, angular woman, who shot out a bony, greedy finger and shrieked convincingly:

"There he is! Look at him! My husband. My *alleged* husband. Look at him, the swine!"

Joe stepped professionally past her, stepped to one side of the doorway and raised his candid camera. The flash bulb blinked piercingly. Swiftly he unscrewed it, and screwed in another, crouching for a shot from another angle.

The angular woman, clutching the arm of the gray-haired man beside her, moaned, "How could he do this to me? How could he, oh, how could he? I've given him the best years of my life, and look at him!"

She sagged, and the gray-haired man put his arm around her, glowering across the room at Frawley.

"Shame on you, Howard," he said angrily. "Shame on you!"

But the angular woman was not satisfied. Behind them was another woman with tortoise-shell glasses and the patient face of a private secretary.

"You saw, Louise?" the angular woman pleaded. "You saw?"

"I saw, Mrs. Frawley," said Louise dutifully.

Mrs. Frawley collapsed against the gray-haired man, clinging to him. "The shame, the shame, the shame!" she sobbed. "I loved him. I always loved him. I still do. The shame!"

The gray-haired man patted her on the shoulder. "Control yourself,

Dorothy," he soothed. "Control yourself. He's not worth it."

The flashbulb flared for the last time, and Suzy lifted her head from Frawley's shoulder. Joe never took more than three pictures. Joe winked at her, and she tried to hold his eyes with a desperate, pleading glance, but he was already backing out of the doorway, thrusting his plates into the leather plateholder that hung at his side.

Mrs. Frawley drew herself up.

"You will hear from my attorneys, Howard," she snapped at Frawley.

Then, in order not to spoil the tableau, she stepped back and slammed the door.

Frawley chuckled, "My wife. You'd think she hadn't been coached for the past week. But that's the way she's been for twenty years. Screaming like a steam whistle."

Suzy tried to disengage herself from the arm that held her across her shoulder.

"It's all over," she tried to sound brisk. "That's all. There isn't any more. I've got a date. Let's break it up."

Frawley's muscular hand tightened on her arm.

"You've got a date all right, baby," he grinned. "But it's right here. I paid that boss of yours plenty …"

"Let me go!" Suzy's voice skirled. "Let me go or …"

"Or you'll scream? Don't kid me, baby. The last thing in the world you'll do is scream. One scream out of you and you bust your boss' racket wide open, so don't try to kid me."

She twisted frantically in the circle of his heavy arm, but he brought around his hand, grasped her jaw and thrust back her head for a heavy-lipped, brutal kiss. He lifted his head slightly.

"The trouble with you," he said heavily, "is that you ain't never been kissed by a *man!*"

He tried to kiss her again, but she turned her head sharply and caught him on the bridge of the nose with her temple. He swore and clasped his nose. She was still holding the glass of scotch, and she swept it around, dashing the contents into his eyes. He howled and clasped his eyes with both hands. She leaped off the edge of the bed.

Her self-possession was entirely gone, and she cried piteously, "Harry, Harry …"

She lunged against the wicker table, tripped and fell. Frawley heard her and made a grab for her, swearing savagely. He got her by the arm and, lunging to his feet, dragged her up.

"I'm going to beat the living daylights out of you for that," he grated. "I'm …"

That was as far as he got.

Suzy heard a meaty smack, and incredulously she saw Joe half crouched over the form of Frawley sprawled across the bed. Joe's eyes were blazing.

She cried, "Joe ..."

His arm went around her.

"It's okay, kid," he said. "The Marines have landed. I thought there was something in that last look you gave me before I bowed out, so I came back. Pretty, ain't he?"

Frawley was out cold, his jaw agape, his eyes glassy.

Joe gave Suzy a gentle smack on the fanny.

"Get your clothes on, kid," he said. "This is no place for a lady."

Suzy walked to the closet on trembling legs. She hurriedly drew on her dress, thrust her slip into her handbag and stepped into her shoes. "Let's go, Joe," she said. "Let's get out of here, please."

He took her by the arm and led her toward the door. He looked back once over his shoulder.

"I really ought to take a picture of that," he said wistfully.

THE ECSTASY OF FULFILLMENT
CHAPTER TWO

It was not until she was downstairs with Joe that Suzy realized how strongly the reaction had set in. He held her arm as they went through the lobby of the hotel, but outside on the sidewalk, he said, "Excuse me a minute, Suzy," and turned to do something with the leather plate case that hung at his side. The moment the support of his arm was gone, her knees sagged beneath her and she staggered against him. He did a double-take, then grasped her elbow quickly.

"It's okay, kid," he said. "The woodchoppers have come and gone, and the big bad wolf is dead. Suppose, Little Red Riding Hood, you and I quaff from the cup that cheers. Namely, coffee."

"I'd like a cup of coffee, Joe," she said gratefully. "What time is it?"

He gave her a shrewd glance, then looked at his wrist watch. "Eight," he said. "Eight pee em. Why do you let yourself in for these rhubarbs, anyway?"

She was recovering her equilibrium. "A nice girl like me," she chanted mockingly. "How did I ever let myself get mixed up in this racket?"

He shrugged and snapped his fingers at the doorman of the hotel, who stood under the sidewalk canopy, cleaning his fingernails with the edge of a match-folder.

"Cab," he said, "get me a cab, Commodore." He looked down at Suzy.

"A nice girl like you? Yeah. Sometimes I wonder myself."

She gave him a lopsided grin. "And a nice boy like you, Joe. A good photographer, a nice personality. How'd you get mixed up in a racket like this, Joe?"

His eyes turned bleak and he watched the doorman sweep majestically to the curb and summon a cab with an upraised arm as pontifical as a bishop's.

"Oh me," he said. "With me, it's just a matter of steak and potatoes. But an angel like you, you can live on manna and Roark Bradford's firmament. Don't disillusion me with talk of economics."

She smiled. You could always depend on Joe to take the sting out of a barbed-wire trap.

"Talking of angels," she said, "what could be more heavenly than a T-bone steak done rare, with french fieds and a tossed green salad? Not," she added, "that I want it now. All I want is a cup of coffee. But I just thought I'd let you know."

He threw up his hands. "What is that but manna described in detail. Here's the cab."

The doorman wiped his dirty gloves on his behind and opened the door for them. Joe gave him a dime.

"Arise ye prisoners of starvation," he said. He settled back into the seat beside Suzy and looked at her. The frivolity dropped from his eyes. "What gave, honey?" he asked.

She avoided his eyes and said, "Oh, the usual."

"I gathered that. You were fighting your way out valiantly when I arrived, and luckily I did arrive or you'd have murdered him. But why do you let yourself in for things like that? You don't have to. You're a beautiful wench, if you don't mind my saying so, and you don't have to go around stooging for jerks. Why don't you get wise to yourself?"

"I'm wise to myself, Joe."

"I wonder," he said morosely. His eyes slid toward her, then widened. His mouth knifed up into his right cheek without grinning. "Let's," he said, sliding down in the seat and resting on his neck, "call it your art."

"That's right," she said brightly. "My art."

The cab driver had been just sitting there, but now he turned and said, "I don't like to butt in at an important time like this, mister, but where to?"

"The Waldorf," said Joe, waving his hand. "The Waldorf Cafeteria on Market Street, Jehu." He scowled at Suzy. "What the hell's a Jehu, anyway? I heard it in a movie once, and it sounded very sophisticated. And speaking of sophistication, I'm crazy about you, by the way. You can put that down to idle conversation. Does the Waldorf suit you?"

She caught her breath. Harry had often said he was crazy about her, and in all tones of voice, but never with quite the pathos that Joe had managed to get in his voice. As flippant as Joe had tried to appear, his voice had gone deep at that point. He had meant it. He was crazy about her.

She pretended not to have noticed. He knew that she and Harry were in love and were only waiting for this crummy business to be over before they married. She did not want to embarrass him. She did not want to have it come to an issue.

"Coffee at the Waldorf," she said. "What more could a girl ask?"

She glanced sidelong at him. His lean, freckled face was not the least pathetic. It was homely and it was tough, but not pathetic. He was not a man who'd pity himself, no matter what happened. He'd always have a wisecrack. He'd always look at you obliquely and grin. He looked something like Ray Bolger, she decided. A very tough Ray Bolger, though she could not imagine Joe kicking up his heels, especially not now.

The cab stopped in front of the Waldorf Cafeteria on Market Street, opposite the Newark Evening News building, and the driver contemptuously knocked down the flag with a flip of his hand. He did not offer to open the door for them. He did not open doors for people who wanted to go to cafeterias.

"Snob," said Joe, giving him a dime tip.

"What was that crack, cap?" said the driver belligerently.

Joe grinned. "I said," he slowly and distinctly, "that you were a snob. S-n-o-b, snob. Also spelled, s-l-o-b, slob. Anything else you want to know?"

The driver started to slide across the seat. "Okay, cap," he started. Joe stepped back to give him room to clear the cab. Suzy grasped him by the arm.

"Joe, please," she begged. "Please no, Joe!"

Joe's grin glittered at the burly cab driver. "Now let me alone, honey," he said softly. "This is something between Junior and me. We want to waltz. You wouldn't cut in on the dance, would you?"

The driver stopped with his hand on the handle of the door. He glared at Joe. His eyes sharpened and became intent, and then he sat back.

"Oh no you don't!" he said triumphantly. "You don't suck me in on this. You just had a scrap with your girl friend and you want to take it out on me. No *sir!* I'm wise to that one. And on top of that, you used to be in the ring. I seen you onct down at the Arena. No thanks, cap. No hard feelings, but no thanks. And no hard feelings, neither." He thumbed his nose good-humoredly at Joe, slid back under the wheel and sent the cab from the curb with a surge of gas.

Joe rubbed his jaw regretfully and watched the cab thread into the heavy Market Street traffic.

"And they say," he murmured, "that there's no such thing as a guy with a camera eye. It's been five years since I was in the ring."

He turned. Suzy was half way up the block toward Broad Street. He ran after her and caught her by the arm.

"I'm sorry, honey," he began contritely.

She did not pull away from him. "Please, Joe," she said.

He dropped his hand. "I'm sorry, Suzy. I ... hell, I don't know. I just ... I just felt like knocking the living hell out of somebody. I ..."

She knew what and why and she put her hand on his arm, relenting. "All right, Joe," she said, smiling. "*I'm* sorry. Let's go and have our cup of coffee."

"You're not sore at me?" he said incredulously.

"No, I'm not sore at you."

"An angel!" he rolled his eyes upward. "An absolute angel. But before we go in, I want to get the evening paper."

He trotted to the newsstand, picked up a paper and loped back with the paper under his arm.

"I'm a jerk," he said despondently. "I'm a revolving jerk. I'm a jerk no matter how you look at me. The first date I've had with you, and what do I do? I offer to fight cab drivers."

"I didn't know you were ever in the ring, Joe," said Suzy.

"Please don't remind me. I used to kick the bejesus out of the kids on the block for the hell of it, and then I went into the ring and kicked the bejesus out of them for money, and then one day I looked into the mirror and said, for a buck I'd kick the bejesus out of you, too. And right that minute I decided it was time to quit. Are you always so nice?"

"I'm not so nice, Joe," said Suzy somberly.

"You are!" he said fervently. "You're an angel. You're a goddam angel."

"Let's have our coffee, Joe."

He looked around with a dazed expression, as if surprised to find himself inside the Waldorf Cafeteria. They each got a cup of coffee and in addition Joe took a piece of cocoanut cream pie, which he carried to the white, porcelain-topped table as if it were rubies. He set it down in front of him and gazed at it, enraptured. But when he lifted his eyes, she saw that they were haggard. His manner changed. He opened the paper he had bought and turned the headline to her.

"Did you see this?" he asked drily.

The headline said:

D. A. TO PROBE DIVORCE MILL

"That, honey," he said, "means us. We're the divorce mill. You and me and Harry. We're the babies the D. A. is going to probe. But I don't see any reason," he went on wearily, "why, if a couple poor joes feel they can't live with each other anymore, they have to go on doing it."

Suzy thought of Frawley. Frawley was certainly not a poor joe. And she thought of the angular, strident Mrs. Frawley. She was not a poor joe. They were getting a divorce, plotted and arranged by Harry.

They were selfish, greedy people, who did not deserve the privilege of divorce.

But right at the moment, Suzy was not interested in the right or wrong of it. Joe was saying something, but it was just a jumble of sound in her ears. She had been badly frightened, and now she felt just a little numb. She wanted to talk to Harry. She wanted to hear his voice, and she wanted to feel his arm around her. She wanted his lips to take away the ache. She pushed back her chair and stood up. Joe looked at her in surprise.

"I have to call Harry," she said. "He likes me to call him when we finish one of these things. I forgot."

She walked to the rear of the cafeteria and stepped into the phone booth. Her heart beat just a little faster, as it always did, when she dialed his number, and when his voice came through the receiver, there was that little catch in her voice before she could speak.

"This is Suzy," she said.

"Oh, Suzy." Then quickly, "How did it go?"

"Like clockwork." He liked her to say it that way. Like clockwork.

He laughed. He had a deep chuckling laugh, and she could feel the warmth of it erasing the memory of Frawley.

"Oh, Harry, Harry, Harry," she said.

"What's the matter?" he asked quickly. "Did something go wrong?"

"Nothing went wrong, Harry. Mrs. Frawley appeared on time with her stooge witnesses and Joe got his pictures. It's ... what would you call it?"

"In the bag."

"Yes, it's in the bag."

"Then what's the matter, honey?"

"I want to see you, Harry."

"About what?"

"Does it have to be about something?" she felt as if she sounded hysterical. "I just want to see you, that's all. Do I have to have a reason? Do I have to have an excuse? Do I have ..."

He broke in soothingly. "Of course not, darling. But why do you have to take these things personally? It's just business."

"A crummy business!"

"Crummy, sure. But it brings in the old moola, sweetheart, and that's what counts."

"I wonder," she said bitterly.

His voice came in smoothly, like milk and honey. "Look, darling. Come over. I'll have a champagne cocktail waiting for you. I'll expect you in fifteen minutes."

She hung up, feeling cheated. So many times, of late, she felt cheated after talking to Harry. But that wasn't Harry's fault. What was it the District Attorney had called this? The divorce mill. That was it. That was exactly right. A mill. She felt as if she had been ground through the mill.

She sat a few minutes in the booth, wondering dully at the emptiness in her, resting her head against the heel of her hand. She felt as if she had been ground to a juiceless powder. It was not merely the unpleasant experience with the amorous Frawley. She had learned to expect that, though not in quite the same extreme. No one before had ever really tried to force his emotion on her in that degree. She had never had to use violence, but the strain of keeping them in hand had always been there. Always. Every time.

But what did it come to? What did she have after she had helped these people get their tawdry divorces? A bad taste in her mouth.

She sat up and gave her head a shake, as if to clear it. This was silly. She was not doing this for her own amusement, or even for the money she received. She was doing this for Harry, so that *he* would have enough money to give himself a front for a decent law practice. That was why she was doing it. That was the only reason. To feel the way she did was selfish.

She walked back to the table where Joe was eating his cocoanut cream pie.

"I have to go now, Joe," she said. "Thanks for the coffee. I needed it."

He looked up with dismay. "But you haven't even touched your coffee," he protested.

But Suzy had not heard him. She was already walking toward the door, eagerly thinking of Harry.

Joe looked at the forkful of pie in his hand, then carefully set it down on the edge of his plate. He knew Suzy had called Harry, and he knew where she was going. He had seen that look on her face. His appetite for pie was gone. His mouth twisted up at one corner.

"Dames!" he said, meaning Suzy. "Why is a dame?"

Outside, Suzy caught a cab and gave the driver Harry's address. She sat back in the seat and wearily forked her fingers through her incredibly blonde hair as the cab snaked through the traffic. She ran her hands down her thighs, unmindful of their loveliness, or of the beautifully rounded flesh. She was merely and completely tired. She longed for Harry's caresses. Her eyes brightened in anticipation. Harry, Harry!

Harry lived in the most fashionable section of Newark, the Forest Hill section. His apartment house had a façade of Italian marble. It had a canopy from the front door to the curb, a doorman, an elevator operator, and bronze urns in the Etruscan lobby. There were discreet murals on the walls, and a flowering jasmine on the handkerchief of lawn. If you were not accustomed to this kind of living, you automatically dropped your voice when you walked into the building, as you would drop your voice when you walked into an expensive mausoleum, for the effect was that of money embalmed and sacred.

The doorman, a gigantic man in the usual field marshal's uniform, knew Suzy, and when he opened the door of her cab, he said cordially: "Evenin', Miss Suzy. And how are you this fine, salubrious evenin'?"

"Very well, Arthur, thank you," she gave him a tired smile and a quarter, but it was the smile he treasured.

He walked majestically ahead of her and opened the lobby doors.

"I don't do this for everybody, Miss Suzy," he grinned. "Only my special people, like you." He laughed liquidly.

It was good to hear his musical laughter. Arthur's world consisted of people he liked or didn't like, and Suzy, feeling deeply touched, said, "Thank you, Arthur," and walked quickly into the lobby, unable any longer to conceal her eagerness to see Harry.

The elevator operator, a cynical ex-bellhop, looked her up and down as she stepped into his car. In one experienced glance he noted the promising curve of her calf, the press of her full thigh against the fabric of her dress, the proud lift of her breasts, the full, almost sensual, width of her mouth.

Within himself he gave the accolade of the wolf whistle, but aloud he said more decorously:

"Hiya, Miz Carr. Gawn up to see the mouthpiece?"

Suzy smiled. Mouthpiece. A tough word, but it brought flooding to the top of her mind the thought of Harry's lips, and suddenly she so yearned for the touch of his lips that she could scarcely wait for the elevator car to climb to the top floor.

She walked quickly down the hushed corridor and thumbed the round ivory button beside Harry's door. When he opened it to her, she surged into his arms, clasping her arms around him, feeling again the thick, comforting muscles of his shoulders and neck. He closed the door hastily, then folded his arms around her and kissed her hair.

"Darling," he said, "darling."

He was a big man, heavy-chested and tall, with thick blue-black hair and a thick, brutal mouth. He was a bull of a man. His face was muscular and aggressive, the way Clark Gable's face was muscular and aggressive. His hands were strong and tufted below the second joint with strong black hair. He was magnificently animal, but his pale gray eyes were a wall behind which he crouched, predatory and dangerous.

He gathered Suzy in his heavy arm and led her into the sunken living room of the apartment. It was a big living room, and very modern in decoration.

The rug was black curly lamb's wool, and the grand piano, at the bank of windows that overlooked the suave green reaches of Branch Brook Park, was starkly white. The walls were gray, but only to accent the dramatically raw reds and greens and yellows of the paintings and draperies. The semi-circular sofa was a harsh grass-green with slashes of bone-white moss edging. It looked so violent that it might almost have been an Aztec altar on which living hearts were torn from the breasts of human sacrifices.

Harry led Suzy to the sofa, murmuring softly in her ear. Before the sofa was a kidney-shaped ebony coffee table. Harry picked up the hammered silver cocktail shaker from it, gave it an experimental shake, and smiled.

"Just right," he said.

He poured the champagne cocktails into the crystal shell glasses.

This apartment cost him five thousand dollars a year, but, as he explained to Suzy, it was invaluable as a front in which to entertain the kind of clientele he wanted to attract. Harry was ambitious.

Suzy lay back in the luxurious sofa and let the cool fire of the cocktail trickle over her tongue. But she was not interested in the cocktail. She drank it merely because Harry had made it for her.

She was on fire with the nearness of him. She wanted his arms around her again, she wanted the brutal thrust of his lips.

But he did not take her immediately. Instead he said, with a little frown:

"Now what's this business that's bothering you, darling?"

She looked down into her glass and said in a low voice, "I can't go through another one of these things, Harry."

"Oh, nonsense!" he laughed. "Just detach yourself and it's easy. I don't know what I'd do without you. Take Frawley, for instance. He's loaded. He's lousy with money. This divorce is only the beginning. I expect to get enough business out of him in a month to pay my rent on Central Park for a year. And *that* is only the beginning, too. He might look like a small town Napoleon to you, but he's Mr. Steamship in person. He owns more shipping lines between here and South America than you and I and a dozen accountants could count in a month of Sundays. He's loaded! And I'm going to get my hands on some of that loose lettuce." He noticed the frozen set of her face, and asked warily, "Is there anything wrong in that?"

"You won't be getting anything more from Mr. Frawley," said Suzy dully.

"I ... what? What do you mean?"

"He made a pass at me and I threw a glass of Scotch in his eyes."

Harry's thick face turned veal-white. He clenched his hands until the knuckles turned white and pointed. "That was a cute trick!" he said with suppressed violence.

Suzy cried, "What did you expect me to do?"

"Not to pull a dumb stunt like that! Great Scott, the guy's loaded and you throw Scotch in his face. Don't you have any sense? You could have eased him out of it, couldn't you? What's the matter with you, anyway?"

Suzy felt the tears roll hotly out of her eyes. Harry was right. She could have handled Frawley, but she had been tired. She had been afraid.

"I'm sorry, Harry," her voice choked in her throat. "I ... I was tired ... and I didn't think ..."

He put his hand on her thigh and squeezed it gently. "It's okay, honey," he said swiftly. "Maybe there's no real damage done. Frawley's a guy, if he sets his mind on something, nothing'll stop him. I think we can patch this up. I'll let him simmer tonight, but I'll give him a ring first thing in the morning."

Very quietly, Suzy said, "What do you mean, Harry?"

"I mean, he's got a yen for you. Okay. We'll use that. To bring him back into the fold," he winked at her. "Get it now? All you have to do is go out on a few dates with him ..."

Suzy cried, "Harry, no! He's horrible! He's ..."

Harry swept her into his arms and kissed her. "We won't talk about it, darling," he murmured. "He gave you a tough time, and we won't talk about it. We'll just talk about us. It won't be long now and we'll be out of this. You and me ..."

His voice flowed over her and around her. His lips stilled the protests that rose to her lips. His kisses became caresses and found the hollow of her throat. He lifted her arm and kissed the hollow of the inside of her elbow.

The world spun around her and disappeared in a glitter of sparks.

She found his lips with hers and her hand cupped the back of his head, pulling him deeper into the kiss. His fingers drew parallel lines of fire on her leg, touched the line of her chin, drew her closer.

She moaned and rolled her head and his lips followed hers. This was Harry. This was her Harry. This was the real Harry, carrying her up and beyond even the chilly spaces, up to where ecstasy dwelt in the dangerous outer-space and only the adventurous dared go.

She cried out as if in pain, "Oh, Harry Harry Harry Harry ...!"

But it was not pain. It was the unutterable agony of ecstasy that was almost beyond bearing.

Her body rose to meet his, her lips buried themselves in his, her arms were cables around him and his arms were cables around her, binding one to the other in the rocketing surge of a blended emotion that was beyond imagining in its intensity.

She cried out again as her soul seemed to lift from her body and soar among the constellations. This was what she wanted more than anything.

Gradually she subsided in his arms, shivering. The tremendousness of it had overwhelmed her. She lay in his arms, turning up her face to the softness of his after-kisses, waiting for the peace to come, waiting for the languid ease of fulfillment.

But this time it did not come.

SUZY'S BAIT FOR THE TRAP!
CHAPTER THREE

Harry kissed her a few times, but they were not the soft, lingering kisses of what he called the "follow-through." He kissed her and looked speculatively over her blonde head toward the foyer, where he could see a corner of the bone-white telephone stand. He frowned thoughtfully. Suzy stirred in his arms and he kissed her again.

"Baby," he said. "Baby ..."

He looked like a blunt, straightforward bull of a man, but actually he preferred to be devious. He preferred the subtle nuances, the sly, circuitous approaches, the triumph by cunning. Not for nothing did he have those pale and predatory gray eyes. He was more cat than bull, one of the great carnivores, with the feral patience of a stalking tiger.

He knew he held Suzy's will at his whim, that he could talk straight and frankly to her, and that in the end she would do what he wanted her to do, but in this he wanted her to take the initiative, to make the offer. And that was the reason for what he called the "old vaudeville." The "old vaudeville" was his name for any act he put on.

He sighed again and shook his head. He knew she was watching him. It sometimes irritated him, the way her great luminous eyes followed him like (what he called) a pair of damn poodle dogs. This time, however, he wanted her to watch him. He wanted her to catch every sigh, every worried motion. He picked up the cocktail shaker, as if looking for another drink, then set it down with a smothered exclamation of, disappointment. He ground out his barely-smoked cigarette, jumped up from the sofa and strode to the window, where he stood looking down into the street and snapping his fingers. He walked over to the piano and played a few abstracted notes of *Melancholy Baby* with his forefinger. Then he sat down and played it all the way through, slow and blue and tearful. Suzy, he knew, responded to the mood of music the way a hungry cat responds to the odor of steak. All this time he did not give her a glance, nor did he say a word to her.

When he finished playing, he let his hands drop to the keys in a worried discord. He pulled out his gold cigarette case, tapped a cigarette on it, then set both the case and cigarette on the end of the piano and walked into the kitchen, where he made the noises of having a compulsory drink with a glass and bottle. Actually he drank nothing. He was a man who did not need to drink. His stimulation came from inside himself. He was a man driven by overwhelming ambition. He wanted, wanted, *wanted!*

He wanted money, not for the sake of the accumulated dollars, but for the force it represented. He wanted money.

He stayed in the kitchen just long enough so that Suzy would think he was having not one but several drinks. He went back into the living room and stood restlessly at the window again. He drew a heavy breath and cocked his head as if thinking deeply.

He knew this was having a definite effect on Suzy. A quick glance in the mirror had showed her sitting up on the sofa, her head turned in his direction. He turned from the window and slowly walked the length of the room, frowning at his shoe tips.

Finally her voice broke the heavy silence. "What's the matter, Harry?"

He pretended not to hear her.

"Harry," she said.

His head jerked around. "Yes, baby?"

"What's the matter?"

"The matter? Nothing's the matter. What makes you think something's the matter?"

"The way you're acting."

"That's your imagination."

"It is not, Harry. You're worried about something. You just went out in the kitchen and had some drinks. That's not like you, darling. What's the matter?"

He shook his head, walked over to the piano and lit his cigarette. He stood smoking with his back to her.

"Harry ..." her voice was pleading.

"Yes, baby?"

"Tell me what's the matter."

"I wish you wouldn't keep saying that, baby. Nothing's the matter." He glanced covertly at his wristwatch. Holy Cow, it was quarter past nine. He had a date at ten. He'd have to get this over in a hurry. He turned and gave Suzy a small, martyred smile. "Anyway," he said, "I don't want to bother you with it. Not tonight, not the way you feel."

"Oh, Harry!" she sprang from the sofa, walked swiftly across the room, took his lapels in her hands and looked up into his face. "Forget the way I acted, won't you? I ... I was hysterical, I guess. I was tired. I won't be able to sleep tonight if you don't tell me what's worrying you."

He looked away, as if reluctant to tell her, then he muttered, "Oh, it's Frawley and the rest of it. Knowing how you feel, I didn't want to bring it up."

She lifted her lips and kissed him lightly on the mouth. He felt the press of her against him and forced back the surge of emotion she could always invoke with the nearness of her body. He congratulated himself with an inner hidden grin. No matter how intense the fleshly desire, he could always subordinate it to the matter at hand. Anyway, it was getting too late to fool around.

"Don't think," he said swiftly, before she could speak, "that I'm fond of this lousy divorce business I'm running, baby. But nothing's ever been handed me on a silver platter, know what I mean? I'm not a Harvard Law School graduate. I had to put myself through law school. I had to earn my way through," (by tending the crap table in Little Augie Larkin's gambling joint on Frelinghuysen Avenue) "and none of the plush law firms offered me a junior partnership when I graduated. Sure, I could have gone into some shyster outfit as a law clerk and sweat my brains out for five years licking envelopes and other things and then, maybe, they'd have put my name on the door in small letters and let me handle the clients nobody else wanted ..."

"No, Harry," Suzy cried. "They'd have recognized your ability. They wouldn't have kept you down!"

"Wouldn't they?" said Harry cynically. "You've got a lot to learn about law firms, baby. What they want is a guy from a hoity-toity family in Forest Hill with a million rich friends. Ability they can hire for peanuts and keep in the back room."

Suzy protested vehemently. "Not *you*, Harry!"

He patted her shoulder, as if wanly amused at her ignorance. "I had another chance, too," he went on. "I could have gone to work for Little Augie Larkin, the gambler. But I didn't want to get mixed up with that crowd."

For a moment, he thought enviously of the golden rewards he might have had with Little Augie—but Augie had a mouthpiece and wasn't interested in law school graduates, no matter how deserving.

Suzy smiled up into the patient, righteous mask Harry had made his face. "Of course you didn't want to get mixed up with gamblers," she said fondly.

His estimate of her I.Q. had never been high, and now it dipped even lower. What the hell did she know about it? What did she know about anything, except the few tricks of divorce routine he had taught her.

"No," he said virtuously, "I didn't want to get mixed up with any mobs. So what choice did I have, baby? I had to go into business for myself—and for six months I starved."

This wasn't literally true. For six months he hadn't had any law practice, but with the aid of a very agile pair of dice, he had been able to afford two hundred dollar suits, a Packard convertible, and all the concomitant luxuries. A police raid on a crap game that missed him by five minutes (he'd had to stop and change a flat tire on the way to the game) killed the gambling urge in him.

"Then one day," he said, "a guy came to me and asked me to fix up a divorce for him. He didn't want to go to Nevada, because those Reno divorces have a habit, sometimes, of backfiring. He offered me a nice chunk of dough. I fixed it up for him, hoping it would lead to some legitimate business with him, but he moved to California. I fixed up divorces for some other guys, but you know about that because you worked with them. Then this guy Frawley came along, my first client who had real important dough. He said to me, 'Harry,' he said, 'do this favor for me. I know you want to get out of the divorce business, but do this for me, and I'll see what I can do about throwing some real business your way. The lawyers the company has now handle a half million dollars worth of business a year for us, but I'm not satisfied with them. They're too conservative.' Now, baby, I ask you, does that sound as if I'm finally on my way out of the crummy divorce business, or doesn't it?"

Frawley, actually, had not even hinted at future business, but Harry was hoping to wangle some out of him.

Suzy's eyes shone and she breathed, "Oh, Harry. That sounds wonderful! Why didn't you tell me this before?"

"We-ll, it's still more or less up in the air—even more now than it was before," he added despondently—but watching her sharply from beneath lowered eyelids.

She responded exactly as he knew she would. She gave a gasp and her hand flew to her mouth. "And I spoiled it all for you!" she wailed.

He sighed. "I'm not blaming you, baby," he said dully. "I'm not blaming you a bit."

"Harry," she clutched his arm. "Isn't there something ... I mean, if I apologized or something ..."

"No! He got what was coming to him. No apologies!"

"But, Harry," she pleaded, "you just can't let a chance like this go. This is the chance you've been working for. Harry, look at me, Harry. I love you," her lips quivered. "I love you very much, and I'll never forgive myself if I've done anything to hurt your career. I'll apologize to Mr. Frawley. I won't mind, honestly I won't. I'll make everything all right. I want to help you, Harry. I want to do everything I can."

"You don't have to do a thing, baby," he patted her cheek, thinking what a fine botch she'd make if he let her try to handle Frawley now. "I won't have my girl crawling around making apologies to old goats like that."

"Please, Harry," she begged. The tears were beginning. "Please, please, please. Chances like this don't come every day ..."

He saw the tears and knew he had her. He made a small negating gesture with his hand.

"I can't let you do that," he said. "And, anyway, who knows how long it'll be before Frawley'll be able to get rid of those prissy lawyers he's got now. He owns those steamship companies, sure, but he doesn't have everything to say. There are other stockholders. Nooooooo ..." Then he brightened and snapped his fingers. "But maybe I can smooth it over."

Suzy smiled mistily. "Try, Harry. Try!"

"But I don't want to get you into anything you don't like, baby," he said softly.

"Don't talk like that, Harry. There's only one important thing, isn't there? Your career, your law practice, and I love you. Talk to him, Harry, please ..."

"Well," reluctantly, "I'll take a shot at it." He tilted her chin and kissed her lightly on her eager lips. "That's my girl." Then he winked and grinned. "The boys used to say I could talk a blind man out of his Seeing Eye hound."

The boys hadn't said "talk"; they had said "chisel."

Harry went to the phone in the foyer and called Frawley at the hotel. Frawley sounded a little drunk and sore when he answered.

Harry said smoothly, "This is Harry Sloan, Mr. Frawley. Joe, the photographer, just called and said everything went off as smooth as silk."

"Sure," said Frawley with heavy irony, "if you can call being half blinded and socked on the jaw as smooth as silk, that's just the way it went over."

"Socked on the jaw? Joe didn't say anything about that, Mr. Frawley," Harry half turned and scowled at Suzy. *She* hadn't said anything about a sock on the jaw, either. "What happened, Mr. Frawley?"

Frawley hemmed and hawed for a moment. He didn't want to come right out and say that the sock in the jaw stemmed from the pass he had made at Suzy.

"It was that dame that works for you," he growled finally. "That lousy tart. After the pictures were taken, I thought she'd like a little drink or something. I made a little friendly gesture, and the next thing I knew she threw a glass of whiskey in my eyes and smacked me across the jaw with a bottle. What kind of stuff is that? I'm going to give you some advice, Sloan. Kick that dame out on her fanny, and the next time you hire somebody, use some sense. What you need, boy, is some personnel training. Let me tell you, I wouldn't hire a man, or a woman as far as that goes, whose actions I couldn't predict to the minute—what, when, where, why and how. Sloppy employment work there, Sloan, sloppy personnel judgment. But that's my advice. Get rid of that girl. She's doing your business nothing but harm." Frawley managed to finish on a virtuous note, restoring his self-respect. Also managing a bit of revenge, too.

"Gosh, Mr. Frawley," Harry purred, "I'm as sorry as hell about this. You know, I had an idea something was haywire somewhere. I saw Suzy Carr a little while ago, and the poor kid was in tears ..."

"In tears!" snorted Frawley. "She ought to be in jail."

"It's one of those things, Mr. Frawley. Let me tell you about it. That poor kid's so upset she doesn't know whether she's coming or going. A girl friend of hers just had a tough break, a really tough break. The worst kind of hard luck. I can't tell you what it is because it's confidential. Poor Suzy's been half out of her mind."

"I didn't know that," said Frawley grudgingly.

"Of course you didn't," Harry said heartily. "How could you? But here's the crux of the matter. She's so broken up about her girl friend that I didn't want to go through with this business today. We'll postpone it, I told her. Mr. Frawley's a right guy, I said, and he'll understand. But do you think that kid would let me do that? Not on your life. No, she said, Mr. Frawley's depending on me. This is an anxious time for him, too, she told me, and I don't want to make it any worse for him by postponing it. And that's the way she is, Mr. Frawley, always thinking of others. Now, mind you, Mr. Frawley, I'm not condoning what she did to you. There's no excuse for it. Absolutely none, and don't think I won't give her a bawling out. When she gets over her girl friend, of course. I wouldn't think of adding woe to her misery right now. I've got a heart, too. I'm giving you this background, Mr. Frawley, so you'll understand, and I know you will. It was nothing personal. It's just that this girl friend she's known since they were in kindergarten together is in such a lousy jam. You know how women are."

Under his hard boiled man-of-business facade, Frawley was as sentimental as a hearts and flowers Valentine, and now he was just drunk enough to make it vocal.

"The poor kid," he said. "Now I feel like a heel. Come to think of it, maybe I asked for it. Now see here, Sloan, you give me that girl's address. I insist. I'm gonna send her a flock of orchids. I'm gonna call up and apologize. I want to show her I can act like a gentleman when I feel like it. Yessir, I'll take her out to dinner, and a show, the works. We'll see if we can take her mind off it for one night, anyway."

The advantages—philanthropic, visual and otherwise—of taking Suzy out for a night of fun seemed to grow on Frawley as he spoke, and his voice got a little fruity as he went on:

"Yessir, that's just what I'll do. I'll do my best to show that little girl a time. Yessir. And you say she went through this hassle tonight because she didn't want to disappoint me? Well, Sloan, let me tell you this, I'm gonna show that little girl my appreciation. That is," an anxious note crept in, "if she'll let me. Do you think she'll talk to me after tonight, Sloan?"

"I can't guarantee anything, Mr. Frawley," Harry turned and winked at Suzy. "But if you tell her you're sorry, I'm pretty sure she'll forgive and forget. You know how women are—all heart and no head. Here's her address and phone number ..."

Despite his maudlin sentimentality, Frawley was still hard-headed enough to know that Harry was anxious for his good will and didn't mind doing a little pimping to get it. Mentally, Frawley smacked his lips at the thought of having Suzy to himself for an evening. After all, she had shown herself to him half-naked, hadn't she? She couldn't be as pure and holy as she pretended. Of course not. Maybe it was just what Harry Sloan said, she had been upset over her girl friend. Though, to tell the truth, he wouldn't take Harry Sloan's word for the straightest route across the street. A smooth shyster if there ever was one. But Suzy, now, that was something different. That girl had something, and not just because she was stacked, either. She was charged. Yessir, maybe they could have a little talk, come to an understanding and have some fun. You only live once, don't you? Frawley was prepared to be generous.

Once he had Suzy's address and phone number, Frawley wanted as little to do with Harry as possible.

"Thanks, Sloan," he said shortly, "I'll give her a ring." He hung up. Harry blinked at the hard click. The S.O.B. Then he smiled thinly. Frawley wasn't getting off the hook as easily as that. He could still get at him through Suzy. Frawley wasn't as tough as he thought. If Harry hadn't fooled Frawley, neither had Frawley fooled Harry. All that gunk about wanting to show Suzy his appreciation. The old malarkey. If Frawley wanted to show Suzy something, you could give odds it wasn't appreciation. But okay. All the better. Suzy could tie him up like a nickel pretzel, and would, too, once she was given the idea that it was for the benefit of Harry Sloan, hereinafter (Harry grinned to himself) to be known as Number One.

He raised his voice and pretended to go on talking to Frawley.

"And now about that other business we were talking over, Mr. Frawley, the law end of your South American freight business ... well, sure I'll call you Howard. Harry is what my friends call me, and I hope we're friends as well as future business associates. So what about it, Howard? How soon can I expect the green light from you? ... Yes, I realize a thing as big as that takes time, and I realize too, that the Board of Directors have the final say. But you control the Board, don't you? ... oh yes, I see. You own only forty-nine per cent of the stock. But what about proxies? Don't you control any proxies? ... Well, that's okay, then. It's just a matter of time till you can get in touch. Sure ..."

Harry turned to Suzy and gave her the okay sign with his circled thumb and forefinger. He turned back to the phone.

"What was that, Howard? ... Oh, sure, sure, I'll go along with you, but here's something that just came to my mind. If I go in with you, I'll be putting all my eggs in one basket, you might say, and I want some pretty iron-clad guarantees ... yes, that's exactly what I mean, a contract for five years. It'll be an iron-clad contract. I'll draw it up myself, ha, ha, ha ... Fine, fine, but in the meantime, I'm going on with business as usual, you know ... sure, we'll get together over lunch someday this week and hash it out. Right. And say, don't forget to call up Miss Carr and apologize, Howard. She's a sweet kid, and deserves the best ... well now, I'm glad you agree with me. If you hadn't, I was all set to put the old sockus-schmockus on you, ha, ha, ha. Well, so long, Howard, so long."

Harry turned from the phone and walked back into the living room, grimacing.

"Did I sound like a Babbitt?" he demanded. "I feel as if I ought to wash my mouth out with Rinso. But that's the only language guys like Frawley understand, Baby. A slap on the back and call me Harry. Nuts. Once I get that contract, there won't be any more of this Chamber of

Commerce rah-rah stuff. I'll run my end of it, and he'll run his."

Suzy's eyes were shining. "You were wonderful, Harry!" She threw her arms around his neck and kissed him lingeringly on the lips. He felt that soaring rise of emotion again at the touch of her, but he quickly smothered it.

This wasn't the time for fooling around, and he was tired of her vocal adulation. Everything was smoothed over—Frawley and Suzy both. He needed Suzy in the divorce business. Sure he could have gotten somebody else, but you never knew what kind of tramp another dame might turn out to be. And if he picked up some dame on the make, it could be a mess. Clients didn't like to be touched for blackmail. Not that Harry had any ethical scruples about blackmail, but it was bad for business. Suzy, he could trust.

Glancing at his wristwatch—holy cow, five to ten!—he broke Suzy's embrace.

"For the time being, baby," he said quickly, "we're going to have to go along with this crummy divorce crap ..."

"I don't mind, Harry. It won't be for long, darling."

"Six months, a year maybe. But after that, it's velvet."

"Oh, Harry, Harry!" Suzy lifted her face for another kiss, expecting his lips to take fire on hers, expecting his big arms to tighten around her as their emotions entwined, became one in a molten, volcanic explosion of ecstatic delirium. Her body was a leaping flame as her lips reached for his kiss.

He kissed her once, briskly, took her by the arm and started her toward the door.

"This time I'm giving the orders," he said. "You're going straight home and you're going to take a good hot shower, and then you're going to bed for a good night's sleep. You've had a tough day. God knows I want you to stay so I can make love to you from now on, but after a night like tonight, what you need more than anything else is rest."

He walked her to the elevator and pressed the button—pressed it hard.

(My God, ten o'clock! Camilla was always late, of course, but this was shading it just a little too fine.)

Suzy cried, "Oh, Harry!" and clung to him as if this were a parting forever. She wanted him, she wanted his strength and his love and his tenderness. Leaving like this, so abruptly, so unfulfilled, was building up that old familiar hollowness and desolation inside her. She clung to him.

Harry heard the whine of the ascending elevator, and he crossed his fingers that Camilla wouldn't be on it. Not that Camilla would mind, really. She would be amused. He did not want Camilla to be amused, not that way. She could make him writhe with cool, witty inquiries about his taste in women, and ask him if he still went to the burlesque, and did he linger over the cheesecake art in magazines? Really, he could hear her drawling, Harry, my pet, I have also a strong notion that your taste in literature still has not risen above the back fence scrawlings of dirty-minded little boys.

She was a witch, Camilla was. Fascinating in her own right. (Her other fascination was her money.) But she wasn't the woman Suzy was. She didn't have Suzy's generosity, nor the superlatively wonderful body, nor the ability to make love. Coolly, Harry knew that making love to Camilla had its terrifying aspects, something like the mating of spiders, after which the female spider calmly ate her mate. Harry could see Camilla calmly eating her mate.

Swiftly, to beat the elevator, Harry kissed Suzy, warmly but finally. "Now promise me," he said, "that you'll go straight home and go to bed. We don't want you to have a breakdown, do we? I'll call you first thing in the morning. Promise me."

A frustrated weariness had settled over Suzy. Yes, she was tired, she told herself. Harry was right. The best thing for her to do was go home and go to bed.

"Yes, Harry," she said submissively.

"That's my girl." He gave her a squeeze, then quickly withdrew his arm as the elevator stopped and the doors purred open before them. Harry gave the interior of the car a quick, clinical glance, and relaxed. Camilla wasn't inside. Suzy was hesitating on the threshold of the door, looking up at him, pleading with her long eyes for a last word of love, a goodnight kindness. Impulsively, with unexpected understanding, he kissed her with a warmth that lifted her spirits.

She whispered, "I love you, darling, I love you, oh, I love you. Do I have to go home?"

"Yes," he said with mock severity. "It wouldn't be much fun visiting you in a hospital, would it? And that's where you'll land if you don't get some rest. You're exhilarated now, baby, but there's always a letdown." He slipped the elevator operator a dollar. "Be sure to see that Miss Carr gets safely to the first floor, Admiral," he said. "Full speed ahead, and damn the torpedoes."

The dollar was blackmail, but Harry's tomcat love life would remain in safe hands.

The moment the elevator door closed on Suzy's yearning smile, Harry turned and walked quickly back to the apartment. He went to the window and looked down into the street. He saw Suzy come out, he saw her hesitate on the sidewalk, then walk to a cab waiting at the curb and get in. The cab drove off. A bare two minutes later, a dawn gray Cadillac convertible prowled to the strip of curb so recently vacated by the cab, and by the light of the street lamp on the corner, Harry saw the sleek and coolly insolent face of Camilla LaFarge, poised on a slender neck, turn and wait for Arthur, the doorman, to come and open her car door for her.

Harry turned and went quickly to the coffee table before the sofa. He scooped up Suzy's cocktail glass and carried it into the kitchen. Then he went into the bathroom and critically searched his face for any remaining traces of Suzy's lipstick. He wiped his mouth thoroughly with a piece of facial tissue. He rubbed a little after-shave lotion on his cheeks to take away any lingering tendrils of Suzy's perfume. He combed his hair and straightened his tie. He looked into the mirror with satisfaction.

"Here we go again, boy," he grinned at his reflection.

DANCE OF FIRE!
CHAPTER FOUR

Camilla walked insouciantly into the apartment and into the living room, where she waited for Harry to follow and kiss her, and after he had kissed her, she looked at him with one eyebrow lifted.

"You've done better," she observed. "I've been kissed more thoroughly by cousins in railroad stations. Have you been tomcatting around this evening, my pet? I seem to detect a sort of jaded enthusiasm. If that's the best you can do, I think I'll go home. I can have more actual fun combing my hair, I assure you."

Harry flushed and seized her, jerking her slender body against him with a violence that bordered on fury. For a moment she hung in the circle of his arm, unresponding, and then her thin, wine-tipped fingers dug into the back of his muscular neck and clawed him down deeper and more hungrily into the kiss. Her body arched rigidly and she fairly bit the kisses from his lips, moving her head with sharp, demanding jerks, tearing the caresses from him. Her other hand taloned on his shoulder. For a moment, they were less like human beings than like eagles, fierce in a suspended, mid-air instant of amatory violence. She lifted both hands to the back of his head and imprisoned him in the kiss, and she became the aggressor, an insatiable succubus. Harry's body was hard and thrusting muscle, but hers was steel. And it was in this bottomless hunger, this predatory search for the more subtle cruelties of love, that

Camilla LaFarge could be terrifying. Her kiss became more than a kiss, became a surgical probe that went deeper and deeper as if seeking to wrench his soul from the darkest and most hidden corners in the pit of him. Her thin hands were inexorable and relentless, chaining him in an embrace that flew madly around the demented borders of terror with a scream frozen in its throat. At every point of contact, wherever her body touched his, there was fire. Not the clean, purifying fire of Suzy, but fire that sought to devour, that sought to find the point at which ecstasy became pain, and pain became torment, and torment became agony.

Many times had Camilla thrust into the quivering darkness of agony, agony that was so great that love became a shriek, but each time she had drawn back. There was something in that dreadful darkness that appalled even her. This was not the shallow agony of the body, but of the spirit. Camilla never indulged in the obvious forms of physical cruelty. She did not scratch, or bite, or rend with her nails. She left no physical marks. The merest thought of inflicting the physical hurt would have filled her with loathing.

But she was seeking something, and it was nameless. She had had love, and now she wanted love and what lay beyond it. That was what precocious sophistication had brought her to. She knew that there was something beyond love, and she knew she could never go there alone. She had to have a magnificent animal like Harry to take her there, even if his brutish sensibilities would not permit him to savor the intricate and elusive delight of it. He would be merely the carrier, but she would be the one who would know the terror and the blinding, transcending ecstasy of it. The times before, when she had approached that dizzy peak, she had drawn back from the fear of being consumed. But never before had she had one so splendidly and arrogantly muscled as Harry. He was a powerful steed she would drive in plunging leaps until his heart burst within him.

That was what she was seeking when she manacled him to the fierceness of her kiss. But not now, not tonight, nor perhaps even tomorrow night. She was waiting for the moment, and she knew she would recognize the moment when it came. But it was not tonight, nor would it be found in the shallower, preliminary searchings of a kiss.

Her hands gradually softened on the back of his neck and dropped to his shoulders, releasing him from the bondage. She tore her lips from his and arched her face back from the slender steel of her neck. Her eyes were closed and her lips lay parted, but evading the baffled kisses he tried to pour on them, like water to quench a fire. Her breath came more evenly, and she let her arms fall from him. He held her for a few minutes longer, his face looking thick and heavy as he groped to understand what had happened. But nothing had happened. There had been nothing but the hint of something to come.

He took his arms from around her and stood staring resentfully at her. There had always been something in her that he had never been able to touch, even with violence, even when she was crying out in the brutal iron of his embrace. There had always been something that had eluded him.

Camilla gave him a thin amused smile of perfect composure.

"Well," she said in a matter-of-fact voice, "that was better. I really think you made an effort that time, my pet. And you're learning, too. You've come a long way from that 'how's-about-it-babe' technique you used to throw at a girl. A long way," her glance was speculative but still amused. "Aren't you going to ask me to have a drink?"

"Sure," he grinned at her. "Why not?"

Her eyes glittered. "You recover fast, my friend."

"Why not?" he repeated with the same grin.

She shrugged, but it was plain that she did not like his facile recovery. It gave him a strength that matched hers, and she liked to be the one who ran the affair. She looked at him, unsmiling, and desire darted within her like the flicker of sword points in the thin light of a cruel moon—but to show it now would be to show him a weakness.

Instead, she said, "A drink, please. Something short and cold. Something with the coolness of an emerald that has fire in its heart." She laughed. "That's a lot to ask of a cocktail, isn't it? Make me a sidecar, and I won't punish you with poetry."

He laughed at her and went into the kitchen to fill the thermos bucket with ice cubes. He wheeled the ebony bar to the side of the sofa and deftly built the cocktails. She watched him fill both glasses.

"You'll drink one," she said, "and, I suppose, as usual I'll drink everything else in the shaker. In the end we'll both be perfectly sober. Liquor doesn't touch me, and you won't let it touch you. You drink so warily. Are you afraid of giving yourself away when you get drunk, pet?"

"You were never more wrong, baby. It's just that liquor doesn't do a thing for me."

"All the same, for clinical reasons, I'd like to see you drunk, just once."

"The hell you would," he told her flatly. "The only thing I get is an uncontrollable desire to smack people in the snoot."

She looked at his powerful hands, tufted along the backs of the fingers with strong black hair—and shivered. Intuitively, she realized a basic truth about him. Sober, he could control his driving ambition, but drunk the bonds were loosed. Drunk and thwarted, here was a man capable of the most violent and completely annihilating kind of murder. For the first time, she realized that she was playing with a dangerous animal, an animal she would not dare torture beyond a definite fixed point. But there was a thrill to be found in that.

"If there's one sensation about which I'm not even infinitesimally curious," she said, "it's the sensation of being smacked in the snoot. You drink your one drink, and I'll drink my eight." She turned her head quickly away from his steady glance. The desire in her was like the forked play of lightning before a storm. But still she held it leashed.

She sipped her cocktail to give her a screen behind which she could recover her composure. She could force calmness on herself. She could hold back the desire for love until, when she did open the dam, it burst forth in tumult and flood. She let the cocktail do the work of blunting the thrust. Then it came, and she was ready to meet his gaze again with long cat-eyes.

"Oh, by the way," she said casually, "LaFarge came in tonight, just after dinner, and in that refrigerated tone of his, informed me that he wanted a divorce."

Harry, caught unawares by the inconsequence of her voice, looked startled, then wary, waiting behind the veil of his pale gray eyes to hear what she was going to say next. Camilla looked amused.

"Relax, my pet," she said. "It has nothing to do with our *liaison d'amour*. It appears he's discovered a yen for some blowsy tart in Maplewood. A redhead, judging from the hairs I've seen clinging tenderly to his lapel. In the most gentlemanly way possible, he told me that her name was none of my business. It's a pity he had to be so stiff-necked, because it might have been entertaining to see what sort of woman who'd have the perverted desire to give herself into the clutches of a walking Frigidaire. I dare say he's dazzled her with tales of my money. I can't think how I could possibly have been so naïve as to have married LaFarge, expecting anything but the joys of a deep freeze locker. He informed me also that he expects a very generous settlement from me after the divorce."

"So?" said Harry. He wasn't committing himself, but his mind was working furiously.

To his credit, he wasn't basically interested in Camilla's money, though she did have quite a pot of it. He was, however, interested in the fact that she was the granddaughter of old Piet Schuyler (deceased), who had once owned a considerable portion of Newark and environs. The family had, morally, more or less gone to pot on the death of old Piet, but the name was still socially powerful.

With a wife like Camilla, nee Schuyler, behind him ... Harry's eyes glowed at the prospect.

Camilla was saying petulantly, "I'm not mean about money, God knows. I have more than I can possibly spend. But dammit, Harry, there's enough of old Piet Schuyler in me to resent being blackmailed out of it. I'd have given LaFarge a settlement, and a big one. Perhaps he earned it, having had to live with me for two years. But I won't be blackmailed."

Harry said sharply, "Blackmailed?"

"Blackmail," Camilla's voice was flat and dry. "LaFarge put it to me bluntly and unadorned. I give him a settlement with the divorce, or else. And he's just the kind of frozen fish who'd go through with that 'or else.'"

Harry turned his glass in his hand and pursed his lips. "Does he have anything to go on?" he asked carefully. "Or is he just talking through his hat?"

"LaFarge never talks through his hat."

"Okay. What does he have on you?"

"That, my friend," said Camilla woodenly, "is something you will never know. It is one of the few things in my life of which I am not very proud. In fact, I have a notion that if LaFarge breathed it, I'd hang my head over a cup of cyanide and take one deep breath. It was very stupid and, as it turned out, rather horrible. But this is what I want to know, is there any way, short of murder, that I can keep from paying LaFarge one single cent?"

Harry knew what she was driving at, but he was going to make her say it. He wanted the suggestion to come from her. That would absolve him. That would, for the first time, give him a sort of whip hand over her.

"There are only two ways of shutting up a blackmailer, short of murder," he said. "One, pay him off and trust to luck. The other way is to let the police handle him."

Camilla cried, "No!"

Harry raised his thick eyebrows. "I was about to remark," he said, "that the second way doesn't appear practical in this case."

"How right you are. Well?"

"Well what?"

"Oh, don't be so deliberately stupid!" Camilla's clenched hands drove her fingernails into her palms. "You know what I mean. I saw that what's-in-it-for-me light in your eyes. All right. Whatever you want is in it for you. Name your own price, so long as I don't have to give LaFarge a cent."

Harry grinned, shook his head and went on grinning. "It's not a matter of price," he said. "It's a matter of what you want done."

She leaned back and smiled, for now she understood him.

"All right," she said. "I want you to fix it so I won't have to pay LaFarge off for keeping his mouth shut. Can you do it?"

"Maybe."

"What do you mean—maybe?" she flashed furiously at him. "Maybe you will, or maybe you won't?"

"Not at all," he said silkenly. "I said maybe because I can't give you anything off the top of my mind. I know what you want. You want the guy framed so you can say to him—okay, chum, you tattle on me, and I'll tattle on you. Right?"

"Right."

"Okay, then. It's got to be worked right. In the first place the frame has to be big enough to scare the living daylights out of him. And in the second place, the frame has to stick. There can't be any chance of it slipping. Once it's sprung, there can't be any chance of it's becoming unsprung. It has to be irrevocable. As far as he's concerned, it has to be a dead end. And it has to be *big*."

Camilla felt a rising excitement. She leaned toward him. He was still standing beside the portable bar, and she leaned over the edge of the coffee table, resting the tips of her long fingers on it for support, her eyes fixed on his face.

"You have something in mind?" she whispered. "Something that big?"

He shook his head. "Not yet." His mind was casting into the dark corners, throwing barbed gang-hooks into the murky pools.

Camilla sat back and said bitterly, "Oh hell, I thought you ..." she made a sound of harsh disgust in her throat. "It's just by-guess-and-byGod and let's hope something'll turn up. You don't have any more idea of what to do than Mickey Mouse. You're a fraud, a big, loud ..." She stopped.

His broad, tigerish face was very still, and he was watching her from behind his pale eyes.

"I take all that back," she breathed. "I think you will come up with something, something altogether ruthless. I actually think you will."

Harry smiled. He looked at the drink in his hand and poured it back into the shaker. He never touched liquor, even in small doses, when he had thinking to do.

"Well," Camilla challenged him, "what do I do?"

Harry spread his heavy, tufted hands. "Tell him okay."

"What do you mean?"

"Tell him," Harry's voice was uninflected, "that you'll give him his divorce, and tell him you'll give him the settlement. But tell him, too," something heavier crept into his tone, "that you won't have a Reno divorce. Tell him that you don't want a divorce that might blow up in your face someday. Tell him you want a divorce that will stay put."

Camilla said irritably, "Details, details. What difference does it make? LaFarge wouldn't care if I got the divorce on the moon. All he wants is to get it. It and the settlement."

"I know that, baby. He doesn't care—but *you* do. *You* want your divorce right here in Jersey, because Jersey divorces are bona fide. Are you beginning to get it?"

Camilla looked at him with more respect. "Yes, I'm beginning to. I forgot, my devious friend, that there's an immeasurable amount of pure animal cunning behind those muscles of yours. We've never given proper value to pure animal cunning, have we? Those single-minded laws of survival have never been repealed, have they?"

"*Your* survival," Harry reminded her. "Not mine."

Camilla murmured, "Now we're being devious again. But go on. I insist on a Jersey divorce. What then?"

"Then it's up to you to see that he comes to me for the divorce. You said he was a gentleman, so I suppose that means he is going to let you divorce him."

"You suppose right. Though," her mouth twisted, "he could have it anyway he wants, if he put the pressure on. But let's say he's a gentleman, and he is letting me divorce him. Go on."

"That's all—for the moment," said Harry blandly. "You just make damn sure he comes to my office for the divorce. I have to have my finger in this, or it won't work. That's flat."

The excitement flashed over her again, like a shadow thrown by the wing of a large bird flying, and unconsciously she swayed toward him.

"*What* won't work?" she asked in a low, low voice. "What do you ... what are you thinking of, Harry?"

"Nothing yet. But I have to have him come to me for the divorce, so I can control it. I don't want him slamming anything through before I'm ready. That's all."

Camilla saw the cold shine of his pale, flat eyes and she cried, "I won't have anything happen to him, understand that. He's not to be killed, even in an accident. A prearranged accident. He's not to be killed!"

Camilla LaFarge was not a woman who lost control easily, but her eyes were wild and she looked as if she were fighting hysteria—which she was. She could not bear the thought of inflicting physical pain, even if that pain were the merest flicker between the swift passage between life and death.

Harry's face congested. He took a long step and clapped his hand over her mouth.

"Keep still, you damn fool!" he said angrily. "Nobody's talking of killing him. Stop talking about killing. These apartments aren't as soundproof as they claim." He looked over his shoulder as if to see if someone were standing in the doorway. He looked into her eyes, then took his hand from over her mouth.

"What kind of talk was that, anyway?" he said roughly.

Camilla touched the sides of her face where his fingers had clamped. "All right," she said sullenly. "But all the same, remember what I said."

Harry mocked her, "I personally and unconditionally guarantee that no one will harm as much as a hair on his head. Does that satisfy you?"

"Yes, that satisfies me. And do you know why?" Her smile was as sudden as it was mirthless. "Because that busy brain of yours is already figuring what it is going to get out of it, and you very well know that if you double-cross me, you won't get paid. And speaking of that, exactly what sort of payment do you expect?"

Payment. He almost laughed aloud at the question. But now was not the time to tell her what he was after. He wanted her. He wanted the prestige of the Schuyler name behind him. He wanted the power of the Schuyler name to help lift him out of this rat-race and into—and why not?—the governor's chair. No, now was not the time to spring it. He'd spring it when he was ready. He'd spring it when he had her and LaFarge tied up in a neat bundle—the kind of bundle that he could unwrap. But not until he had that would he have her.

"We'll talk of payment later," he said easily. "We can't think of anything until the guy walks into my office, asking for a divorce. That's enough to think about for now."

His mind cast again, and this time came up with Suzy. Ah. That was a beginning. Suzy. Yes, he'd be able to use Suzy in this somewhere. He didn't know where, yet, but there'd be a place. She was a natural for it. There wouldn't be any kickbacks from Suzy. He had Suzy in his back pocket. With a little soft crap, Suzy would do anything he asked. *Anything!* Suzy. He could start figuring an angle from there.

"I'm beginning to get an angle," he said. He hadn't meant to say it aloud, but it was his habit, when fixing something in his mind, to repeat the thought vocally.

He was startled when Camilla said, "I'm sure you are, my pet."

His head turned and he found her looking at him with the same cool insolence she had worn when first she had walked into the apartment. She had regained her composure and was regarding him with amusement.

"Yes, I'm sure you are," she smiled. "And I'm certain it will be something thoroughly unpleasant."

"Not at all," said Harry, thinning his lips with irony. "I was just planning to go to LaFarge and appeal to his better nature."

Camilla laughed and it was like the metallic tinkle of hidden bells in a dark city street.

"You're precious," she said.

She lifted her forgotten cocktail and tasted it. She grimaced. It was flat and sweet, and the fire seemed to have gone out of it, or perhaps her thirst was demanding a more subtle flame. She put down her glass on the cocktail table and demanded:

"Do you have any champagne?"

"Yes."

"I mean decent champagne. Not just fizz water. Piper-Heidsieck?"

"Mumm's."

"A man with a wine cellar!" she jeered. "All right. Now do you have any cognac ..."

"Not just any low-brow brandy," he interrupted, mimicking her. "Will Napoleon 1812 suit you?"

"Don't be so smug. Do you know how to make French Seventy-fives?"

"Half cognac, half champagne."

"Make it, make it for me," she said intensely. "Make me a bucketful of it!" The desire for him strained and danced and leaped within her. She still held the leash, but she was beginning to let it slip through her fingers. Still, she held to the last inch. She wanted to go to him with complete abandon. They had fought with words, but the force of his body and sinew and muscle had been behind the words, and the excitement of the conflict had been like the excitement of actual physical contact.

But first she wanted to drink. There were certain things she wanted to anesthetize first—the raw nerve ends, the physical revulsion she had felt at the thought of LaFarge being hurt.

"Well, are you going to make it, or aren't you?" she demanded.

Smiling secretly, Harry went into the kitchen for the bottles of champagne and brandy. He brought them back to the bar and stirred the explosive mixture in a tall bar-glass. Camilla reached for it.

"Don't bother pouring it," she said. "I'll drink out of this. Turn on the player. Put on some records, something blue, something really blue, like *St. Louis Blues* or *St. James Infirmary* or *Mood Indigo*. I want to dance."

Harry said, "Sure," and went over to the Capehart. He stacked the record changer with blues. He waited until the music started, then turned down the volume and adjusted the bass until it was like the throb of a fevered pulse. He turned—and his eyes sprang wide.

Camilla was standing, nude, in the middle of the floor, her shoulders hunched, her head canted on one shoulder, her long fingers knotted together at her waist. She was beginning to sway to the throb of the music. This was what she had meant by wanting to dance. Harry stared. He had never seen her like this.

She was beginning to dance. From her submissive, half-crouched position, she slowly straightened and her arms lifted above her head, her fingers again entwining. Her eyes were closed. Slowly, she lifted one long, delicately rondured leg, pivoted sharply on the other foot and brought her leg down sharply. It was an exclamation rendered in sheer motion. She was making a statement.

I am Camilla.

She repeated the motion, this time slowly lifting the other slender leg, bringing it down more emphatically.

I AM CAMILLA!

Harry was not esthetic. He had been once to a ballet, and its inarticulate, symbolic pantomime had bored him—but this was different. He forgot her nudity, he forgot everything that had gone before, in the swift fluidity of her body.

It was less a dance than an autobiography in motion, stripped of adjectives and adverbs, its statements as stark as an Icelandic Saga.

What the movements of her legs had proclaimed, her arms affirmed.

I am Camilla. I am unpossessed.

Her arms came down to her sides without touching the flowing body, hovered and rose again. Her eyes remained closed. In the darkness, she was wrestling with devils. Her silken body turned lithely, intricately. For an instant, stretched upward from her toes, slim and tall, momentarily immobile. Her breasts declared:

We are the challengers. Who will stand before our spears?

The dance never once became wild or frenzied, but there was a dangerous Circean languor in her movements. There were moments of harsh emphasis, repeated and repeated.

I am Camilla. I am unpossessed. I will be unpossessed.

She was no longer a naked girl with proud breasts, dancing. She was a woman who stood afraid on a lonely mountain, speaking this language through her supple body to hide her own fear of the height she had climbed, to hide her fear of the sheer mountain face that rose before her, unclimbed. She was dancing to exorcise the devils of fear.

I am Camilla, I am Camilla.

The dancing became slower, less emphatic. The statement was not enough. It was not enough to be Camilla, and now her pride was admitting it.

When she stopped dancing, she was facing Harry. She opened her eyes and looked full into his face. He was standing with his legs astride, his head thrust forward between his powerful shoulders. The emotion that leaped and crackled between them was more naked than the unclothed girl. Their eyes were as thin as the eyes of two great hunting cats. Harry walked heavily toward her, reaching with his hands. He touched her shoulders and his fingers flowed down the satiny smoothness of her sides. Her chest rose and fell, lifting her breasts from the depth of her breathing. Her demanding eyes raged wordlessly into his. Then, with a hoarse growl, Harry scooped her up in his arms and strode across the room.

She cried out once, piercingly, exultingly.

INVESTMENT FOR BLACKMAIL
CHAPTER FIVE

When Suzy walked out of Harry's apartment and into the street, a weary gloom had settled on her. She did not want to go home, tired as she was. She did not want to face the loneliness she thought she would find there, not knowing that the loneliness was within herself. She hesitated on the sidewalk, and someone called her name. She turned and saw the cab at the curb. Joe's freckled grinning face appeared in the window.

"Going my way, honeybun?" he asked.

"Joe!" she exclaimed. "What are you doing here?"

"I had something I wanted to talk over with the Boss," he prodded his thumb upward at Harry's apartment. "But it'll keep. Come on, get in."

It was a small lie. He had been waiting for Suzy. When she had left him in the cafeteria, he had known she was coming to see Harry, and he knew, also, that Harry would hustle her out this night. He had been glumly waiting in the cab for her for an hour. To pick up the pieces.

Suzy said, "Well, thanks, Joe!" She walked across the sidewalk and got into the cab beside him.

"How about a drive around the park?" he asked. "Washington Park."

Washington Park, in downtown Newark, was two blocks long and shaped like an ungenerous piece of pie. At one end, a statue of George Washington sat on a horse, staring fixedly at the double feature advertised on the marquee of the Broad Street Theatre.

"I feel sorry for George," Joe said. "He's never been to the movies. Did you like the drive around the park?"

Suzy smiled. "It was wonderful," she said—but nine-tenths of her mind was busily trying to find an excuse to go back to Harry's apartment. She wanted to see him just once more that night, even if it were only for five minutes.

"Well," said Joe, "if the drive around Washington Park was as wonderful as all that, let's crowd our luck and try a drive around Lincoln Park this time."

Suzy smiled her okay.

"To our right," said Joe, as the cab began a slow circuit of the park, "we see the inspiring spire–inspiring spire, I'll have to remember that—to our right we see the inspiring spire of the Medical Tower. It teems with every kind of specialist known to medical science, who, for a modest fee, will gladly remove any organ from your innards that you might care to name. Except an appendix. The appendix is beneath them. Even barbers are removing appendixes these days. Tell you what I'll do. I'll match you to see who goes in to have a gland removed."

"Take me back to Harry's," said Suzy.

"Aw, wait a minute ..."

"Please, Joe. There's something I have to ask him. It's important." She had just thought of her excuse to see Harry once against that night. Frawley. She wanted to ask him about Frawley. What should she do when Frawley called? If he asked her to go out with him, should she go? It was ticklish, because she was sure Frawley would make another pass at her. Wouldn't that jeopardize Harry's opportunity with the Frawley Steamship Company? It was a flimsy excuse, but she would see Harry again.

Joe squirmed and said, "It's a long ride back, honeybun. Call him on the phone. It's simpler. You know what a phone is. Don Ameche invented Alexander Bell, and Alexander Bell invented the telephone. Over it you can insult a guy ten miles away and not get punched in the nose."

He had an excellent reason for not wanting Suzy to go back to Harry's apartment. He had been in Harry's office that afternoon when Camilla called up and made the date for that evening. He had seen Harry's lecherous grin and had heard Harry say:

"No, I won't come over to that mausoleum of yours. It gives me the creeps. Come up to my place and I'll show you how to break a full nelson. No, there won't be any tramps around except you and me. Sure, ten o'clock's fine with me. Be seeing you, baby."

And Harry had turned to Joe and winked. "Camilla LaFarge," he had boasted. "Granddaughter of old Piet Schuyler, the guy that held the first mortgage on Newark. I met her one night playing crap down at Little Augie's on Frelinghuysen Avenue. What a dish!"

No, Joe did not want Suzy to go back to Harry's apartment. "Tell you what, honeybun," he said. "We'll send him a telegram. I've always wanted to send somebody a telegram."

"Are you going to take me back, Joe?"

"Now wait a minute. Let's talk this over like two civilized people. There's no reason why we can't be friends, even if I did try to smack you with a sledge hammer last week. And anyway, I had something important to say to Harry, but I thought it over and found it would keep. Now why don't you think it over ..."

Suzy started to get out of the cab, but Joe reached out and caught her by the arm. He pulled her back into the seat.

"Don't try to get out of a cab while it's moving," he growled. "You'll give the driver an anxiety complex. Okay, I'll take you back to Harry's."

Suzy said gratefully, "Thanks, Joe. I'll only be a minute, and afterward we can go someplace and dance."

Joe knew how much she was going to feel like dancing after she saw Harry with Camilla LaFarge. He had seen that LaFarge dame and nobody, not even a trusting little innocent like Suzy, would ever believe that Camilla was in a guy's apartment after ten o'clock at night to discuss the theory of law as propounded by Blackstone.

"We'll dance on my grave," said Joe gloomily. "But honestly, honey, Harry's not going to appreciate your busting in on him."

"Why not?" Suzy laughed.

"He's up to his ears in work. I know. Every night he stays up till three, four o'clock in the morning, briefing a brief, or whatever it is lawyers do. Give the guy a break. Let him get his work done and go to bed. Tell him about it in the morning."

Suzy just smiled. Of course, Joe couldn't know how Harry felt about her. Fondly, she pictured in her mind how he would look when she walked in. He would be in his shirtsleeves and his tie would be pulled away from his collar. His hair would be rumpled, and he'd be wearing those tortoise-shell glasses he sometimes put on when his eyes were tired, but which made him look as if he contained the wisdom of a college professor. He'd be carrying some papers in his hand when he came to the door. "Suzy!" he'd exclaim, his eyes lighting up. Then chidingly, "You should be in bed, you know. Golly, am I glad to see you!"

This was a dream-Harry, who had never existed. Harry, for instance, had never said golly. He said holy cow or damn—but Suzy preferred to think of him as saying golly.

Joe tried again, but with waning hope. "You know," he said, "this might not be as important as you think it is, and if it isn't important, you'll just be making him sore. You know how he is, honey. He'll bawl the hell out of you, and wouldn't that be nice!"

"He won't be sore," said Suzy confidently.

"You hope you hope you hope. I don't know why everybody can't be as simple and uncomplicated as I am. Me, all I want is a cup of coffee. I just found out something about coffee, by the way. When you buy it alone, it's only a nickel and I love tuna fish sandwiches. Tell you what, if you're a good girl and don't bother Harry tonight, I'll buy you a bacon and tomato on rye with mayonnaise. And match you to see who tips the waiter."

Suzy turned and looked at him. "Why are you trying to prevent me from seeing Harry, Joe?" she asked seriously.

He flushed. "Aw," he mumbled, "I'm just a mad, jealous fool."

Suzy patted his hand. "You're nice," she said maternally.

Joe groaned. All he could hope for now was that Harry would have the sense to keep her out of the apartment. He would, of course—but there was always a chance that Suzy would catch a glimpse of Camilla when the door opened. Or smell her. What was that perfume? Cobra. Well, Camilla not only smelled like it, she looked like it. Joe crossed his fingers. He did not want to have to see that hurt, dazed look on Suzy's face when she came down from Harry's apartment.

The doorman was not on duty when the cab drew up before Harry's apartment again. He had gone off duty immediately after Camilla LaFarge had driven up. Her dawn gray Cadillac convertible was still parked at the curb, and though Joe did not actually know it was hers, he had a pretty strong notion. It was the only car around. He groaned again. He had been half-hoping that she and Harry might have gone out, to a night club or someplace, but it had been a very faint hope. Harry was not a one to take a girl to a night club when he could stay at home and teach her to break a full nelson.

Joe jumped out of the cab. "I'll go up with you," he said desperately. "There's a couple things I wanted to tell Harry, too."

"Wait here for me, Joe," said Suzy serenely. "I'll be right down." She turned and walked into the apartment. Her step was light. All she wanted was to see Harry for a few minutes. But if he asked her to stay … She smiled. He'd ask her to stay. She knew it. She knew it in her heart.

The foxy-faced elevator operator was sitting in his car reading the *Racing Form*, but when he looked up and saw Suzy, his eyes sprang wide and he jumped up from his stool. Here was trouble. He could see it coming. Two's company and three's a crowd. No guy wanted two dames around unless one of them was his mother.

"Forget something, Miss Carr?" the operator asked warily.

"No. There are a few business matters I have to talk over with Mr. Sloan." She started to enter the car.

And now the unexpected dollar that Harry had given the operator earlier in the evening became less a blackmail fee than an investment.

The operator pretended surprise. "Mr. Sloan?" he said. "Did you see him? He walked out of here not more than two minutes ago, Miss Carr. If you looked down the street, you'd of seen him."

Suzy showed her disappointment. "Did ... did he say where he was going?" she asked.

"Nah, he didn't say nothing. He looked like he had a lot on his mind, if you know what I mean."

Suzy bit her lip. "Perhaps he just went down to the store for cigarettes. Maybe I ought to go up and wait for him. For just a little while."

"It wouldn't be such a little while, Miss Carr," said the operator glibly. "I think he was going down the awfiss. He said something about a long night ahead of him. And he was carrying that briefcase. It was fulla stuff. Why doncha try the awfiss, Miss Carr? You might catch him there."

"Thanks. I ... I will."

As she turned away, the operator called after her, "I'll tell him you called, Miss Carr. Want him to give you a ring?"

"No. No, thanks. I'll probably catch him at the office."

She walked out quickly. The elevator operator grinned. He'd tell Mr. Sloan how he got him out of this one. It'd be worth a fin, anyway. But whatta man, he thought enviously; two dames in one night, and both of them honeys. But to tell the truth, he couldn't see why Mr. Sloan took the thin one when he could have the blonde. The blonde was stacked, and he meant stacked.

Joe was leaning against the cab, smoking an anxious cigarette, and when he saw Suzy walking toward him, he pushed himself away and went to meet her. His spirits lifted when he saw her face. She hadn't seen Harry. She wouldn't be looking like that if she had.

"Get everything settled?" he asked cheerfully.

"I didn't see him. The elevator boy said he just left to go to the office. Do you mind driving me to the office?"

Joe had been able to see the lighted windows of Harry's apartment from the sidewalk, and twice he had seen Harry's passing silhouette. Thank God for smart elevator boys!

"Sure I'll drive you to the office," he said, taking her elbow. "Come on, hop in. There's nothing I like better than driving around from place to place with a beautiful woman. I'm just a sucker for a beautiful dame, I guess."

He bundled her quickly into the cab before she, too, looked up and saw the lights in Harry's apartment, or Harry's silhouette with a glass in its hand. Then there would be hell to pay.

Harry had an expensive suite of offices in the National Newark and Essex Trust Building, opposite the Prudential on Market Street—but of course he wasn't there.

"Too bad," said Joe cheerfully. "But there's no sense going back to his apartment if he went out with a briefcase full of torts and writs and stuff. Maybe he went out to write a will. Anybody dying tonight that you know of?"

Suzy smiled. She was feeling better. She had wanted to see Harry, but Harry was busy, and it was all right. She knew where he had gone, naturally. To see Mr. Frawley. Mr. Frawley was probably just as anxious to get Harry to work for him as Harry was to get out of the divorce business.

"No, there's nobody dying that I know of," she said lightly. Then, thinking of Frawley and Harry's opportunity, "But something might be born."

"That sounds very profound, and it probably is. If it has anything to do with babies, I'm for it. I always say, television will never replace the great American baby. And now, honeybun, who shall we visit next? And not find at home, I mean."

"You said something about dancing. I feel like dancing."

At that moment, a nude and cold white flame, Camilla was dancing by herself in Harry's apartment, but she was dancing out of a desperate need in herself, because she was afraid, and because she had drunk a full bar glass of champagne and cognac. Suzy wanted to dance simply because she was happy. If Harry had gone to see Mr. Frawley this late at night, it would surely mean something.

"*Vive la danse*," said Joe still clowning. He wanted to make Suzy laugh. It had been a long time since he had heard a clear ringing laugh from her. "We will go to some low dive, my lovely, and there I will ply you with liquor and smother you with pulsating kisses—but who the hell'd want a pulsating kiss except a goldfish?" He pushed his lips in and out to illustrate.

Suzy laughed. "That's just what we'll do," she said. "We'll go to a low dive and you can smother me in goldfish."

"Driver," said Joe, "hie us to a low dive."

"Sure, Cap," said the driver. "I'll take ya to the Oasis Club."

The Oasis Club had soft lights, a quiet orchestra, honest drinks, good food and intimate little booths. He was a smart driver.

THE BIG DEAL
CHAPTER SIX

Suzy awakened the next morning on a bright new world. She felt fresh and relaxed. She wanted to call Harry and ask him how things went with Mr. Frawley last night, but she was willing to wait. She knew Harry would call her the moment he woke up. He'd want her to be the first to know the good news. She stretched and smiled contentedly. It had been fun with Joe last night. Joe was full of fun, always clowning. When you were with Joe, you didn't have to walk around with your defenses showing.

She got up, took a lengthy shower, but it was not until the coffee was snorting in the percolator that the phone rang. It was Harry.

"Oh, hello, darling!" she cried. "Hello, hello, hello!"

Harry grunted. He was feeling lousy. Camilla hadn't left until dawn, and he felt as if a pair of husky wrestlers had been practicing body slams on him all night.

"Sorry I was out when you dropped by, baby," he said.

The elevator boy had tipped him off. (And it *had* been worth a fin.) Harry was cautious because he knew you could see the lights of his apartment from the sidewalk, and he didn't know if Suzy had stood down there, spying on him. She sure would have gotten an eyeful, Camilla acting the way she had. He was all ready with a fast story that a guy, a classmate from law school, had come to town and the super had let him and a dame into his apartment. Rummies, both of them, too. Was the apartment a mess when he got home at four in the morning! He didn't want Suzy to get sore now. With this LaFarge thing coming up, he needed her more than ever.

His apprehensions were dissipated when she said gaily, "And how are *you* this morning, Mr. Counselor?"

"I feel like an old girdle," he grumbled. It was the truth. "What a night! I didn't get in till four this morning."

"And what did Mr. Frawley say?" asked Suzy eagerly. "Please tell me, Harry. Don't keep me on pins and needles."

"Frawley?"

"But wasn't it Mr. Frawley you went to see last night?"

"Hell no."

Suzy said, "Oh ..." on a falling note of disappointment.

Harry reached for the bourbon he had brought from the kitchen and drank straight from the bottle. This was one morning he needed an artificial stimulant.

"What made you think I went to see Frawley?" he growled.

"Well ... the way he spoke to you over the phone, making all those promises ... I thought ..."

Harry felt the hundred proof liquor course into his bloodstream. He sat up a little straighter on the phone bench. That was better.

"No, I didn't go to see Frawley," he said. "But this is something better, baby. Bigger and better."

"Harry!"

"Bigger and better," he repeated with satisfaction. And wasn't it the truth! Once he was married to Camilla, he was out of the rat race. "Ever hear of the Schuyler family, baby?"

"Of course. Everybody in Newark knows of the Schuylers."

"Well, here's how it goes. This dame is one of the Schuylers. She's married to a drip named LaFarge, but she wants out. And who did she call in? You guess."

"Oh, Harry. Another divorce?"

"Why don't you wait till I'm finished?" he snarled. "What's the matter with you? Why do you always have to jump to conclusions? Just hold on a minute."

"I'm sorry, Harry. Honestly I am. I ... well, I'd thought that maybe you and Mr. Frawley had gotten things settled last night. Know what I mean? It's what you've been wanting ..."

"Sure, sure, but I told you it'd take from six months to a year, didn't I? So how could we get it settled in one night? Use your head, will you?"

"I'm sorry, Harry, I'm sorry."

"Okay, baby. And I'm sorry, too. I didn't mean to yap at you like that. But between that dame and her screwy husband, I had a tough night. All they did was scrap. It was like pulling teeth to get the facts out of them, to get them to agree on anything. What a pair of screwballs!"

That was the stuff, he congratulated himself. Let Suzy think of them as screwballs, then when he spent time with Camilla, she wouldn't go getting ideas.

"The divorce end of it isn't settled yet," he went on quickly. "But it seems this LaFarge was kind of managing his wife's estate, and if you know the Schuylers, you'll know that estate's loaded. Well naturally, she's not going to let the guy go on managing it now. So she put it up to me—get her the divorce, get rid of the guy for her, then I can manage the estate. Of course," he threw in to make it sound legal and authentic, "I'm going to have to put up a fifty thousand dollar bond or something, but I'm not worried about that end of it. Now what do you think, baby? Are we on our way, or are we on our way?"

"It sounds wonderful, Harry, but ... is it as good as Mr. Frawley's offer?"

"Frawley? Don't make me laugh, baby. The Schuyler estate runs into the millions. Of course, I don't want to let Frawley drop. I can handle his stuff on the side. Did he call you yet?"

"Not yet."

"Well, he will. Handle him with kid gloves, baby. 'Yes' him to death, know what I mean? He's got the dough, and I'd like to get my hands on some of it. I mean," he added hastily, "his account should be good for twenty, twenty-five thousand a year easy. It's nothing to be sneezed at. But I don't have to tell you how to handle him. You know what's at stake, so use your head. Okay, baby?"

"Okay, darling," cried Suzy in a delirium of flooding happiness. "I'll flatter Mr. Frawley's precious ego till he purrs like a pussy cat. Oh, Harry!"

"Yeah, it won't be long now, baby. But it all hinges on how we handle the LaFarge divorce. There can't be any hitches. I said the guy was a screwball, didn't I? It's not going to be a pushover, but I know you'll take care of your end. It might be a little tough on you, baby, but just keep remembering that this is the last crummy divorce case we're going to handle. So, if the going gets rough, just clench your teeth and take it. But hell, I don't have to give you a pep talk. You're a trouper."

The hell he didn't have to give her a pep talk, he thought sourly. He didn't know what LaFarge was like, but this was one time she wasn't going to go around smacking guys with a bottle just because they made a little pass at her. This time she was going to take it and like it.

"Oh, Harry, I can hardly believe it's true! Look," she cried gaily, "I'm coming right over and I'll make your breakfast for you. You go back to bed, and I'll bring it to you on a tray."

The thought of even seeing a woman this morning, made Harry feel like crawling off into a corner.

"Baby," he said, "there's nothing I'd like better. Honest. But I can't, I've got a million things to do. Inside fifteen minutes I won't know if I'm coming or going. I've got more paper work than the Pentagon. I'll give you a ring later in the day, if I can take a break."

Suzy put her lips close to the mouthpiece of the phone and whispered, "I love you, darling."

"There's nobody like you, baby."

He hung up and stared dully at the phone. Then he picked up the bourbon bottle and shambled back toward the bedroom.

DELUGE OF ORCHIDS!
CHAPTER SEVEN

An hour later, a box of orchids arrived for Suzy from Frawley. Twelve white orchids. Apparently, no one had ever told Frawley that you didn't send orchids in bouquets, like chrysanthemums. You sent one orchid or you sent a corsage. But, on the other hand, Frawley had never sent anyone orchids before in his life. It had never occurred to him to send an orchid. His wife's standard of horticultural royalty had been long-stemmed American Beauty roses. Or dahlias.

In fact, Frawley was not quite the tycoon Harry had pictured him to Suzy. Frawley did not own steamship lines. He owned three freighters that operated between Cuba and Tampa, carrying tobacco for the Tampa cigar factories and whatever other cargo they could pick up. Frawley was not a millionaire, but he was a little better than comfortably fixed, and when he bought a car he did not have to worry about how many miles he got to the gallon.

Suzy would not have been feminine had she not been delighted with the orchids, but part of the thrill was missing because Harry hadn't sent them. She brought a vase from the kitchen and set the orchids on the console table at the window. She stepped back to admire them—and, woman-like, suddenly discovered that they made the whole apartment look so shabby that there was nothing she could do but give it a thorough house-cleaning.

Frawley called. He sounded chastened, but Suzy put him at his ease immediately.

"Your flowers are lovely, Mr. Frawley," she said. "I've never seen so many orchids before in all my life."

"Then I'm forgiven?"

"We-ll, you were a little impetuous, you know."

"We were both a little impetuous, if you ask me," he said. Ruefully, he felt the side of his jaw where Joe's hard knuckles had raised a blue-black lump.

"It was a very trying situation," Suzy soothed him.

"I guess so—but I shouldn't have acted the way I did, all the same."

"You're forgiven."

Ah, if Harry could only hear her now!

"Well, that's fine," said Frawley heartily. "I'm glad to hear that. I certainly am. Yessir. Uh ... how's your girl friend? The one that's been having the trouble, I mean."

Suzy had to think for a moment before she remembered the mythical girl friend Harry had conjured up to sooth Frawley's ruffled ego. "Oh, much better," she said, "much better."

"Well, that's fine. I'm certainly glad to hear that."

"Mr. Sloan paid all the bills," said Suzy slyly. "I don't know what she would have done without him."

"He's a fine fellow, Sloan. Yessir." But to himself, Frawley thought—if Sloan paid the bills, he must have been mixed up in it somewhere. He was sure now that the mythical girl friend had been, in his language, an unwed mother.

"And, uh, how are you feeling today, Miss Carr?" he asked.

"Wonderful. Your flowers brightened up the whole day for me."

"They did, eh? Well, what do you know about that. I'll have to send 'em more often, ha, ha, ha." Clumsily he was trying to lead up to an invitation for that evening. "I sure felt like a heel after last night. I was sore for awhile, sure, then I realized that you'd helped me out, and I'd sure like to show my appreciation."

"But, Mr. Frawley, I was just doing my job. If anybody helped you out, it was Harry Sloan. He managed everything for you. If it hadn't been for him, it wouldn't have gone off so smoothly."

He wished irritably that she'd stop talking about that shyster, Sloan.

"What I meant to say, uh, is this," then he blurted, "what are you doing for dinner tonight?"

Suzy laughed, remembering a wisecrack Joe had made. "I never do anything for dinner," she said. "It's up to dinner to do things for me."

"It's up to … say, that's a good one, ha, ha, ha. I'll have to remember that one. Well say now, if I found a restaurant that'll put up a good healthy dinner to do things for you, how's that sound?"

Suzy said, "Wonderful." Oh, Harry!

"Huh?"

"I said, it sounds wonderful."

"Yeah, that's what I thought you said, ha, ha, ha. But I couldn't quite believe my ears, after … uh … well, well, well. Yessir, I think it's wonderful, too. Suppose I pick you up, say, around six. And how do you feel about a show afterwards? Something like *Guys and Dolls* or something?"

"My, my, Mr. Frawley, you really must have influence to be able to get tickets for *Guys and Dolls* on such short notice."

"Well," he said modestly—but knowing he was going to have to pay through the nose to get a pair of tickets from the scalpers, "I do know a few of the boys. Six o'clock be okay with you?"

"I'll be ready, Mr. Frawley."

"Well, that's fine ... yessir ..." he floundered, not having any more to say, yet not knowing how to break it off gracefully.

Suzy came to his rescue. "I'll have to run now, Mr. Frawley. Thanks loads for the flowers, and thanks loads for your nice invitation. I'll see you at six." She hung up.

And in his hotel room, Frawley also hung up, with the satisfying feeling of having concluded a very difficult operation. His satisfaction, however, was not quite complete. In the back of his mind, though he would not admit it to himself, he knew that it was really Harry who had managed this for him, and that was what kept him from patting himself on the back. Whatever his other faults, Frawley was an honest and really quite simple man, yet shrewd enough to spot the touch of Harry's devious hand. He did not like to have other men procure women for him. He had a hard, ugly name for such men. But—there was something different about this girl, this Suzy Carr. She might be mixed up with Harry Sloan and all that, but she was sweet and clean and, well, an all-round nice kid. Yessir.

Within five minutes after she had hung up, Suzy had quite forgotten all about Frawley—except, of course, that the time six o'clock was pegged in her mind.

It was about three that afternoon that Joe, as sloppy and grinning as usual in his baggy tweeds, sauntered in.

"I brung yiz something," he said, tossing her a brown paper bag. "Indian nuts. Do you know why the Indian's practically extinct? He starved himself to death on Indian nuts, and on top of that worked himself to death cracking the shells. Holy cow, what's that?"

"Orchids, silly," Suzy laughed.

Joe whistled and walked over to them. He peered in among the petals, looked all around them, under them, behind him. Suzy watched him.

"What *are* you doing?" she asked finally.

"Looking," he said.

"Looking for what?"

"The ribbon."

"The ribbon? What ribbon?"

"You know what ribbon. That gold ribbon they always put on things like this. The ribbon that says Good Luck, or Rest In Peace."

"Oh, for heaven's sake."

"My deepest apologies, fair lady. I'm just a humble wayfarer, and never before have I seen such a staggering assemblage of floral pulchritude. I mistook it for a wreath. Who sent them, by the way? The House of Morgan?"

Suzy hesitated. It was funny, but she didn't like to tell Joe who had sent them. "Mr. Frawley," she said a little defiantly.

"Frawley?" Joe lifted his eyebrows. "Isn't that the senior wolf we gave the special Harry Sloan treatment for the matrimonially misunderstood last night? The same, I'll bet. Well, all I can say is, damn handsome of him, ma'am. I think I'll have an Indian nut."

He reached into his sagging pocket and pulled out a nut. He looked at it and muttered, "I'll bet there's more nourishment in ball bearings." He slouched across the room, dropped onto the sofa, kicked off his shoes and propped his feet comfortably on the edge of the coffee table. He slid down and lounged on the back of his neck. He waved a lanky, freckled hand.

"I have just come," he said, "from taking some very enjoyable pictures of a bevy—what the hell's a bevy, anyway?—a group of practically naked ladies. In addition to a miserable fifty bucks, the gentleman in charge gave me a couple passes to his establishment, namely the burlesque. How's about you and me stepping out tonight for a nice low-brow evening? Of course, if you don't like low-brow evenings, we can make it a high-brow evening. We can go as intellectuals and sneer. Root, snoot?"

Suzy was dusting the radio, and very carefully she did not turn and look at Joe when she said, "I can't tonight, Joe."

He made amiable noises as if he had more than half expected that answer. "Well," he said, "I'm not selfish. If you want to give poor old Harry a little time now and then, I won't object. I realize he's your boss, and I know what a girl has to go through these days to keep her job. But when I'm elected to Congress, bosses who force girls to go out to dinner with them, will be summarily executed. Unless, of course, he pays them time and a half for overtime."

Suzy suddenly found that she could not lie to Joe, nor even let him go on thinking she was going out with Harry. She could lie to almost anybody, when necessary. She had even lied to Harry because, well, sometimes he was funny, and the lie was the easier way. But she couldn't lie to Joe.

"I ..." she tried to frame it in her mind, then went on reluctantly, "I'm going out with Mr. Frawley tonight. He's taking me to see *Guys and Dolls*."

Joe's hand stopped in mid-air, with an Indian nut pinched between his thumb and forefinger. A moment before, his face had looked so easy-going and good natured, but suddenly it was all hard, flat planes, and his mouth a thin slit. He took a breath and seemed to draw himself together in a hard, compact unit.

"What's Harry up to?" he asked very quietly.

A little panicky, Suzy cried, "Harry? What's Harry got to do with it?" What was she panicky about? Furiously, she went back to dusting the radio.

"Don't give me that stuff!" Joe sat up on the sofa. "You're not going out with that middle-aged comedian because you want to."

"I'm going," said Suzy, "because he asked me."

Oh, why couldn't Joe just go on being amusing, making wise-cracks? Why did he have to be like this and spoil everything?

Joe knew he was walking close to a narrow edge, and he knew, also, he wouldn't be doing anybody any good if he stepped over the line. Suzy would not let him say anything against Harry and, what was worse, she wouldn't even believe him. His fists knotted angrily. If there were only something he could do!

He temporized. "Look, honeybun," he said, "I'm not trying to butt in, but ... have you ever heard of the birds and bees?" Shrewdly, he knew she would listen to him and perhaps even remember what he said, if he made it funny.

"The flowers, too," said Suzy, eager to get back on the old easy going, wisecracking level with him.

"And flowers, too. Orchids in particular. All of which gives rise to a very interesting biological speculation." His eyes became intent. "What will you do if this joker makes a pass at you tonight?" He was hoping to be able to tell by her face if Harry had given her orders to play along with Frawley.

Suzy did not flush or look guilty. "He won't," she said confidently.

Joe felt a little better. Not much, but a little. "Maybe not," he said, "but like Al Smith always said, let's take a look at the record. I'll lay you odds that Frawley has made more passes than the whole Notre Dame backfield since 1912. And I'll give you even longer odds, that the Salvation Army hasn't gotten around to reforming him yet, either."

Suzy laughed, then asked reasonably, "But what have you got against Mr. Frawley, Joe?"

"Not a thing, honeybun, and I hope I never do. But you've got to face it, Suzy, sooner or later sometime tonight our little dumb chum is going to come down with a bad case of wayfaring fingers, and don't ask me how I know. A little bird told me. A vulture. So, what will you do? Slap him down again?"

"If a girl keeps her head, Joe, she can always handle a man."

She said it so calmly and sounded so convinced that Joe was more than half persuaded that Harry was not involving her with whatever it was he was trying to promote with Frawley. Could be. Could be, too, that this was just a kind of trial run. Later Harry would put the pressure on her. Joe knew how Suzy felt about Harry, but he had his fingers crossed that she hadn't gone overboard—that Harry had not yet brought her to the point where she'd do anything for him, anything he asked. Including keeping guys like Frawley happy.

Joe's opinion of Harry was succinct—a stinker.

Then, all of a sudden, he found himself hoping that Frawley would make a pass at her. Now he was pretty sure that Harry hadn't put the real pressure on her yet. So it would be a damn good thing if Frawley made a real college try. Suzy was smart enough not to let herself get boxed the way she had been last night in that hotel room. She wouldn't let herself be trapped in any parked cars on lonely roads, nor could she be persuaded into letting Frawley show her his stereoscopic views of Boulder Dam. So okay, thought Joe gloomily, let Frawley make a pass. Suzy would slap him down. Then when Harry bawled her out, or tried to steer her into another date, maybe she'd begin to get an idea of the kind of guy he was.

He gave Suzy a lopsided grin. "That's right, honeybun," he said. "Any smart girl can handle a dumb male, if she keeps her head. But here's something a little more practical, a set of brass knuckles. Keep these, in addition to your head, and you'll be okay."

Surprisingly, he pulled a set of brass knuckles from his pocket and tossed them to her.

"A guy gave them to me the other day," he explained. "He owed me a couple bucks, but he didn't have it, so he gave me these. I got a stuffed Dachshund the same way. I use it for a doorstop. Know how to use that thing? It's easy. Just slip your fingers through those rings and swing. That's all there's to it. I'm telling you, I've seen more discouraged-looking guys wandering around trying to count their fingers after just one teensy-weensy little poke in the snoot, honest."

Suzy turned the knuckle-duster over in her hand. "For heaven's sake, Joe," she said; "what do I want with a thing like this?"

"Call it a keepsake, from me to you," he said earnestly. "A token of undying love and affection. Put it in your purse and keep it with you, and every time you smack some guy in the kisser, you'll think of me. Ah yes, it's tender moments like that make me almost wish I'd taken the blow torch to my poor old father."

"Oh, Joe, be sensible. I don't want this thing."

"But you do. You don't realize it, but you do. For instance, you're standing on the street corner some day, and up comes a Boy Scout. How are you going to keep him from making you cross the street? Smack him."

"Here, Joe. Take it back."

He slouched across the room and closed her hand around it. "Put it in your purse," he said.

"But why?"

"Have I ever asked you to do me a favor before?"

"What's a favor got to do …"

"Put it in your purse and take it with you … as a personal favor to me."

Suzy was half laughing, half exasperated. "Well, all right," she surrendered. "But it's only because this is all getting so silly."

"Promise?"

"Yes, I promise, I promise."

Joe grinned. Now let Frawley press a pass!

"Honeybun," he drawled, "you don't know how lucky you are."

LOVE'S INCANDESCENT BRILLIANCE
CHAPTER EIGHT

Harry was lying in bed, still sleeping, when the phone rang. It rang four times before he reached out a heavy arm, plucked it from its cradle and mumbled, "Okay, okay …"

Camilla's peremptory voice snapped at him. "Don't you ever go to your office?"

"What's that, what's that?" he asked stupidly.

"Are you drunk?"

"Hey, wait a minute!" He sat up indignantly. Then lazily he grinned. "Hiya, baby."

"Do you have any particular baby in mind?" she asked acidly. "Or was that a blanket baby?"

Harry scowled. "What's eating you?"

"Oh my God, what's eating me! Are you sober?"

"Yes, I'm sober."

"Then why aren't you at your office?"

"Because I'm taking a day off, and what the hell is it to you, anyway?"

"Don't you dare talk to me like that!"

"No?"

There was a tense, hating silence, but neither of them hung up.

Camilla was the one who capitulated.

"You're quite a rat, you know," she said.

Harry yawned. He'd known she'd come around. He had her. She'd always be the one to come around first, not him. The thought made him feel more good-natured.

"Sure I'm a rat," he said. "But don't tell me you don't love it."

"Are you trying to put me in my place, by any chance, my pet?" There was a coldness in her voice that warned him.

"I'm nuts about you," he said, "and last night you said you were nuts about me. Is it different today?"

"Oh God, don't let's get sloppy. Now see here," she said briskly, "you told me last night to get LaFarge down to your office. Well, I did, and he just called me to say you weren't there. I told him to wait for you."

Harry swung his legs over the edge of the bed and sat up. "Fast work," he said. "I'll be down there in a half hour. See you tonight?"

"Tonight nothing. You'll come straight here the minute you get finished with LaFarge."

"Surest thing you know, baby."

They hung up simultaneously. Harry was out of the apartment in fifteen minutes. He felt wonderful. Right on the beam. That's all he'd needed, a little sleep. Thank God he hadn't hit the bottle.

LaFarge was waiting in the reception room when Harry walked into the suite. Harry eyed him curiously. LaFarge was tall, about six feet, but his blond hair was faded and there were unhealthy pouches under his eyes. His eyes were bright, very bright. Otherwise, he looked worn out.

He rose languidly from the chair and said, "Sloan? My wife said you're the chap who'd ..."

Harry cut him off shortly. "Let's go in my office where we can talk in private. This isn't something to discuss on the corner of Broad and Market."

"Anything you say, old boy." LaFarge couldn't have sounded more disinterested.

He followed Harry into the inner office and dropped into the chair beside the desk. His hands dangled limply from the ends of the chair arms. He looked worn out—except for his eyes.

Harry looked at him from the ends of his eyes as he walked around the desk to his own chair.

From Camilla's description, he had expected somebody different—somebody cold, thin-lipped and uncompromising. Not this washed out dishrag.

He sat down. "Well, Mr. LaFarge?" he said.

"Well what, old boy?"

"Well, what's on your mind?"

"The divorce, of course. You know all about it. At least, that's what Camilla told me. Or don't you?"

"People sometimes change their minds."

"My dear chap, Camilla hasn't changed her mind since the Hoover administration. I suppose you want to ask me some questions, what? Fire away, old boy, fire away."

LaFarge's languid, off-hand manner nettled Harry. It was too soft, nothing to get your hands on. "Your wife tells me you want a divorce," he said curtly.

"I?" LaFarge looked wanly surprised. "Not at all. It's Camilla who wants the divorce. Not that it matters who, I daresay. However, her mind is quite made up. She said you'd arrange the grounds and all that. Personally, I can't see why she doesn't go to Reno, but she seems prejudiced one way or another and insists on having it in this dreary place. By the way, isn't there some talk of a divorce mill investigation by the district attorney?"

"That won't affect us." Harry peered intently at the man across the desk from him. There was something about LaFarge, something ... Involuntarily he slapped the desk. Of course! The guy was a hophead. And right now he was full of hop and bliss. That's where he got those bright eyes. A hophead! Harry's mouth curled contemptuously.

"The district attorney's investigation won't affect us a bit," he repeated. LaFarge shrugged. "No? Just thought I'd mention it, that's all."

"Thanks, but I read about it, too. Now, Mr. LaFarge, sure you're not the one who wants this divorce?"

"Not at all sure, old boy. Come to think of it, it'll be quite a relief. Do you know my wife?"

"Casually."

"Well, she's quite mad, you know. I mean literally. A cog or two loose, here and there. Makes things a bit difficult at times."

"And are those the grounds for the divorce?"

"Good heavens no, old boy. Wouldn't think of mentioning it. I doubt that you could get her certified, anyway. She's very clever at it. You have to live with her quite awhile before you realize it. It came as quite a shock. Absolutely and utterly crazy. You wouldn't believe it."

"You don't say."

"But I do. It's a relief to get it off my chest. But, I say, you think I'm talking drivel, don't you?"

Harry just grinned.

For the first time, LaFarge showed agitation. His pale hands fluttered and his face twitched. "Ask her about that room on the third floor," he cried a little wildly. "The one she keeps locked, the one where she goes. Ask her about that!"

Harry thought, the hell with humoring this hophead! "Let's get back to the point, pal," he said brusquely. "If you're not using that as grounds for divorce, let's forget it. All I'm interested in is the divorce."

LaFarge sank back in his chair as if exhausted by his brief outburst. "That's your end of it, old boy."

"Your's too, pal. I lay out the blueprint. *You* follow it."

LaFarge looked pained. "Righto," he said at length. "Just what is my little chore? Something unpleasant, I'll warrant, if Camilla has anything to do with it."

"It might not be so hard to take, pal," Harry jeered. "All you do is get to a hotel with a beautiful girl and wait there till your wife busts into the room with a photographer and catches this tomato sitting on your lap in her scanties. Will that be so hard to take?"

"Sounds terribly, terribly interesting." LaFarge tried to stifle a yawn.

Harry reached in his desk and pulled out an eight by ten glossy of Suzy in a swim suit.

"The dame," he said.

LaFarge peered at it. "Buxom, isn't she?" he said finally. "Quite an artless face too, when you come to look at it. And this is the one who will perch herself on my lap in her, ah, scanties?"

"Right the first time, pal."

"Then I'm quite certain she won't realize what she's doing. Not with that guileless face, old boy. Unless, of course, this photograph was taken years and years ago."

"It was taken two weeks ago."

"Fancy that. Really quite a lovely face. Really, I've never seen such complete innocence. She must be rather on the stupid side, what?"

"Don't count on it, pal. She'll set you right back on your heels."

"This is very interesting. I say, may I keep this photograph?"

Harry waved his hand. "It's yours. Now that part of it's settled, right?"

"Ra-ther. I shall be looking forward to it, in fact."

"Good. We'll clean up the rest of the details and then you can go home and play with your picture. The settlement from your wife." Harry's eyes sharpened on LaFarge's face.

"A hundred thousand dollars," said LaFarge indifferently.

"That's quite a chunk of dough," said Harry.

"Is it? I've earned it, I suppose. Actually, I didn't ask for a penny. It was Camilla's idea. A hundred thousand dollars. She said you'd arrange it so that I wouldn't lose too much to the income tax chappies."

"All her idea, eh?"

"Yes, quite. I have no head for money at all, you know. Never have had a head for money."

"Enough of a head to promote an easy hundred grand though, eh, pal?"

"What was that, old boy? Sounded rather nasty. However, it's not important. Is there anything else?"

"Not at the minute. I'll have some papers for you to sign, and I'll let you know a little later when we're ready for the hotel stunt."

"Make it soon, will you, old boy? Sounds as if it might be rather diverting."

"Yeah, doesn't it!" Harry spread his forearms along the edge of the desk and leaned over them. "How long have you been on the hop, chum?" he asked.

LaFarge jerked and his eyes glittered with hate. "You know," he said evenly, "it would give me the greatest pleasure to cut your throat—slowly."

He twisted lithely out of his chair and walked from the office, carrying Suzy's photograph with him.

Harry pulled his hand down the side of his cheek and looked at the shine of perspiration on it. "Hophead," he muttered. That was wonderful. That was just dandy. One minute LaFarge looked dead on his feet, and the next minute he was gliding out as quick as a mink. A nice guy to have waiting in some dark doorway for you. *It would give me the greatest pleasure to cut your throat—slowly.* Nice people Camilla married. But Harry had no real physical fear of LaFarge. He had supreme confidence in his ability to handle himself. It was a complication, that was all, and he didn't want any hitches. He wanted this one to go through like silk. Well, the next time he saw the hophead, he'd butter him up and smooth it over.

Harry opened the bottom drawer of his desk and brought up a bottle of Old Granddad. It had lain there for six months, untouched. He filled a small silver jigger, downed it and filled the jigger again. Ah, that felt better. He downed the second one, and poured himself another refill. A sense of well-being began to spread warmly over him.

Hopheads.

Harry had a right to be leery of hopheads. He didn't like having to work with them. Especially with this damn D.A.'s investigation on the fire. The guy might blow his top at the last minute and sing like a canary. Then it would be, so long, Harry, nice to have known you. Harry clenched the third jigger of bourbon in his meaty hand, looked at it, drank it off. Hopheads! He reached for the bottle and caught himself in the act of pouring his fourth drink.

He growled, "Don't let it get you, chum!"

Here was a hophead and he had to work with him. This hophead had to be separated from Camilla. This hophead had something on Camilla. So here was the problem—to separate LaFarge from Camilla and to shut him up at the same time.

In five minutes, Harry had the answer. He picked up his jigger, drank it carelessly, and went out into the reception room.

"I won't be back today," he told the girl. "If anybody calls," he hesitated, thinking of Suzy, "I'm out of town and may not be back for several days. Take this telegram. Miss Suzy Carr ..."

"Do you mean *Susan* Carr?" asked the girl brightly, her pencil poised over her stenographic notebook. She was new.

Harry gave her a cold glance. "Do you want to write the telegram, or shall I?" he asked.

The girl colored. "I ... I'm sorry, Mr. Sloan."

"Okay. Miss Suzy Carr, Mt. Pleasant Avenue, Newark, New Jersey. Darling, out of town for big game, keep the home fires burning, may need the heat to grill the steak I'm bringing back. Harry. No, wait a minute. Better make that—love, Harry. That's all."

He went downstairs, caught a cab and fifteen minutes later was in Forest Hill, where Camilla was awaiting him.

Her house was a tomb-like pile of brick and marble, built by old Piet Schuyler in his heyday. It was solid, substantial and would last forever, worse luck. It looked as if in it were interred all the hopes of subsequent generations of Schuylers.

Camilla was pale. She led him into the high-ceilinged drawing room and after she closed the doors, her first question was: "You saw him?"

"I saw him."

"Well?"

"Why didn't you tell me he was a hophead?"

"Is that the kind of thing you go around telling people?" she asked bitterly. "Should I say, My husband takes dope."

"You might have told me so I'd have known what to expect."

"I'm sorry. So you guessed."

"I didn't guess. I could *see* it."

She made a small gesture that meant nothing. She was a very subdued Camilla.

"All right," she said. That didn't mean anything either. She was waiting.

"How long has he been on it?" Harry demanded.

"What difference does it make?"

"It makes a hell of a lot of difference. I want to know how far gone he is."

"Oh."

She walked over to the veined marble fireplace that had a mantle two feet higher than her head. "Years and years and years. It started he told me, during the time he was recovering from a broken back after a plane crash in '32. He was in great pain, he said, and they gave him cocaine.

I don't believe it, though. I think he's just dope prone, the way some people are accident prone. He was really quite decent when I married him, however. It's been only during the past few years that he's become so awful."

"Why don't you have him put away. You could do it."

"In case it hasn't occurred to you, my pet," she said frostily, "the Schuylers just don't happen to care to have members of the family put away as dope addicts."

He could see that she was still lying to him. No, not lying. Evading. Lying and evading. But he knew how to get at her.

"He told me," he said deliberately, "that *you* were nuts, that you were very clever about it and kept it out of sight, but every once in awhile you went up to a room on the third floor, locked yourself in, and something very funny went on."

She clenched the side of the fireplace. "He told you what?" she cried shrilly.

Harry shrugged. "Who believes a hophead?"

"No, no. I want to show you, I want to prove to you ... the third floor. Come with me. I'll show you that room on the third floor."

"Relax, baby." Then he repeated significantly, "*Who believes a hophead?*"

"No, no, no, I want to show you!" She seized his hand and took him across the room and out into the marble hall that arched to the roof, three floors above their heads. A stained glass skylight dismally lighted the stairs. "It's true that I do lock myself away up there, but I won't let him make something horrible out of it. I want you to see. I want to prove to you!"

Harry whistled. She was in a state, all right. They climbed to the third floor. She threw open the door to a bright, sunny room. "There! This is the room!"

It was a nursery. Not a nursery for a modern child, for the toys and dolls scattered around the room were all period pieces, toys of children who had grown and had children of their own. Some of the toys were a hundred years old, or older. A toy fire engine of a type that hadn't been used since men stopped dragging them through the streets with their own muscles, a toy Conestoga wagon, complete even to the broad iron rims on the wheels.

Barely audibly, Camilla said, "Some of these toys were my mother's, and some were my grandmother's. This was my room when I was a child. No one has used it since. When I come up here, I do lock myself away, I shut out the world. There's peace here." Then tonelessly, she asked, "Do you really think I have a yearning to die, Harry?"

He was gaping at the toys. He hadn't expected anything like this. A place with a little bar, a place for some private drinking maybe, but nothing like this.

"Huh?" he said.

"Nothing, Harry. This is the room, however."

"So, just as I told you," he said. *"Who believes a hophead?"* He hammered that home again.

It was out of her averted silence that he plucked the clue—the final piece of the puzzle that made it a complete picture. She wasn't crazy, as LaFarge had said, she wasn't nuts. Okay. He had never believed that part of it anyway. The truth came when you turned it the other way around.

LaFarge was crazy. Of course. All the things he had said, and the way he had said them. LaFarge had been describing himself and laughing at Harry when he did it. What were his exact words? Harry had a good memory.

I doubt that you could get her certified, anyway. She's very clever at it. You have to live with her quite awhile before you realize it. It comes as quite a shock. Absolutely and utterly crazy. You wouldn't believe it.

The sly cunning of the madman putting something over on the world of the sane. *I doubt that you could get her certified.* What LaFarge had really been saying was, "They can't get me certified." And immediately after that, *she's very clever at it.* He had been boasting, "I'm too clever for you."

Harry did not build this step by step. His mind took shortcuts, but he knew it just as certainly.

LaFarge was not only a hophead, but his brains were loose in the bargain. Of course, the two went hand in hand, but they didn't usually hang around that long.

And Camilla knew it, too.

So, it all came down to the fact that, looney or not, LaFarge had something on her.

"What does he have on you?" Harry said suddenly.

She stood rigid, her head turned away. "I'll never tell you," she said. "I've never told anyone. I didn't tell *him,* but he knew. I don't know how he knew, but he knew!"

"Are there any proofs?"

"There couldn't be."

"Then it's just his word against yours."

"Yes," her face was sunken and bitter. "But if anyone looked in my face and asked me and I denied it, they'd see that I was lying."

"It sounds rough."

"It was something ... horrible. Worse than I let you think the other night. Different than I tried to lead you to believe. And I'll never tell you what it is, my friend. I don't trust you that far."

"Why don't you have him picked up and locked away before he knows what happened to him? It can be done."

"Oh, you fool!" she cried piteously. "Don't you see, if I had that done, and he talked, people would know."

"Well," he put his forefinger under her chin, tilted up her white face and kissed her, "you can stop worrying. I've got it all figured out."

She cried, "Harry!" and clutched his lapels. She was trembling. "How? How?"

"And the beauty of it," he said, "is that *you* won't even figure in it."

Her face darkened. "I won't have him hurt, remember that!"

"Okay. He won't be hurt. But why are you so worried?"

She shivered. "I ... can't tell you," she whispered.

"That's your business," he pretended no interest, but he knew he would get it out of her sooner or later. "But to get back to this other business. The cops'll take care of everything."

"The police?"

"Hold your stuff, lady." He put his arm around her. "LaFarge won't even know what hit him." He glanced into the nursery. "Let's get out of this kindergarten and go someplace we can talk. I stopped playing with dolls so long ago that I've started playing with them all over again." He grinned and tightened his arm.

Sometimes, the way she regained her composure disgruntled him. Just when he thought he had her going, she snapped back.

"Well, well, well," she said coolly. "The old how's-about-it-kid technique of yours, I believe. But all right. We'll go downstairs. This," her voice saddened, "this really isn't the place to talk."

She took him down to the second floor, hesitated, then led him to a small sitting room in the south wing of the house. It adjoined a bedroom, and he could see the canopied bed through the open door between. Camilla went to a mahogany Sheraton cupboard, took out a decanter and two glasses, then crossed the room and lay in the chaise longue.

"Sit here," she said, making room with her knees. "Do you like bourbon?"

"Mother's milk," said Harry, grinning.

She gave him a brimming glass. "Now tell me about your scheme."

She drew up her leg to give him more room and her skirt fell away, showing the white slenderness of her thigh, striped by an emerald garter that ran elusively from her stocking.

"Dammit, tell me!" she cried urgently.

"Sure," he said quietly. "You know the D. A.'s promoting a divorce mill investigation, don't you?"

"Yes, but what of it?"

"That's the wedge, baby, that's the wedge. LaFarge brought it up himself this afternoon. The next time, I put it to him, see?"

"No, I don't see."

"Wait, can't you?" he said irritably. "Damn women anyway. They can't wait till you finish. Now shut up for a while. So, as I said, the D. A.'s investigation is the wedge. Now I can tell LaFarge that it would be better not to pull that phony hotel raid in Jersey, but I got him fixed up in a hotel just across the north Jersey line in New York. He'll drive the dame up, of course, register, and so forth. Now do you get it?"

"No," she said.

He grinned. "I thought you'd get that one. That's wedge number two. He drives the dame across the state line and registers in the hotel under a phony name. Now you see where he's put himself. Right in line for prosecution under the Mann Act—transporting a female across a state line for immoral purposes."

"Oh God!" she said scathingly. "I thought you said ..."

"Hold your stuff," he grinned. "That's only the beginning, the wedge. That dame's going to be full of hop before she leaves Newark. She won't know where she got it, but I'll fix it so that she thinks LaFarge gave it to her in a drink, or something."

Now he had her attention. "So?" she said tensely, hanging on his words.

His hand moved to the neckline of her blouse. Slowly he began unbuttoning it.

"Also," he said, "I'm going to spend about five hundred bucks that you're going to give me, and buy a nice big bottle of cheap hop. It doesn't make any difference what is as long as it can be identified as hop. It can be diluted all to hell, but it won't make any difference. As far as the cops are concerned, it's hop."

She was breathing very shallowly, her eyes fastened on his lips, fascinated.

"Now something very mysterious happens," Harry said softly. "The cops are tipped off that a guy in this hotel has brought in a dame for immoral purposes, the good old Mann Act, and believe me, there's nothing quite like a hick cop to put the boots to a stranger. To wit, LaFarge. So, when they bust in, they find this dame coked to the eyes. These days, even a hick cop knows a coke job when he sees it. So they go through LaFarge's luggage and what do they find but this bottle of cheap hop I mentioned a while ago. Now they've got something, and don't think they won't squeeze it."

Camilla did not even notice what Harry was doing to her blouse. Her chest rose and fell and her breasts lifted with each breath, but she could not seem to take her eyes from Harry's mouth.

"Okay," he said. "Now they've got LaFarge and this dame in the caboose. This dame is clean, by the way. She hasn't got a record."

He pushed her blouse back from her bare shoulders. He leaned forward and kissed her lightly in the hollow of her throat. She moaned, then tangled her fingers in his hair and thrust him away. He grinned.

"Now," he picked up the story, "the dame comes out from under the hop. Where'd she get it, they ask her. She doesn't know. They show her this bottle they found in LaFarge's luggage and ask her if LaFarge gave her a sniff. No, she says ... then she begins to remember that he's been giving her some drinks. And there it is. As far as the cops are concerned, he's been slipping it to her in the drinks. Now they've got him on three counts—violation of the Mann Act, illegal possession of narcotics, and they've got him as a 'pusher' because he slipped some to the dame. There may be another count there some place because he gave it to her without her consent or against her conscious will or something. That's the blueprint. They'll put him away for so long that kids'll be making atomic bombs in the back yard out of mud by the time he gets out. He'll scream, but nobody'll pay any attention to him. He'll accuse everybody of everything, and nobody'll even listen. It's just what I've been saying, baby—*who believes a hophead?* Especially when they've put the arm on him."

Camilla moved her mouth. "This girl," she said finally. "What becomes of her?"

"Nothing becomes of her. She's an innocent victim of a hophead. They let her go."

"But ... but ..." words were coming to her with difficulty. "Suppose he suspects something, Harry?"

"How can he suspect anything? He won't know what's going on till the cops walk in and grab him."

"He'll do something horrible to that girl!"

"Nuts. He's got a yen for her. Hell, he even asked me for her picture before he walked out of the office this afternoon."

"Her picture?" Camilla moistened her lips. "That's very odd. He's never shown any interest in women before. Are you sure he *asked* for it?"

"Hell yes."

"Harry, he's planning something. He's not interested in women. I know. I've been married to him. He's plotting something ghastly. You don't know him. You haven't seen him in his bad moments. He's ...

diabolical!"

Harry remembered the glittering look of hate LaFarge had given him, the even voice saying, *It would give me the greatest pleasure to cut your throat—slowly.* LaFarge had meant that, every word. Harry remembered the lithe, sinewy, mink-like swiftness with which LaFarge had left the office.

"What's the matter with you?" Harry asked uneasily. "Are you trying to throw a monkey wrench in the works? Nothing's going to happen to anybody. In fact, I'll slip LaFarge some hop before he leaves Newark, and by the time he gets across the line into New York, he'll have a skinful and be out of this world. He'll be like a lamb when the cops grab him off."

Camilla looked at him, her eyes enormous. "You know," she said with a trace of her former brittle manner, "you're really quite a monster, aren't you?"

"And you hate it." He leered at her.

"Yes, I hate it!" Her voice fell away. "But there's nothing I can do about it. I'm a monster, too."

Harry's face congested. "What the hell goes on here?" he said savagely. "I'm a monster and you're a monster. What are we supposed to do about it? Lay ourselves down in a crossroads at midnight and let them drive stakes through us? Come on, baby, snap out of it!"

He grasped her blouse and ripped it away. Her body arched.

She cried, "Harry! Oh Harry! Now, now, now!"

She stabbed her lips to his. She moved her head as if in pain. She taloned her fingers into the small of his back, taking fierce joy in the resistance of his thick muscles. She felt the breath rush out of her when his arms tightened around her. She felt herself lifted and carried. She cried out for him. They were swept to a height that transcended even the dizzying peaks they had mounted before. They were shaken by a turbulence neither of them had ever dreamed possible.

Their emotions mingled and crashed, one following so quickly after the other that it was a succession of mounting shock until it crested the tidal wave that suddenly engulfed them in a burst of incandescent brilliance that seemed almost beyond bearing.

A darkness flowed over them, and it was deeper than exhaustion.

COMPROMISING SITUATIONS!
CHAPTER NINE

They sat side by side, each with a glass of bourbon. The decanter stood on the night table at Harry's elbow. He tossed off the drink he was holding and poured himself another.

"It's a funny thing," he said reflectively, "but I never appreciated this stuff before."

Camilla's eyes glinted with amusement. "You know," she said, "you'd make a magnificent rummy, my pet."

"What kind of a crack is that?"

"It was a compliment, really."

"The hell it was. When you start talking about rummies, you're not complimenting anybody."

"Don't be such a peasant, my friend. I merely meant that if you started drinking, your toots would be something really historic. Or perhaps not," she added thoughtfully. "You're really quite wily. And you've a positively ruthless mania for the survival of the fittest. Meaning yourself, of course. No, I've changed my mind. Your drinking would be very secretive."

Harry was too full of the after-languor of love to let anything bother him for very long. "Go ahead, insult me," he said generously. "But don't forget that I'm the chum that's getting you out of your jam with LaFarge."

"Surely you don't expect gratitude."

"I wouldn't know what to do with it."

"But you're expecting something. What is it?"

He held up his glass to the light and turned it slowly, looking at the gold in the heart of the bourbon. His expression was smug. "I've been thinking of getting married," he said.

"Indeed! That's a novel idea—for you. And just who is the girl? Or should I say victim?"

"You," he grinned.

Her first impulse was to laugh in his face, but it was followed so quickly by anger that her eyes blazed. She was debased, she knew she was debased, but she wasn't *that* debased. It was absolutely absurd!

But just as quickly, the anger and surge of high Schuyler pride died in her eyes and rotted there. She had this coming. This was judgment, this was her sentence and her punishment. This was retribution. First there had been the obvious horrors of LaFarge, and now would come the more subtle horrors of being married to Harry Sloan—and all the dark torment that had gone before and that lay ahead. It was only through suffering that she would be able to mitigate the self-loathing that came with the remembering. She almost welcomed it.

"Yes," she cried, "we'll be married!"

His jaw dropped. He hadn't expected it to be as easy as this, and he had been prepared to do a little threatening, to let her know who held the whip hand now.

But on the other hand, why shouldn't she want to marry him? He was a good-looking guy, wasn't he? A helluva lot better looking than LaFarge had ever been. And he had shown her what a *man* could do, too, hadn't he? He was willing to bet she'd never had a real *man* before in her life. She had never gotten anything from LaFarge, and that was a cinch. Yessir, she could do a helluva lot worse than marrying one Harry Sloan.

"You and me, baby," he said, "we'll go places. But we won't live in this dump. It gives me the creeps. We'll sell it to an undertaker or somebody. We'll move into a place with some style."

"A love nest," cried Camilla with a glittering smile. "And perhaps we can have it decorated by Sam Goldwyn or the Warner Brothers. Or perhaps Boris Karloff."

"Huh?"

"Nothing, my pet, nothing. I was just making plans for our post-nuptial bliss. Isn't it a pity that we can't become formally engaged so we could have parties and receptions and everybody would gather around and congratulate the bride-to-be. A party for hundreds at the Roney Plaza in Miami Beach, champagne and expensive gifts, and all the girls standing around, green with envy. I've always loved being engaged. You live in such an improbable Never-Never Land. That means a lot to a girl, my pet. It gives her something to look back on," and somberly she added, "later."

"Yeah? Well, we got to get rid of LaFarge first. It's settled now. Right?"

"Right," said Camilla hopelessly

"You're not going to change your mind now."

"No, I'm not going to change my mind."

"You don't look too damn happy about it, if you ask me."

"But I am. Madly. See?" She gave him another glittering smile.

Satisfied, Harry poured himself another drink. "You know," he said, "I've been thinking."

"Please don't. Something horrible always comes out of it."

"Now wait a minute ..."

"What were you thinking, my pet?"

"Well," he scowled, "I'm taking a couple days off, so why don't we take a plane down to Miami or someplace, just you and me. We could have some fun. What do you say?"

"No."

"Why not?"

"Because it's not necessary. And furthermore, I want this business with LaFarge settled as quickly as possible. How much *fun* do you think I'd be able to have in Miami, or anywhere else for that matter, with this hanging over my head? No, my friend," she said flatly, "you're going to go to work on that, and you're going to go to work on it immediately. There are details that need your very adroit attention, if I'm not mistaken."

"I guess you're right," Harry agreed.

Taking time out had only been an impulse. He'd wanted to go down to Saxony and loll in fantastic luxury, but what the hell, she was right. The main thing was to get LaFarge out of the way. Then everybody would breathe easier.

"Tell you what," he said. "Suppose we set the date for Saturday. That'll give me a couple days to get things set, papers signed and all that. We won't have any trouble getting him to go on Saturday, will we?"

"No. He'll go. You might pour me a drink, you know."

"Sure. Anything else you want?"

"Oh for Pete's sake, give me a drink, will you!"

Grinning, he poured her drink and as he was setting the decanter back on the night table, there was a slight cough from the doorway.

His head swivelled. Camilla froze, and her eyes distended. LaFarge was leaning there.

"Charming, charming," he murmured. "Had you noticed my wife's *décolletage*, Mr. Sloan? If not, let me point it out to you. In some lights it really approaches a work of art."

Camilla snatched for the nylon robe on the chair beside the divan and covered herself. LaFarge smiled.

"Dreadfully sorry to have interrupted your *tête-a-tête*, old girl," he said. "But I seem to be low in funds. I squandered my last penny on something or other that quite seems to have slipped my mind. Let me have a check, will you? So sorry to have interrupted your romp with Mr. Sloan."

Harry recovered from his stunned surprise and leaped from the bed with a growl, swinging. LaFarge went down and lay still. Camilla screamed.

Harry turned, stammering, "But I ... I ..."

Her face was sick. "You hit him," she whispered. "You hurt him." Her shaking hands clenched. "Get out of here!" she cried hysterically, "Get out, get out, get out! I told you that you weren't to hurt him, I told you. Get out, get out!"

Harry yelled back at her. "Shut up, will you? I never touched him. He's faking. Look at him."

LaFarge was lying on his side, his arm propped on his elbow, his head resting on his hand. He was laughing softly.

"I'm not quite a fool, you know," he said. "Why should I have remained standing and let Mr. Sloan hit me? That would be silly, wouldn't it? Calm yourself, dear Camilla. I assure you that Mr. Sloan's fist missed me by at least two feet."

Camilla whimpered and covered her face with her hands. LaFarge regarded her brightly, his head cocked to one side.

"I wonder, Mr. Sloan," he said, "if you noticed my wife's quite pathological reaction when she thought you had struck me. The normal thing would have been for her to *urge* you to beat me to a pulp, for I did make myself quite objectionable, didn't I? Quite intentional, I assure you. But don't you think it odd, Mr. Sloan, that my wife should have such a morbid horror of the infliction of pain? Strange, isn't it?"

Camilla cried piteously, "LaFarge!"

LaFarge went on as if he had not heard her. "Oh, there's something in back of it all right, Mr. Sloan," he said sweetly. "Hasn't she told you of it? All things considered, I really think you have a right to know …"

Camilla moaned, "You promised, you promised …"

"Oh dear, so I did. What a bore. Sorry, Mr. Sloan, but I can't tell you. Can't break a promise, y'know. And now may I have that check, darling? I really have to go."

Camilla tottered to the Sheraton writing desk at the window and scribbled out a check. LaFarge lounged to his feet. He looked mockingly into Harry's lowering face.

He took the check and walked out, humming.

Camilla watched him go. She stood like stone. Her eyes turned to Harry.

"Saturday," she said, "Saturday without fail. Promise me!"

"You're not kidding," he growled.

DRUNKEN EMOTIONS!
CHAPTER TEN

Suzy got Harry's telegram at four o'clock, shortly after Joe left her apartment. Her hands trembled a little as she opened it. Telegrams meant bad news. She read it.

"Darling, out of town for big game, keep the home fires burning, may need the heat to grill the steak I'm bringing back, love, Harry."

She read it again, her heart lifting. This was something new. *Out of town for big game* ... Things were beginning to break for Harry at last. Now he had three irons in the fire—Frawley, that LaFarge-Schuyler woman, and now this new thing. If only he had given her a hint of what it might be, just a hint. Maybe somebody wanted his advice about the formation of a new company, or maybe it was an offer from somebody like Western Electric or General Motors. Suzy danced around the room, singing.

There was a knock, the door opened and a dark girl with tousled red hair poked her head into the room. She lived down the hall.

"Hey, Suzy," she called, "want to take a break and come to a party?"

"Sure!" She was ready for a party. She wanted to celebrate. "What kind of party?"

"Oh, you know. A couple kids dropped in, then some more, and the first thing we knew it was a party. Come on down."

"Give me a minute to get into some clothes."

The redhead eyed the playsuit Suzy was wearing. "Come as you are," she advised. "If I had legs like yours, I'd never wear anything but a G-string, believe me. And say, you should see tall-freckled-and-homely that we picked up in the hall on account of we needed some men. I swoon! I get the quivers all over every time he looks at me. What a hunk of man! Compared to him, Van Johnson is a back number. But I have to run now on account of some dizzy blonde might grab him off while I'm gone. See ya in a couple minutes, keed."

She was gone.

Suzy ran into the bedroom, stripping off her playsuit. She felt light-headed and gay and blithe as a flying bird. For a moment she stood and looked at her wonderful sun-tanned body in the full length mirror—the long, intoxicating thighs, the high breasts. She was glad she had a body she was proud of. She was glad to be able to bring such a body to Harry.

She dressed quickly. She wanted the sound of laughter around her, the sound of music, people dancing. She was in a high mood. But before she skipped out of the apartment, she picked up Harry's telegram and read it again. She kissed it and whispered, "All the luck in the world, darling!" Then she propped it against Harry's picture on the radio and ran out into the hall.

Though the apartment house was reasonably soundproof, she could hear the swing of the music the minute she stepped into the corridor. She didn't have to stop to listen. Nobody played a trumpet like that but Louis Armstrong. She didn't knock when she came to the apartment of the party. No one would have heard her, anyway. She opened the door and walked in, calling:

"Anybody home?"

The redhead was dancing and she waved. "Hiya, Suzy. Hey, somebody pour Suzy a drink."

The man she was dancing with turned his head and grinned. It was Joe. He winked. A bulky young man with football shoulders loomed. He took Suzy possessively by the arm.

"You're mine," he announced. "I saw you first and you're all mine. If anybody else wants you, he'll have to fight me for it."

"I can hardly wait," Suzy smiled.

"Now what'll you have to drink? We've got rye in bottles and rye in glasses. Which way will you have it?"

"In a glass, please."

"Yez go!"

He lowered his head and plowed through the dancers, yelling, "Gangway," and hauling Suzy after him into the kitchen. There was the usual kitchen group in there—two couples very seriously trying to harmonize. That is, *all* of them were harmonizing and no one was singing the melody, which made it a little difficult to know just what it was they were trying to sing. And over by the window were two men, clutching glasses, buried in the usual profound discussion, which would keep them happy for hours. Of course, their girl friends or wives would be in the other room, either fuming or having the time of their lives, depending on whether or not they had been able to pirate a man.

The bulky young man maneuvered Suzy over to the sink, where the bottles of liquor and soda were standing.

"I'm Mush," he said. "Who're you?"

"Suzy."

"Suzy, Suzy, quite contruzy, heh, heh, heh. I hope not. Okay, here's the rye," he picked up the bottle and splashed a generous amount into two glasses. It was obvious that he'd been here before. He handed Suzy one of the glasses and raised the other. "Happy days," he said.

Thinking of Harry, Suzy echoed gladly, "Happy days!" Unconsciously imitating Mush, she drank it off in one happy gulp.

Mush set down his glass, rubbing his hands together.

"That'll do for a starter," he said, "but if we're going to do any serious drinking, we've got to have something we can carry around with us from place to place, something in a glass. Now how'll you have yours—we've got soda, light ginger ale, dark ginger ale, Tom Collins mix, and strawberry soda."

Suzy was glowing, partially from the rye, it was true, but more from exaltation.

"Let me see," she said, pretending to consider. "I don't want to make any mistakes. I think I'll have dark ginger ale and squeeze some lemon juice into it."

Mush chanted, "The lady wants dark ginger ale with lemon juice," and reached for the bottles.

He was evidently an accomplished lush, for he managed to sneak himself two fast straights as he was mixing the drinks. Suzy's thoughts were soaring out to Harry, and she did not notice that Mush poured a good five ounces of rye over the cracked ice in the glass, sprinkled it with ginger ale, and deftly squeezed the juice of a quarter lemon into it. He stirred it with a spoon. The glass frosted. He handed it to her.

"You're delicious, you're delightful, you're delirious," he said. "Taste it and tell me if it needs any more ice."

Suzy sipped. It was rather like a whiskey sour. Tart. She liked it tart. "Ummmmm, good."

"Praise de Lawd. Now I'll mix myself one."

He had another straight. He really didn't want a girl. All he wanted to do was drink, but he had to have someone to stand next to the bottles with him. Later in the party, he would not be so self-conscious. He propped himself comfortably against the sink and began to tell Suzy about all the cocktails he knew how to mix, the innumerable kinds of liquor he had drunk and how to tell a good rye from a bad rye by reading the label on the back of the bottle.

But Suzy didn't care what he talked about. It was a party and she was happy. She could see the couples dancing in the other room and she could hear the music and all the voices. She didn't care if she didn't dance. It was Harry she wanted to dance with and as he wasn't here, she'd just as soon go on listening to Mush's earnest voice explain the art of drinking a Swiss Lick.

"It's like this," he told her, "you hold a quarter lemon in your right, no, left hand and you sprinkle salt on the back of the same hand. You take your gin in your right hand. Then …" he paused dramatically, "you lick the salt, drink the gin and suck the lemon! Here, I'll show you. I'll be using rye instead of gin, but you'll be able to get the idea."

He showed her.

Some time later when Suzy had practically finished her drink, he was illustrating the esoteric movements necessary in shaking a Puerto Rican Bomba cocktail, and his flailing elbow knocked the glass from her hand to the floor. He gave a cry of anguish.

"Jeez, I'm sorry, toots. I can't tell you how sorry I am. Honest, I'm sorry. That's something I hate to do, spill a drink. I'd rather give it away, or have somebody steal it, than spill it. I hate to see good liquor go to waste. I apologize. I'll make you another one right away."

Suzy was floating just a little. Never before had she drunk this much liquor so quickly. But she didn't feel drunk. She felt gloriously happy. Gloriously, but quietly, inside herself. New vistas of rosy thoughts, as wide as prairies, had been opened before her. It was wonderful just to stand there and think thoughts. The thoughts did not have form, nor did they have much coherence, but they were so wonderfully rosy, and they all had to do with Harry, and that was the wonderful part of it, to be able to stand there without any effort and think all these wonderful thoughts about Harry and how wonderful everything was going to be.

She hardly noticed Mush busily mixing her another drink and sneaking himself fast straights at every turn. Then the fresh glass was put in her hand and she sipped it. Then Joe appeared.

She gave him an angelic smile and said, "Hello, Joe. How'd you get here?"

"We-ll, I'll tell you," he said. "When I left you, I felt a strong need to be depressed. Then when they asked me to this party, I came because there's nothing, absolutely nothing as thoroughly depressing as a souse party. Shall we dance?"

"I'm Mush," said Mush belligerently.

Joe looked at him thoughtfully, then poked Mush's bulging middle with a clinical forefinger.

"No," he said, "you're not mush yet, but soon."

"That's my girl, and if you want her, you'll have to fight me for her."

"I don't feel like fighting, Mush, but I'll do something better."

"What's that?"

"I'll let you make me a drink."

"*Amigo!*" cried Mush. He turned joyfully to the bottle.

Joe led Suzy into the other room.

"You look higher than a kite," he said as they danced.

"I am." She laughed softly.

"Are you drunk?"

"Of course not. Have you ever known me to get drunk, Joe?"

"We-ll ... but that guy in the kitchen looked like a double-handed drink-spiker from way back. You sure you're okay?"

"Of course I'm sure, Joe. Don't be silly."

"I don't want you to go on this date with Frawley tonight if you're potted."

Suzy giggled, then said very rapidly, "Peter Piper picked a peck of pickled peppers if Peter Piper picked a peck of pickled peppers where's the peck of pickled peppers Peter Piper picked? How's that?"

Joe was silent. He was not convinced, but on the other hand she walked okay and she talked okay. Maybe she was okay.

The small apartment was crowded, and dancing was hardly more than a slow intimate shuffle, and it wasn't made any easier by the four swing fans who sat on the floor in front of the gramophone, solemnly telling each other that no matter what you said there was nobody like Armstrong, nobody. From the kitchen, the singing had become recognizable as either the Cornell alma mater song or *Just Before the Battle Mother*, and Mush had found another bottle friend, for whom he was enthusiastically mixing a drink.

"Having a good time, Suzy?" Joe asked suddenly.

"Mmmmmmmmmmm."

"Then give Frawley a ring and tell him you can't make it. This party'll go on all night. I know the signs. You can go right on having a wonderful time."

"Uh-uh."

"Have it your own way."

"What time is it, Joe?"

"Five ... twenty-five exactly."

"Good heavens, my date is at six. I have to run; see you later ..."

She was out of his arms and squirming through the crowd of dancers before he could blink. She ran down the hall, reaching up her back for her dress zipper.

She was showered and dressed by five minutes to six. She'd have made it by quarter of six, but her fingers had been just a little inclined to fumble, and once or twice she had stood perplexed in the middle of the bathroom, wondering what she had come in for. But she didn't think of this as being drunk. She didn't think of it at all.

Frawley arrived promptly at six with a box of candy under his arm. "Oh thank you," said Suzy. "Schraffts. How wonderful. I love Schraffts. See your flowers? Aren't they wonderful?"

Frawley said, "Yeah," not taking his eyes off her. "You look kind of nice yourself. But, uh, I hope you don't mind my saying this, but you're kind of undone on the side."

Suzy looked down, she had not pulled up the zipper, and the gap revealed a satiny gleam of skin between the top of her panties and her brassiere. She laughed merrily and zipped it.

"Would you care for a drink before we go, Mr. Frawley?" she asked brightly.

"Well say now, that sounds good. Yessir. I could do with a drink, to tell you the truth."

"Well, you sit right down and I'll make it in a jiffy. I know all about making drinks. I was told all about it this afternoon."

She floated into the kitchen. Two glasses, that was right. Now what came next? An ice cube. She hesitated with the Scotch poised over the glasses. What was it Mush said was the perfect drink—three fingers or three inches? She held up three slim fingers and shook her head. That couldn't be right. That would be hardly anything in these tall glasses. She poured in three inches of Scotch—though it turned out to be four because it was very hard to judge unless you crunched down. She had a bottle of soda, and Mush had told her about that, too.

You use, he had said, exactly twice the amount of whiskey as you do soda. He had been very emphatic about that.

Suzy poured about an inch of soda over the four inches of Scotch and floated back into the living room, where Frawley was sitting carefully on the edge of the sofa.

She looked at him and suddenly discovered, to her delight, that he was really very nice, the flowers and candy and all, and sitting there being a perfect gentleman and not making passes the way Joe had said. She suddenly discovered that she was really quite fond of Mr. Frawley. And, of course, all the things he was going to do for Harry with that company and all. But he was just naturally nice, anyway.

She gave him his glass with a smile and perched herself on the arm of the sofa.

"Happy days," she said, the way Mush had said it, raising her glass.

Frawley said, "Happy days," and took a deep swallow. He blinked in surprise and looked at the liquor in his glass. "Say," he said, "that's a real drink."

"Oh yes," she said. "I used real Scotch." Then conversationally, "Have you been doing much drinking these days, Mr. Frawley?"

His eyes narrowed. "Not very," he said shortly.

"I was told all about it this afternoon. It was very interesting ... whoops!" She had been teetering on the arm of the sofa, and, had she not thrown up her leg for balance, she would have toppled off.

Her skirt slipped up, but she made no move to pull it down again. Her thigh gleamed, the silken tan of it excitingly rounded against the thin white line of her garter. Frawley could not take his eyes from it. He tried not to stare. He tried looking across the room at the radio, at the doorknob, at the picture on the wall, but each time his eyes were dragged back to that six inches of thigh above her stocking top. Vainly he tried to keep from thinking of how she had looked yesterday in that hotel room in just her panties and brassiere, and how she had looked when she moved, and of the excitement there had been in her.

Dammit, if she doesn't want me to make a pass at her, why doesn't she pull her dress down, he thought almost angrily—angrily because he was wary about making a pass. So early in the evening.

He said gruffly, "Uh, suppose we polish off our drinks and get going, okay?"

"Root, snoot." She had heard Joe say that. She wondered if it meant, Right, snite. But that didn't sound right either.

She had two thirds of her drink left, and she drank it down without taking the glass from her lips. She jumped down from the arm of the sofa, and his eyes leaped for the last fleeting glimpse of her thigh.

She could walk straight, she could stand without swaying, she didn't see double, and she could talk without slushing—but she was nevertheless over the edge. She was—anesthetized. Everything was wonderful.

"Shall I wear my sport coat, Mr. Frawley?" She really wanted to please him. "I mean, if we're going any place sporty, I should wear a sport coat, don't you think?"

"Sure. Tonight we'll be a couple sports. Wear your sport coat."

"I'm glad you agree, because my other coat's too warm for this time of year, and I don't like it very much, anyway, a girl friend sold it to me, she needed the money. And it is too warm this time of year, isn't it?" She couldn't seem to stop talking, and furthermore, she didn't want to. There were so many things to say, and she had to keep Mr. Frawley interested, didn't she, but he was nice.

Then they were outside the apartment, walking toward the elevator, when she remembered. She put her hand on his hand, the one that was somewhat insistently and quite unnecessarily cupping her elbow. "I'll be right back, Mr. Frawley. There's something I forgot. It's very important. Don't go 'way."

She ran back to the apartment. She walked over to the radio and looked into Harry's picture. It had a wide, expensive silver frame. It had come with a clear Lucite frame, but Suzy had substituted the silver. She smiled at the picture, then put her finger to her lips, kissed it, and touched the lips of the picture.

"The bestest and the bestest and the bestest, darling," she whispered.

She started to turn away, then spun and snatched up the telegram.

"You get one, too," she smiled. She kissed it and propped it again against the photograph.

She felt a sudden, swift wave of dizziness, and she swayed, clutching the edge of the radio. She had been moving too fast and turning too quickly. The liquor was warning her. Then it was gone.

"My goodness," she said. Then, cryptically, "At my age."

She ran out of the apartment. Her purse slapped heavily against her thigh as she ran. Joe's brass knuckles.

Frawley watched her as she came toward him, and something alien stirred within him, a flickering of tenderness. How young she looked! Her silvery blonde hair was in slight disarray, her eyes were shining, and she was smiling. A kind of eternal adolescence ... But it was an alien thought, and Frawley got rid of it. He didn't approve of aliens in the first place.

As Suzy pushed the button for the elevator, she told him, "We only have a self-service elevator here, but it's better for people to do things for themselves, anyway, don't you think? On their own initiative. Self-service elevators, and you can stop where you want, on any floor, just by pushing a button. I used to do that. Do you think it's coming? Sometimes it doesn't work at all."

It worked.

Frawley's car was parked out front. It was a black Ford coupe he had hired from the U-Drive. He had enough money so that he could afford not to hire a Cadillac. His hands were a little more than assisting when he helped her in.

"And now, young lady," he said jovially as he slid in behind the wheel, "is there any place you want to go specially to eat, or do you want to take pot luck?"

He put his hand paternally on her knee and gave it a fatherly squeeze.

"Mario's," said Suzy. "I want to go to Mario's. And have spaghetti, French bread and red wine. They've got candles in bottles on the table." And her voice lifted as she thought of all the times Harry had taken her to Mario's for spaghetti, French bread and red wine. It was at Mario's, in the parking lot, that Harry had first told her he loved her. She had been a little in awe of him then, so handsome *and* a lawyer. *I'm nuts about you, baby*, he had said, *how about it?* She remembered how the inexplicable tears had come into her eyes, because she had been in love with him for exactly twenty-three days. *I love you, too*, she had said. She remembered how she had risen to his kiss, and the sweet, unbelievable delirium that followed.

But Frawley was saying something to her, and she turned and gave him a glowing, inquiring smile.

"Mario's?" he was saying. "You want to go to Mario's?"

"I want to go to Mario's and have candles in bottles on the table!"

"Uh, which Mario's do you mean?"

"The one on River Road."

Frawley shook his head. He couldn't understand it. Here this girl could have asked him to take her to dinner at the Stork Club, and he would have done it, too. But where does she want to go? The cheapest, crummiest, darkest little spaghetti joint on the Passaic River!

"Now look, uh," he started uneasily, "it's up to you, of course, but wouldn't you like to go to a place where they, uh, have some music?"

"Oh, they have music at Mario's. The most wonderful juke box in the world."

"I didn't, uh, mean that. I meant orchestra. Know what I mean?"

"But a juke box plays orchestras, doesn't it?" Then, pleadingly, "Take me to Mario's. I want to go to Mario's. I want spaghetti and French bread and red wine and candles in bottles on the table and *Smoke Gets In Your Eyes* on the juke box. Please."

Frawley did the only manly thing left to him. He said heartily, "You're the boss, little lady," and flipped the old, prostituted Ford into low gear.

Before he headed for Mario's, however, he drove downtown to the huge Garden State Liquor Shoppe and bought himself a bottle of rare old Royal Henry V Scotch, that set him back exactly sixteen dollars and forty-nine cents. (Special This Week Only.) Then he turned the car toward Mario's.

As the familiar streets fled past, Suzy let her head rest on Frawley's shoulder (as she had so often let it rest on Harry's) and happily watched the road ahead, anticipating every remembered landmark—the cemetery, the railroad bridge, the big gasoline storage tanks, the oily shine of the river after they had made the turn down past the cemetery.

Frawley dropped his hand on her leg with seeming carelessness. She did not object. He moved it a little, experimentally. He felt her stir against him and said hastily:

"I was just thinking of a little restaurant on the Prado down Cuba-way. You'd have liked that joint. Full of atmosphere. I forget what they call it now, but they had, uh, candles on the table, too."

The restaurant was entirely mythical.

Suzy smiled up at him. "You're nice," she said. "Harry's going to take me to Cuba sometime."

Frawley thought cynically, *don't kid yourself, girlie*.

Mario's parking space stretched for two vacant lots along the darkest hundred feet of river bank between Newark and Paterson. A line of tree trunks stopped even the most inebriated from driving their cars into the polluted river.

Though the parking lot was practically empty (no one with any sense dined at Mario's, unless he was broke), Frawley drove the Ford to the farthest and darkest corner.

Suzy looked up at the trees. Her whole body was now a delicious languor. A smile hovered over her lips, not quite descending. She was remembering. This was the exact spot where Harry always parked, and she wondered vaguely how Frawley had known that. But, of course, he was nice, he just naturally knew, and that was why.

She turned and kissed him on the cheek. "You're so nice," she said.

Before she could withdraw, he grabbed her with a kind of clumsy fury, ground his lips into hers. His thrusting lips mashed hers back from her teeth, and their teeth grated together. His hand became trapped in the folds of her sport coat, unable to find her. Her arms were caught between them and, without resentment, she pushed until he released her.

With detached, irrelevant serenity, she murmured, "You're nice," and felt in her purse for her lipstick and compact. Her conscious mind, the part of it untouched by the unaccustomed amount of liquor she had consumed, had wandered back in time, plucking the memories of the evenings she had spent here with Harry.

"Would you mind turning on the overhead light?" she asked. "I've got to paint the front porch, and I can't see."

Breathing heavily, he snapped on the light and watched her repair her makeup.

Okay, he was thinking, *okay, the evening's young*.

But he was puzzled and uneasy. He couldn't figure her out. Last night she had damn near killed him for laying a finger on her, and now look. And it wasn't an act, either. But maybe that was the kind of kid she was impulsive and hard to figure. At least, he thought so.

She dropped her lipstick and compact back into her bag. The compact clanked against the brass knuckles. She smiled at him.

"Ready?" she asked, as if he hadn't been sitting there waiting.

She opened her door, and as she slid from the seat, her skirt clung to the stiff mohair of the upholstery, and there was a flash of legs before she stood outside and the skirt fell again.

The blood was pounding in Frawley's temples. His whole face felt congested. He knew she wasn't deliberately exhibiting herself, but all the same, by God, a guy was only human, wasn't he?

He took the bottle of Scotch from the ledge behind the seat and turned off the lights. It was so black outside, that he had to grope to find her. He slid his hand under her upper arm.

"Now watch your step," he said. "Don't fall."

She lurched against him several times as they walked toward the yellow lights of the restaurant, but he attributed it to the unevenness of the ground. Now and again, he could feel the swell of her against the back of his hand, and he grinned secretly in the darkness.

Mario's had no *maitre d'hotel*, no head waiter. You walked in, picked out a table and sat down, and after awhile a waiter came up and disinterestedly pushed a menu at you. It was as easy as that.

Suzy sat down happily and looked at the familiar stained red-and-white checkered tablecloth.

"Play me *Smoke Gets In Your Eyes*," she said to Frawley. "And tell them I want some candles in bottles on the table. There aren't any."

Frawley went over to the juke box and peered self-consciously at the list of titles. He had never played one of these things before in his life, but he wasn't stupid and the directions were plain enough. He found *Smoke Gets In Your Eyes* and he was relieved, because he knew she wouldn't be satisfied with *Stardust*, even if it was with Artie Shaw. He looked at the money slots—nickel, dime, quarter. He dug in his pocket and looked at the change in his hand. Then, very astutely, he selected two quarters, dropped them into the machine and pressed the *Smoke Gets In Your Eyes* button ten times.

Carrying his bottle of Royal Henry V Scotch, he walked over to the linoleum-topped bar and beckoned the barkeep. He set the bottle on the bar.

"This," he said, "is what the lady and me are drinking. Tell the waiter to keep 'em coming. I don't want to have to order any drinks. We want our glasses to be full when we reach for them. And another thing. The lady wants some bottles with candles in them. She happens to like them, and I don't want any arguments. Get some candles, stick 'em in bottles and put 'em on the table, even if you have to send a cab down to the hardware store to buy 'em." He put a five dollar bill on the bar and put the bottle on top of it. "Any questions?"

The barkeep looked a little dazed, but he repeated, "Keep the drinks coming, candles in bottles on the table for the lady." The five dollar bill disappeared from under the bottle. "No questions."

Frawley marched back to the table. It always took five or six minutes for these Napoleonic moods to wear off.

The much-used juke box was playing a very tired *Smoke Gets In Your Eyes*, and Suzy was sitting at the table, wearing a vague, faraway smile. In a flash of intuition, Frawley knew he would never find her in a more acquiescent mood, and he had sense enough to sit down without making any remarks. At the moment, she was lost in the music, lost in remembrance.

A waiter came briskly from the bar, carrying two drinks on a tray, and he set the glasses before them with a flourish. He whipped two menus out from under his arm, opened one before Suzy, trotted around the table and opened the other before Frawley.

At least, thought Frawley, that five buck tip got service, if nothing else.

Suzy did not even glance at the menu. Still smiling vaguely, she ordered spaghetti, French bread and red wine.

"And candles in bottles on the table," she added, smiling up at the waiter.

"Lady," said the waiter, and threw out his arm toward the bar.

Clutching two plumber's candles and two Chianti bottles, a grinning, panting boy in faded denims came running across the floor. He laid them carefully on the table.

"Okay, lady?" he panted. "I hadda go clear up to Sweeney's."

Suzy hardly heard him. She reached out and gently inserted the pared ends of the candles into the Chianti bottles. Impulsively, Frawley gave the boy a dollar.

The waiter drew a match from his pocket and lighted the candles, with the air of a Prometheus bestowing the gift of fire on all mankind.

Suzy sat, misty-eyed, watching the candle flames restlessly twitch and dance. She had only to look into them long enough and she could see Harry's face grinning at her.

Frawley lifted his glass. "Happy days," he said.

That awakened another memory and she lifted her glass. "Happy days, Harry," she murmured. She drank.

With increasing vagueness, she ate, she drank again and again, listened to *Smoke Gets In Your Eyes* over and over and over, smiled and smiled at Frawley across the table, he was so nice, he was going to do so many wonderful things for Harry, answered questions, talked—but all with a remoteness that was practically disembodied.

Then Frawley was showing her something—a wristwatch!—and saying:

"I hate to break this up, little lady, but tempus fidgets and the curtain goes up at eight-four-five. Suppose we skip the dessert and scram while the scramming's good. We still gotta drive the Lincoln Tunnel and park when we get over to New York. So let's finish our drinks and beat it. But don't think I'm rushing you, now ... happy days."

Suzy lifted her drink. Happy days. Happy, happy, happy days! She was content just to sit and think of the happy days, but she rose dutifully to her feet when Frawley stood and dug in his hip pocket for his wallet.

She looked very lovely as she walked across the room toward the door. The light over the door was brighter than the lights inside, and the disarray of her silver blonde hair threw a glowing aura around her head. In her face was a look of innocence and eagerness, the look of brides. Her long eyes were dreamy, and the full, generous width of her mouth curled in contentment. She looked entranced.

If only the liquor had affected her legs, or her speech, or her vision, but it had affected only her mind. And her mind was out of this world, ranging in some improbable realm with an unlikely Harry. There were no sensations left in her body, and what happened to it, or what it did, meant absolutely nothing to her in that enraptured moment.

She clung to Frawley's arm and leaned heavily on him as they carefully walked the inky length of the parking lot to the car. Frawley hurried her as fast as he dared. He had been with her too long now, he had been staring at her too long and thinking too much about it. He was on fire.

The moment he closed the car door, he swept her against him and poured furious kisses into her face, her eyes, her lips, her neck—but he was holding back a little, still wary. At her first resistance, he pulled back. It was still early in the evening. He didn't want to rush things. He knew she was in a very acquiescent mood, and he didn't want to spoil it by scaring her.

But there was no resistance. She just lay limply. It was impossible to know what she was thinking anymore, her mind was so completely befuddled. If she had any reaction at all under the fury of his overeager kisses, it was faint and it could be that she was imagining herself in Harry's arms, for this was the place where she had lain in his arms.

Exulting, Frawley pushed her head against the back of the seat and found her mouth with brutal urgency. He was not making love; he was assaulting her with the long-frustrated, incoherent turbulence of his emotions. Never before had he held a really lovely girl in his arms. Never before had he made love at all. When it came to love, it had always been a short, brutal encounter, followed by a sense of having been cheated. But this time, this time it was going to be different. His shaking, overly-urgent hands ranged over her, but lingering nowhere, really taking nothing, so greedy were they to take all at once.

He lifted his head to take a panting breath—and to his horror her head fell limply over on her shoulder. In a spurt of panic, he gave her a shake. Her head bobbed and rolled as if her neck were made of rubber. The thought of liquor never crossed his mind—well, hell, they'd only had a few drinks—and she was so limp that he thought she'd had a stroke or something. Nobody got drunk this early in the evening. He shook her frantically, babbling:

"Miss Carr, Miss Carr!"

My God, what a mess it would be if he turned up with a dead girl on his hands!

A light flashed in the window and a tough voice said, "What's going on here?"

Frawley blinked up into the light. "I don't know," he bleated. "We just came out of the restaurant, got in the car and—look at her!"

The flashlight was already on Suzy. She was sprawled in the corner of the seat, breathing shallowly.

The tough voice said, "She passed out. She's potted."

"It sure looks that way, officer." Frawley felt weak under the sudden flood of relief, "But we only had a few drinks. Ask the bartender. I guess she just can't take it."

"She had a mess of drinks," the tough voice said sadly. "She was higher than a kite before you even picked her up."

"I think you're right about that, officer. I think you're absolutely right. I thought there was something. I mean, the way she acted. But I didn't have anything to do with this, officer. You can ask the bartender. All we had was a couple drinks."

Frawley did not know how much had been seen. He hadn't *done* anything when you came right down to it. Kissed her a couple times, was all. But you never knew what these cops would try to make out of it. Accuse him of getting the girl drunk for immoral purposes, or something.

He plucked hurriedly at his pocket. "We were on our way to a show in New York, officer. Look, here are the tickets. We were a little late and I wanted to get going and she passes out on me ..."

"Ah, shut up, for crisake. Move over."

Frawley slid to the middle of the seat and sat there sweating. My God, was he under arrest? In the faint light from the dashboard, all he could see of the man was a hard profile. But some cops were reasonable. If you showed them a hundred bucks or so ...

The car whirled and sped up the parking lot to the front entrance of Mario's. Frawley's eyes darted, but he couldn't find the squad car. A cab was parked there, but that was all. The man beside him slid out of the car. He was a tall freckled man in crumpled tweeds.

"Give me a hand with her over to the cab," he said shortly.

So he wasn't a cop!

"Wait a minute," said Frawley.

"Wait nothing!"

"I said wait a minute, buddy," it was Frawley's turn to sound tough.

"Who the hell do you think you are? Whattaya mean, give you a hand over to the cab? I'm not handing this poor girl over to you or anybody else. What authority do you have, anyway?"

"Look, mister, I've been aching to give you a good poke in the nose and ..." Then, wearily, "Ah, hell. Look. I'm a friend of hers. The name's Joe McBride. In case you don't recognize me, I'm the guy who took your picture last night in that hotel room. Now are you satisfied?"

"I'm satisfied that this is none of your damn business," Frawley snapped. "*I'm* taking Miss Carr home!"

"Go right ahead, mister. But I'll be right behind you all the way." Joe turned and went back to his cab.

By the time Frawley reached Suzy's apartment, he was glad enough to have Joe with him to help carry her upstairs. They laid her on the sofa, and Joe put a pillow under her head. All Frawley wanted now was out. He wanted to wash his hands of the whole business. He didn't want any more to do with it. He had been badly scared, and now the very sight of Suzy filled him with vicious dislike.

But he couldn't leave Joe there alone with her, not with her like that. No, sir. Suppose the guy took advantage of her. Who'd be blamed? Him, Frawley. And she'd have witnesses she could bring up—the waiter and the barkeep at Mario's. No, sir, he wasn't letting himself in for anything like that.

He looked at Joe and said sourly, "Well, what do we do now?"

"I don't care what you do, but I'm going to try to bring her out of it."

"Why don't you just let her sleep it off?"

"Why don't you go to hell?"

Frawley compressed his lips and looked around the apartment. He found the phone and strode over to it. He called his wife at her hotel. "Listen, Helen," he said in a low voice. "I want you to come over to this address right away. I need a witness. You'll be doing me a favor, but you'll be doing yourself a favor, too. There's something here that can turn nasty."

"Are you mixed up with a woman already, Howard?"

"I'm not mixed up with anybody. But I need a witness. Look, I don't want any arguments. If I get sued for something, that'll affect your settlement and don't forget it. Now are you coming or aren't you?"

"I shouldn't lift a finger for you, Howard Frawley ..."

"Get over here as fast as you can." Frawley gave her Suzy's address and apartment number and hung up.

He turned to find Joe regarding him with cool contempt.

"Suspicious sonuvagun, aren't you?" said Joe.

Frawley shrugged. He was indifferent to Joe's opinion of him.

"Where Harry Sloan's concerned," he said flatly, "I'm as suspicious as hell, and this girl's mixed up with Sloan. I'm not taking any chances."

"You got something there," Joe admitted. He looked worriedly at Suzy. "I wish I knew what the hell to do. We can't feed her black coffee ..."

"Wait till my wife comes. She was a registered nurse once."

Joe lit a cigarette and prowled the room. He went in Suzy's bedroom, came back with a blanket and covered her. Frawley stood at the window, scowling around a cigar.

Mrs. Frawley walked in about fifteen minutes later. She was a tall, angular woman, but there was a kind of patience in her eyes. She looked at Suzy on the sofa.

"What's the matter with her?" she asked quietly.

Frawley felt a rush of affection toward her. You could always depend on Helen. Yessir.

"She passed out—but I didn't have anything to do with it. You can ask this young man. I was just taking her out to a show, was all. That's right, isn't it, young feller?"

Joe said wearily, "She was high this afternoon. But look, Mrs. Frawley, I want to bring her out of it ..."

The woman walked over to the sofa. She felt Suzy's skin, listened to her respiration, took her pulse.

"Well," she said to Joe, "she doesn't have alcoholic poisoning, if that's what you're worried about. My advice is to let her sleep. Does she always drink herself into a stupor?"

"Never. I've never seen her drunk before."

"Then why'd she do it this time?" Mrs. Frawley was a practical woman.

"I don't know for sure," said Joe slowly, "but it's got something to do with Harry Sloan."

"Well, if you ask me, there's something wrong with a man that'll make a girl drink like that."

"You can say that again, lady!"

Frawley was feeling better. There was no doubt about it, there was nobody like Helen to get things straightened out.

"If you were such a friend of this girl's," he said to Joe, "you'd get her away from that Sloan."

Joe made a gesture of despair. "I know ..."

"He's not doing her any good," warned Frawley. Then, in a burst of honesty, he blurted, "To tell you the truth, it was Sloan who arranged for me to go out with that girl tonight. And he as good as told me over the phone I could go as far as I wanted."

Joe turned white. "You're sure of that?"

"Do you think I'd say a thing like that in front of my own wife if it wasn't true?" Frawley was as close to an unselfish act as he would ever be. "Take my advice, boy, and get her away from Sloan. He's no good." He looked at his wife. "And as far as you're concerned, Helen, I want you to withdraw your petition for divorce. Take it out of Sloan's hands. I don't want to be mixed up with him."

"Do you want me to go to Reno, Howard?" the asked evenly.

"Well," he looked down at his hands, remembering how she had come over and helped him out of this mess, remembering all the other times, remembering how comfortable and how dependable she was, and he was suddenly filled with a distaste for all young women. All he wanted to do was go home again. "Well,'" he repeated, "maybe we've been hasty. Maybe we should talk this over a little more. Oh, dammit!" his eyes were suddenly filled with tears, "do you want me to get down on my knees?"

She put her hand on his arm. "Come, Howard," she said. "Let's go home."

But before she left, she threw a blanket over Suzy and gave Joe some very crisp directions.

"If the girl gets cold and starts to sweat, and her face turns a pasty white, and she keeps gasping, call a doctor. But I'm sure you don't have anything to worry about. You'd have known before this. If she wakes up and gets sick, let her get as sick as she wants. But don't, for heaven's sake, try to pour hot black coffee into her. If anything, give her a teaspoon of bicarbonate in lukewarm water. It'll make her feel better in the morning."

"Thanks," said Joe gratefully.

Mrs. Frawley hesitated, then said in a low, swift voice, "And don't think harshly of Howard. He's not a bad man, only headstrong. He can be very generous. And I think he's had a lesson that convinced him that he's really fat, bald and fifty-five."

She turned and rejoined Frawley, who was waiting for her in the hall. He took her arm.

"I've just had an idea about a little trip, Helen," he started eagerly.

Joe closed the door. He looked at Suzy, then went over and touched her cheek. It was warm and dry. She was breathing shallowly, but evenly. Her silver blonde hair was tumbled around her face, and she looked like a very young girl sleeping there, an unkissed schoolgirl dreaming.

Something choked up in Joe's throat and he turned away angrily. It wouldn't take long for Harry Sloan to change all that. Imperceptibly, step by step, he'd make her over, muddy her essential innocence, destroy her.

But what had he done, he, himself, Joe thought with self-loathing.

What had he ever done about it? Nothing. He'd just stood around, making wisecracks and *hoping* something would turn up to open Suzy's eyes. Hoping!

He paced the floor, sucking short, angry puffs from his cigarette. He saw Harry's silver-framed photograph on the radio and he snatched it up, intending to smash it, but instead; he held it up and looked at it, noting the heavy, animal handsomeness of the face, the arrogant eyes, the sensual mouth.

"You rat," he muttered, "you lousy rat."

He put the picture back on the radio and stooped to pick up the telegram that had fluttered to the floor. As he was replacing it, his eyes caught the words, "love, Harry." His eyebrows lifted. Why should Harry send Suzy a telegram? He opened it.

"Darling—out of town for big game—keep the home fires burning—may need the heat to grill the steak I'm bringing back—love—Harry."

Joe's lips compressed. What the hell was going on? That telegram might fool a kid like Suzy, but it wouldn't fool anybody else. Out of town for big game. Who was he trying to kid? Harry was in the niche where he belonged, the cheap divorce racket. Nobody'd trust him even to draw up a bill of sale for a pack of cigarettes, and the people with the kind of law business that could be called "big game" wouldn't touch him with an asbestos pole.

But now Joe could see why Suzy had gotten high. She had swallowed this phony line and was celebrating Harry's success. Joe felt sick. He knew Suzy was in love with Harry, but he hadn't known she was so deeply in love that even the hint of a business success for Harry could send her into a state of elation. And a lie, at that.

On impulse, Joe went to the phone and called Harry's receptionist at her home.

"Hiya, Dimples," he tried to sound as cheery as usual. "This is Joe McBride. You know, the guy that worships the ground you walk on. But look, I've got to talk to Mr. Sloan, and it's pretty important. Have you any idea where I can reach him?"

"He's out of town for a few days, Mr. McBride."

"I know that. But did he leave an address with you?"

"No, he didn't."

"But don't you have any ideas?"

"I'm sorry, Mr. McBride."

She was a help! Joe clenched the phone. "Look, Dimples, this is very, very important, and I have to get in touch with Mr. Sloan. Now I know he didn't just walk up to you and say, I'm going out of town for a few days."

"But that's just what he did, Mr. McBride."

"Hold your horses, sweetheart. I'm coming to it. Now—did anybody call him up just before he told you he was going away? Or was there a telegram? Think hard."

"No-o-o ... but there was a Mr. LaFarge in to see him."

"LaFarge?" Joe's eyes thinned. "What'd he want to see Mr. Sloan for?"

"It was about a divorce. But, Mr. McBride, I don't think I should be telling you all this. You really don't work for Mr. Sloan."

"Of course I do, Dimples. In fact, from now on, I'm going to be one of the busiest little workers he's got around him. Thanks a lot. You've been a big help."

Joe hung up. Thoughtfully, he ran his fingers up and down the phone cord. He knew that Harry was running around with Camilla LaFarge. Okay. So now LaFarge himself wanted a divorce. It couldn't have anything to do with Harry, or he wouldn't have come to Harry to make arrangements. So Camilla must have sent her husband to Harry, which meant ... just what the hell did it mean?

Joe thought he had something, but it was too slippery to get a grip on. Then he pursed up his lips and reached for the phone. Could be. If Camilla LaFarge was out of town, too, that was the answer.

But it was Camilla who answered the phone.

"Whatever gave you the idea I know anything of Mr. Sloan's whereabouts?" she asked coldly.

"His receptionist. She thought it might have something to do with your pending divorce. I'm sorry I bothered you, Mrs. LaFarge, but something just blew up, and I wanted Harry to know about it."

Camilla hesitated. It could be something important. "Well," she said finally, "I happen to know Mr. Sloan changed his mind about going out of town. Have you tried his apartment?"

"Well say, thanks. I'll call him right away."

Joe hung up with a feeling of grim satisfaction. His conclusion wasn't quite accurate—he thought Camilla and Harry had planned to slip away together for a few days, but something had come up to change their minds. He was near enough, and it was something to work on. What a fool he had been last night, trying to persuade Suzy not to go back to Harry's apartment because Camilla was there! That would have done it—but he hadn't wanted Suzy to get hurt. Brother, what a fancy piece of simple-minded thinking *that* had been!

Then, just so there wouldn't be any kickbacks or immaturely aroused suspicions, he called Harry and told him the Frawleys were calling off their divorce.

Harry snapped, "What am I supposed to do, play *Hearts And Flowers*?"

"I just thought you'd want to know, that's all."

"So now I know."

Bang!

Joe winced at the crash of Harry's receiver in his ear. Nice boy, Harry. This could have been a favor. In fact, it was. It would save Harry the trouble of filing the petition in the morning. Joe grinned. What had he expected, anyway—a pat on the back and a merit badge? He didn't give a damn about doing Harry a favor, or getting gratitude for it. He'd just been covering all this phoning around he'd been doing.

Maybe he needed a drink, he thought. He did feel kind of beat.

He went over to Suzy again and felt her cheek with the back of his hand. It was still warm and dry, and her breathing was still just as even and peaceful. He bent over and kissed her lightly on the cheekbone.

"I earned that one," he told her solemnly.

Then he went into the kitchen and came back with the Scotch bottle. He sprawled in the arm chair and lounged down on the back of his neck. He might just as well be comfortable, because here's where he was going to spend the night.

OUTSIDE INTERFERENCE
CHAPTER ELEVEN

When Harry got down to his office the next morning at ten, he found LaFarge waiting for him.

"Camilla said you wanted to see me, old boy," he yawned, "so I humored her and came down. But I say now, couldn't we sort of wind up all this nonsense this morning? It's no fun for me, you know, having to keep looking at that loathsome, meaty face of yours. No offense, of course, but you are rather disgusting."

Harry said shortly, "Let's go in the office. Any calls for me?" he barked at the receptionist.

"Well ... Mr. McBride called me last night. He had something important ..."

"I talked to Mr. McBride. Anything else?"

"That's all, Mr. Sloan."

"Take that gum out of your mouth and stop trying to look so dumb. Try to get some work done around here, will you? Let's go, LaFarge."

He was in a foul mood, and the girl was the handiest victim. Her face turned fiery red. He was going to snap at her just once too often …

Harry went around his desk and sat down.

"It's set for Saturday," he said to LaFarge. "All right with you?"

"My dear fellow, I have absolutely nothing to say about it, so why shouldn't it be all right with me?"

"Okay. Saturday it is. You'll pick up Miss Carr at her apartment at two o'clock and drive to the Rockland Hotel, in Rockland, New York. That's just off Route 9-W. Your wife, the witnesses and the photographer will break into your hotel room at exactly eight o'clock, so be there—unless you want to have to do the whole thing all over again. Here's the address of the hotel, Miss Carr's address, and I have also written down the important hour." He gave LaFarge an envelope. "Have you got that straight now?"

LaFarge merely looked amused.

Harry went on. "At the hotel you will register as Mr. and Mrs. John Smith. I've written that down also."

"Well, I suppose it's usual, but it's going to make me feel quite an idiot."

"What is?"

"Writing Mr. and Mrs. John Smith. And it has a touch of the sordid that I might have expected from you. I say, why can't we make it Mr. and Mrs. Baron de Sade?"

"We'll leave it John Smith," said Harry.

LaFarge's glittering eyes thinned with amusement.

"There are a few other things," Harry went on. "Bring luggage. That's a respectable hotel, and you have to have luggage. It's not a riding academy. You won't have to worry about anything once you get in the hotel. Miss Carr will take charge. She knows exactly what has to be done, so please let her make all the arrangements, even if you think they're screwy. That's important, and all I want is for you to keep it in mind. Mrs. LaFarge's witnesses will not know that this divorce has been arranged, and things have to be just so when they bust into that hotel room. Miss Carr knows all about that, so when she tells you to do something, do it."

Though Harry knew that there would be no fake raid, that the police would be the ones to do the actual busting-in, he enjoyed bullying LaFarge.

"Got that straight?" he demanded.

"Oh yes, old boy," said LaFarge inattentively. "Quite straight, quite straight."

"One more thing and we're finished." Harry leaned over the desk and tried to sound casual. "Bring along a bottle of Cointreau. Miss Carr is very fond of Cointreau. But," he held up a finger, "don't let her get hold of the bottle. You can give her four or five drinks, but don't let her as much as see the bottle."

LaFarge looked interested. "She's a tippler? What a pity."

"We won't discuss the lady—but keep that bottle out of sight. I've been through this with her before. She'll pretend not to know what it is, she'll ask to see the bottle, and all that. Pay no attention. Give her a silly answer. Anything. But don't let her see the bottle—because the first time you step out of that room, she'll grab it out of your bag or wherever you've shown her it is. I don't want her drunk."

"Cointreau, Cointreau," repeated LaFarge. "I'll keep that in mind. Righto, I'll keep it hidden."

Harry grinned to himself. That was it. As far as he knew, Suzy had never tasted Cointreau, but it was the kind of thing she'd like, and he knew she'd show a natural curiosity. Then later, when the police questioned her about where she'd gotten the hop, she'd remember how suspiciously LaFarge had acted about showing her the bottle. This was going to be a pushover. The guy would never know what hit him.

"Now to wind it up," he said, taking a paper from his folder, "this is the settlement agreement in which your wife agrees to pay you the sum of one hundred thousand dollars and so forth and so forth. This is your acceptance. Read it over and sign at the bottom."

LaFarge scrawled his name without as much as glancing at the body of the text.

"My dear fellow," he said, "Camilla wouldn't dare try any hanky-panky. Is that all?"

"That's all. I'm just as sick of your face as you are of mine."

"Thank you. That shows spirit, if nothing else. Though I suppose you feel rather frustrated at not being able to punch me in the nose and all that, what?"

"Frustrated," said Harry, "doesn't even begin to describe it, pal."

LaFarge cocked his head and gave Harry an odd, glittering glance. "I'd really believe you, but the fervor was missing, old boy. I'd say you've figured out something rather unpleasant for me—or think you have, which is a horse of quite another color," his lips pursed in a veiled smile. "Perhaps you recall that yesterday I ventured the pleasantry that it would fill me with ineffable delight to cut your throat. D'you know, it really would. You're such a beefy, bulging boor. However, I'd just as soon we got this divorce nonsense settled first."

"Ducky. Now scram, will you?"

"Tut tut tut tut, old boy. You've had your innings. Now it's my turn at bat. I'm really putting up with quite a lot from you two, Camilla playing Juliet to your rather meager Romeo, and all that. I think I'm entitled to one demand now, don't you?"

Harry smothered an impulse to throw him out of the office—but in a moment of unaccustomed generosity, he remembered that the guy was as good as in the clink for the rest of his life, and he said, "Why not?" Humor the guy.

LaFarge's smile became a little more hidden, and his voice was not quite so off-hand when he said, "I want to meet the girl. What did you say her name was? Miss Carr. I want to meet her."

Harry felt a shiver, remembering how Camilla had cried—*he's not interested in women. He's plotting something ghastly!* He looked into LaFarge's eyes, and looked quickly away.

"But why?" he asked uneasily. "She's just another dumb dame, that's all."

"Oh, I don't know. Let's say the complete innocence of her face rather intrigues me. I mean, one can't help wondering if the innocence is really as complete as it seems. I know she's in a rather tawdry business, and I know that association with you, old boy, would corrupt angels, but I have the odd notion that hers is the innocence of the spirit, which would be too delightful, if true. Yes, I really must meet her. And don't think you're going to refuse me, old boy, because you know damned well that if you don't indulge my whim, I'll simply tell the pack of you to go to hell. And wouldn't Camilla be delighted to know that it was all because you refuse to introduce me to this girl."

Harry reached heavily for the phone, picked it up and called Suzy.

"Hiya, baby," he said. "Can you come down to the office right away?"

Suzy had been up for barely an hour and she was feeling terrible, but for a moment she lifted at the sound of his voice and she cried, "Darling! I thought you were away for ..."

"I know, I know. But it blew up. One of those things. But come on down to the office. We're going to work on this LaFarge thing."

"Couldn't it wait, Harry?" she pleaded wanly. "I'm not feeling so good."

"Whattaya mean you're not feeling so good?"

"Well ... I got potted last night. I'm awfully sorry, Harry, honest I am. I had a date with Mr. Frawley ..."

"Forget it. Frawley's out. And I don't care how you're feeling. I want you down at the office right away!" He caught himself and went on smoothly, "I really need you, darling. This is important. If you got a hangover, I'll tell you what to do. Drop in at the Robert Treat Bar and have a couple of whiskey sours. You'll feel like a million. Okay? See you in a half hour." He hung up.

Joe came out of the kitchen, holding a cup of coffee in one hand and a piece of toast in the other. "There's nothing quite like a telephone," he observed interestedly, "to bring the rosy bloom of health into a maiden's cheeks. Good news? Did a rich old uncle die and leave you his kennel of Airedales and a tinted reproduction of the Gettysburg Address?"

"I have to run, Joe. I'm sorry," Suzy ran for the bedroom. "Harry's back, and we have to go right to work on the LaFarge divorce."

A look of hard bleakness crossed Joe's face, but he said lightly, "A woman's work is never done. And, to tell the truth, I'd like to get some of it myself. Then maybe I wouldn't have to worry where the next job's coming from."

He was preserving the character of good old wisecracking Joe, the working girl's friend. Suzy looked on him as a friend, and he wanted to keep it that way. She was going to need a friend.

"And say, honeybun," he called, "I have to do a little salt mining myself. There's a guy thinks he makes better kosher pickles than anybody else, and he wants to put it in the paper. He asked me, as a special favor and for fifty bucks, to make a few artistic photographic studies. I'll call you later."

"Please do, Joe." She appeared briefly in the doorway, holding a long bath towel to cover her not-quite-obvious nudity. She gave him a grateful smile. "And ... thanks for last night, Joe."

"Ah," he said, "think nothing of it. I used to do the same for my poor old mother, night after night."

He walked out, whistling jauntily.

Harry and LaFarge sat waiting in the office. Their silence was absolute. Harry wanted to throw him out, or tell him to go sit in the reception room, or something, but he didn't dare. If LaFarge kicked over the traces now, there'd be hell to pay with Camilla. So okay, he'd humor the guy—but LaFarge gave him the creeps all the same. It's just what he always said—you can't depend on a hophead.

For the most part, LaFarge sat indolently in his chair, watching the rhythmical beat of his foot, but every now and again he shot Harry a veiled look of blazing, demoniacal hatred. He never let Harry catch him at this. Whenever their glances crossed, LaFarge smiled and nodded, and once he waved. He could see Harry was jittery, and it amused him.

"I say," he said, suddenly thinking of another way to needle, "what sort of cuisine has this Rockland Hotel?"

"How should I know?" Harry growled. "I've never been there."

"I say, old boy, that's rather thick now, isn't it? Surely you don't expect me to dine on some aboriginal mess, do you? Be a good fellow and get me a menu, will you?"

"What difference does it make?" Harry shouted. "You're only going to be there till eight. You can go out and eat afterwards."

Only there wouldn't be any afterwards, smart guy!

LaFarge smiled. "Of course," he murmured. "Do they have a decent bar?"

"I told you I've never been there, didn't I?"

"Don't get so excited, old boy. You're the meaty type that pops off from apoplexy."

When Suzy walked into the office, glowing and fresh (she'd had a bromide) Harry rushed to greet her almost with gratitude. He threw his arm around her and led her to the desk.

"This is Mr. LaFarge," he told her. "You know about the divorce. He wants to know you better before that hassle at the hotel."

LaFarge leaped to his feet. "I say, Sloan old boy, she *is* a beauty, isn't she! You're a man to be congratulated, all right. There aren't many girls like this around, I can tell you. And Miss Carr," he bowed slightly over her hand, still smiling. He had seen that look of intimate happiness in her eyes when she looked at Harry, and he knew she was in love with him. "Delighted to meet you, Miss Carr. Though good old Sloan here hasn't come right out and announced it, I gathered from his conversation that you're the one and only in his life, eh? Such rhapsodic descriptions and all that. You needn't blush. It's quite all right. And really, you know, you're quite a lucky girl, too. It's not every girl, either, who can get herself an up and coming ambitious young fellow like Sloan here." He slapped Harry on the shoulder and chuckled. "Come, come, old boy. Don't look so modest. You know it's true!"

Suzy looked up at Harry and smiled happily, and all he could do was give her a frozen grin in return. This speech of LaFarge's had made him feel as if someone had laid an icy hand in the small of his back.

LaFarge looked at Suzy and gave an embarrassed laugh. "I daresay I'm a bit of a fuddy-duddy, and all that, but I'm absolutely miserable with strangers. I'm really quite shy. Good old Sloan here has just told me that we'll have to spend a bit of time together before the, ah, event. I'll be frank with you. I absolutely dread it. So, if you don't mind, it would be really quite kind of you if you'd come out with me and we could have a cup of tea and become a little better acquainted. What I mean to say is ... oh dash it. You tell her, Sloan old boy. My tongue gets all gumdiddled."

"He wants to get better acquainted," said Harry stonily.

"Exactly," beamed LaFarge. "I couldn't have put it as well myself, but that's it exactly. It would really be a great kindness, Miss Carr. But please, if I'm imposing, if you have other plans, it's really quite all right. Oh dash it, I wish I had good old Sloan's easy manner with strangers. It would make things simpler all round." He seemed quite overcome in an excess of diffidence.

Suzy said impulsively, "Of course I'll have a cup of tea with you, Mr.

LaFarge. And you're not imposing at all. Unless Mr. Sloan needs me for something." She looked at Harry.

"Get him out of here," said Harry harshly.

LaFarge took Suzy's arm, urging her toward the door and exclaiming, "I really can't tell you how grateful I am, Miss Carr." But he turned in the doorway and gave Harry a look of such cold malevolence that Harry felt the chill go through him like a stab. The door closed with a bang.

Harry stood gripping the desk, then walked stiffly around it and sat down in his chair. He reached in the bottom drawer for his bottle of bourbon. This was one time he needed a drink and needed it bad. If ever he had seen naked, gibbering insanity in a guy's eyes, he had seen it in LaFarge's. The guy was a maniac. Camilla should have him shoved in a straightjacket and chained in the sub-cellar. A guy like that shouldn't be around loose. And all that guff about throat cutting. Harry's animal courage had been shaken since yesterday.

He felt steadier after four drinks, so he took just one more for luck. Today was Friday. Tomorrow was Saturday. By tomorrow night it would be all over. He straightened his tie, gave his head a sharp jerk and walked out into the reception room.

Having no typing or anything else to do, the girl was looking pensively out the window at the dreary Newark skyline.

"Is that what I'm paying you for?" Harry snarled—it was a relief to let off steam. "What's the matter with you broads anyway? The minute you graduate from business school, you seem to think you're ready to retire on your boss' money. Get out your book and take a telegram."

The girl bit her lip and shakily reached for her stenographic notebook. "Telegram to Rockland Hotel, Rockland, New York. Please reserve room for self and wife. Arrive Saturday afternoon. Deposit enclosed. John Smith. Got that? Okay. Draw ten bucks from petty cash and have Western Union send a voucher. I'm going out now, and I might not be back for the rest of the day."

He walked out of the office without giving her another glance. He walked down to the liquor store on Raymond Boulevard and bought a bottle of Cointreau, then hailed a cab and gave the driver the address of Little Augie's joint on Frelinghuysen Avenue. He leaned back in the seat, grumbling to himself. If only Suzy had Camilla's dough and Camilla's brains. But what the hell. You can't have everything. And it was going to give him a lot of satisfaction putting the boots to LaFarge tomorrow night.

Little Augie's place was called the Melody Club, and was decorated with chrome, plastic and colored mirrors that were as standard as handlebar moustaches were in 1890. It was closed, but Harry knew that Augie's office, in the back, was open for business twenty-four hours a day. He went down the alley, knocked on the door, was peered at by a gorilla with two cauliflower ears, and was admitted with profane enthusiasm and a slap between the shoulders that snapped his neck.

"Cut it out, you punch-drunk ape," he growled. "Is Augie busy?"

"Maybe." The pug opened a second door, thrust in his head and yelled, "Ya busy, Aug? It's that Sloan monkey." There was a rumbling answer, and the pug pulled back his head and grinned at Harry. "Oke. How's tricks, kid? Say, I juss hoid a new one ..."

"Don't bother me, will you?"

Augie was playing solitaire on his desk and he merely grunted when Harry walked in. He was short, squat and swarthy. His office was as modernistic as bleached wood, tortured forms and bad taste could make it. One entire wall had been torn out and had been replaced by a sheet of clear plate glass. "It's modernistic, see?" That it faced the sheer, red-brick wall of the factory behind the club, meant nothing. Plate glass walls were modernistic.

Harry sat down in the chair beside the desk and lit a cigarette. Augie went on playing solitaire. Neither of them spoke. Harry knew that Augie would open the conversation when he was good and ready. That was Augie's way.

Augie played for about fifteen minutes, then with an irritable, "Aaaaaaaah!" sent the cards flying from the desk with a sweep of his arm. He lit a cigar and finally admitted Harry's presence.

"Well, hiya, Harry-boy. What's on your mind?"

"I want to buy about five hundred bucks worth of hop."

"Well, why doncha then?"

Harry said nothing. He waited.

Finally Augie said, "What makes ya think I got any hop?"

Harry waited.

Then at length, Augie grumbled, "What kinda hop?"

Harry shrugged. "Any kind."

"Novocaine?" Augie jeered.

"You know what I mean, Augie."

"So now I'm a mind reader? Okay. But I'm telling ya, five hundred bucks don't buy hardly enough to get a rear these days. Thinking of pushing it, pal?"

Harry just grinned. He took a flat aspirin bottle, about three inches high, and stood it on the desk. "I want that full."

Augie guffawed. "Are you nuts, pal?" He held out his hand and flickered his thumb across the tips of his fingers. "Start talking real dough, pal."

"You can't dilute the stuff, I suppose?"

"Well, that's different. Sure I can cut it. But y'know it comes cut in the first place, so don't try to push the stuff on anybody that knows."

"I'll worry about that."

"I can see you worrying. Now what?"

Harry was taking the bottle of Cointreau from its paper bag. He put it on the desk beside the other bottle.

"I want you to stick a charge of something in that, too."

"Why?"

"It makes a difference?"

"Look, pal, who's doing who a favor? I'm a guy that likes to know, see? Tricky characters like you int'rest me, and I'm always willing to learn something. You want me to do you a favor, okay, but give."

Harry said reluctantly, "It has to be fed to a dame in a way she won't know."

"You that hard up?"

"It's a divorce case."

"Oh, one of them." Augie wasn't interested in how divorces were framed. He never bothered getting married, and when he wanted to get rid of a woman, he just kicked her out. He looked clinically at the Cointreau. "You want laudanum. It dilutes easy."

"What does it do?"

"Puts 'em to sleep, and she'll dream she's the Queen of Sheba with a thousand Gregory Pecks flopping all around her."

"How many will it take?"

"She can drink the whole bottle and it won't kill her. Hell, there's only eight drinks in the bottle. She'll be happy on the third or fourth. Okay?"

"Whatever you say, Augie."

Augie picked up the two bottles and waddled out of the room. He was gone about twenty minutes. The aspirin bottle had been filled with a white powder. The government stamp had been steamed from the cap of the Cointreau bottle, then carefully glued back in place.

"That sets ya back exactly six hunnert and fifty bucks," said Augie.

Harry knew Augie was giving him the business, but he wrote out the check without question. Augie waved the check in the air to dry it.

"Scramming outta town won't do ya any good if this thing bounces," he informed Harry pleasantly. "And another thing. There's other guys around town pushing the stuff, so if you try to peddle it in any of their drops, yer gonna get yer neck in a sling. And don't hang around with this stuff in ya pocket. Now beat it. I don't want ya around here neither."

Harry was annoyed when he got outside to find he had forgotten to tell the cab to wait for him. He walked to the drugstore on the corner, called another cab, then sat down at the counter to have a cup of coffee. Looking in the mirror behind the counter, he saw Joe walk in, and he turned suspiciously.

"What're you doing down here?" he demanded.

Joe patted the camera that hung around his neck and pointed back over his shoulder. "New roller skating rink opening down the street. The Frawleys get in touch with you?"

Harry shrugged to show his complete disinterest in the Frawleys. Joe sat down at the counter beside him and ordered a cup of coffee. "When're we pulling the LaFarge divorce?" he asked.

Harry scowled. He hadn't intended to ring Joe in on that—but then he remembered that Joe and Suzy went around a little, and that Suzy would be sure to spill it. But what difference would it make if he told Joe? It'd be all over by the time Joe got up there anyway.

"Yeah," he said, "I was just going to call you, Joe. It's set for tomorrow night. The Rockland Hotel up in Rockland, New York."

"New York!"

"Don't you know there's an investigation on, pal? We don't want the D. A. nosing in on this. It's fixed for eight o'clock in the Rockland Hotel. They'll be registered as Smith as usual. Mrs. LaFarge'll meet you in the lobby." Camilla wouldn't be within a hundred miles of the place. "I don't want any hitches in this one, Joe."

"I hear and I obey, O lord and master. Have an Indian nut?"

"Grow up, will you?"

Harry turned sourly to his coffee. His nerves were jangling. He'd be glad when this mess was over. He wouldn't give a damn if so much didn't depend on it. About ten minutes later, a cab drew up outside the drugstore and honked its horn.

"Whoops," said Joe, putting down his cup. "There's my iron horse."

Harry started pugnaciously, "Wait a minute ..." when another cab drew up behind the first one. He knew Joe was grinning at him, and he walked out scowling. Joe trotted at his side right up to the cab.

"I had a brand new idea to give your divorces some class, Harry," he chattered. "Infra-red flash bulbs. No flash, no glare. Of course, they cost a few cents extra ..."

Harry said peevishly, "All right, all right," and turned to the cab and gave the driver Camilla's address.

Joe called after him, "You'll be sorry when your competitors start operating with infra-red. Just remember I warned you, that's all."

Harry sat brooding. Twice he touched the small dope-filled bottle in his pocket to make sure he hadn't dropped it. He shook himself angrily.

What the hell was the matter with him?

Camilla, on the other hand, was calm and composed when she met him at the door and led him to the south wing glass-enclosed sitting room. She patted his cheek and kissed him.

"You look all fussed and bothered, my pet," she murmured. "Did you have a rotten morning? Let me make you a drink."

"I can use it!" He glanced jumpily around the room. "There a phone here? I want to call the office."

"Over there. Anything special?"

"I want to make sure that dumb girl sent the telegram off to the hotel in Rockland. It'd be sweet if they got up there and there wasn't any reservation."

"Oh, calm down, darling. You're all jittery."

"Shut up, will you?"

He strode over to the phone and called his office.

"Did you get that telegram off?" he demanded when the girl answered.

"An hour ago, Mr. Sloan."

"Well for once you used your head!"

"Miss Carr called," said the girl primly. "She wants you to call her back at this number."

Harry scribbled the number on the back of the telephone book and hung up. Camilla was watching him with raised eyebrows.

"You *are* jittery," she said. "Or do you always talk to your secretaries like that? Here, drink this. You'll feel better."

He took the glass and drank the bourbon thirstily. She stood with the bottle and poured him another.

"Drink it down," she said. "It'll work in a moment."

He drank it down—and felt the nerve-blunting warmth begin to spread out from his chest. He grinned and patted her under the chin.

"One more call," he said. He picked up the phone and called the number Suzy had given the receptionist. It was a tea room on Broad Street, but Suzy was waiting for the call and answered almost immediately.

"Hello, darling," she said. "Mr. LaFarge wants to take me to the Short Hills Jockey Club for lunch. Should I?"

LaFarge's voice broke in cheerily, "Hello there, good old Sloan, d'y'mind if I abduct your lovely fiancée for an hour or two? Actually, she's the first female I've been able to talk to for years and years and I can't seem to stop. But of course you don't mind, do you, old boy?"

"Would it make any difference?"

LaFarge laughed softly, and Suzy's voice came back. "Is it all right, darling?"

"Sure, sure, sure."

"Will I see you tonight?"

"Oh hell, I'm up to my ears, but I'll give you a ring. So long."

When he turned from the phone, Camilla was watching him with thin eyes. "That sounded like LaFarge," she said.

He shrugged. "He's taking the girl out to lunch."

"Harry, you shouldn't have let him! I don't know what he's up to, but he's not interested in women. I'm sure he's planning something hideous …"

"Aw for God sake, what can he do to her in a restaurant full of people? Use your head."

"Of course you're right, but I can't help feeling …" She walked back to the cocktail table in front of the sofa that faced the garden, picked up her glass and poured herself a drink. "I must be a little jittery myself," she confessed. She patted the sofa beside her. "Sit down and tell me how everything is going."

"Like silk," said Harry. There was a warm glow inside him now. "But there are a couple things for you to do." He sat down beside her and took out the small, flat bottle of dope he had gotten from Little Augie. "This is it, baby. This is the evidence. I want you to slip it into the lining of his luggage. Can do?"

"Very easily. Is that dope? It glitters."

"So do the guys that use it. They glitter all over the place. But here's the other thing. He's going to be packing a bottle of Cointreau. I want you to switch it with this one."

She looked at both bottles, then set them on the cocktail table in front of the sofa.

"I'll be glad when this is over," she whispered. "But he won't be hurt, will he, Harry? I wouldn't want that on my conscience—too. Promise me he won't be hurt."

"Of course he won't be hurt. They'll just grab him and stick him in the booby hatch. He won't know what hit him. I'll tip off the cops that he's a hophead, and they'll know how to handle it. It's in the bag."

She turned and her arms went around him convulsively. "Hold me tight, Harry," she whispered, "hold me tight, hold me tight!"

He grabbed her almost brutally and crushed her slender body against his. Their lips met fiercely. Their inflammable emotions exploded. Camilla moaned and strained into his kiss as if seeking to be swallowed by it. Harry felt the wrench and tear of his own emotions as the storm of her passion leaped and crackled around him. Her body twitched and convulsed in his arms as if shock after shock of high voltage electricity were being shot through it. Her fingers were like daggers, clutching him to her. His hands sought her hungrily. She jerked her lips away.

"Draw the blinds, darling," she panted. "Draw the blinds. There's one of the gardeners leaping about in the shrubbery. Draw them, draw them!"

Harry leaped up.

Later, they felt sodden, but still, with all passion spent, they clung to each other, each desperately seeking the after-comfort of fulfillment, but it wasn't there.

It was about four that afternoon when LaFarge strolled in. He did not come any farther than the doorway.

"Well, well," he said, "if it isn't good old Sloan. I just dropped your charming little assistant off at her humble abode. Delightful girl, old boy, utterly delightful, and with an innocence of spirit that you really ought to treasure as a jewel. I can't tell you how it intrigued me. However, I dropped her off safe and sound and in parting, gave her a posy—with the proper shy respectful diffidence, of course. It warmed my heart to hear her girlish cries of delight. Altogether I believe I spent one of the most innocuous afternoons I have ever spent in my life. We'll probably have an even more delightful time tomorrow. By the bye, I'll be using the Cadillac convertible tomorrow, Camilla my dove, so please don't vex me by dashing off with it somewhere." He smiled once, vaguely, and sauntered out.

Harry saw the look on Camilla's face and he growled, "He was just trying to needle you, baby."

"I know, I know. He's always doing that. But this time he seems to be making a special effort. Oh, Harry, isn't there any way we can do this without letting him take that girl with him tomorrow?"

"Are we back to that again?"

Outside the room, flattened against the wall beside the door, LaFarge pursed his lips in a small, secret smile, then softly walked away.

THE BEGINNING OF THE END!
CHAPTER TWELVE

To Suzy, this was like none of the other divorces she had ever worked on. It was more like a nice date. Mr. LaFarge picked her up in a beautiful dawn gray Cadillac convertible, and the drive up Route 9-W was wonderful.

She had talked to Harry just before leaving, and he had been very brusque, but she knew he was nervous. This meant so much to him, being offered the handling of the Schuyler estate and all, but she didn't have any difficulty at all being nice to Mr. LaFarge. He was so easy to be nice to. He was so thoughtful. He had brought her a corsage of violets. None of the other men had ever been so thoughtful.

And he was very gay today, pointing out the little sailboats that fluttered on the Hudson River far below at the foot of the Palisades, and driving her down through Edgewater where she could see the river lapping against the shore only a few yards away. He was very gay and his eyes were very bright. You'd never have thought he was getting a divorce. To Suzy, divorce was a calamity, or a painful cure for two people who were matrimonially sick.

"Aren't you even a bit sorry you're getting a divorce, Mr. LaFarge?" she asked him.

"My dear charming little Suzy, two people do grow away from each other."

"Not if they're in love," said Suzy firmly.

He glanced at her. "Can you keep a secret?" he asked, sounding wistful.

"Of course I can."

"Well ... I'm very deeply in love with my wife."

"Then why ..."

"It's all rather hard to explain, Suzy. But ... I'm quite convinced," that wistful note again, "that my wife is still very deeply in love with me, too. Perhaps she won't realize it before the divorce, but I'm hoping that ... afterward ... there's always a chance of our being remarried. Promise to keep your fingers crossed for me, will you, Suzy?"

"Of course I will, Mr. LaFarge! But I hope she finds out before the divorce."

"That's what I'm praying for, Suzy," said LaFarge devoutly. "But let's talk of something else. Let's not spoil our outing. Have you traveled much, Suzy?"

She laughed. "I've been to Staten Island, Jones Beach and Atlantic City. Oh yes, and once I was in Philadelphia."

"I'll tell you a secret, Suzy. People don't enjoy traveling as much as they pretend. They'd rather be home and comfortable—though you do see some curious things, I'm bound to admit. I was in France a number of years ago and watched them eat live fish. Not just swallow them, the way the college chaps did, but actually eat them, bite off the heads while they were still wriggling. Very odd."

He watched her face clinically and smiled at the swift disgust that crossed it.

"That's ... horrible!" she cried.

"Oh, not really, you know. One becomes detached. The sport of pig sticking in India, for instance. They hunt from horseback with lances, and how the brute squeals and bellows and throws up great gouts of blood all over the place. It's a good deal more gory than watching a chap nip off the head of a guppy, and rather unpleasant for the pig, I should imagine, but it's sport, really. It's the way you look at it."

"But I don't want to look at it," Suzy shivered. "I don't ever want to look at it."

"No? It's not like the stockyards and slaughterhouses of Chicago, you know, where they knock the poor brutes over the head, then cut their throats and the blood runs in gutters and they rip the poor things up and everything spills out. Pig-sticking is a gentleman's sport in India, my dear."

He watched the sick horror settle on her face, and his eyes glinted with amusement. How remarkably plastic she was. How easy it was to play on her emotions. A turn of a word and she was as happy as a meadowlark; another turn and there were tears in her eyes. Remarkable. Such lively emotions. She was altogether delightful—and not at all like that leathery old harpy, Camilla. His mind darkened evilly for a moment at the thought of Camilla. How she had patronized and bullied him for years—until that night she'd gotten maudlin drunk and he'd wheedled that stupid secret out of her. Ah yes, and how he'd made her dance to his tune ever since. But he was tired of Camilla. She was so unversatile. All she did was suffer. She had a positive mania for suffering. Well, she had one last bit of suffering coming to her, and then ... LaFarge wondered idly how deeply Suzy was really in love with Harry Sloan. It was more a matter of hypnotized infatuation, he thought. The fellow did have a tremendous amount of blatant animal magnetism. But there wouldn't be any trouble getting rid of Harry Sloan, however. In fact, he looked forward to it.

He glanced at Suzy and saw that the joy had gone out of her face. Well, he wasn't going to permit that!

Within three minutes he had her laughing merrily over an account of his first solo flight in a plane.

"And there I was," he said, "at three thousand feet, and all of a sudden it struck me that I hadn't the foggiest notion how to get down again, and I had the most dreadful feeling that I was going to spend the rest of my life sitting up there, wistfully watching the good old earth whirl away beneath me. Fortunately, I ran out of gas."

He listened to her laughter. Really, she was wonderful. Like a violin. They had dinner on the Palisades, and it was six-thirty before LaFarge drove the dawn gray Cadillac convertible into Rockland, New York. He drove past the Rockland Hotel and up the street to the Empire House, where he had wired ahead for reservations. He parked the Cadillac in the lot behind the hotel, and when he registered at the desk in the lobby he used a deliberately grade-school scrawl and signed—Arthur J. Wiedemeyer and wife. No one would, even accidentally, discover LaFarge under the granite respectability of Arthur J. Wiedemeyer.

They had a front room. He had specified that in his telegram. He wanted a front room. After the bellhop had left the luggage at the foot of the bed, LaFarge went to the window, lifted back the curtain about an inch, and peered down the street. He had an excellent view of the entrance of the Rockland Hotel. Marvelous, marvelous. He turned back to Suzy, smiling.

"I say," he murmured, pretending diffidence again, "good old Sloan emphasized that once we arrived in this rather less than Imperial Hotel you were in charge and your word was law on the pain of death and all that, but I do hope you're not going to insist on a stroll through this dreary hamlet. Would it be all right if we just sat here and talked? What I mean to say is, I caught a glimpse of the bar downstairs and saw some rather badly mounted owls and partridges and things standing about, and I have the ominous feeling that the moment I set foot in it, I would be seized by some local taxidermist and stuffed."

Suzy laughed. "I'd rather stay here and talk," she said. She would never have said that to any of the men on the other divorce cases, but Mr. LaFarge was different.

"You're sure you won't be compromised, or whatever they call it, will you?"

"Of course not. I'd rather stay here, anyway."

"Good girl. To show you that I'm a gentleman and that my intentions are thoroughly honorable, you can have first whack at the johnny to freshen up."

He was glad when she walked out of the room. He was beginning to feel the strain of all this light banter. He opened his bag on the bed, glanced quickly over his shoulder, then hurriedly slipped a case containing his hypodermic needle into his pocket. He spied the bottle of Cointreau he had brought for Suzy and, remembering Harry's warning, wrapped it in a towel. Not that her drinking habits made any difference to him, one way or the other, but it would be very dull if she got potted.

Finally he put into his pocket a small leather case containing four delicately chased silver cups of Spanish design. He went to the window again and glanced up the street at the entrance of the Rockland Hotel, smiling sardonically.

Suzy was fresh and glowing when she came from the washroom.

LaFarge patted her on the cheek and said, with a touch of sadness, "Ah me, if I were a bit younger and a lot less tired … good old Sloan. He's a lucky dog."

Then, as quickly as he could without running, he went into the bathroom, locking the door behind him. With suddenly shaking fingers he shoved up his sleeve, baring his arm to the elbow. He took out his hypodermic, filled it hurriedly from a small bottle also contained in the same case, then, with practiced dexterity, slid the needle into his arm. He sat down on the edge of the bathtub and waited for the first clammy effects to wear off. There was the usual bad moment, and then he was lifted on wings of ineffable light. He jumped up, turned on the faucets and splashed and laughed, singing. He dried himself vigorously on the thick Turkish towel, then looked around the room for a hiding place for the Cointreau bottle. He found the metal waste basket. There was a newspaper in it, so he tore off several sheets, dampened them under the faucet, and tossed them back in. A bit of psychology there, he congratulated himself. A woman would pick up dry paper and look underneath, but she would not touch wet paper. You're a fox, LaFarge, old boy. But how odd that little Suzy should be a drunkard, now. There was a reason for it, of course, and he hadn't any doubt that a few adroit questions could weasel it out of her. It would be a simple exercise for him. He knew people, and he could make them do anything he wished. It was a wonderful feeling, knowing that you had this subtle power over people, that you could control them without their knowing. A bit like God.

He filled one of the silver cups with Cointreau, then hid the bottle under the wet newspaper in the waste basket. He concealed the cup in his hand behind his back when he walked into the other room. Suzy didn't look around, anyway. She was trying to tune the radio.

"Feeling awfully guilty about keeping you incarcerated in this cupboard," he said gaily, "I have said abracadabra and whisked a liqueur out of the air." He handed her the little silver cup of Cointreau.

"Well, for heaven's sake!" she said. She smelled it, then sipped. "How lovely. It tastes like oranges. What is it?"

LaFarge lifted one eyebrow. That's exactly what Sloan had said she'd say.

"Ambrosia," he said, "just plain good old ambrosia."

"I didn't mean that, silly. It has a name, hasn't it?"

"Has it? I really wouldn't know. I'd always thought of ambrosia as … just ambrosia."

"You're making fun of me now. Let me see the bottle. The name'll be right on the label. I'd really like to know. Things you drink always taste like ... well like whiskey. But this tastes just like oranges. Please tell me what it is. I'd like to buy a bottle for myself sometime."

I'll wager, LaFarge thought. He smiled.

"I'll make you a sporting proposition," he said. "If, by the end of the evening, you can guess the name of it, I'll buy you a whole case of it. Tonight."

Now go ahead and sweat, old girl, he thought. Let's see how adroitly you can squirm out of this pretended ignorance. It would be amusing to watch her try.

"Well, I'll never be able to guess, I can tell you that," said Suzy helplessly. "Even whiskey isn't called whiskey. It's called old crow or wedding bells or old grandfather or something."

"Try," smiled LaFarge. "Just think it over." Oh, she'd come around to it, he knew. She'd manage to say Cointreau, as if it were something she'd read in a magazine once but hadn't quite known what it was. She'd come around to it, and it would be amusing to watch. But not for long. It was too childish.

"I'll just drink it," she said. "I'll never guess. It's delicious."

When she was playing with the radio again, he slipped into the bathroom, filled the other three little silver cups and brought them back without her noticing.

By seven-thirty, she had drunk all four. They were so small, and he was so amusing that she hardly noticed when he put a full cup down in the place of an empty one.

"What time is it?" she finally asked, in the voice of a small girl who was growing awfully sleepy but wanted to stay up because so many wonderful things were happening.

He told her, and she said, "I have to get undressed now."

He watched with interest as she took off her dress and slip and sat down on the edge of the bed to strip off her stockings.

She really had a wonderful body—and she was so unconscious of its loveliness, too. She walked across the room to hang her dress in the closet and he cocked his head to one side, watching her, feeling an unaccustomed excitement arising in him. Since he had become really addicted to drugs, women ceased to interest him physically, but there was something here that stirred him. Perhaps it was the essential and universal femininity of her long legs, the calves curving into the knee, the thighs flaring warmly, the hips molding into the torso, the width of her mouth and in her eyes that one thing of which he had talked so much—the basic innocence of spirit.

By God, he cried within himself, as if making a discovery, here was Woman. He was excited. He had never thought of this before, never having dreamed of the possibility. Suzy was the embodiment of Woman, the zenith of femininity, she was all of it. Most women had bits of it. The more fortunate ones had it in a large measure. But Suzy had all of it! LaFarge's excitement mounted. To possess her. To possess her body, to possess her soul, but most importantly, to possess that infinite innocence of spirit. He became quite agitated. His hands twitched on his thighs and a pulse beat in his cheek near his left eye. His eyes sparkled. It would be like possessing the greatest of them all, the great mother Eve, which was the fundamental desire of all men. And here it was. His, his!

But, with subtlety, he curbed the desire for the moment. That was the after pleasure. First he wanted to savor the crushing blow he was serving Camilla. A cloud came over his mind again at the thought of her, and he had all he could do to keep from leaping to his feet and lashing her with savage invective. But invective was unnecessary. Within a very short while, she would start to know what suffering was. She and her bumbling paramour, Sloan.

At eight o'clock, she would walk into the Rockland Hotel, expecting to find him there with Suzy. But he wouldn't be there! During the last two days, he had shown an unnatural interest in Suzy. Deliberately. He knew what kind of conclusions she would draw—that he had something rather horrible in mind. Dear, dear Camilla. What a disgusting mind she had! And what fun she was going to have!

During the first hour after she found that he wasn't in the Rockland Hotel with Suzy, she would suffer, wondering what he was up to. During the second hour, the suffering would become agony—and before the night was out, she'd be stark, raving mad. There was absolutely no doubt about it. She would feel responsible, just as she felt responsible about that other stupid thing, she would feel the corrosive guilt, the guilt that kept her whimpering in the night, and awakening with the sweat of madness on her. Oh, it would take only this little touch to send dear Camilla over the edge. Her and her morbid dread of inflicting pain. Let her wonder what he was doing to Suzy, let her suffer, then let her mind splinter, as it would, into the void of insanity.

LaFarge's only regret was that he would not be there to watch the process. But later, he would visit her in whatever institution she was incarcerated, and he would watch her and look through her eyes into the mind he had emptied. The greatest pleasures in the world, he told himself, were these, the pleasures of the spirit.

He watched Suzy walk back across the room. He watched the movement of her thighs and touched with his eyes the soft texture of her skin. Later, dear Suzy, later. But not too much later.

"Do you mind?" she asked him drowsily, "if I lie down a while?"

He smiled with anticipation as she lay down and closed her eyes.

Harry Sloan picked up the telephone and, with Camilla standing whitely tense at his elbow, called the Rockland Police. "Police Headquarters?" he said in a hoarse voice. "Look, there's a guy over at the Rockland Hotel registered as John Smith, and he brought a dame in from Jersey. Not that I give a damn how a guy gets his fun, see, but this guy's got that poor little tomato filled with hop, and it goes against the grain. I'm down here at the corner of ..." He pushed down the bar of the phone, as if they had been cut off, and replaced the receiver. He looked up at Camilla. Their eyes were bleak and empty.

LaFarge lifted himself indolently from the chair, sauntered across the room and sat down on the edge of the divan. His eyes were veiled and he looked down at Suzy from under his eyelids.

"Dear universal Suzy," he murmured.

He put his hand on her thigh and let his fingertips move slowly and gently down to her knee, then up again. He smiled. He traced the contour of her lips with his forefinger, he spread his fingers and encircled her neck. He ran his hands over the full richness of her hips, feathering his touch. There had always been something harsh and demanding in Camilla, but Suzy with her silver-blonde hair ... His eyes fell on his wristwatch. Seven-forty-five!

He leaped from the divan and sprang for the window. Suzy would have to wait. He wanted the pleasure of watching Camilla walk into the Rockland Hotel, and he wanted the greater pleasure of watching her coming out again, tottering a little under the first pangs of the fears and torture.

He stood against the wall, lifted back the curtain and stared down the street. He would recognize her insolent carriage, even at this distance, and when she came out, the insolence would be gone. He watched. No one was going in or coming out of the Rockland Hotel, but in a few moments, she would be driving up in a cab, if she had taken the train, or in the green Lincoln, if she had driven herself.

LaFarge's mind glittered with anticipation.

Then his hand tightened on the curtain. A black car, with a police insignia on either side, swooped silently to the front of the Rockland Hotel and four heavily-walking detectives strode for the entrance, while two uniformed policemen conferred for a moment on the sidewalk and one of them ran around toward the back of the hotel while the other took up a post beside the front door.

LaFarge's hand convulsed and with a faint, ripping complaint, the curtain tore from its rod and came tumbling down over his arm. He did not notice, so rigidly was he staring. That louse Sloan. He should have known. He shouldn't have underestimated that animal cunning. He had intellectualized too much, as usual. He had let Sloan out-fox him! Then, slowly, he rose above it. He was standing high, high above it and looking down at the frantic scurryings far below, like a god in a cloud, smiling at the impotence of such puny human machinations. As if these clumsy plots and stratagems could touch *him!* The glitter in his mind became an incandescence of showering sparks.

Like a god, he must strike! He must destroy! And he knew now how to bring the deepest horror to Camilla before he destroyed her.

He walked back to the divan and sat down on the edge of it.

"Dear Suzy," he said with genuine sorrow, "you and I may not have found a new world, but we may have discovered an old, lost truth. I hope you will forgive me, but I am about to do something rather shocking."

He put his hands to her throat, but the fingers would not constrict. He tried to flood his mind with the poison of the memory of Camilla and Sloan, but his hands had touched Suzy before in a semblance of love, and they could not destroy her now. He jumped up from the divan and looked around angrily. There was nothing heavy enough in the room to smash in her head, and he ran into the bathroom. As long as his hands did not have to touch her, he could do it. There was nothing— a light metal wastebasket, a small Cointreau bottle—his eye lighted on the heavy porcelain top of the toilet tank. He lifted it with both hands and turned back to the door. He stopped. There was a man coming in from the hall, a tall, freckled man.

With a skirling cry, LaFarge ran at him, lifting the heavy porcelain slab. The man leaped away from him and LaFarge whirled. Destroy! Destroy! He flung the slab and jumped out into the hall, sprinting for the stairway but two state troopers were pounding up the steps, cutting off his escape. He turned and ran down the hall to the rear stairway. He heard voices below, and he leaped up the stairs toward the roof, pushed open the scuttle and scrambled, panting, out on the graveled roof. Before him lay a large rectangle, empty except for the brick columns of four chimneys. He ran to the edge of the roof. There was nothing beyond but the open street. No houses abutted the hotel. It stood on a narrow island of its own.

LaFarge ran from one side of the roof to the other, then turned. He lifted his chin. Why was he running? What had he to fear from these fumbling yokels? He folded his arms and waited until the first state trooper climbed cautiously out on the roof, followed by another. He laughed at the way they crouched with guns in their hands. What clowns! He gave a cry to catch their attention, and when their heads turned, he sprang up to the parapet of the roof, then leaped out into space. For a moment, as he soared, he felt as if he had finally become God ... but then he began to fall.

Harry was savagely pacing the room, sucking at a cigarette, when the phone rang. He snatched it up, listened for a moment, then held it out to Camilla.

"For you," he said. "The Rockland police."

She took it from his hand, gave him a swift glance, then held it to her ear.

"This is Mrs. LaFarge," she said.

Harry watched her face undergo a terrible change. The phone dropped from her hand. She stood for a moment, frozen. Then she whirled on him, her face convulsed.

The first words came out of her choked, "He's dead ... he jumped off the roof when they went after him. *He's dead!*" The shriek seemed wrenched out of her very soul. She looked at Harry. Her eyes became enormous. "You! You promised. You said he wouldn't be hurt. You said no one would be hurt. You ... get out, *get out!*"

Harry scrambled back before the ferocity of her eyes. She walked toward him, her eyes seeming to become larger and larger. Her hands clawed.

"I'm warning you. Get out of here ..."

Harry stammered, "Wait a minute. It was a ... was it my fault? Wait a minute!"

"*GET OUT!!*"

He jumped back, found the door and jumped out into the hall. He did not see her crumple to the floor. "The hell with you!" he yelled, and slammed out of the house.

He stamped down the walk. What a lousy break! What a stinking lousy break! Who'd have expected the guy to jump off a roof? But that was a hophead for you. This was the last time he'd have anything to do with hopheads.

But he wasn't worried. Okay, so it had been a shock for Camilla, but she'd feel different in the morning. She'd know it wasn't his fault. She was rid of LaFarge and that was the main thing. And when you came right down to it, maybe it was better this way. It saved a lot of grief.

He found a cab on Mt. Prospect Avenue and had himself driven to his apartment. What he needed was a drink. He stumbled a little as he ran for the kitchen. He'd been drinking heavily since five o'clock that afternoon. He wrenched off the cap and drank straight from the bottle.

What a lousy break, what a lousy, lousy break!

He took the bottle with him to the bathroom and put it on the floor while he bent over the sink and splashed his face with cold water. He rubbed the water into his eyes and held his cold hands behind his neck. He felt better. He scrubbed himself vigorously with the rough towel. It brought a glow to his skin. When he walked back into the living room, his step was almost jaunty. What was he worrying about? Camilla'd get over it when she finally realized that LaFarge was out of the way permanently. It couldn't have gone off better, in fact.

He fumbled around for several moments before he realized he was looking for his bottle, and then he couldn't remember where he had put it. He went back into the kitchen and took a fresh bottle from the cabinet over the sink. He carried it into the bedroom, lay down on the bed, tore off the plastic cap wrapping with his teeth, and tipped the bottle to his lips. He stretched out. He wouldn't call Camilla tomorrow, that's what. She'd been getting too snotty lately anyway. Make her call him. She was nuts about him, wasn't she? Okay. Let her call him. She'd damn soon realize who'd fixed it up for her.

But there was something nagging in the back of his mind, and only liquor could kill it. An hour later he was dead drunk.

THE WALLS COME TUMBLING!
CHAPTER THIRTEEN

He was awakened the next morning by a hammering. He groaned and paid no attention to it, but gradually the hammering became distinguishable as something different from the hammering in his head. Someone was hammering on his door. He lurched out of bed, stumbled into the living room and fumbled the door open. A big, heavy man came in and jostled him back, and another man, just as big and solid, followed, closed the door and leaned against it.

Harry tried to hold his balance, saying angrily, "Hey, what the ..."

The first man showed a badge in the palm of his hand and said pleasantly, "The name's Feeney, Sloan. The D.A.'s office. The boss'd like you to drop in for a little talk."

Harry's survival instincts gathered and sobered him instantly. He pulled himself together and straightened up.

"Sure," he said. "Why not? But why bust in like this?"

"It's kind of informal, Sloan," said Feeney. "We didn't have time to send out engraved invitations. Let's go."

"I'm not going in these clothes," said Harry sharply.

"Oh no ..."

"Do you have a warrant? Because if you don't, pal, you're going to have to drag me out of here, and I think we can go round and round for quite a while."

The detective leaning against the door growled, "Ah, let him change his damn clothes, but keep an eye on him."

Grinning, Harry went back into the bedroom, tagged by Feeney. Round one for him. He didn't know what was up, but all he had to do was keep his head. They didn't have a thing on him. He changed slowly into a conservative gray worsted suit, white shirt and blue tie. Then he went to the bathroom. He stopped Feeney at the door.

"The window in here, pal," he said, "is eight inches wide and sixteen inches long. Even a rat'd get stuck in it."

Feeney glanced at the window and stepped back. "I think I can count on that," he said.

Harry slammed the door. His eye fell on the bottle he had left in there the night before and he grabbed it up greedily. God, how he needed a drink. He took two long pulls from the bottle then turned to the sink. He dashed cold water into his face and combed his hair. He took another pull from the bottle before he went outside.

"Sorry to keep you waiting, boys," he jeered, "but a guy's got to look his best for the D.A. these days."

They didn't bother to answer. It was a silent ride to the court house.

The first face Harry saw when he walked into the district attorney's office was Camilla's. Her face was drawn and stony, and she did not look up when he strode in. Then he saw Suzy. How white and sick she seemed, and when she looked up at him it was as if she were looking at someone she hadn't seen for several years and whose face she couldn't quite remember. That shook Harry. She had never looked at him like that before. Behind her chair stood freckled Joe McBride.

Joe's eyes were merciless. Harry swaggered into the room. The hell with them! He could take care of himself.

The District Attorney was professionally bland. "Have a chair, Mr. Sloan. Mrs. LaFarge has a statement to make, and she insisted on your presence."

Harry said, "Okay with me," and sat down. He shot Camilla a wary glance. She could talk, all right, but thank God she had no proof.

A gray-haired man—who looked like a doctor—bent over Camilla's chair and tried to say something, but she waved him away impatiently.

The District Attorney said smoothly, "It's quite all right for her to speak, doctor. This is not a formal inquiry. If Mrs. LaFarge has something she wants to get off her mind, perhaps it will be better to permit her to do so. Are you ready, Mrs. LaFarge?" With a quick flip of his hand, he signalled to the stenographer in the corner of the room to be ready to take it down.

Camilla's stony expression did not change. "First I want to confess that I killed my mother and my father," she said in a colorless voice.

The doctor started to protest, but the District Attorney silenced him with a sharp wave of his hand.

Camilla went on tonelessly. "I was to blame for their deaths. We were out in the Gulf of Mexico in the speedboat. My father liked speedboats. There was a storm coming up. My mother asked my father to go back. He laughed and told her the boat could outrun any storm. It was a very fast boat. I was lying on the bow, smoking. I flipped my cigarette behind me. It fell into the boat. Later they told me that the gas tanks were not properly ventilated to allow the gas fumes to escape. The spark from the cigarette ignited the fumes and the boat exploded. We were all thrown into the water. I saw my mother drift by me, bleeding and burned. I heard my father feebly call for help. At that moment there was a clap of thunder and the storm struck. I was terrified. I swam away and later I was picked up by the Coast Guard. I did not try to save either my father or my mother. I killed them."

The doctor said hurriedly, "Of course you realize, Mr. District Attorney, that the guilt in this case is entirely in Mrs. LaFarge's mind. Even if she had tried to save her father or her mother, she would have been unable to do so because of the storm, and ..."

The district attorney raised his hand. "Please let Mrs. LaFarge tell it," he said. "Mrs. LaFarge ...?"

Camilla continued mechanically, "I knew I had done a horrible thing, and I resolved never to bring pain or suffering to another human being. The mere thought of bringing pain or suffering brought terror to my mind. I knew that I could atone only through suffering myself. I knew that the real evil in the world was causing pain and suffering, and I couldn't stand to see others suffer ..."

The District Attorney cut in suavely, "We sympathize with you very deeply, Mrs. LaFarge ... but what has this to do with the suicide of your husband?"

"My husband discovered that I had killed my mother and my father," her voice sounded inhumanly mechanical. "I hated him. I wanted a divorce. I promised him a large settlement, but I wanted to be sure that he would never tell my crime to another living human. I went to Mr. Sloan. Mr. Sloan and I plotted to have my husband arrested by the police in Rockland, New York. We had placed a bottle of drugs in my husband's luggage and also a bottle of Cointreau, which was heavily doped. Mr.

Sloan had arranged to have my husband give this drugged Cointreau to the girl who was with him. We told my husband that we were arranging a divorce, and that the girl was necessary for evidence of infidelity. We told my husband that a photographer would take a picture. At a quarter of eight last night, Mr. Sloan called the Rockland police and told them ..."

Her voice broke, and the doctor bent quickly over her, but she pushed him away. The silence in the room was like something squeezed in a fist.

She went on woodenly, "Mr. Sloan told the Rockland police that my husband had drugged the girl after taking her across the state line from New Jersey for immoral purposes. Shortly thereafter, I learned that my husband had killed himself. I am guilty, and I want to be punished."

The doctor walked quickly over to the district attorney and began a hurried, whispered conversation. The District Attorney nodded several times and finally said:

"Of course. It's quite obvious. It's in your hands, not mine."

He signalled to a detective standing at the door, and the detective helped the doctor lead Camilla out of the room. She really needed assistance. Her head was high, her face white, but she tottered as if she would fall any moment.

The District Attorney waited until the door had closed behind her, then he leaned over his crossed forearms and said, "Well, do you have anything to say, Mr. Sloan?"

"Sure," said Harry easily. "She's nuts, and you wouldn't dare bring her into a court room."

The District Attorney raised his hand, and a detective brought the flat dope-filled aspirin bottle and the drugged bottle of Cointreau to the desk. The District Attorney looked at Harry.

"Have you ever seen either of these bottles before, Mr. Sloan?" he asked.

"Never," said Harry.

The District Attorney reached into his desk and took out two strips of photographs.

"These are photographs," he said, "taken by Mr. Joseph McBride with, he tells me, a telescopic lens and infra-red flash bulbs. One set was taken from the top of a wall behind the Melody Club, owned by a Mr. August Szabo, and the other set was taken from the shrubbery behind the home of Mrs. LaFarge, looking into a sitting room in the south wing of the house. Look them over, Mr. Sloan."

Without a quiver, Harry took the strips of photographs. He didn't even blink when he saw the pictures of himself and Little Augie at the desk, the two bottles standing between them. The other strip of photographs showed him and Camilla in the south wing sitting room, and again the same two bottles were standing on the cocktail table before the sofa that faced the window. The last two pictures on the strip showed him and Camilla almost frantically clutched together.

Harry's face was still, but his mind clicked savagely. That rat Joe. So that's what he was doing down at Little Augie's yesterday. He'd take care of Joe later.

He handed the photographs back to the District Attorney and said, "So what?"

"Those bottles on Little Augie's desk," said the District Attorney "seem to bear a strong resemblance to these two bottles on this desk."

Harry looked amused. "So I'm responsible for the bottles on Little Augie's desk?"

"Perhaps not, but there seems to be a strange similarity again between these bottles and those photographed on Mrs. LaFarge's cocktail table."

"Maybe Mrs. LaFarge likes bottles. How do I know?" He leaned forward. "Look, pal," he said, "off the record, the LaFarges wanted a divorce. I was helping them out, but all this took place up in New York state, so it's out of your jurisdiction. All this gab about bottles and photographs and stuff is just so much horse apples, and you know as well as I do, that you'd be laughed out of court. On top of that, if you ever tried to put that LaFarge dame on the stand, I'd have forty psychiatrists who'd prove she was squirrel bait before you could open your mouth. So why don't you stop trying to make like a big shot, and let me go home? You don't have a case."

The District Attorney held up a wallet. It had Harry's name embossed in gold letters.

"Have you ever seen this before, Mr. Sloan?" he asked.

Harry's hand shot to his hip, then his eyes glinted up at Feeney at the door. "So now the cops are grabbing it even before you can get it out of your pocket," he said nastily.

The District Attorney smiled briefly and coldly. "You can't possibly deny that this is your wallet, Mr. Sloan," he said. "It has your driver's license, signed, in it, and other private papers. It is your wallet, isn't it, Mr. Sloan?"

"You forgot to mention the two hundred bucks that were in there too," snapped Harry. "Are they still there?"

"Oh yes, they're still there, Mr. Sloan. But there's something else, too. Your fingerprints. During Mrs. LaFarge's confession, we had them compared to the fingerprints on this bottle of dope and this bottle of drugged Cointreau, and oddly enough, Mr. Sloan, though you deny ever having seen either of these two bottles before, your fingerprints appear on both of them. *What do you say now, Mr. Sloan?"*

Suzy leaped up and fled from the room so that she would not have to watch Harry struggling with Feeney and another burly detective as he tried frantically to smash the two bottles on the District Attorney's desk.

LOVE'S CHASTENED FACE!
CHAPTER FOURTEEN

Suzy sat woodenly on the sofa. At her side, Joe had slid down comfortably on the back of his neck and was eating Indian nuts. Harry's picture was gone from the radio—Joe had given it to the policeman on the corner, complaining that it was annoying the neighbors—Mr. Frawley's orchids had wilted in their vase at the window, but otherwise the apartment was the same. The same, except for Suzy.

She was numb, but she could not understand why she did not feel worse. Mr. LaFarge had turned out to be a maniac, and she had lost Harry ... no, she hadn't lost Harry. She had never had Harry. But there was something wrong. There was a depth of grief and heartbreak that was missing, that she could not feel.

"But I can't understand how you ever found us in that hotel, Joe," she said for the third time.

"Aw," he said, "you're just trying to make me feel like a hero because I am. But this hero business is a racket. All you had to do was look at Rockland, New York, and you knew right away that it was a Ford, Chevrolet and Plymouth town and a Cadillac is a curiosity. So all I did was walk up to a guy and say, where can I find a dawn gray Cadillac roadster? It was humiliating, because by that time everybody in town except me and the cops knew that there was a Cadillac parked behind the Empire Hotel. I hate to admit it, but all you need to be a hero is a press agent."

"No, Joe. You came up to the room ..."

"Oh that," he said quickly as her voice broke. "Believe me, I'd never admit this to anybody but you. When that guy came galloping out of the bathroom, waving a toilet seat over his head, I hit the carpet and prayed dear God don't let me be knocked off with a toilet seat, the ignominy of it. He must have heard my prayer, because the next thing I knew, the guy had gone by with a whoosh. Believe me, it would have been more humiliating than choking to death on an Indian nut. Which reminds me, I hate these damn things. They've got tough, cynical shells, and when you get to the inside ... huh! even the squirrels laugh at me."

He looked anxiously up into her face. He had seen the way she looked when she fled from the District Attorney's office, and he had expected her to take a nosedive into a Grade A wingding—but she hadn't. So far. Of course, she didn't quite believe it yet. She was in a state of shock. But when the shock wore off, well, he wanted to be there to catch her when she fell so she wouldn't bump her head on the sidewalk.

That was the reason he'd been chirruping along in the character of good old wisecracking Joe, the modest stumblebum. He knew that as long as he could keep her talking a little and if he could keep those wisecracks coming, it would postpone and ease the rude awakening—when she finally realized that Harry was in the clink to stay and that he had been more of a heel than O'Sullivan ever dreamed.

"Joe," said Suzy, "I never lied to you."

Joe groaned. "That takes care of me," he said. "Show me a guy a dame doesn't lie to, and I'll show you a guy she thinks of as a brother."

"I'm serious, Joe. I never lied to you."

He sat very quietly, knowing that she was talking because she wanted to say something that was important to herself, important to her self-respect. Harry didn't leave a girl much self-respect.

"I never lied to you, Joe," Suzy said, speaking with a kind of difficulty, "because I just couldn't lie to you. No matter what you asked me, I had to tell you the truth. I lied to Harry. I lied to lots of people. But I never lied to you. I don't know why, but I couldn't do it."

Unobtrusively, Joe sat up on the sofa. "I kind of like that, Suzy," he said.

"Do you, Joe? Do you really?" She seemed pathetically eager for someone to like something about her.

He put his arm around her. She stiffened.

"You don't want me on the rebound, Joe!" she cried.

"Whattaya mean I don't want you on the rebound?" he said indignantly. "If I don't catch you on the bounce, the fielders'll run in, scoop you up and toss you to first base for a put-out. You won't even be credited with a hit and, believe me, honeybun, that kind of thing plays hell with your batting average."

"Please, Joe, I'm grateful and ..."

"And that leads me to another point, Miss Carr," he said. "I don't want to have anything more to do with this business of rescuing females in distress. The Galahad racket is a deadend. My mind is made up. As far as females in distress are concerned, what I want is a wife to protect *me!*"

The stiffness went out of Suzy's shoulders and she leaned into the circle of his arm, and she was grateful that it was there for her to lean into. It was a comfortable, comforting arm. With a pang, she remembered Harry—and then she remembered something else. Whenever she had sat like this with Harry, sometimes wanting just to sit and talk, or listen to music on the radio, it had lasted for just a few moments, and then he was reaching for her body or reaching for the hem of her dress.

She felt the warmth of Joe's arm around her shoulders, and it was demanding nothing. It was just offering her a place to lie. And then she was confused. Love was Harry raging at her with naked emotions—love was the drained and frustrated aftermath—love was worry and strain and tension. If love were as easy as this, anybody could fall in love.

"Joe," she said in a small, meek voice, "will you do something for me?"

"Name it!"

"Give me an Indian nut," she asked humbly.

THE END

LORENZ HELLER BIBLIOGRAPHY
(1910-1965)

As Frederick Lorenz

Novels:
A Rage at Sea (Lion, 1953)
Night Never Ends (Lion, 1954)
The Savage Chase (Lion, 1954)
A Party Every Night (Lion, 1956)
Ruby (Lion, 1956)
Hot (Lion, 1956)
Dungaree Sin (Chariot, 1960)

Stories:
Backbite (*Justice*, Jan 1956)
Big Catch (*Justice*, July 1955)
Living Bait (*Justice*, May 1955)

As Dan Gregory

Three Must Die! (Graphic, 1956)

As Laura Hale

Novels:
Wild is the Woman (Rainbow, 1951)
Lovers Don't Sleep (Falcon, 1951)
Kiss of Fire (Rainbow, 1952; reprinted in Australia as *Kiss Of Death*, Phantom, 1953)
Woman Hunter (Falcon, 1952; reprinted in Australia, Phantom, 1953)
Desperate Blonde (Beacon Australia, 1960)
Lessons in Lust (Beacon, 1961; rewrite of *Woman Hunter*)
Sensual Woman (Beacon, 1961; rewrite of *Lovers Don't Sleep*)
The Zipper Girls (Beacon, 1962; rewrite of *Wild is the Woman*)
The Marriage Bed (Beacon, 1962; rewrite of *Desperate Blonde*)

As Larry Heller

Novels:
I Get What I Want (Popular, 1956)
Body of the Crime (Pyramid, 1962)

Story:
Blood Is Thicker (*Guilty Detective Story Magazine*, Mar 1957)

As Larry Holden

Novels:
Hide-Out (Eton, 1953)
Dead Wrong (Pyramid, 1957)
Crime Cop (Pyramid, 1959)

Stories (alphabetical listing):
...And Death Makes Ten (*Detective Tales*, June 1947)
Another Man's Poison (*Shadow Mystery*, Apr/May 1948)
Any Corpse in a Storm (*Dime Mystery Magazine*, Aug 1949)
Anybody Lose a Corpse? (*Mammoth Detective*, Aug 1946)
The Big Haunt (*10-Story Detective Magazine*, Oct 1948)
Blackmail Means Homicide (*15 Story Detective*, Feb 1950)
Bloody Night! (*Dime Mystery Magazine*, Oct 1949)
Bodyguard (*Thrilling Detective*, June 1951)
Bullets for Beethoven [Dinny Keogh] (*Mammoth Mystery*, June 1946)
Coffin Key (*Detective Tales*, Oct 1951)
A Corpse at Large (*Ten Detective Aces*, July 1949)
Corpse in Waiting (*New Detective Magazine*, Nov 1950)

BIBLIOGRAPHY

A Corpse to His Credit (*Dime Detective Magazine*, May 1947)
Criminal at Large (*Suspense Magazine*, Summer 1951)
The Crimson Path (*Detective Tales*, Sept 1947)
Cry Murder (*New Detective Magazine*, Oct 1952)
The Crying Corpse (*Ten Detective Aces*, Sept 1948)
Death Brings Down the House (*10-Story Detective Magazine*, Apr 1948)
Death Carries the Mail (*F.B.I. Detective Stories*, Aug 1950)
Death for Two! (*Detective Tales*, Dec 1952)
Death in Dirty Linen (*Shadow Mystery*, June/July 1947)
Death in Six Reels (*Doc Savage*, July/Aug 1948)
Death in Thin Ice (*Shadow Mystery*, Feb/Mar 1948)
Death Is Where You Find It (*Suspect Detective Stories*, Nov 1955)
Die, Baby, Die! (*Detective Tales*, June 1948)
Don't Crowd My Shroud (*10-Story Detective Magazine*, Dec 1948)
Don't Ever Forget (*Detective Story Magazine*, Mar 1953)
Don't Wait Up for Me (*Triple Detective*, Fall 1955)
The Eighteen Screaming Corpses (*Detective Tales*, Jan 1948)
The Expendable Ex (*Dime Detective Magazine*, June 1952)
Face in the Window (*Detective Tales*, June 1951)
Fall Guy (*Detective Tales*, Aug 1953)
Forger's Fate (*Dime Detective Magazine*, Apr 1951)
The High Cost of Chivalry (*Dime Detective Magazine*, Dec 1951)
Home for Christmas (*Thrilling Detective*, Dec 1947)
House of Hate (*10-Story Detective Magazine*, Apr 1949)
Humpty-Dumpty Homicide (*Detective Tales*, June 1949)
If the Body Fits— (*Dime Mystery Magazine*, Dec 1947)
If the Frame Fits— (*Detective Tales*, Dec 1951)
I'll Be Home for Murder! (*Detective Tales*, Apr 1948)
I'll See You Dead! (*Detective Tales*, May 1947)
In Her Mother's Best Bier! (*Detective Tales*, Dec 1948)
Keeping Honest (*Doc Savage*, Winter 1949)
Kickback for a Corpse (*All-Story Detective*, Apr 1949)
Killer's Kiss (*Detective Tales*, Aug 1949)
Lady in Red (*Detective Tales*, Oct 1948)
Lady-Killer (*Dime Detective Magazine*, Dec 1952)
Lethal Boy Blue (*Detective Tales*, May 1949)
Love Me, Love My Corpse! (*Detective Tales*, Aug 1948)
Make Mine Mayhem (*New Detective Magazine*, Jan 1949)
Man with a Rep (*Detective Tales*, Dec 1949)
Mayhem at Eight (*New Detective Magazine*, May 1950)
Mayhem's Mechanic (*Detective Tales*, Sept 1946)
Morgue Bait (*New Detective Magazine*, Dec 1951)
Murder and the Mermaid (*Dime Detective Magazine*, Oct 1952)
Murder Never Gets Too Old (*Private Detective*, Jan 1950)
Never Dead Enough (*New Detective Magazine*, Sept 1947)
Never Turn Your Back (*Mike Shayne Mystery Magazine*, July 1959)
Nightmare (*Detective Tales*, Oct 1952)
No Dead End (*Triple Detective*, Spring 1955)

On a Dead Man's Chest (*Thrilling Detective*, Apr 1953)
One Dark Night [Dinny Keogh] (*Mammoth Mystery*, Dec 1946)
One for the Hangman (*Suspect Detective Stories*, Feb 1956)
Operation—Murder (*F.B.I. Detective Stories*, Aug 1949)
Orphans Are Made (*Mobsters*, Feb 1953)
Out of the Frying Pan... (*15 Mystery Stories*, Oct 1950)
Port of the Dead (*New Detective Magazine*, July 1947)
Prelude to a Wake (*Dime Detective Magazine*, Feb 1952)
Red Nightmare (*Dime Mystery Magazine*, July 1947)
Sailor, Beware! (*Detective Story Magazine*, May 1953)
Save Me a Kill (*New Detective Magazine*, June 1953)
Self-Made Corpse (*Detective Tales*, Apr 1949)
She Cries Murder! (*New Detective Magazine*, June 1952)
Sing a Song of Murder (*Dime Detective Magazine*, Aug 1952)
Snow in August [Dinny Keogh] (*Mammoth Mystery*, Aug 1946)
The Spice of Death (*Private Detective*, Dec 1950)
Start with a Corpse [Dinny Keogh] (*Mammoth Mystery*, Jan 1946)
There's Death in the Heir [Dinny Keogh] (*Mammoth Mystery*, Aug 1947)
They Played Too Rough [Dinny Keogh] (*Mammoth Mystery*, Mar 1946)
This Shroud Reserved (*New Detective Magazine*, Oct 1951)
Those Slaughter-House Blues (*Mammoth Detective*, Feb 1947)
A Time for Dying (*Dime Detective Magazine*, Aug 1951)
Too Many Crosses [Dinny Keogh] (*Mammoth Mystery*, Feb 1947)
Tragedy in Waiting (*Invincible Detective Magazine*, Mar 1951)
The Trouble with Redheads (*Mike Shayne Mystery Magazine*, Apr 1959)
Two-Headed Killer (*15 Mystery Stories*, Feb 1950)
Undressed to Kill (*New Detective Magazine*, Sept 1949)
Vicious Circle (*Detective Tales*, Nov 1949)
The Voice That Kills (*15 Mystery Stories*, Aug 1950)
Wake of the Ermine Chick (*15 Story Detective*, Dec 1950)
When Cops Fall Out (*Detective Tales*, June 1953)
With Hostile Intent (*Fifteen Detective Stories*, Dec 1954)
With Love and Bullets! (*Detective Tales*, Feb 1953)
Written in Blood (*Ten Detective Aces*, May 1948)
You Can't Live Forever (*New Detective Magazine*, Aug 1952)
You Die Alone (*Fifteen Detective Stories*, Oct 1953)
You'll Die Laughing (*Detective Tales*, Oct 1950)
You're Killing Me (*Detective Story Magazine*, Sept 1953)

Dinny Keogh series:
Start with a Corpse (1946)
They Played Too Rough (1946)
Bullets for Beethoven (1946)
Snow in August (1946)
One Dark Night (1946)
Too Many Crosses (1947)
There's Death in the Heir (1947)

As Lorenz Heller

Novel:
Murder in Make-Up (Messner, 1937)

Stories:
Blood Money (*Suspect Detective Stories*, Nov 1955)
A Tasty Dish (*Suspect Detective Stories*, Feb 1956)
Twilight (*Short Stories*, Nov 1956)
The Hero (*Mystery Tales*, Dec 1958)
The Last Hunt (*Adventure*, June 1959)

As Burt Sims

Television Scripts:
1953: "Death Does a Rumba" (Season 2, Episode 12, *Boston Blakie*)
1953: "Island of Stone" (Season 2, Episode 1, *Chevron Theater*)
1954: "Tailor-Made Trouble" (Season 1, Episode 11, *Waterfront*)
1956 - 1959: Seven episodes of *Sky King*
1958: "Beautiful, Blue and Deadly" (Season 1, Episode 14, *Mike Hammer*)
1958: "Texas Fliers" (Season 1, Episode 18, *Flight*)

Rediscover the hard-hitting, character-driven fiction of

Lorenz Heller

The Savage Chase (as Frederick Lorenz) · $19.95
Three 50s noir thrillers in one volume. "...a sexually frank, violence packed thriller with vividly crisp dialogue."—*GoodReads*.

A Rage at Sea / A Party Every Night · $19.95
"Lorenz's characters are what keep the pages turning."
—Alan Cranis, *Bookgasm*.

Dead Wrong · $9.99 · Black Gat Books #26.
"These interesting, well-developed characters propel this rather standard crime-noir plot into something special and unusual."—*Paperback Warrior*.

Hide-Out / I Get What I Want · $15.95
"In Lorenz's fiction, it feels like he moulds the plot from organic character confrontations, his writing is electric and alive with unpredictability."
—Paul Burke, *CrimeTime*.

Crime Cop / Body of the Crime · $15.95
"One of the better entries, outside of 87th Precinct, in the paperback police school." —Anthony Boucher, *New York Times*

Woman Hunter / Kiss of Fire · $15.95
"What makes this one ding is not necessarily the plot, but the great characterizations which serve to humanize all the players. A terrific read."—Dave Wilde

Hot / Ruby · $17.95
"[Heller] writes in a hard, fast, crisp style and he has a feel for colorful language and characters that makes the story sing."
— *Mammoth Mystery*

Pulp Champagne: The Short Fiction of Lorenz Heller · $15.95
"... a complete delight and showcased Heller's superior characterizations.... terrific collection by an author worth remembering."—*Paperback Warrior*

Stark House Press, 1315 H Street, Eureka, CA 95501
griffinskye3@sbcglobal.net / www.StarkHousePress.com
Available from your local bookstore, or order direct via our website.

www.ingramcontent.com/pod-product-compliance
Lightning Source LLC
LaVergne TN
LVHW021808060526
838201LV00058B/3282